The Horrors Hiding In Plain Sight

Rebecca Rowland

www.DarkInkBooks.com

First Published by *Dark Ink Books*, August 2018

www.AMInkPublishing.com

Dark Ink Books is a division of *AM Ink Publishing*. *Dark Ink* and *AM Ink* and its logos are trademarked by *AM Ink Publishing*.

For twisted friends… who are so difficult to keep.

Contents

About suffering they were never wrong,
The old Masters: how well they understood
Its human position: how it takes place
While someone else is eating or opening a window or just
walking dully along...

-W. H. Auden (1940)

This world doesn't need no opera
We're here for the operation
We don't need a bigger knife 'cause we got guns
We got guns: you better run

We're killing strangers
We're killing strangers
We're killing strangers so we don't kill the ones that we love.

-Marilyn Manson (2015)

It Comes Around

It had been a long time since 13-year-old Elio Harmon had enjoyed the feel of the sun on his face. The winter had been long and hard, with just enough snow to keep his feet in a constant state of cold but not enough to rack up snow days on a regular basis. It was April now, and the smells of pollen and grass and earth filled his nose as he pushed the pilfered grocery cart down Powell Avenue, the long side street where most of his customers lived.

He stopped at almost every house on the block, snatched an orange-bagged newspaper from the pile, and ran up the walkway before placing the bundle gently inside the screen door or in the mailbox. He had 59 customers this Sunday. That number dwindled in the summer, when families packed up for vacations at the Cape or southern Maine coast, but he had a steady customer base for the most part, due to the neighborhood being mostly old and relatively free of Millennial families who didn't read newspapers. They got their news from Yahoo or Google or their Apple watches. Even his own parents didn't subscribe.

As he maneuvered the uneven sidewalk where the concrete had split and broken from frost heaves and minimal upkeep, the rickety carriage sputtered and jangled, announcing his presence to the sleepy trees and occasional ambitious squirrel that darted across the lawns. Elio looked at his watch: it was almost seven. He had to be finished well before eight or the endless wave of angry phone calls would begin.

He grabbed an orange bundle and ran up the walkway to Mr. Pratt's house, a tall, white Colonial with black shutters and a broad front porch. As he stood in front of the door, a fat orange cat watched him suspiciously from his place on the stoop, opening one eye and shifting the limbs he had tucked beneath his furry loaf. Breaking the morning stillness, the sound of a screen door opening and slamming shut echoed from next door. Elio glanced sideways, his breath catching a bit. He knew who he would see before their bodies came into view.

Elio had grown up with the James twins; they had played in the same playgrounds, eaten the same sandbox sand, and taken drool-inducing naps on the same carpet squares in Mrs. LeMay's kindergarten class. Elio had even attended a birthday party or two at the James' house, and when Tim, the older of the two by three minutes, had broken his ankle after a cringe-worthy tackle on the pee wee football field, it was Elio who held his hand until the ambulance came.

Of course, that had been five years ago: a lifetime in middle school years. Tim and his brother Jake had joined the ranks of the chosen: the cool clique of seventh graders who monopolized the sports teams, clubs, and general social interactions within Carter Junior High's walls—and terrorized other children outside of them.

Elio placed the newspaper carefully within the space in front of the front door and delicately closed the screen, doing everything in his power not to attract attention. If they didn't see him, he could continue on unmolested. He held his breath and watched the two boys bound recklessly down their cement stairs and onto the tree belt. Tim shoved his brother and cackled as Jake fell onto the grass in a half-somersault. The latter grabbed his brother's calves and pulled him to the ground, playfully punching him in the abdomen.

Elio let his breath out slowly. They were wearing cleats and carrying baseball gloves, and likely were off to practice in the park across from the church a half mile away. Elio said a silent prayer of thanks that they weren't carrying their bats.

"Well, looks like you two fags have an audience," said a voice from the sidewalk in front of the Pratts' steps. Elio jumped, startled. Jamie Payson had crept up without Elio seeing him coming. That was how it usually was with Jamie: he'd leap out from the lockers between classes, or appear like an apparition from behind the tall, green vinyl seats on the bus ride home. And there was that one time he had pounced on Elio in the showers after gym. Elio didn't shower after gym class anymore.

Jamie was almost a foot taller than the twins and looked like his mother had been surreptitiously sprinkling steroids over his Frosted Flakes. Just one year into his teens and he was already sporting a spotty beard and mustache; at sixteen, he'd likely be the one sent to the package store to buy beer for townie graduation parties—at this rate, he'd probably be grey by then.

Jamie lived a block over from the James' house and was the unofficial leader of the cool kids' pack, and this honor included the prerogative to harass, bully, and terrorize anyone he deemed worthy of victimhood. Elio had been at the top of his list for quite a while, but fortunately, soccer, basketball, and now baseball occupied most of his free time. If Elio was careful and monitored where and when he walked alone, he could all but avoid the trio of boys and their reign of terror. This morning, his luck had run out.

"Oh, Jamie, it's you," Elio said, trying to sound casual. He used every ounce of focus in his body to steady his walk as he padded softly down the steps.

Jamie put a hand on Elio's shopping carriage and drummed his fingers like an impatient mother waiting out a toddler's temper tantrum. "Well, now, look who it is, boys: my good friend Elio!" His tone dripped with sinister foreshadowing. Elio could practically see the planning wheels turning in the boy's head when he met his eyes, so he looked away quickly and said nothing and busied himself with rearranging the remaining newspapers in the cart. Jamie responded by grabbing the carriage and flipping it violently away from Elio so that it landed on its side and its contents spilled over the dew-soaked grass.

As Elio squatted to pick up the pieces, Jamie was on him like a wild animal, tackling him and pushing his face against the sidewalk. "Now that's not very *polite*, Harmon. Can't you say *hello* to us like a good boy?" He accentuated the words *polite* and *hello* by picking up Elio's head by the hair and shoving it back into the cement each time. Elio felt the scrape forming on his cheek, the gravel digging into his skin, the warm blood against the cool, wet pavement. Within seconds, two sets of feet joined Jamie's on the sidewalk next to Elio, who tried to flop onto his side to get a better look at the situation at hand.

"Where'd ya get the shoppin' cart, paperboy?" Elio heard Tim (or Jake?) say. He didn't dare look up out of fear of being punched in the face. The question was punctuated by four hard metallic bangs as the interrogator kicked the exposed bottom of Elio's carriage. A second set of feet were closer, though. Elio could see them in his peripheral vision— two black cleats with white swooshes decorating the sides— so when he saw one of them swing purposefully backwards, he knew to brace himself for the impact.

The foot struck him once, twice, three times, square in the stomach. *Right in the breadbasket*, some unrecognizable but strangely familiar voice echoed in his head. It was a good thing he *hadn't* eaten breakfast yet: whether it had been bread, or eggs, or cereal, it would have sailed quickly out of him during this assault. Elio curled into a ball and covered his head with his arms and waited for it to be over. He knew by now that it was pointless to fight. No one was around. No one would come to his aid. If he played possum, they might bore quickly and go away. He felt hot bile rising in his esophagus, sizzling against the mucous membrane and burning as he forced it back down again.

The sound of a screen door opening creaked above them, screeching on its rusty hinge, followed by a gravelly adult voice. "What are you kids doing?" it called. It was Mr. Pratt. His seventy-year-old body emerged onto his front porch cloaked in a black waffle-textured bathrobe and ragged grey slippers. Elio uncurled himself and looked up to meet Mr. Pratt's black-rimmed glasses shining down at the group from four feet aloft. "Tim, Jake, what's going on here?" he asked.

Jake's (or Tim's? Elio wasn't sure from his vantage point) broad frame moved into Elio's field of vision and blocked eye contact with Mr. Pratt. "We're just horsing around, Mr. Pratt. We're on our way to practice." His body moved to the right and away from Elio's body, and the two other boys began to follow. Elio wiggled himself onto his knees and pushed himself back into a standing position. His belly felt like it had been trampled on by horses.

Jamie and the twins collected their gear from the James' lawn and bounded down the street toward the intersection with the main road. Elio did his best not to stare in their direction, but he wanted to make certain they were out of earshot before responding to the question he knew would follow.

"Are you alright, son?" Beneath their furry caterpillar brows, Mr. Pratt's kind blue eyes pitied Elio. "Would you like some water? Juice, maybe?"

Elio brushed the gravel from his legs and righted his shopping cart, then began tossing stray papers back inside the metal cage. *Yeah, a glass of juice is really gonna fix this*, he thought. *'Nothing like a big glass of OJ to help you forget that some douchebags assaulted you.* "It's okay, Mr. Pratt. I'm okay. We were just fooling around." Even as he heard himself speak, he knew it sounded lame. He fixed his eyes on a small rock that had stuck to his calf and pretended to be fascinated by it.

Mr. Pratt was silent for a moment. "Okay, Elio. Keep your chin up. What goes around, comes around." He paused and scratched his face with his thumb. "You have a good day, now." He walked back into the house, retrieved the bagged newspaper from the floor of the doorway, and shut the door. Elio put his hand on his cheek and felt for the blood that had already dried to a brick-colored crust. If he hurried and delivered these last few papers, he could clean up before his parents saw the damage. He didn't want them to worry. He didn't want to disappoint them.

It was the last day of classes before the first day of spring vacation, the day students savored and schoolteachers dreaded because they knew, no matter what effort had been put into planning an important and engaging lesson, no one's mind would be on learning. It was also the last day of swimming for Elio's gym class; when they returned from break, class would be held outside, alternating between the tennis courts, the baseball diamond, and the soccer field.

Because it was the final day in the pool before vacation, the gym teachers declared the class would be "free swim," an announcement that signaled dread for Elio: free swim meant free range bullying. Without a structured activity to contain them, the trio whose beating he'd escaped less than a week previous had a full hour to splash and side-swipe Elio at their leisure. When the teacher blew his whistle to signal that all of the students should enter the water, Elio dove quickly from his place near the diving board, hoping to avoid detection by spending most of the period underwater.

As he rocketed toward the drain at the floor of the pool, the echoes of children's laughter and screams muffled until they were nearly a whisper. He hit the silver cover with the tip of his finger, giving it a pseudo-high-five, and propelled his body as far down the length of the pool as he could hold his breath. When he felt his lungs begin to ache, he kicked toward the surface, feeling the cacophony grow louder again.

Elio resurfaced halfway down the length of the pool, at the point where the five-feet plateau plunged toward the drain in a slope too steep for a swimmer to rest his feet comfortably. He opened his mouth wide as soon as he broke the surface to engulf as much air as he could muster. However, as his head materialized from the water, it was met with resistance, and before he could take a full breath, before he could see what was holding him, something pushed down hard on his shoulders, forcing him back under the water.

His eyes darted around his body. All he could see were torsos and swim trunks. Boys' torsos: three of them, with their arms stretched out, their hands touching him. He pushed his arms against the resistance of the water, trying to force his body upward, but it was as if a cement block had been placed on his shoulders. His lungs felt like were going to explode. Unfiltered, primal panic set in, and he began to flail wildly, scratching and clawing at his captors' arms, trying to dislodge himself from their grasps. He felt his heart race into his throat as his body, now out of his control, opened his mouth to the chlorinated water and sucked it in, hoping for oxygen.

Elio Harmon choked. His lungs rejected the water, trying to force it from their depths with stilted wet thrusts, but it was only replaced with more water.

Elio's mind froze.

Everything slowed, like a paused image on the television being nudged forward, frame by frame.

Click.

He reached out twice more.

Click.

With one final thrust, he felt his nails scratch skin.

Click.

And then the water clouded

Click.

and was black.

Jamie Payson jumped back like he'd been bitten. "What the hell? That fucker scratched me or something!" He let go of his grip on Elio and pushed his torso up from the water to catch a glimpse at his own chest and felt the skin under his nipple, searching for signs of a scrape. Tim and Jake removed their holds on the boy as well and stared blankly at their leader as if waiting for further instruction. All around them, students splashed and yelled and laughed and screamed.

On the bleachers, Mr. Dandry, the thirty-something gym teacher with the shaggy, Beatles-era haircut and a pair of Beats headphones perpetually encircling his neck—even when he was teaching—was explaining to Billy Henderson that yes, he had to take off his t-shirt before getting into the water. He was trying desperately to explain this as sternly as possible while keeping a close eye on the blonde, ponytailed student teacher. She always wore a grey tank top and tight black shorts. Did she wash the clothes every night, or did she own five grey tanks and five pairs of identical shorts? Mr. Dandry imagined her walking into her spotless, girly apartment, peeling the tiny t-shirt and shorts from her body, and dumping them into a washing machine in her tiny, pink kitchen. She wasn't wearing anything underneath those clothes. He saw her pick up the tiny teakettle from on top of the stove, fill it with water from the sink, and replace it on the burner—all while naked as a jaybird. As she waited for the water to boil, she leaned her body to rest her head on the pink granite countertop, crossing one pink-sneakered ankle over the other, pushing her tiny, perfectly round buttocks presentably into the air as the blonde hair from her ponytail spilled across the counter like a feather duster.

Mr. Dandry was building the scene in his mind with great ferocity while trying to maintain a firm demeanor with Billy Henderson, who was, for his part, firm on never parting with his faded Abercrombie t-shirt, which is why when the girl with the unflattering pixie cut whose name he could never remember began to point at the middle of the pool and yell, "He's drowning! He's drowning! Somebody do something!" Mr. Dandry was not quick to acknowledge her. There were only so many things he could juggle in his head at once. And then the student teacher with the blonde ponytail was running down the length of the pool, not stopping to remove her tiny pink sneakers before diving in and breast-stroking to the center of the water—and he realized what was happening. He could see a small, dark shape sitting on the floor of the pool, slowly drifting deeper as it slid softly down the sharp decline and toward the drain. He paused to remove his headphones, handing them to a wide-eyed Billy Henderson, and jumped into the water, but he was too late.

Elio Harmon was dead.

The news about a young boy drowning in the junior high's indoor swimming pool blanketed the news for weeks, not only in Elio's hometown but everywhere across the state, and in some cases, across the nation. Teachers' unions cited understaffing as the catalyst for the tragedy; principals and superintendents cited underqualified educators as the culprit. Elio's parents were too devastated to blame anyone: they just wanted their son back. For weeks, Mrs. Harmon did not leave her sanctuary under the aubergine comforter of her bedroom; the blackout shades were drawn twenty-four hours a day. A week and two days after their son's death, an irate newspaper customer phoned the Harmon house, screaming into the answering machine that she wanted her paper delivered immediately. Mr. Harmon responded by walking out to the garage, picking up the sledgehammer he had procured years ago when he installed the brick walkway, and slamming it over and over into Elio's pilfered shopping carriage until it was a battered, melted tangle of metal and black-ringed plastic wheels. Then he called the customer back and calmly told her to go fuck herself.

Nobody blamed Jamie or Tim or Jake. Nobody had seen them, and they never spoke out loud about what had happened—not once. That is, until the thing at the fountain happened.

Sure enough, by the time Jamie Payson turned sixteen, his scrape of facial hair had bloomed into what his mom joked was "a goddamn face sweater," and he had to shave every day to keep it in check. Women—not just teenaged girls, but bona fide women—loved his broad shoulders, movie star smile, and bad boy attitude, and after he easily made the varsity team his freshman year, the college recruiters began skulking around his baseball games, sniffing here and there, weighing their chances at wooing him to Vanderbilt, Duke, or Louisiana State. He was only a sophomore, but his swing guaranteed Central High a win game after game. It was May, the prime of the season, and Jamie begged a Saturday afternoon off from practice and cross-training in order to hang at the mall with his perpetual shadows, the James twins, and a handful of girls the three had met at a suburban kegger the night before.

The Windsor Mall was three towns away, but when they could manage to find rides, all Central High students would travel there: to shop and eat, to gossip and peer-watch, and of course, to get high behind the Friendly's Ice Cream Shoppe exit door off the food court. The Windsor was three

stories tall with cathedral ceilings to boot—a palace, really—
and boasted more than 150 stores. Its second and third levels
of retail eye candy overlooked the bottom floor's expansive
food court, and everything was connected by a zig-zagging of
escalators that surrounded a great glass elevator like a Willy
Wonka fever dream.

The penny fountain, a staple at the mall for decades,
stood at the far end of the food court. When Jamie was just a
toddler, his mother had stopped for a hot dog at the stand
nearby and let go of her son's hand for just a moment, but it
was long enough for his chubby, restless legs to propel
himself up and onto the seat-like lip along the front of the
fountain.

"Is that your boy?" the fast food employee asked Mrs.
Payson apathetically, and she turned just in time to see her
only child belly-flop into two feet of coin-dirtied water,
splashing some nearby patrons. She dropped her lunch and ran
to retrieve him, certain this near-death experience would leave
him fearful of water for the rest of his life. Instead, when she
pulled him from the fountain by the back of his OshKosh
overalls, he only looked at her wide-eyed and began to laugh.
He was clutching two dimes and a penny in his left hand.

While the three girls took turns lobbing spare change
into the water, Jake and Jamie sat at the lone table nearby and
watched them. "So, what do you think of Natalie?" Jake
asked. "She's hot, right? I mean, look at those tits."

Jamie eyed the busty brunette and returned his
attention to his friend. "She's kind of a bitch, dude," he said,
raising an eyebrow. "You really want to put up with that level
of demand for just a taste?"

As if she had heard them, the tallest of the trio turned
from the fountain and yelled over to the boys. "Hey, I'm outta
change. I need some change. You got anything?" She paused.
"Jaay-ake?" Natalie stretched his name into two syllables.

"Could you get me some change, please?" She tilted her head slightly to the side and smiled at him prettily.

Without hesitation, Jake patted his chest and stomach, but there were no pockets in the oversized t-shirt he had exhumed from the hamper that morning. He dug around deep in the pockets of his jeans. Jamie sighed audibly and shook his head. Ignoring him, Jake turned to his brother who was sitting alone at the far end of the fountain. "Hey, Tim," he called. "Hey! Tim! You got any change?"

Tim was staring at the fountain, into the water. He appeared lost in thought. This had been happening a lot over the past few years: Tim distracted, Tim drifting off in the middle of a conversation, Tim spontaneously tuning out like a television set being unplugged. His father explained it away as hormonal overload, a side effect of literal growing pains. The boy had shot up six inches in under a year and Mr. and Mrs. James told neighbors they thought they could actually *hear* their children growing while they slept.

"TIM!" yelled Jake. "What the fuck? Do you hear me?" Jake was growing too, though not as fast as his twin, and he didn't seem to have any problem staying on planet earth: what was his brother's problem? "Fucken retard," Jake said under his breath. He stood up and walked over to where Tim was sitting.

Without taking his eyes off of the water, Tim stood up as well. He leaned onto the fountain's seat, resting his weight on one knee, and leaned his face toward the water. When he was only an inch from its surface, he turned his head, dipped his ear into the fountain, and held it there. He closed his eyes and frowned. He seemed to be listening to something.

Jake grabbed his brother by the shoulder and yanked him back. "Jesus, what the hell are you doing?" he asked, then lowered his voice. "You look like a psycho, dude. Cut it out." He glanced over at the girls. The blonde one was standing very still while the short one with the blue streaks through her hair was checking the blonde's face for something. She brushed something away from under her friend's eye, then examined her fingertips as if trying to verify she had removed the invisible culprit. Natalie was looking down and checking her phone.

Tim put his hand over his wet ear, then pulled it away. "I gotta get something," he said. "I'll be right back."

"Where are you going?" Jake asked him. "Seriously? You're leaving?"

"I gotta go to…" Tim paused. "Brookstone. It'll just take a minute." He began to walk toward the escalator.

Jamie passed him on his way over to join the group. "Where is he going?" he asked. "I'm starving." He turned to the girls. "We're getting something to eat." Without waiting for them to reply, or even checking that any of the four were following him, he turned and walked across the food court and stepped into line at a popular burger joint.

He was reading the menu when Jake appeared next to him. "The girls say they want Diet Cokes. No food," he said.

Jamie snorted. "Typical." Five minutes later, balancing their overflowing trays, the two returned to the fountain. Someone was now sitting at the table where they once were, so the boys sprawled out on the fountain seat, spreading their takeout like a picnic.

Natalie snatched up a soda and jammed a straw into the lid. She shoved the straw between her lips without bothering to thank either of them and continued to paw at her phone. For a long while, the group ate and drank in near silence, exchanging only strained, choppy bits of conversation. When he had finished his second sandwich, Jamie balled up his wrappers and craned his neck, looking for a trash receptacle. The rest of the group glanced about as well. They were a decent walk's distance from most of the food establishments, but there were rows of white metal tables and chairs about twenty feet over that bathed in the natural light of the skylight far above their heads.

The blonde girl turned her head and squinted her eyes. "Hey, isn't that Tim?" she asked. "What is he doing?" She was looking upward, toward the elevator. Jake followed her gaze and focused his vision.

It was Tim alright, but Jake was confused. What was he doing? Tim appeared to be standing right on the edge of the third-floor walkway, facing toward them. He could see that his brother was clutching a Brookstone bag by the handle in his right hand. His left hand was holding onto the railing as his knees pressed against the chest-high glass enclosure surrounding the third-floor level. He wasn't looking down at the food court but rather staring straight ahead, across the open space at the up escalator.

Jake felt his stomach drop into his legs. The frightening height of the third level had always given him the willies, especially since the glass barricade gave the illusion that one could walk right off the edge and plunge the forty-foot distance to the food court floor. Even today, he couldn't bring himself to ride the glass elevator.

Jamie cupped his hand around his mouth. "Hey, Tim!" he yelled. "Get down here, dude: 'food's almost gone!'"

Tim turned his head slightly and looked in the group's direction. His expression was blank. Then, without a word, he let go of the bag, allowing it to fall to the ground by his feet. To Jake's horror, Tim leaned forward like a gymnast readying a pummel horse mount, pushed himself up, and climbed over the glass enclosure. He stood balancing his toes on the slim edge on the outside of the transparent wall.

Jake felt all of the color drain from his face. He thought he might vomit. "TIM!!!" he screamed. His voice caught and squeaked at the end, but he didn't care. "TIM,

WHAT ARE YOU DOING?!" He dropped his food and ran toward the escalator. "Don't move!! Don't move! I'm coming! Please, please just stay there!"

Tim stood, still facing the barricade, holding on with both hands. As his brother's screams ricocheted across the food court, prompting shoppers and eaters alike to stop what they were doing and watch what was happening, he barely registered a change in his expression, but he craned his neck sideways to look in the direction of Jamie and the girls. No— it wasn't them he was looking at; it was the fountain. He was looking at the fountain.

Meanwhile, Jake reached the bottom of the escalator and in his frenzy to reach his brother, began running up the moving steps, taking two at a time. He made it up the first escalator in record time, ran around the corner, and began to bound up the next one, but on his first leap, he tripped. When he fell, he cut his chin on the sharp metal treads of the step, and the pain took him by such surprise, he paused a moment, stunned, before getting up. When he attempted to stand, however, he found his body being held tight to the stairs—the loose bottom of his t-shirt had been sucked into the side of the moving stairs and must have become entangled in the gears. Jake was frozen in a perpetual push-up, his torso pulling closer and closer to the side of the escalator as he rode silently upward.

By the time Jake could see the top of the stairway, his face was pressed against the side of the stairs so tightly that he could no longer turn his head. Once at the top, the motor seemed to kick into overdrive, and it maintained its iron grip on Jake's t-shirt despite his furious kicking and struggling. The cotton blend material tightened around Jake's throat like a boa constrictor, and he felt another wave of nausea as the bones in his neck strained and cracked, one by one, like sinewy twigs. He smelled something burning: a metallic, chemical odor.

He could hear a woman screaming, but his vision was restricted to the brown speckled cement floor and a tiny silver corner of the escalator's frame. He felt a stabbing pain in his throat, and when tried to take a breath, he couldn't: his mind willed his body to obey, but his throat and chest somehow had dislocated themselves from his brain's communication center. Somewhere far away, he felt his arms and legs flailing in frustration, but his vision had faded to a deep purple cloud. He lost consciousness before the blood seeped into his lungs and he drowned in his own fluids.

Jamie stood up and tried to see what was happening, but the metallic frame of the escalator was blocking his view. One minute Jake was there, and the next, he wasn't. Jamie looked at Tim for a clue, but Tim had not broken his gaze from the fountain.

"Tim!! TIM!!!" Jamie screamed, and finally, Tim looked at Jamie. He continued to look at him as he pulled his hands away from the barrier and stepped backwards into nothing. His body plummeted straight down into the food court and onto one of the white metal chairs, where, had his neck not broken first, the twisted metal frame impaling him through the chest would have been the cause of death. His body twitched and skipped for ten seconds, then went limp.

Natalie dropped her soda, and Jamie leaned his body toward the fountain and threw up chunks of chewed chicken sandwich into the green water.

Jamie stared at the peach-brown siding on the front of his Cape Cod style house. From his vantage point in the passenger side of Jennifer's Pontiac, he could see the Pratts' orange tabby crouched under the evergreen bush, stalking a mouse or mole. When Jennifer rested her hand on his left thigh, he jumped slightly but did not turn to face her.

"Jamie, baby... you okay?" she asked, curling her red-lacquered fingers around the inside of his leg. She checked her makeup in the rearview mirror. "'Your mom home?" she added, then pressed her slippery, glossed lips together and squeezed his quadricep. Jennifer once thought that dating a guy seven years her junior would come with more advantages than drawbacks—I mean, the bedroom stamina alone was a selling point—but after six months of sneaking into Jamie's bedroom and tip-toeing around his parents' work schedules, the novelty was wearing thin. Besides, ever since the tragedy in the mall two months back, Jamie was relatively useless in bed. When he wasn't vegging out in front of the television or staring stupidly out into space—like he was as they sat there—he was sleeping. The kid slept about fourteen hours a day: was she dating a sixteen-year-old or a six-year-old?

Jamie pushed her hand off of his leg and opened the car door. "Gotta go. Thanks for the ride." He got out and shut the door behind him, then jogged up the walkway without looking back.

Jennifer tapped the button on her door panel to roll down the passenger window. "Don't bother calling me again, Jay," she called out to his back. She waited for his reaction, something to indicate that he had heard her and understood, but there was none. He climbed the three cement stairs, unlocked the front door, and disappeared inside.

The house was quiet. The previous year, Jamie's mother had purchased one of those germ zappers that used ultraviolet light or something similar—she had heard hospitals used them, and it had been a particularly bad flu season—but the motor had died, and the white noise it had elicited for more than a year had been replaced with dead silence. Jamie kicked off his sneakers in the front hallway and padded to his bedroom at the end of the hall.

He didn't need to draw the shades—he kept them closed twenty-four hours a day. He hadn't let sunlight into his room since returning home from the twins' funeral. That day, he hadn't bothered going to the James' house for the after-party, or whatever they called it. He had stayed at the gravesite even after Mr. James had to pry Mrs. James' hands from the silver caskets and stuff his sobbing wife in the stretch limousine. Jamie had been the only one left when the last car pulled away and the cemetery workers began to collapse the folding chairs and sweep up the errant flowers and discarded Kleenex, and he had walked home, despite the cemetery being a good four miles from his neighborhood. The trek had provided Jamie with enough time to recall, over and over, the look on Tim's face before he let go of the barricade railing. It was an image he saw imprinted on the darkness as he tried to fall asleep at night, and it was the first thing he considered when he woke up screaming from another nightmare.

His parents shipped him off to a psychologist twice a week, every week, beginning a week after the mall incident. The shrink—or Paul, as Jamie was supposed to call him—pressed him not about the deaths of Jake and Tim, but rather, about Elio Harmon's drowning.

"That happened, like, three years ago," Jamie said, nudging a tiny piece of paper on the blue Berber rug with the toe of his shoe. "Why do you want to talk about that?"

"Well, he was a classmate who died rather tragically, and your parents told me that you were present when it happened. You were present when Jake and Tim died, too. That's an awful lot of terrible stuff to witness," Paul said.

"You sayin' I had something to do with Tim and Jake?" Jamie sat forward in his chair and crossed his arms over his chest.

Paul paused a beat. "No. Do you feel responsible for their deaths?"

Jamie shrugged and resumed kicking the paper.

"Do you ever think about your classmate who died…" Paul checked his notes. "Elio? Elio Harmon?"

Jamie looked toward the lone window in the room. A single, dead leaf had lodged itself on the screen and waved helplessly in the summer breeze. "Nope."

Paul made a note in his pad, put his pen down, and folded his hands together in his lap. The two said nothing more for the remainder of the session, and Paul had not brought up Elio's name since. Twice following the appointment, Jamie dreamed of Elio. The content was the same both times: Jamie was getting ready to step into a hot shower after baseball practice. He was covered in mud and sweat. When he stepped into the tub, he leaned down to adjust the water temperature, and when he stood up again, Elio was standing in the water's spray, staring at him. His face was pale and swollen, his eyes bloodshot and empty. Jamie began yelling at Elio to leave the shower, but Elio's only response was to open his mouth wide—wide like he was a serpent who was trying to swallow Jamie whole—and reddish-brown water poured from his throat and onto Jamie, staining his skin everywhere it touched. Jamie couldn't move—he was rooted to the spot—and the water's temperature turned scalding hot. He could still feel the burning sensation when he woke, covered in sweat.

Jamie grabbed his earbuds and prepared to assume his afternoon position, a dead-man's float atop his unmade bed, to zone out for a while. Maybe he'd smoke some weed if he had any of that skunk he had scored from one of Jennifer's friends. He opened his nightstand drawer and was rustling through its contents, looking for the bag, when he heard a voice in the kitchen. "Mom?" he called out, still holding the earbuds in his hand. He hadn't heard her come home, and she was never around this early in the day.

He wandered into the hallway, glancing into the living and dining rooms as he went. The same voice drifted from the kitchen. *It's you,* he thought he heard it say. It wasn't his mother's voice… who could it be? Who was in the house? Should he bring a weapon? He backtracked and grabbed his baseball bat from behind his bedroom door: if there was an intruder, he would be ready.

He entered the kitchen, bat held high in the air like he was swinging for the Green Monster. There was no one there. He walked to the back door. It was locked from the inside.

He heard it again—just a whisper this time, but it was clear what it said.

It's you.

Jamie blinked his eyes repeatedly. Was he asleep? He could have sworn it was coming from… the sink? He looked in and around the stainless-steel basin, feeling like a fool. *No one can hide in a sink, you fucken idiot*, he thought to himself. *Jesus, it's a good thing you* didn't *smoke yet.*

And yet, there was the whisper again.

It's yooooou.

Jamie leaned his head into the sink and bent his ear toward the drain. Was it coming from the pipes? That was it! Someone was in the house and speaking through the pipes to mess with him. Well, he'd show them.

He opened the doors to the cabinet under the sink and inspected the contents. A wide, white pipe snaked down from the sink and disappeared into the floor.

The cellar. They must be in the cellar. He smiled. "Okay, fucktard," he said, keeping his voice even. "You asked for it." He readied his bat, opened the door to the basement, and switched on the light.

His father's woodshop monopolized most of the left side of the area; tools, two-by-fours, and random metal doodads scattered his workbench, and an overworked wall outlet sprouted at least five different cords, all intertwined and running off of one another, practically begging for an electrical fire. His father had taken a new miter saw out of its box and added it to the cord jamboree: Jamie had given it to him for Father's Day the previous Sunday. The other side of the basement was practically sterile: other than a washer and dryer and the ancient furnace, the area was barren, even of dust bunnies.

No one was there, and yet, Jamie heard the sound again.

It's you, you, yooooooooou, it repeated.

He spun around wildly, trying to determine the source. It seemed to be echoing off the walls, swimming along the ceiling, trapped within the pipes running above his head.

That was it. It was in the pipes.

"I found you!" Jamie called. "You think you can hide from me? Fuck THAT!" He held the bat at a right angle to his body, repositioned his hands to line up the swing perfectly, and slashed with the bat as hard as he could at the copper pipe above his head. The impact ricocheted down his arm, vibrating painfully like he had struck his funny bone against a door frame. He hit it again, and again, and again, until he saw that the joint was beginning to warp and give way. One final hit cracked the pipe open and water began to spray onto Jamie like celebratory confetti.

It's you, it's you, it's you, it's you! the voice cheered.

Jamie hit another pipe. He knew his shoulders would ache and his palms would chafe, and he'd likely be unable to do anything but run around the field during practice for the next week, but it felt good. He sweated profusely as he ran around the basement, striking every plastic and metal pipe he could see. The water rushed out of every broken fixture, soaking his hair and clothes and spreading the length of the cellar floor, and soon his feet sloshed through a growing lake.

As he readied his swing to strike a vertical pipe running near the stairs, his bat caught something behind him. Startled, he whirled backwards to face what had surprised him, and in the process, the tip of the bat leaned on the big red switch on the top of the miter saw. It growled to life and Jamie watched in horror as it glided effortlessly, like a ghost, off the workbench and into the pool of water on the ground, sending an electrical charge through the cellar and into Jamie.

The water swirling around his ankles felt instantly hot, so hot that his instinct was to bend his knees and hop, but he was frozen in place. At the same time, it felt as if someone had reached into his chest and was squeezing his heart in a vice. He tried to take a breath, but his lungs were paralyzed, and as what felt like fire ripped through his flesh and up his legs, filleting his torso like a fisherman with a hunting knife, he felt the warm urine soak the remainder of his dry clothing and saw the cellar go dark. His last sensation was of his cheekbone fracturing as it struck the wet cement floor.

Bent

I. Jesse

Confucius said, "if you choose a career that you love, you'll never work a day in your life." I didn't become a nurse because I like to help people. I didn't become a nurse because I have an affinity for keeping cool in hectic situations or because I have a preference for soft-soled shoes with solid instep support. I became a nurse because it seemed like the most obvious transition after practically consuming anatomy books throughout my adolescence. To say that I was fixated would be an understatement. There were times when I wanted to peel the images from the glossy pages, drape them over my forearms like perfectly formed crepes, and carry them daintily to the solace of my bedroom where I could consume them still warm from the pan.

No, I didn't enjoy anatomy book drawings like every other adolescent boy "enjoys" them—as if that isn't the euphemism of the year—I mean, their ultimate purpose was by-proxy masturbation material of course, but not in the way you think. You see, I didn't use the illustrations to view naked bodies. I used them to investigate. To formulate. To plan.

Sure, maybe it all stems from that somewhat traumatic incident when I was about eight and the babysitter was curled up on the couch, watching *The Exorcist* on HBO. I needed to pee, so I crawled out of my bed and crept down the hall in my Ninja Turtle footie pajamas and did my business. For whatever reason, I chose not to return straight to bed; instead, I padded further down the hall and tip-toed into the shag-rugged living room, pitch dark save for the strobing alien glow of the television. It was just my good fortune that the scene that was playing on the screen was the one where

Ellen Burstyn is trapped in her daughter's bedroom, furniture sliding along the floors and blocking the exits, while Linda Blair hacks away at her hoo-ha with the business end of a crucifix. I froze, completely transfixed by what was going on. And then Linda's head turned in a way I had never seen a head turn. It was as if all of the joints and cartilage and muscle and bone in her body had melted. In that moment, I realized: there was nothing keeping a human body from becoming a life-sized Stretch Armstrong.

The funny thing is, the creepy back-bending spider walk scene wasn't reintroduced by William Friedkin until the movie was rereleased in 2000. I can't fathom what kind of effect that scene would've had on my sexual identity.

After that night, I became obsessed. I needed to know every detail of the human skeletal and muscular system. I dumped all of my GI Joes into a big pile on my bedroom floor and spent hours trying to bend them into yoga poses even the Kama Sutra would frown upon. Zarana and Zanzibar were my favorites, and looking back now, I can see why: unlike most of the hero Joes, those villains were half-naked, clothed in what I, a now rational and somewhat worldly adult, can only describe as "daddy bondage wear." Zanzibar, with his swarthy eye patch, midlife crisis ponytail, and brown and silver codpiece, sported a ripped orange t-shirt like a bizarre fetish club stripper. Zarana, the decidedly more butch of the two, wore ripped jeans, a pink halter, and elbow-length leather gloves. The red knee pads draped over the tops of her boots are a detail crystalized in my memory, one that immediately came to mind when Samantha, my rich, blonde, dumb-as-rocks girlfriend in high school, decided to deliver a special present for my sixteenth birthday but insisted on kneeling on the throw pillows from her parents' Sunpan Modern Bugatti grain leather sofa while doing it.

I spent hours, more likely months, of my tween years

trying to bend Zanzibar and Zarana and their merry band of Tom Savini Sex-Machine-costume inspired action figures into human pretzels. After my father took me kite flying on Wells Beach one summer, I swiped the spool of string and repurposed it as fixing rope, manipulating tiny Joe bodies into contortionist tableaus. After weeks of careful, systematic stretching, I managed to turn Zanzibar's head completely around until he was a fortune teller in Dante's *Inferno*, forever doomed to look only behind himself and tickle his silver skull pendant with the tip of his hair. Unfortunately for Zarana, though, I became too impatient, and frustrated after weeks of trying to make her elbows entwine behind her back, she broke in two, her torso spilling a dried-out black rubber band and her splayed legs held together only by a tiny metal hook.

Twenty-five years later, I still have her legs. Sometimes I think about attaching an ornament hook to them and hanging them somewhere out of sight on the town's Christmas tree, but that might give the police a clue to my identity, and it's best not to be reckless after what I've done lately.

II. Rebekah

My name means "tied up" in Hebrew. I shit you not. When I was a kid, a bunch of us looked up our names in my mom's old baby book shoved way in the back of the old, musty bookcase. Apparently, it had been a real party game in the late 1970s, deciding what to name your little bundle of post-Roe v. Wade joy. When we cracked open the spine, a few dog-eared pages pulled us right to our brood's namesakes. My older brother, Matthew? His name means "Gift of God." My sister Abigail? "Gives joy." And my cousin Adam, his name translates into "Son of the red earth," whatever the fuck that means. Rebekah? "Bound." Restrained. Confined.

The irony kills me.

I didn't set out to become a dominatrix. I mean, I know everyone in the sex trade says that, unless they're lying and/or coked up so high they'd say just about anything to keep the camera rolling. When you're sitting at that worn wooden desk in third grade, tracing the scratches and graffiti with your finger, all the while cursing the son of a bitch whose etchings cause your pencil to make holes in your papers because the surface below isn't perfectly flat anymore, you don't daydream about one day, maybe someday, wearing a latex cat suit and cracking a whip against some thirty-something-year-old district attorney whose suit jacket shoulder smells a little like sour milk and Fruity Pebbles. You don't go shoe shopping with Mom the summer before you begin junior high and imagine the sales clerk licking the toe of your brown Candies t-strap loafer. You don't fantasize about hog-tying your senior prom date and stuffing him in the trunk of his dad's Dodge Aries while you stab your undercooked chicken cordon blue and listen to your best friend whine about her stiletto heels *totally killing her feet*.

I mean, maybe you do think about all of those things. But you don't make it a career choice. When Mrs. Zahn, my high school guidance counselor, called me into her office in October of my senior year to have "the talk"—you know, since I hadn't expressed any interest in applying to college, entering the military, or even pursuing a dead-end career as a Citgo convenience store attendant or IHOP waitress—I had nothing to offer her, not even a half-assed line of bullshit about wanting to become a kindergarten teacher or a famous fashion designer. I simply stared at her and waited out the five minutes of silence that hung between us until the bell rang for next period.

I loafed around community college for a few years,

even honed a trade working for an engraver part-time to pay my rent. The place was called "Stanislau's Personalized Gifts," and Stan, the mild-mannered owner with the heavy Polish accent, was patient and taught me first how to engrave metal plates using a machine. After a few months, I was using the hand stencils and detailing calligraphy like an ancient stenographer on papyrus. I even tried my hand at stone etching a few times and seriously considered going into the tombstone design business. I still might. It's an art, transcribing someone's last identity onto a marble slab. I dabbled in wood carving a bit, too, and was even hired to create a set of "special edition" paddles for Pi Beta Phi's Rush Week; the sorority liked my work so much that they let me keep one of them afterwards. I still personalize paddles for wedding shower gifts every now and then. It's the gift that keeps on giving.

Anyway, one night after work, a bunch of us headed up to Sophia's Bar for the usual obnoxious binge-drinking and beer goggling, and I met this guy and we really hit it off. His name was Chris, and he had this beautiful light brown skin, big, brown doe-eyes and a headful of soft, curly brown hair. When he laughed, his whole body shook, like the joy was ricocheting off of his insides like Pop Rocks. We sucked down Mind Erasers first through those tiny cocktail straws, then finally by pouring them down our throats without swallowing, sometimes ice cubes and all. We shared a cab back to my apartment, and while I didn't make it a habit to bring strange men into my home, I knew my two roommates would be there within the hour; I figured I could survive his plan to knock me out and rob the place and still live to tell the tale if worse came to worse.

Almost immediately after stumbling through my front door, we began making out like newlyweds on honeymoon. I pulled him into my bedroom, the second door off the hall of our railroad flat, and he held his hands against the sides of my face and said, "Tell me what to do."

I laughed and tried to untie my sneaker without falling over. "Um… help me get my stupid shoes off," I joked.

Chris leaped to my feet and began to furiously untie my muddy Keds, and when my socks were finally exposed, he quickly peeled them off and bowed down like a devout Muslim facing Mecca to kiss the tops of my feet. "Tell me to clean them with my tongue. I'm a very bad boy. I need to be punished," he wailed suddenly, not looking up at me at all.

I was confused. The evening had taken a really weird turn. This kind of kink dialogue was usually reserved for steady relationships that had cooled or cheesy late-night cable movies. "Uh… yeah, okay. Go ahead. Lick my feet. Consider yourself warned, though: I've been on them all day. They have that not-so-fresh-feeling," I said, suddenly wondering how I could manage a graceful exit to grab a glass of ice water: my mouth was fetid and dry with post-alcohol tackiness.

Chris wrapped his meaty hands around my ankles and bent his head back, finally meeting my eyes. "I want you to slap me," he said, his face completely serious.

I laughed. "You came home with the wrong gal, buddy. I'm a pacifist. I don't even kill spiders—I scoop them up in Dixie cups and escort them outside."

He smiled but didn't move his hands from my lower legs. I shifted my weight a bit, more to assess how easily I could wiggle away to get that glass of water than out of nervousness. When he felt my movement, his grip tightened. "I'm not letting go until you slap me across the face," he said. "Hard."

I tried to move my feet again, and when I was unsuccessful, I glanced quickly around the room, running the situation quickly through the rational filters in my brain. He was drunk and wobbly. He was on his knees and would need an extra second or two to push himself up into a running position if I needed to get away fast. Defense weaponry was scarce, but I spied the barrel of my curling iron peeking out from a pile of discarded laundry on the floor near the hamper, and in a pinch, I still had my roommate Sharon's duck-handled umbrella stuffed underneath my bed where I shoved most of my acquisitions. I tried to think of what to say next, but only one-liners from man-hating Lifetime movies came to mind. "Get your hands off of me," I said with as much menace as I could gather. "Right. Now."

A hard second passed. Chris didn't blink. "No."

I paused. Now I was angry. Who the fuck did this guy think he was, bullying me into slapping him?

I pulled my arm back and smacked the side of Chris's face as hard as I could—so hard, the sting on my palm made me wave it around immediately to shake off the pain. He winced a bit, then returned his head to its original position. "Again," he said softly.

This time, I slapped him with my right hand and followed with my left, a one-two strike. I didn't wait for him to react. I continued alternately slapping and punching his face until he let go of my ankles, and then, instead of using my newfound freedom to run out of my bedroom, I began to kick him in the stomach. He did nothing to defend himself, even repositioning himself on his back on my nearby futon mattress so that more of his body was exposed. My assault continued for a good five minutes, until blood began to run from his nose and my toes and wrists started to ache. I sank to the floor in exhaustion, panting and wiping the sweat that had begun to form on my forehead.

We were quiet for a long while, and then Chris got to his feet, grabbed a tissue from the box on my nightstand to wipe his face, and walked over to me. I was still crouched in the same place on the floor. He touched my shoulder gently.

"You're one sexy fucking pacifist," he said. Then he opened my bedroom door and left.

We never saw each other again, but I slept better that night than I had in years.

III. Jesse

I want to go on record and say that I have never viewed prostitutes as lesser human beings. I don't subscribe to that conservative crap, and I have never treated a patient differently because he or she was poor or white trash. I have little patience for stupid people, that's true, but poor doesn't always translate into dumb. And I know prostitution doesn't necessarily mean poverty either. You always hear about those bored suburban housewives who get their rocks off selling it while their corporate husbands are at work, and I am here to attest that it is not, in fact, an urban myth.

In the beginning, I only ordered custom call girls— the kind where you call a service, tell the operator what you want—height, hair color, hold the anchovies—and within an hour, she's on your doorstep, hotter and fresher than a Domino's pizza. Thank you, American Express. One of the women, a petite but curvy gal named Mary Jane with a strawberry blonde Jennifer Aniston haircut and a meticulous manicure, stayed in bed with me for a bit after my deeds were done. Truth be told—I fell asleep immediately after, having worked a double the night before, and I had neglected to untie her wrists from her ankles before inspecting the insides of my eyelids. She had no choice but to watch her tiny, pedicured feet transform from dark pink to slightly purple after her attempt to unravel my intricate braiding had only managed to cinch the restraints tighter. A half hour into my snoring, she lost all feeling in her toes and nudged me awake.

I apologized profusely and gave her an extra tip for her trouble, and that's when she confided in me. "I'll have to stick to pants for a little while," she laughed, rubbing the marks the rope had burned into her lower legs. "My husband wouldn't understand."

And that's when she did it. Sore from having been held in one position for too long, Mary rolled her shoulders back and reached her arms above her head to stretch. She plaited her hands together, bent her elbows, and cupped the top of her head like a finger yarmulke. Without thinking, I jumped behind her, grabbed each of her elbows, and pulled them back hard, trying to make them touch. I recall wanting to mimic the Monarch butterfly I had seen resting on a flower in my garden earlier that week. Wings outspread, wings folded.

Her arm sockets cracked with a loud popping sound, and Mary screamed: a high-pitched, primal screech of both surprise and pain. I had not only dislocated both of her shoulders, but I had ruptured one of her coracobrachialis, the muscle running just under the top of the bicep where it attaches to the shoulder. Still holding her elbows together, I shifted my arms slightly from side to side and felt the new freedom with which her no-longer-tightly-tethered extremities could move. Mary buckled, made a terrible wail, and fainted, falling forward and back onto my bed, face-first.

In that moment, I saw my two choices as plain as day. I could carry Mary to my car and drive her to the hospital. I could pay for her medical treatment and maybe even throw her a few bucks in hush money. I was certain the service would never accept an order from me again, but that was to be expected.

I pondered that option for about two seconds, then chose the other one. I grabbed the rope from the floor and tied Mary's elbows tightly together, weaving the rope in and out along her forearms until I could tie the ends together at her wrists. I gently turned her face so that she could still breathe—I'm not a monster, for God's sake—and stood back to admire my work. From the side, her silhouette resembled that of a great white shark, her teepeed elbows the tip of an ominous fin. I grabbed my phone and took photo after photo from every angle: I had to commemorate this image—my Zarana had finally been achieved, and I hadn't broken this one, at least not irreparably. My excitement almost reaching a climax, I climbed onto the bed and straddled her thighs, preparing to achieve what would surely be the greatest orgasm of my life, when Mary came to and began to moan. She opened her eyes and immediately began to cry, not because I was preparing to violate her but because she was in so much physical pain.

I lost my erection. I could not perform if I knew she was in pain. I was a rigger, but apparently, I wasn't a sadist. Fuck. What a way to find out.

I climbed off of the bed and quickly began to untie her.

Before helping her into the wheelchair at the hospital I put five hundred dollars in her back pocket.

Her husband wouldn't have understood.

IV. Rebekah

Have you heard of Fetlife? It's a social media site on the border of the Dark Web for individuals with sexual fetishes. If it whips, chains, bullies, cowers, pees, peeps, poops, licks, diapers, or switch-hits, you'll find it there. There are even in-person "club meetings" and game nights. Profiles are free, but you do have to run through a verification process. Nothing is too freakish, nothing is too vanilla. When I first joined, more as free advertising than to expand my social calendar, I saw my old Philosophy professor's picture in a profile. If I had registered sooner, I might have scored an A in that class after all.

Now that I have a regular rotation of clientele, I'm not as desperate to glean new business, but I do still check my Fet mailbox every now and then. That's how I met Jesse.

One of my best friends, Johnny, is an out gay man. He's extremely handsome and as fabulous as they come, but he tells me that his biggest problem in the sex department is finding a compatible partner. He's a self-described top, and for whatever reason, he finds himself attracted to men who, as he finds out later, are also tops. Two tops don't jive: it's like trying to attach two screws together. You need a nut, or everything falls apart. Although we operate in separate sexual toolboxes, albeit neighboring ones at that, Jesse and I are both tops. We could never connect as sexual partners. We did, however, thrive as friends once we learned to interact as a team.

Jesse had misunderstood my ad and booked a "meet and greet" over breakfast at a greasy diner near my apartment. I always required this public meeting for new clients: why waste my time with wishy-washers or endanger myself with potential kidnappers, rapists, or serial murderers? Not that I could tell if someone had the potential to kill someone by the way they dipped their toast into their eggs: I mean, I certainly didn't recognize it in Jesse.

When I walked into O'Brien's Corner at seven in the morning on a Tuesday, I knew right away which man was him, even though he didn't look at all as I had imagined. He was tall, but not too tall, and very thin, but muscular in the upper-arm region. His hair was wavy and a little too long on top, so it swooped over his eyebrows like a ballet dancer. The strangest part of about him was his face—I knew he was in his mid-thirties, but his face was that of a thirteen or fourteen-year-old boy, complete with Cillian Murphy lips and freckles. I suspected he had made a concerted effort not to color the streaks of grey in his hair so that he wouldn't be carded on a regular basis. Without them, he hardly looked old enough to drive a car.

I stood by the booth and offered my hand. "Morning," I said. "J?"

He clasped my hand in his. "Good morning yourself, R." His hand was smooth and cool, like a doctor's, and it too was sprinkled with tiny freckles.

I slid into the seat across from him. "What are we eating?"

He laughed, and his wet blue eyes danced with amusement. "A gal with an immediate appetite is always appreciated." He brought his water glass to his lips and drank a healthy swallow, his lips grinning and his eyes still focused intently on me. I liked him immediately, which is good, because twisted friends are hard to find.

They're even harder to keep.

V. Jesse

My Mary Jane experience was one from which I learned a number of things.

1. Don't do anything hurtful, damaging, or that might otherwise require a trip to the emergency room with someone to whom my credit card is tied

2. Don't meet prostitutes in my own home or drive them anywhere in my own car, especially those with whom I wish to push the boundaries of flexibility

3. Don't push those boundaries of flexibility with prostitutes without doping them up with pain-killers first

4. A hospital visit costs a fuckload of money without insurance

But most importantly,

5. I liked dislocating Mary's shoulders. I liked seeing her arms pinned back in an unnatural posture more than I had enjoyed anything in my life thus far.

It took a while to master my new technique. I rented cheap but clean motel rooms on the other side of the city, then picked up a pro or two in a seedy bar not far away. I couldn't risk transporting a girl in my own vehicle again, so walking to my room was a must. I swiped a few Fentanyl patches and a handful of the lozenges from the pharmacy at my work when I knew Stacy, whose two-pack-a-day smoke habit couldn't keep her from slipping out of the back door every half hour or so, was careless enough to let the door swing open just long enough for me to stick a card in to block the auto lock feature while she escaped to shove another oral cancer welcome mat in front of her mouth. I cut the patches into quarters and sealed the pieces in a Ziploc baggie, then packed them alongside my ropes into an overnight duffel bag.

As exciting as the spontaneity of folding Mary Jane's arms had been, I needed to plan things carefully from then on. If I broke a woman's knees or ankles, if I dislocated hip flexors or tore Achilles tendons, it was likely my little rope bunny would pass out from the shock or perhaps even die from spinal cord injury or blood loss. I was a smart man, smart enough to know that it is nearly impossible to get rid of a dead body without a trace. Besides, I had no interest in fucking a corpse. What was the point of folding these women into flesh accordions if I couldn't stick my cock in them as a grand finale?

When it was time for my first foray under this new protocol, I checked into the motel, slipped a lozenge into my pocket, and walked the three blocks, past the dilapidated housing and run-down Mini-Mart to The Atlas Cafe, a tavern with the square footage of my living room whose wood-paneled walls and cement floors I guessed hadn't seen a bright light in about a decade. There, sitting with her gazelle-like legs folded neatly around each other under the barstool, was my first experiment. Her hair was long and shaggy and dyed a teenie-bopper purple color over black and grey roots; her eyes were large and brown and heavily lined in black. She looked to be at least forty years old, even in the dim lighting, and had a silver ball piercing in her cheek dimple like a metallic beauty mark. I slid into the stool two chairs down from her: close enough to start a conversation but with enough distance as to not raise suspicion. She nodded her head at me and within a record twenty minutes, Keri (spelled like the lotion, she made certain to explain) and I were walking back toward my room, me fingering the door key in my pocket and her tonguing the lozenge she had accepted from me without a quiver of suspicion.

By the time I wrestled the sticky door open, Keri had begun to sway a bit on her feet. "Phew," she said dreamily, the word coming out as *foooyood*. "This really does pack a wallop." She draped her long fingers along my shoulder like she was trying to regain her balance.

"Have you taken an opioid painkiller before, miss?" I asked, somewhat amused. I was starting to suspect I wouldn't need to slap one of the patches on her skin after all. It was just as well: they could take hours to take full effect. Keri walked purposefully over to the polyester-quilted bed and sat down on the edge. She rubbed her palms over the tops of her thighs over and over, like she was petting a cat. The faraway look in her now-glassy eyes told me that she was ready. I crossed my arms in front of my chest and waited for her to initiate payment specifics.

Instead, she stuck her hand out toward me like a

parent beckoning a child. "C'mere, you big silly," she said, half smiling, half yawning. She crossed and uncrossed her slender legs, then crossed them again; her legs were so thin, she could tuck her foot around her calf, a second cross. This phenomenon made my mind race.

I unfolded my arms and walked over to the bed. Keri looked up at me expectantly. "I have a very specific preference when it comes to sex," I said. "How flexible are you?" I touched her hair. It felt like matted straw, and I pulled my hand away in disgust.

She smiled a drunken smile and put her hand on my stomach. "Oh, I've been known to do an impossible yoga pose or two," she said. "For the right price, that is. $200 for straight sex, but for anything kinky, the price doubles."

"Good," I said, reaching over to my duffel bag and unzipping the top. "Because I'm a big fan of achieving the impossible." I snatched the pile of fifties I had laid beside the Ziplocked patches and grabbed the thin, yellow rope from the top of the bag.

For a moment, I thought I saw a flash of concern fall across Keri's face, but it was soon replaced with contented calm. The Fentanyl was working overtime; I hadn't considered the interaction it might have with the alcohol, or how much Keri had drunk before I arrived, for that matter. She began unbuttoning her shorts and pushed them to the floor, along with her panties. As she lifted her t-shirt over her head, I felt the same pang of conscience I had felt with Mary Jane. I had wanted the Fentanyl to numb my partners; I hadn't wanted to dope them beyond the point of rational consent. I counted out eight fifties, folded them, and shoved them into Keri's shorts pocket on the floor.

"Thanks, darlin'," she mumbled. "My goodness... mmmmm, I don't think I can feel my face anymore," she said. "Hey, slap me across the face."

I snorted and unrolled the rope.

"I said, slap me," she repeated. "Come on, baby… I just want to see how it feels."

Laying the rope on the mattress, I grabbed Keri gently by the shoulders and pulled her so that her head could lie comfortably on the pillows at the top of the bed. She obliged without objection, and when her head touched the pillow, she lowered her eyelids into a squinting position and smiled at me again. I drew my hand back and slapped her half-heartedly across the face. She did not react but kept smiling.

I back-crawled down to her legs and grabbed her left calf firmly by her ankle and beneath her knee. Holding it parallel to the floor, I folded her leg backwards so that her knee was touching her hip. She still did not react. Now was the time to see if my plan would work. I tightened my grip on her leg and with a quick jerking motion, pushed it toward the mattress as hard as I could, feeling the tight snap as the knee ligaments ruptured. Keri's face changed but she did not cry; instead, she looked confused. I tested the new freedom of her appendage by wiggling her lower leg in her knee socket. It felt disconnected, like her knee had turned to Jell-O. When I straightened and dropped her leg onto the mattress, it bounced once, and I could see the outline of her kneecap shift freely beneath her pale skin.

I picked up her right leg and repeated the process, feeling the snap of the ligaments and the gelatin wobbliness once more. Once again, Keri moved her head but did not cry out in pain or protest. I could feel my heart racing in my chest in excitement. My groin throbbed. I snatched the yellow rope and moved it into a pile between Keri's upper thighs. Grabbing her right calf again, I turned it inward, then pulled her foot upwards to rest next to her right hip so that her leg formed a V-shape. I mimicked the action with her left leg and leaned back to admire my work. I had made a perfect W. *W for   Why-didn't-I-think-of-this-sooner?*   I   thought,   and chuckled to myself.

I ran the yellow rope back and forth, around and under each calf and thigh, pulling the V's closed so that they resembled chicken wings. Keri began to moan, and I wondered if the lozenge had begun to wear off. Reaching into the duffel bag, I felt for the plastic bag of snipped patches. "Don't you worry, my little yoga master," I said. "This will make it all better." I peeled the backing from the patch piece and pressed it firmly onto the left side of her abdomen. Then, in one swift motion, I flipped Keri over onto her stomach and her tightly folded legs spread to each side of her hip. I grabbed the ends of the rope, brought her wrists together to the bottom of her spine, and tied them securely together.

When I was done, I climbed from the bed and stood at its foot, admiring my work. With the bright purple hair concealing her face, Keri resembled a strange insect of some sort, her tiny leg wings splayed helplessly to each side. I angled my phone to take my photos before allowing myself the final indulgence, but I found I could only take three shots before giving in. "I can't feel my feet," Keri called out weakly from under the nest of hair.

"I know, sweetheart," I said. "And that's probably for the best." I unlatched my belt, unbuckled my pants, and climbed onto the bed.

VI. Rebekah

I had just finished the three-hour session with one of my regulars, a high school Special Education teacher who called himself Sean, when my cell phone buzzed with vibration from the dresser. Sean, who was shaped like a fleshy Weeble-Wobble but sported an incongruous sandy blonde crew cut like a Marine, was in the hotel room bathroom, running his arms under cold water to quell the sting of the burns he'd special-requested at the start of our meeting. Ever since America had banned clove cigarettes, I'd had to special order packs from Canada on eBay just to avoid the disgusting remnants of Newports or Marlboros in my mouth and hair. You'd be surprised how many people want their flesh singed as part of their session. I've seriously considered a GoFundMe page to finance an indoor grill and fire poker set. Nothing shocks me anymore.

"Speak," I commanded into the receiver. This was my business-only iPhone; I deducted it and the separate bill off of my taxes as a work expense.

"It's Jesse," said the voice on the other end of the line. "I need your help. Can you come by?"

Sean poked his head into the room. "You got any more of those Band-Aids?" he asked. I moved the phone to my other ear, felt around in my travel case, grabbed the blue and white box, and tossed it to him. "Thanks," he said and disappeared back into the bathroom.

"I'm a little tied up right now," I said, "and not in the way you'd prefer." I tried to wrestle my suit pants back on with my one free hand.

Jesse was silent on the other end, and for a moment, I assumed he had hung up. Then he said, "I can wait. You're the only one who can help me with this."

I tucked my wallet, now fat with earnings from the day, into my case and glanced at the digital clock on the nightstand. "Let me drop some stuff off at my apartment and I'll be over. Where are you, exactly?"

Two hours later, I was walking briskly along American Legion Highway after departing the subway, glad my wallet was hidden safely away in my jacket's inside pocket. A plane flew by low overhead, temporarily deafening me. The only thing separating me and the traffic whizzing by was a battered guard rail, and each time a particularly noisy car sped by me, I flinched, readying my body to take the impact of a hit and run. The sun was just beginning to set, and I was relieved to see the rainbow-accented blue hotel sign just ahead of me in the exhaust-filled haze. I made a mental note to call a car service to take me home later.

Jesse was sitting in the lounge of the hotel's resident Mexican restaurant, Tio Juan's, at a counter-height table with three other stools, his back to the window. He was sipping a dark-colored beer. "'Pick a shady enough location?" I asked. "What's the matter: all the motels in downtown East Rob-Me booked solid?"

He smiled and put his glass down. "Well, you know the old adage: *Lynn, Lynn, City of Sin: You never come out the way you went in.* Gotta represent."

The waitress, a tiny waif of a thing with thinning hair and an owl tattoo on her inner elbow, appeared at my side. "What can I bring you?" she asked.

"Uh… an appletini, I guess," I answered.

When she was out of earshot, Jesse leaned back in his stool and looked at me, wide-eyed. "Well, don't you look fancy," he said, motioning to my pantsuit and tidy hairstyle. "Just outta work, are we, madam?"

"Yes, wiseass," I said, suddenly self-conscious. "Now what is the emergency? And you're buying this drink, by the way," I added, as Owl Tattoo placed the light green martini in front of me. I fished the maraschino cherry from the bottom of the glass and popped it in my mouth.

Jesse stopped smiling and started to run his index finger along the rim of his beer stein. "So, I think I may have killed someone." He said it so nonchalantly that I thought I had misheard him. He didn't take his eyes off of his glass, and he didn't remove his finger.

"I'm sorry—what?" I asked, taking a big gulp of my drink.

"I told you about the Fentanyl, right? How I've been using it?"

Ever since our first breakfast together, Jesse and I had been meeting for monthly meals in seedy diners. It was our chance to swap stories in our self-created judgement-free zone. Neither of us were out to our friends or family: hell, my mom still brags about her daughter landing a corporate office manager job in the financial district with only a handful of college courses under her belt. I didn't know where Jesse lived or even what his last name was, but I knew he was a nurse by trade and that he was fixated on turning human bodies into unnatural shapes: it was his own little fetish puzzle, a Sudoku or New York Times crossword to be completed naked and with a lot of illegal painkillers.

He stopped touching his glass and rested his hands on the table between us. "Well, I finally ran out. But a few weeks before that, this patient came into the emergency room, whacked out on some drug—we initially thought it was a heroin-speed combo of some sort—and since he was stable, we let him fester in the waiting room for a bit. You know, give him time to ride the high down before monopolizing a bed. We could still see him from the desk, just in case anything *did* happen.

"He was sitting in one of the chairs on the end of a row, his left arm kinda dangling over the side, toward the floor. All of a sudden, this guy, this twenty-something-year-old guy who's there with his grandmother, he gets really irate with the in-take staff, screaming that his nana's sugar is through the roof and they're out of insulin and we need to see her right away. The triage nurse took a blood reading and yes, her sugar was high, but not astronomical, so she told him to have a seat and we'd get to her as soon as we could. The guy was so pissed, he wheeled her to the back of the waiting room, practically running while he was doing it, and he wheeled right by our zonked-out druggie. He cut the chair too close to the row of seats, though, and as he passed, he caught the man's dangling hand in the wheels of the chair and mangled it, almost severing the damn thing off. Blood everywhere. The grandmother starts yelling in Spanish, the girl next to the druggie starts screaming like it's *her* hand that just got Ginsued, even the damn grandson is screaming in panic. But the guy? He just looks down at his hand like he's watching a movie on his cell phone screen. No cries of pain, not even a complaint."

"What? How is that possible?" I asked, swallowing the rest of my martini.

"Our orderly ran over to him with a wheelchair and threw him in it and brought him back for medical attention," Jesse continued. "And while he was in recovery, his hand all stitched up and bandaged like a mummy, I stopped in to ask him how he was feeling. The drug he had taken had long since worn off, but he was on an opioid drip and was still feeling pretty fine.

"I asked him, 'Off the record, what did you take this evening? I've never seen anyone react to such a traumatic accident as calmly and coolly as you.' 'Grab me my coat, would you?' he said, and motioned to the plastic hospital bag of his clothing on the other chair. I did, and he fished a tiny vial half-full of white powder out of his tweed pocket and threw it at me. 'One snort and you're on the moon, buddy. A hundred bucks and you can keep it,' he said."

"So, what did you do?" I asked.

Jesse drank a healthy gulp of his beer. "I gave him the eighty I had in my wallet and told him to count his blessings." He fished his hand in the front pocket of his pants and pulled out a plastic vial with a red cap and placed it on the table.

"They call it Apache Chief. Twice as effective for numbing as Fentanyl with none of the drowsiness."

"Apache Chief? Like the SuperFriends character?" I picked up the container and turned it over in my hand. "Wow, way to disparage the Native American one more way, America: name a deadly street drug after one of their few cartoon superheroes."

Jesse emptied his glass and pointed at me. "I'm not sure Apache Chief is considered part of the graphic novel canon, but point taken, Elizabeth Warren."

I handed the vial back to Jesse. "So, what do you need me here for? What happened?" I looked down at my fingertips. "Fuck: now my prints are all over it."

Jesse smiled and put the container back in his pocket. He waved at the waitress for the check. "You're only at the top of the rabbit hole, sister. Just wait until you see what I have in my hotel room."

VII. Jesse

It's not enough to be sorry when you commit a crime, even if it's purely by accident; society mandates that the offender must pay. That seems like a pile of bullshit to me. If I honestly—for real—*honestly* did not mean for someone to die, and whoops, someone's airway is closed off for longer than allotted by natural law, am I *really* at fault? Isn't God, or Allah, or fate, or insert-magical-deity-here the one at fault?

I never intended for her to die. Her name was Lisa, just like the perfect teenage-spank-bank-fantasy girl in *Weird Science*, the one Anthony Michael Hall and that other guy create while wearing bras on their heads as Robert Downey, Jr and his terrible pre-capped teeth snicker and seethe. Just like that Lisa, my Lisa was a dream girl: buxom breasts, firm stomach and thighs, round hips and ass, a headful of bouncy hair like a Wella wet dream. Truth be told, I wasn't thrilled with her teeth: they were about three sizes too big for her mouth, forcing her to keep her lips slightly parted to make room at all times—but come on, if she had been perfect, she probably wouldn't have been working as a prostitute. There are no Julia Roberts walking Hollywood Boulevard, *Pretty Woman* fans. There are no Elisabeth Shues riding the barstools in old Vegas. Sorry, Virginia, there isn't a Santa Claus after all.

But Lisa was a bargain, especially since she had to transport herself all the way to this airport hotel a good mile away from any subway stop. I'm not sure why I chose that hotel in the first place, except that I never used the same location twice and I could see the Mexican restaurant sign from the road and suddenly had a hankering for a chile relleno. I actually had met Lisa at a bar at the airport, just having returned from a nursing symposium in Oregon. We were the only two in the bar at eleven in the morning, and I got her number, passed her a fifty, and made arrangements for her to meet me later that afternoon at a location I would text to her. I knew she'd show up: I had made certain to work in that I was returning home from a medical conference, and it's always been my experience that women, whether pros or not, can't resist the idea of fucking a doctor.

In any case, she was right on time—I appreciate punctuality—and came directly to my room. I had ordered a pitcher of margaritas from room service and poured us each a glass. I sat in the faux leather swivel chair and she lounged in the grey-upholstered easy chair, and we used the desk as a makeshift cocktail table. I casually mentioned my Apache Chief, telling her it was a pharmaceutical sample I had procured from the conference, but to my dismay, she shook her head.

"I don't do drugs," she said. "Sorry. I don't even take Tylenol for headaches. I'm not even much of a drinker, to be honest."

I squinted at her. "Really? Interesting." It wasn't interesting. It was irritating.

"Yeah," she continued. "I'm a vegetarian too. Vinyasa yoga three times a week, guided meditation daily. It's so important to be centered, you know?" She clicked her giant horse teeth together for emphasis, then stood up. "I'll be right back," she said suddenly, giving me an awkward grin, and wandered into the bathroom and shut the door.

As soon as I heard the water running, I pulled out the vial of white powder from my pocket, removed the red cap, and tapped a bit of the substance into Lisa's margarita. I felt zero guilt as I did it: after all, I was preventing her from experiencing pain or discomfort. If anything, she should thank me for stealth drugging her, I thought. Besides, if she was stupid enough to still drink from her glass after leaving it unattended with a strange man, well, I washed my hands of responsibility.

She was stupid enough.

For such a centered person who didn't drink, Lisa downed her margarita awfully fast after returning from the bathroom. In less than sixty seconds, she had replaced the glass on the table, empty save for a handful of ice cubes; she had given them so little time to melt, they still showed sharp edges. She leaned her body against the dresser and placed her hand on her hip. "So, any special requests?" she asked.

I crossed my right leg onto my opposite knee. "You do yoga, do you?"

She attempted a tight-lipped smile, but half of her teeth burst forth from her lips. "I do. Pilates too. Is there a pose you'd like to see?"

After the incident with Mary Jane, I had spent hours

surfing through yoga and Pilates, contortion and gymnastic websites, adding image after image to my fantasy gallery. I had done my research. "Can you do an inverted grasshopper, a full locust pose?"

Lisa clapped her hands excitedly. "I can! I'm so impressed you know that pose!" She pulled off her shoes and began to kneel down on the floor.

"No," I said. "On the bed. And naked."

She seemed embarrassed at forgetting where she was but quickly recovered. She briskly unzipped and removed her dress, then unclasped her bra and peeled it and the matching panties from her body. She climbed onto the light brown bedspread, not bothering to push aside the red bed runner draped along the foot as decoration. "I don't know if this is the best place to balance," she told me. "Not a lot of grounding support here. The mattress is kinda squishy."

I uncrossed my legs. "We'll make do."

Lisa lay on her stomach in the middle of the king-sized bed and placed her arms at her side, palms down. She lifted her head and rested her chin on the bedspread so that she was looking at the pillows but kept her breasts firmly on the mattress. "Ready?" she asked. I stood up and positioned myself at the foot of the bed to get a better view.

I watched in amazement as she lifted her legs behind her, keeping them almost perfectly straight and hip-distance apart, and when her shins were perpendicular to the floor, I saw her pelvis and stomach follow, until her entire torso formed a straight line starting with her shoulders, which were pressed hard against the bed, and ending with her toes, which pointed directly at the ceiling. She clasped her hands together on the bed like a kickstand. She had made herself into an upside-down T.

We were both silent in the moment, and then I whispered, "Keep going."

She tilted her legs forward toward the headboard, then bent one knee and pressed her toe against the pillows. She followed with the other leg, stretching it first toward the top of the bed as far as she could, then pulling her lower body until both of her feet were planted firmly on the bed in front of the pillows, where she could gaze at them facing her.

I stuck my hands inside the duffel and silently removed the yellow rope. I pulled my dress shirt over my head, not bothering to remove my undershirt, and practically ripped my pants and shorts off. I was still wearing my black dress socks when I climbed onto the bed and stood in back of her, holding the rope with one hand while positioning my feet on either side of her still-clasped arms. I put my free hand on her stomach and felt her abdomen; the muscle felt like heavy, raw steak beneath her taut skin. I moved my hand to the front of her thighs, which were now nearly parallel to the bed, and stroked their smoothness.

"Okay," said Lisa. "I have to pull my legs back now. It's starting to hurt a bit. I told you: this mattress is too soft. It isn't supporting my neck."

She didn't see me pull the rope under her thighs. She didn't know what was happening at all until she felt me pull the rope tight, sealing her thighs together. I weaved the rope back and forth along the entire length of her legs to her ankles, knotted it, then ran it back to her torso, securing it at her ribs. Unable to bring her legs back to the original position, Lisa began to panic. "Please… oh my god: please untie me," she said, starting to cry. "Please… I'll do anything you want."

I climbed off of the bed and fumbled around my bag for another rope. I had to affix her arms and head in order to complete my masterpiece. It wasn't until Lisa began to cry that I realized the drug I had placed in her drink wasn't having any effect. Perhaps one couldn't simply ingest it, or perhaps putting in a drink had diluted it too much. It had worked like a charm on the two women I had used it with previously, but they had snorted it and rubbed it on their gums without argument. Did Apache Chief have to be snorted or smoked to have any effect?

As I gazed upon Lisa's beautiful, contorted shape, twisted like a fishhook in the middle of my hotel bed, I realized: I no longer cared. I tied a noose into the second rope and climbed back onto the bed.

VIII. Rebekah

I had prepared myself for the worst, but at the same time, I couldn't fathom walking into a hotel room with a corpse in it. After that day, I would know someone who had actually killed someone. I mean, sure, you fantasize about following that asshole who cut you off in traffic, walking up to his driver's side window, and smashing it with a rock, maybe even pulling him out by his neck and scaring the bejesus out of him, but you don't *actually* attempt it—I mean, most people don't. The sane ones don't.

Jesse seemed sane. He seemed normal. I know that sounds like a weird thing to say, but in my line of work you come to realize something: there are only two types of people—those who engage in sexual practices that might seem strange to others and those who wish they had the balls to engage in those sexual practices. (There *is* a third category: those who read the *Fifty Shades of Grey* series and think they're hip and dangerous but are really just in need of some serious education on literary merit, but that's a discussion for another time.) Above all, Jesse was a medical professional: if anyone was qualified to engage in sexual pursuits that pushed the boundaries of traditional fucking, it would be him. Wouldn't it?

He pushed his keycard into the door slot and the light lit green. I noticed he had placed the "Please Do Not Disturb" hanger on the knob. I turned the handle and walked slowly inside, Jesse following behind me and shutting the door.

Three steps into the room, the stench of urine hit me like an ocean wave. Jesse switched on the lamps next to the bed and on the desk. On the bed was a woman—but at first, my brain didn't process that it was a woman, or that it was a human at all. She was on her side, but her arms stuck out awkwardly straight in front of her. They were covered in blue rope woven so heavily that there was more blue visible than skin. More unnerving were her legs, which were bent backwards at the hip, the back of her ankles almost touching the back of her head. They, too, were bound, but with yellow rope, and tethered to her neck and torso. The skin that bulged between the strands of rope was purple and deep red, and in some places her flesh seemed to be stretched to the point of almost bursting. By far, the most disturbing part of the tableau was the woman's head: it lolled unnaturally to the side, her mouth partly open with a brown substance dried and caked where it had dribbled onto her cheek and along her broken neck. Her eyes were open and black, like those of a cheap plastic doll.

I turned and looked at Jesse. "Holy Christ, J! What the fuck happened?!" Jesse was standing motionless, staring at the body. He was not smiling, but he wasn't frowning or furrowing his brow in worry either. He wasn't answering me, so I grabbed his shoulder and shook it.

"She wouldn't take the drug," he said. He walked nonchalantly to the other side of the bed, keeping his eyes on the body at all times. "And I guess I pressed down too hard at one point... broke her neck." He started to laugh a little, making my skin crawl. "And you know, I'm not exactly sure *when* she died: I was flipping her around and taking her every which way, and after a while, she just stopped complaining, you know?" He let out a hearty cackle at that point, and I stepped backwards instinctively.

I rested my hand on my left temple, like I was warding away a pending migraine, but I was really doing it to block the woman's corpse from my field of vision for a minute. "When did this happen, exactly?" I asked.

"Two days ago," Jesse said. "I wasn't sure what to do, you know, and then it finally hit me: a plan. I just needed a companion to lend me a hand."

I let out an audible breath. "Wow, Jess, I mean—this is beyond my field of expertise, I have to tell you." I allowed myself to look at the body again. "You don't want me to help you cut her up, do you? I'm not really a... manual labor kind of gal."

Jesse laughed. "No, no, nothing like that." He reached down beside the bed, out of sight, and reappeared with a large, wheeled suitcase. "I'm gonna stuff her in this, but I thought it would probably look weird if a single guy was carrying all of this big luggage through the lobby. If he had a wife with him, well, that might look a little less weird—you know?"

I frowned. "Let me get this straight. Is this some sort of misogynistic pantomime? Like, women are clothes whores, so people won't think twice if she's making her man haul her giant suitcase around?" I put my hand on my hip, only then realizing the absurdity of the whole situation. I was missing the point—the bigger problem was that Jesse had killed someone and had now involved me in the cover-up. If I didn't tell the police, I could be implicated and charged as an accessory.

As if reading my mind, Jesse said, "Listen. I called you because I trust you. Did I make a mistake to think that?" His face went blank, like a robot whose batteries had been suddenly yanked out of its head. There was something in his eyes that made the bottom of my stomach drop.

"No, Jesse—you weren't wrong," I said quickly. "But that's all I have to do? Just walk next to you in the lobby with the suitcase?"

He unzipped the side of the case and dropped it on the floor in front of him. "Yep, that's it." He quickly gripped his hands around the woman's wrists and ankles and began pulling her body toward the edge of the mattress. For a moment, I thought of a checkout clerk pulling a frozen turkey down the conveyor belt at my local Star Market grocery store. The body made a heavy thud as it dropped off the side of the bed and out of sight, and Jesse bent down to do some rearranging in the suitcase. Where the woman had once been there was a distinct imprint and more than one visible puddle of various colors and wetness. When Jesse reappeared, his eyes followed mine along the bedspread, and he reached over and pulled the blankets this way and that, concealing the evidence and making the bed appear slept in. It was soiled and filthy, but easily interpreted as having been utilized by living people.

We said nothing to each other as we walked coolly down the long hallway to the elevator, rode the five floors to the ground, and sauntered across the lobby past the front desk. When we reached the sliding glass door exit, however, Jesse stopped. He rested his hand on top of the case. "I have to check out," he said, as casually as if we had just completed a relaxing vacation at a spa in the Hamptons. He walked to the concierge, exchanged a few words, turned in his key card, and returned without breaking a sweat. I bit my lip as we walked side by side to a long, silver sedan in the parking lot.

Jesse clicked a button on his keys and the headlights flashed. "This is me," he said and opened the trunk. "The passenger door's unlocked. Go ahead and get in and I'll take care of the luggage."

I hesitated. I guessed I couldn't make an excuse and call a car service now. If anyone was watching, it would look weird. I would have him drop me at the subway and be on my way.

He opened the driver's side door and climbed inside. "So, where to?" he asked. "Hey, are you hungry? I'm starving. Want to get something to eat?"

"No… that's cool. I really have to get home," I said. "Why don't you just drop me off at the subway? It's right down the street, and then you can do… whatever you plan to do with your girlfriend. If you don't mind," I added.

Jesse turned on the engine and shifted the gearstick into drive. "Don't be silly, R. I owe you big-time for this. And we are intimates now, don't you think? We may not have fucked, but I think *this* trumps fucking as far as a bonding experience, don't you?" he laughed.

He seemed so at ease, so normal, that I started to question if what had just transpired had really occurred at all. Maybe this was all some sort of colossal joke. Or maybe I had taken a drug or was dreaming. Whatever it was, I knew Jesse was not going to take *no* for an answer, and there was nowhere I could pass off as my home without rousing his suspicion. I gave him my address, he plugged it into his GPS, and we rode home in the dark, making strange small talk and discussing plans for the upcoming long holiday weekend.

When we had reached my address, Jesse lowered his head in order to glean a better view of my building through his windshield. "This is you, huh? Nice building."

I shrugged my shoulders. "Yeah, I guess. Thanks." I patted my coat pockets to make certain I hadn't dropped anything in his car and took my keys out. "Thanks for the ride."

He reached over suddenly and grabbed both of my wrists and held them together. "I want to let you know that I really appreciate you helping me today," he said. "You can't ever tell anyone about this, though: do you understand?" He tightened his grip on my skin.

I tried to yank my hands away but found I could not. He was stronger than he looked. Much stronger. "Jesse, I make a living off of keeping people's dirty little secrets. I think I can manage to keep this one." I didn't know if I could, but Jesse was making me very nervous. I had never seen him look the way he was looking at me. In the dim glow of the streetlights, his eyes were blank, cold, and steady. Dead. Dead like the woman's. "Now let me the fuck go," I said with as much steadiness as I could gather.

He maintained his grip for five seconds longer, then released his hands and turned his face back to the steering wheel. "I'll see you soon," I said, and opened the car door and slid out.

As I walked up the steep cement stairs to my entrance door, I felt Jesse's eyes boring holes in my back. I turned my key in the lock and waved at him. He rolled down his window. "Just want to make sure you get in okay," he said. "I'll see you soon." I heard his window roll back up as I walked inside my building.

My apartment was the first one on the right, the same apartment I had had so many years back when I brought Chris home. Many roommates had long since moved away and into shared homes with husbands and partners, but I had kept the place, repurposing their bedrooms as guest space and storage. I flipped on the hall light, took off my coat and hung it on the rack in the living room, then kicked off my shoes and walked to the front picture window to pull the shades. As I grabbed hold of the shade, I glanced down into the street; I had to cup my hand over my eyes and press it against the glass to look closer. Jesse's car had not moved. I put my other hand against the side of my face to block out more of the glare. Jesse wasn't inside the car.

I stepped back from the window, and as I did, I saw his reflection in the glass. I turned to run, but I was trapped—there was nowhere to go. "What the fuck, Jesse?" I yelled. "What are you doing?" It was only then that I saw the rope in his hand.

He walked toward me, slowly but methodically: a cat trapping its prey. "I don't want you to think I am ungrateful. That couldn't be further from the truth." He pulled the rope through one of his hands, letting it glide along his fingertips like a lover's skin. "It was a mistake to involve you... I can't have loose ends, not if I want to keep doing what I'm doing. And I will never stop. I'm getting too good at it, and it's best not to be reckless, you know?"

He stood in front of me, his pale eyes wet and amused, almost excited. I stared at him, saying nothing. He raised his free hand and placed it on my cheek; it was smooth and cool, just as it had been the morning we first met. "I've always wondered what it would be like to make you my rope bunny. To tie up the dominatrix, make *her* helpless for once."

My mind raced, but I kept my eyes steady. Jesse was smart. He would see me formulating a plan if I didn't keep my face a blank slate. "Well, why didn't you say so?" I raised an eyebrow and painted on my best mask. "Would you like to see my room before you go?"

Jesse moved his hand higher, almost touching my eye with his index finger. "Clever girl," he said. We were both silent, staring at each other. Then, he roughly grabbed my wrists and pulled them in front of me, wrapped the rope around them tightly until I could feel the blood pool in my hands, and tied the ends. "Show me," he instructed.

I walked down the hall to the second doorway; the door was open. "The switch is on the left," I said, and Jesse turned it on. I walked over to the futon mattress and turned to face him, then lifted my arms above my head in resignation. "You'll have to unbutton me," I said.

Jesse looked at me for a moment, then ripped the front of my dress shirt open, exposing my bra. I fell backwards onto the mattress and scooted away so that my head was almost hanging off of the other side. I stretched my arms as far back as I could so that my fingers brushed the edge of the old radiator that was sandwiched under the window. "You can tie me to this," I said.

I watched and held my breath as a smile spread across Jesse's face. He began to walk around to the other side of the futon, and in that instant, I turned my body onto its side and bent my arms so that I could reach under the bed frame. As Jesse leaned down with his rope to grab my arms, I pulled out the souvenir Pi Beta Phi paddle I had stored beneath my bed, garnered as much strength as I could with my arms bound and from a prone position, and I hit Jesse across the face. The sound of the wood on flesh made a satisfying crack. He pulled back in surprise, and I sat up, managed to swing one knee beneath myself, and tried to wobble to my feet, but Jesse grabbed me by the shoulders and held me in place.

I swung the paddle again, this time aiming the edge against his neck. I slammed the wood directly onto his Adam's apple and heard a sickening crunch. Jesse let go of me and began clutching at his neck and jaw, his eyes bulging from his face. I pushed myself to my feet and pulled the paddle back far into the air, then brought it down on his head as hard as I could, feeling the skull give way. When I brought the paddle back again, red blood gushed from the wound on his scalp, and where I had made contact, there was an actual dent. I had made a dent in his head—the idea seemed bizarre and unreal—but I had no time to process it, as Jesse lunged for me in pure rage.

I don't remember exactly what happened for the five or ten or thirty minutes that followed immediately after, but I know what I did. I've seen the photographs. The police showed them to me again and again when I was questioned. The psychiatrist that evaluated me showed them to me as well, although I question her motivations in doing so. Perhaps she wanted to see if I'd show any remorse? Any signs of trauma? *Lady, you're wasting your time*, I wanted to tell her. *You forget what I do for a living. There's nothing I haven't seen.* In the pictures, there is nothing left of Jesse's face but some matted, bloody pulp. I think there may have been part of a jaw, some teeth I think, sticking out from where his neck used to be, but no nose, and certainly no eyes. Apparently, I had hit him so hard and so many times in the upper cervical region, that I almost cut his head—or what was left of his head anyway—clean off.

Nothing shocks me anymore.

Of course, when the police discovered Lisa's body in the trunk of Jesse's car, they had no choice but to rule my actions as self-defense. When his driver's license photo hit the news, women were coming out of the woodwork in droves to report incidences of torture and abuse.

I was a lucky lady, the cops said, and I was. Jesse's name? It comes from the Hebrew word *Yishay*.

It means "gift."

The Last of the Janet Leighs

It always struck Christina as ridiculous, all of those people making resolutions at the first of the year. I mean, why quit a bad habit unless it's causing more harm than good? Or, unless the quitting is part of a court order.

Haha.

Christina chuckled to herself morbidly as she stared at the shower tile, letting the hot water beat on her throat. Her sister was in court-ordered rehab, the second stint in five years. She had been caught driving with a suspended license again, but instead of going straight to jail—do not pass Go, do not collect $200—the girl had turned on the waterworks for the judge, claimed an abusive childhood, absentee father, cult imprisonment, some shit like that, and POW! she was whisked away to a cushy 28-day program... again. The last time, they let her out after only 21: just in time for her sister to attend her daughter's school awards ceremony at the middle school, carrying a travel mug full of box wine and yodeling *Woo Hoo!* each time the poor kid's name was called. Humiliated by her mother's behavior, Christina's niece had run off the stage in embarrassment.

So, January resolutions were a complete line of bullshit, as far as Christina was concerned. If you wanted to quit doing something badly enough, you could do it in March. Or August. Christina couldn't think of anything she needed to quit anymore. She'd quit smoking three years ago after watching her mother slowly waste into a dried-up stick person on a ventilator. And she didn't do drugs, except for the occasional pot now and again.

The walls of the shower were tiled an earthy brownish tan, tiny squares of natural stone surrounded by grout unnaturally white and clean, like a game show host's smile.

She hated cleaning the shower; the smell of the cleanser coupled with the claustrophobia hovering over her head when she folded herself onto the tile floor with a scrub brush: it was too much to bear. Knowing that Thomas's claw-like feet sloughed dirt, dry skin, and general stench on this floor didn't sweeten the pot. She swore she could smell him while she scrubbed the tile. Thus, the tile didn't get cleaned as often as it should, unless Thomas broke down and washed it himself as payment for some marital offense: a forgotten anniversary, an off-hand comment about her make-up being too garish, a too-long look at a waitress's cleavage during dinner with her father and one of his vapid girlfriends. Last week, high on vodka martinis at his office's "after-holiday" party, he had bragged to a group of co-workers that Christina gave the best blowjobs in Savannah. Christina had flashed him a look of horror and quarantined herself in the ladies' room until it was time to leave, secretly pleased with both the compliment and the knowledge that this would earn her some housecleaning payback. Sure enough, the entire bathroom was spotless the next day.

Who had picked out this tile, anyway? It must have been Thomas. Everything about him was earth tones, even his appearance: wide, brown eyes the color of a tiger's eye gem, deep brown hair that reflected auburn in the sunlight, and a splattering of light brown freckles across his body like confetti that at times made him appear a full decade younger than he was. In the summer he turned an even, light tan like coconut beginning to toast. There was no getting around it: he was handsome, and although she'd never admit it to him, Christina knew that if Thomas only presented himself with more confidence, he'd have women fawning over him everywhere. Instead, he had held tight to his boyish charm and a too often utilized body stance of looking slightly out from under his hair, like a child trying to trick his babysitter into letting him stay up an hour past his bedtime. Christina had once found this wildly attractive, but now she loathed it, found it weak.

They had met in graduate school: Christina, pursuing her master's in accounting and being actively recruited by a number of prestigious corporate healthcare firms and Thomas completing the final practicum hours for his M.S.W. with a specialization in elder care. Immediately following graduation, he had signed on to work for a hospice care center, and he never vocalized or displayed any ambition to move elsewhere. In his spare time, he volunteered for a local advocacy group to support the Death with Dignity Act in Georgia, an interest Christina had always found a bit morbid. She was certain that when it came time for her to receive palliative care, she'd be unlikely to trust a social worker with a copy of *The Peaceful Pill Handbook* displayed so prominently on his office bookshelf. "You'd be blown away with the kind of detail and step-by-step instructions this baby contains," Thomas had explained excitedly when it arrived in the black-swirled cardboard shipping box from Amazon. Christina envisioned her husband, ever the Millennial hippie, marching up the steps to City Hall, waving a Right to Die sign while yelling gardening tips for growing hemlock and shucking cyanide from apple seeds through a bullhorn.

"Welcome to the government watch list," was all she said in return.

She was clean, nothing left to shave or scrub, but she didn't want to get out from under the water yet. She was probably using up all of the hot water. She turned around and bent down to touch her toes, letting the water beat on her lower back. In an hour, they would be meeting her father at an upscale Italian place that had sprung up on Hutchinson Island last spring, so she couldn't hide for much longer. She turned off the shower and rubbed her temples, watching steam surreptitiously escape out the sides of the curtain and into the cold bathroom.

Ten minutes later, as she padded across the cream-colored carpet toward the kitchen to grab a glass of ice water, Thomas called to her from the living room.

"I'm not dressed yet—can it wait?" Christina yelled back. She untucked and tucked the top of the towel from her cleavage. She grabbed a handful of ice cubes from the freezer and plopped them into a short glass, then topped them with tap water. "Okay?" she called. When he didn't answer her this second time, she decided to investigate in person.

Thomas was reclining in the worn desk chair in front of the computer. Christina stood in the doorway, alternately sipping water and resting the cold glass against her temples. Her husband always kept the place so damn hot in the winter. It was Savannah, for Christ's sake: it didn't need to be 90 degrees year-round. "Did you call me?" she asked.

Startled, Thomas jerked forward nervously and grabbed the computer mouse. "Yeah—sorry: I didn't realize you were still getting ready. Just wanted to see if you had seen the party invite. Joe will definitely bring it up tonight, and we should have a game plan for how to deal with it."

She leaned over his shoulder and he scrolled to the Facebook invitation to her father's annual St. Patrick's Day shindig. She could smell the faint musk of Thomas' deodorant, a woodsy, earth scent. *Fitting*, she thought.

"Jesus. Why can't there be an 'attending under duress' RSVP option?" she asked, more annoyed than ever. The photo for the invitation was of her dad and his newest blonde companion, both of them wearing floppy sun hats and Hawaiian shirts while smiling widely into the camera.

Thomas squinted at the screen. "Looks more like a Betsy Palmer than a Janet Leigh," he said.

Christina's mind raced through other pixie-haired starlets of the '60s. "Who's that?"

"Jason's mom in *Friday the 13th*. The first one. You know, the killer," Thomas said. His voice stretched and curved, the auditory equivalent of a funhouse mirror. "*Kill her, Mommy! Kill her! Don't let her get away!*" He laughed.

"Well, if nothing else, I can fantasize about beheading her with a machete," she answered dryly.

A smile spread across Thomas' face. "Very nice."

They all had been incarnations of mid-century screen siren Janet Leigh: creamy blondes with pageboy or pixie cuts, streaks of black roots peeking only slightly, and well-defined eyebrows. Some looked like they were physically counting her father's money on their fingers, each certain she would be the one he would ask to marry him. He never did. Christina knew her father's game better than they did: he liked telling anyone within earshot that he had inherited more insurance money from her mother than he would ever spend in his lifetime, and he liked making his blondes salivate over this. The whole business made Christina uncomfortable: her mother had been a brunette with deep brown eyes. And, he hadn't given her a dime of her mother's money. She and Thomas made more than enough to never need his charity, but that wasn't the point, really. Christina had spent her childhood watching her mother return home each evening, exhausted from working long hours to earn that insurance money and pension, and now she was spending her adulthood watching her father shed the fortune on lavish gifts for parasitic bimbos like a pathetic strip club patron making it rain.

Ironically, it was her father's first girlfriend after her mother's passing, a woman Christina had nicknamed *Psycho* Janet Leigh in her head, since the woman popped psychiatric pills like a reverse Pez dispenser, who didn't bother Christina one bit. That Janet became as dependent on her father as all of the others did, and yet, there was something about her nervous, darting eyes and bird-like mannerisms that Christina found endearing. Perhaps she saw a little of herself in the woman, so when *Psycho* Janet appeared spontaneously in Christina and Thomas' backyard, peeking into their kitchen windows just hours following the recitation of Joe's *I'm-just-not-ready-to-commit-to-one-person* dumping speech, Christina invited her inside and poured her a Manhattan with extra maraschino cherries.

That night at dinner, Christina had been wrapped up in some daydream or another when *Touch of Evil* Janet erupted in a fit of giggling, snapping her attention back to the table.

"So, I set him straight," her father was saying. "Canada only has two exports worth accepting: hockey players and prostitutes." Joe leaned back in his chair and vomited a boisterous *hehhehheh* laugh that made diners at the neighboring table look over sharply. *Touch of Evil* Janet slapped Joe on the shoulder like she was brushing off a ladybug and continued her giggling.

Thomas grabbed Christina's knee under the table and flashed his Eddie Haskell grin at Joe. He hated her father more than she did but he understood the politics of family. Christina pushed the remaining pieces of key lime pie around on her plate, making fork indentations and crisscrosses until her dessert looked like the after effects of a tiny chicken stampede. She hadn't eaten much of her dinner, either. Lately she had been finding herself overcome with a choking sensation at the most inopportune times: when she was driving, when she was eating in a restaurant, even when she was riding an elevator. Suddenly, she would feel her windpipe narrow, and out of sheer instinct she'd claw at her neck as if to remove a tight scarf until it passed. She'd even scratched herself once, prompting the Spanish Inquisition from Thomas. *What happened to her neck? Had it bled? Is it infected? Shouldn't she put some Neosporin on that? Did they even have*

Neosporin? Maybe she should pick some up the next time she went food shopping. Yep, I'll get right on that, Tom, if I don't choke on my own saliva in the middle of aisle four.

"You know, Christina, you and Thomas will never adjust to being parents if you don't learn to be a little less selfish," Joe said, directing his dessert fork at her, making a swirly O with it in the air. "Your lavish lifestyle of marble floors and swimming pools—it doesn't pay for private college tuition."

"Christina and I aren't sure we want a family," Thomas interjected before his wife could roll her eyes. "We're happy with just the two of us."

Touch of Evil Janet took a big gulp from her wine glass and painted a Wile E. Coyote sideways grin across her face. "Joe, dear, it's not polite to talk about having children to the kids. They've been married six years now: not everyone can have children, you know." She winked at Christina. The gesture made Christina want to grab the wine glass from her hand and jam its stem into Janet's eye.

"Jesus, Tom: is that true? Buggers not strong swimmers, eh?" Another belly guffaw. "Because I know it's not my daughter's doing. She's built like her mother—all tits and ass. If that isn't a baby-making body, I don't know what is!"

Christina continued to mash her pie into nothingness, pretending not to hear him. *Touch of Evil* Janet swirled her wine and pointed a burgundy-painted nail at Thomas. "Don't listen to that filth. But you know, it may be all fun and games now, but what're you gonna do when you're elderly? I mean, do you wanna die alone in a rest home? I know MY boys will always take care of their momma."

"I'm not sure elder care is a valid reason for procreating," Thomas said dryly. He had taken his hand off of Christina's leg and was feeling around in his suit jacket, a sure sign he was getting the car keys ready for a quick getaway. They had had this conversation so many times previous, both Thomas and Christina could recite their responses in their sleep.

Christina pulled her napkin from her lap and balled it in her fist. "If you'll excuse me—I'm going to go to the ladies' room," she said, pushing herself back from the table.

Touch of Evil Janet snatched her purse from the floor and stood up as well. "Oooo! I'll join you!" she exclaimed like a small child who'd been asked to accompany an adult to a candy store.

As she weaved her way around tables to reach the archway marked *Restrooms*, Christina could feel herself having to actively concentrate on walking straight. The two martinis were using her empty stomach as a bounce house, and the straight black design lines slash-marking their way across the brick red carpet seemed to tilt and bend as the archway loomed closer. Christina pulled the C-shaped handle on the wooden door with her last two fingers and slipped inside, not bothering to hold it open for her father's girlfriend. When she emerged from the stall, *Touch of Evil* Janet was standing at the sinks, staring into the mirror and holding a maroon colored lipstick in the air like a conductor's baton.

"I think he's waiting until we walk to the parking lot to tell you," she said, not taking her eyes off of her own lips' reflection, "but I might as well save you the surprise. Joe's asked me to move in."

Christina turned on the faucet and ran her hands slowly under the water, taking her time rubbing each and every cuticle. "Oh?" she said, half in disbelief. Her father had only been dating this one for a month: her timer was nearing the alarm stage.

"Yes," *Touch of Evil* Janet said flatly. All of the playful affability had drained from her tone and her expression. She turned to face Christina. "You know, if you had married smarter, you wouldn't have to work for a living. You could travel and shop and make babies, or adopt babies, or hell, even BUY babies if you damn well wanted them… and even if you didn't, you could afford to pay a full-time nanny to care for them too." She paused and recoiled her lipstick back into its tube, then forcefully slapped its cap back on.

Christina switched off the faucet and shook her hands in the sink. "Listen, I…" she began.

Touch of Evil Janet continued talking as if Christina hadn't spoken. "Do you think I had to work a day in my life? I've always had a husband to take care of me. First there was Al—he died in a car crash—and then there was Richie—I got the house *and* a lifetime of alimony outta that transaction." She smiled, but it was a dead smile, one that made Christina grateful she could turn to the towel dispenser. "Your father is a lonely, self-absorbed man. He needs a woman who will laugh at his stupid jokes and fawn over his ridiculous proclamations, and…" She cocked her head to the side as if listening for the precise word to be whispered into her ear. "And an ornament to decorate his sad, pathetic life."

The door to the restroom opened, and a sharply dressed woman with coifed white hair entered behind them. Christina tossed her wadded up towel into the trash and walked out of the room without saying anything else.

When she returned to the table, she saw her father, too, was returning from the restroom. He pulled out the chair next to his own, and *Touch of Evil* Janet appeared next to him, her approach silent as a ghost's. She sat down prettily and allowed Joe to push in her chair. Christina yanked her own chair back from the table and sat down, hard.

"You know, Dad, I'm not feeling so hot tonight. I couldn't even finish my dinner." Christina looked at her father, diagonally across from her, in the eye for the first time that evening. He had a lot more broken blood vessels than she remembered. He was turning into Ted Kennedy right before her eyes. She hoped *Touch of Evil* Janet knew how to tuck and roll from a moving car, or at least how to swim after drinking a bottle of wine. "I think we're going to call it a night."

Thomas put his arm around Christina and rubbed his palm along her upper arm. "Right after limoncello." He motioned to the four cordial glasses of bright yellow liquid in the center of the table. "Your dad was kind enough to order them before he left for the men's room." Thomas retracted his arm, selected two of the glasses from the group, and placed them in front of Christina, keeping his fingers on the side of one of them.

Joe chose a glass from the last two, and *Touch of Evil* Janet picked up the remaining one. "To love," Joe said, raising the digestif into the air. Without waiting for the other three at the table, he put the glass to his lips and consumed the lemon alcohol in one gulp. *Touch of Evil* Janet and Thomas followed suit. Reluctantly, Christina put the glass to her lips and swallowed the tangy liquid.

Joe placed his empty glass in the center of the table. "Alright, sweetheart. I hope I didn't upset you. I just worry about you." He draped a meaty arm around his current Janet. "We both do."

We, my ass, Christina thought. Without meaning to, Christina imagined a cardboard cutout of her father standing with his arm around a petite blonde. The eye and mouth holes on the blonde were empty. *Manchurian Candidate* Janet had filled them during Thanksgiving; *Vikings* Janet had filled them over Christmas. Why her father liked to play the twisted game of house with girlfriend after girlfriend was beyond her, but she was too tired to question it. "I appreciate that," she said, and smirked, her lips pursed together tightly. *No teeth for you, Dad.*

Thomas stood up from the table and placed his hand on the back of Christina's chair. As she began to stand, her father began to wave his hands strangely in front of his face, like he was brushing cobwebs away. Then he began to cough. Next to him, his girlfriend rolled her head backwards. Christina glanced at the ceiling to see what she was looking at, but as *Touch of Evil* Janet's head snapped forward and she began to cough as well, Christina felt her heart skip. Something was wrong.

Her father pushed himself up from the table with one hand and grabbed at his own throat with the other. He continued to cough a wheezy, dry hacking cough, like a man fruitlessly trying to force out something that did not exist. White foam formed at his lips, then poured from his mouth, and Joe began to shake back and forth. Janet's mouth also began to froth, and her eyes rolled back into her head as her body tipped sideways and started to convulse on the floor.

Thomas grabbed Christina and pulled her close to him, stifling her screams of panic.

It was over before the manager had finished dialing 911.

An hour later, as the emergency services wheeled the sheeted stretchers carrying Joe and *Touch of Evil* Janet's bodies out of the restaurant, Thomas guided his wife to their car. They would meet the police at the hospital morgue.

"I'll always take care of you, Christina," Thomas said, reaching his hand over to squeeze his wife's knee. As he did, a clear, unmarked bottle of homemade orange capsules spilled out of his suit jacket pocket and onto the car mat under her feet. Seeming not to notice, Thomas put the car in reverse, backed out of the parking space, and turned his face to look at Christina.

He tilted his head down slightly and looked up at her from under his hair. "Always," he repeated. Then he looked forward again and shifted the car into drive.

Annabel, Me

We loved with a love that was more than love —
I and my Annabel Lee

-Edgar Allan Poe

It's our two-week anniversary today, and I know she'll remember. Annabel was always good about things like that. I stopped at the supermarket to pick up an assortment of Gerbera daisies, her favorite flowers, to surprise her before dinner. Yes, I know: the supermarket isn't the best place to score a romantic bouquet, but I was short on time and lousy at planning, and besides, I needed to grab a few household items as well. I needed cat food, a couple rolls of paper towels, and a couple of nice steaks, maybe some button mushrooms and a handful of fresh green beans. And I needed a refill for my plug-in air freshener. It had to be vanilla. Annabel loves vanilla. I only know this because of the perfume she wears; it smells like cake fresh from the oven, a potpourri of cinnamon and sugar and vanilla beans and orange peel. I can still smell her a half hour after she's left a room. I so closely associate the scent with her that when I walk into a bakery, like a Pavlovian mutt, I feel my heart beat faster and my stomach fill with nervous butterflies.

It seems like I've loved Annabel forever: like, from even before we met or from the beginning of my adult life, or maybe even from before time itself began. That's the kind of love we have. And it was instant, you know? The moment I saw her, I knew: she was the girl for me, and I, the man for her.

We had so much in common, right from the get-go, and our few differences completed each other's gaps. I have always been a pathological introvert. The fact that I can gather up the courage to stand in front of twenty-five teenagers, six times a day, every weekday still astonishes me. Then again, I'd rather lose a finger than be trapped in an intimate work cocktail party. This past December, Annabel convinced me to go with her to the school's Christmas party; it was held at a fancy steakhouse downtown, and the principal, a perpetual jock and good-time-guy, was known to let the bar tab run amuck on his own dime. I lasted all of twenty minutes. Between the noise and the crowd and the general obnoxiousness associated with free-flowing liquor, my panic meter shot to overdrive, and Annabel had to double-time it to follow me outside and into the parking lot, where I leaned forward, put my hands on my knees, and tried to force myself to breathe.

"It's okay," she said softly, rubbing her hand on my shoulder and upper back. "We don't have to stay. How about we see a movie instead?"

My lungs relaxed and I stood tall again. "That sounds great," I said, and straight to the movies we went; we didn't even check back in at the party to say goodbye to anyone first: just out and gone, the perfect Irish goodbye.

We met at the beginning of September last year: we were both first-year teachers and just happened to sit next to one another at the orientation meeting. Kismet. On the third day of school, Annabel knocked on my classroom door and inquired how my first classes had gone, and from that day forward, we were a team, two blossoming educators standing tall against the masses of hormonal adolescents. A trial by fire is always easier when there are two of you holding hoses.

There were strange coincidences that linked us. For instance, Annabel lives on Seaside Drive; I live on Ocean Avenue, on the other end of the city. Our street names are ironic since we are in the middle of the Pioneer Valley, a quiet, hamlet-filled area of Western Massachusetts, a good hour and a half from even a whiff of salt water. Neither of us have roommates, despite being just out of college and practically selling off body parts to finance our student loan payments. We spent much of our hangout time in my apartment, though; it's larger, with a separate bedroom and kitchen, and the building is so well insulated that we can blast movies as loud as we want, as late at night as we want, without worrying about neighbor complaints.

After a few awkward weeks of getting-to-know-you lunches in the school cafeteria or shared prep time in the library, we began spending most weekday afternoons and a handful of evenings together outside of school. We spent so much time together, in fact, that people began to gossip that we were an item. We were, of course, but we had never consummated it: a year and a half later, I hadn't even summoned up the nerve to kiss her, which is just as well, because sometimes the anticipation is the best part anyway.

As far as work went, everywhere our attendance was required outside of the classroom, there was Annabel, and there was me. Two peas in a pod. We practically became one entity: Annabel, me. Some afternoons, as we sat across from one another in my empty classroom, I'd stare at her face, committing every freckle and line to memory. Truth be told, Annabel has one of those faces that isn't always pretty. I mean, she's not an ugly girl by any stretch of the imagination, but there are times when she is confused or worried and the lines on her forehead fold up like a paper fan; when she is angry, her eyes narrow and pierce like tiny, wet BB gun ammunition. Sometimes, when I stare at her face, she looks plain and even haggard, and I think of the ways she could be perfected with a little more, or a little less, makeup. When I share that with her, her eyes get that ammunition look and she tells me it is hurtful and mean to make such comments, but I never understand why. I mean, if you had a flaw, wouldn't you want someone to point it out so you could rectify it? It's what true friends do.

Other times, though, when I look at Annabel, I can't imagine there being a more beautiful woman on earth. In those moments, she is the epitome of the perfect woman: smart, funny, kind, pretty, and sexy. In those moments, I want to envelop myself in her cake batter-scented skin and spend all day with her under the covers of my bed, draping my arm over her bare chest and resting my head in the crook of her neck. In those moments, I want to consume her.

It wasn't until Annabel began to branch out and make other friends that I realized how jealous my co-workers were of Annabel's and my special relationship. She, the more social of the two of us, began attending Friday afternoon drinks at Nathan Bill's bar with fellow members of the Humanities departments. All of a sudden, she was spending some of our lunches with them, partnering with them for field trip planning and club advisories and sports team coaching, and even going to the movies with a guy here and there. The movies had always been our thing: there's nowhere I feel safer and more content than in the dark recesses of a theater, and despite the excessively loud speakers, it is my happy place. Saturdays were our regular movie date day, but since the Christmas party, we haven't spent many Saturdays alone together anymore. I guess that's what they mean when they say that relationships evolve. We were once in the infatuation stage, and now we are in the comfort zone. It doesn't mean we aren't just as madly in love. Come to think of it... my co-workers weren't *jealous* of our special bond: they were envious. Jealousy implies that they had something and were afraid of losing it. They never had what we had, and they never will.

Two weeks ago, Annabel and I were spending lunch together alone in my classroom. She nibbled on an energy bar as I stabbed forkful after forkful of salad with crumbled goat cheese and Caesar dressing. "Come on," I chided her. "You never spend Friday afternoons with me anymore. What's going on?"

She bent one of her legs and pointed the toe of her shoe straight down at the ground, like a ballerina preparing a pirouette. "Bradley... you know I kind of have a thing with Chris now. We've been dating for almost a month, and Fridays are..." she paused. "Fridays are like our group date night: you know, where we hang with everyone else. Saturdays we go out alone."

I sat in my desk chair, swiveling it slightly to shake off my irritation but saying nothing.

"You know you're my bestie," she said, stretching her arm toward me and placing her palm on my shoulder. It was warm where she held me, and it was everything I could do not to lean my head down toward her hand and rub my cheek on her alabaster skin. "Why are you cock-blocking all of a sudden?"

I shook her hand from my shoulder. "Cock-blocking? Really?" I stared at her face. It hadn't even occurred to me that she might be sleeping with Chris, or even that she might want to. I decided to switch gears. "Listen. I'm having a really hard time right now. Monsignor Pee-Paw has been kind of sick, and it's been so cold outside this winter that I haven't had much opportunity to get outside and run, and it's all just ganging up on my mental health at once."

"What's wrong with Pee-Paw?" she asked. Monsignor Pee-Paw, my feral cat turned fish-scented roommate, was an acquisition from the previous year, when Annabel casually mentioned her disappointment at not being able to have a pet in her tiny studio apartment. I've never been a fan of pets: they're dirty, they smell, and quite frankly, I have better things to spend money on than litter and canned stink meat. However, the day after Annabel's comment, I bought a can of tuna fish, left it open on the back deck of my garden apartment, and crouched down next to my gas grill, gripping the handle of the mesh skimmer I borrowed from the complex's pool house. When a skittish grey tabby crept over to the malodorous can, I slapped the net over him and dragged his hissing body, along with the overturned tuna, into my living room through the sliding glass door. It took a few weeks, as well as a few gallons of Nature's Miracle urine treatment, to train him to use the litter box I slid under the sink in my bathroom, but he finally acquiesced, though he developed a strange OCD habit of stepping in his deposited urine immediately after it began to harden in the clumping litter, leaving bizarre paw-print garden stones behind. Thus, I named him Pee-Paw, only adding the title of Monsignor after acknowledging that Mister and Doctor just didn't have the same musical cadence.

I thought quickly. "Oh, he's been kind of yowling when he uses the box. You know, I'm so afraid of blockages. Cats get them, you know, and then, poof, they're dead without warning." I scrunched my brow and mouth into an expression that I hoped communicated concern and sensitivity.

Annabel stared at me for a long minute. "I haven't seen the Monsignor in a long time," she said. "What time should I swing by?"

I wrestled a mushroom onto my fork while I thought for a moment. "Want to order a pizza and make it a night?" I said, trying to sound casual. "There's that new doc on Netflix that—"

"Bradley," she interrupted. "I have plans tonight. But I can come by for a few hours after school, if that's okay?"

I placed my dirty silverware in my empty Tupperware container and resealed the lid. "Sure, sure. The Monsignor will be happy to see you." I shoved the plastic container in my backpack and took a swig of water. "Why don't you come by at 3:30 or so? I have to do a few errands before I go home."

Annabel swung her leg backwards and kicked the floor lightly with her toe a few times. "Okey-dokey." She leaned down and gave me a light hug around my shoulders. "I'll see you at 3:30. Have a good last two periods!" She turned and started to walk toward the door, tossing her lunch wrapper in my trash barrel.

"Of course I will: we're doing Poe today. I always have fun teaching Poe," I said, smiling and watching her yellow cardigan catch the breeze as she spun. She waved and left without another word, and I leaned my head down toward my shoulder and breathed in the delicate haze of vanilla sugar she had left behind.

I left the door unlocked as I tidied up my apartment. Despite the chilly weather, I opened all of the windows to let some fresh air circulate. Monsignor Pee-Paw followed me from room to room, crying to me in his gravelly Danny Trejo meow, until I realized I hadn't fed him since the previous evening. I was terrible about things like that. Thank goodness Annabel is so organized and on top of things; otherwise, our children will likely starve! I poured a small amount of dry food into his bowl, promising to give him moist canned food, which he favors, later. I was fluffing the bouquet of daisies I picked up on my way home from school when Annabel walked into the kitchen and dropped her purse onto the counter.

"Oh my goodness, Bradley: it's freezing in here!" she exclaimed, wrapping her arms around herself. "Did you turn off your heat?"

"Oh… oh, I'm sorry: I opened a few windows to get some fresh air, and I forgot to close them," I said and ran to the sills to shut them quickly. When the apartment was air-tight again, I walked over to Annabel and rubbed my hands furiously along her upper arms in an attempt to warm her up.

She laughed. "That feels good, actually," she said. "My shoulders and arms have been killing me this week—so much correcting with the research papers being due and all."

"Well, why didn't you say so?" I said. I pulled her gently by the shoulder and guided her into one of my kitchen chairs. "Sit down and relax for a minute." She sat down without a fight and leaned her head down into her hands.

"Oh, Bradley, I am so stressed out," she said through her fingers. "I have all this correcting, and my parents want me to come home for a few days at Easter next week, but it will take me a day to drive all the way to D.C. and then another to come all the way back here. I have the sick time saved up, but I feel like… like a bad worker bee taking sick time to go on vacation."

I stood behind her, positioned my hands on her shoulders, and began to rub her muscles. They were tense and warm beneath her cold sweater. "Why? Because you want to see your family during a holiday? You haven't called in sick all year. I think you should just do it." I moved my hands upward to her neck and kneaded gently. She responded by sitting up and being silent for a breath.

"I guess so," she said finally. "It's not like I can take the sick time with me, right? I don't plan on retiring from that school or anything." She paused. "I mean, do you?"

I thought for a moment. I felt pretty comfortable in my classroom. And I hated change. However, I couldn't imagine going to work every day without Annabel being there. I rubbed her neck harder and moved my hands back down to her shoulders again, continuing to massage her skin. Annabel couldn't leave and go to another school. She just couldn't. What would happen to us?

"Ow, Bradley: that hurts a little bit," she said, putting

one of her hands over mine. I eased my grip but did not take my hands off of her. "Anyway, I'm just... I'm just overwhelmed right now, you know?" She turned her torso to look at me. "Listen, I think we need to talk."

I remained in my position, my hands resting softly on her. "Okay. What do you want to talk about?"

She pulled away slightly, shaking my hands from her body. "I don't think we should see each other as often as we have been."

I felt my mouth go dry. "What? What do you mean? We hardly see each other at all these days. You're always with your new friends and Chris and—"

"And I think that's normal, Bradley," she said. "I don't think it's normal for two people to spend as much time in isolation as we used to spend." She touched her cheek and stared into space for a moment as if searching for the right words to say. "I... I think people were starting to think that maybe something was going on between us."

"What do you mean?" I said, confused. "I mean, we weren't doing anything wrong. We're just two people who like each other and get along and like spending time together: what's wrong with that?" I felt my cheeks burn hot. Suddenly, I wasn't feeling well. "We're doppelgängers... Bonnie and Clyde, Spencer and Katharine: two stars in the same constellation. Of course we should be together all the time."

Annabel looked down at her lap. "Oh, Bradley... you're my friend, and I love you. But that's all we are, and that's all we're going to be: don't you see that?" She looked up at me, and I searched her face. The skin next to her mouth was starting to wrinkle with age. She had a few new freckles under her left eye: eventually, they would turn into age spots. And her hair was looking limper these days. I wondered if it was her diet or a new shampoo that was causing its heaviness. "Do you understand what I'm saying, Bradley?" she asked.

I looked into her bright eyes. "Yes. You're in love with me," I said. "I'm in love with you, too, Annabel." I smiled at her.

She adjusted the neck of her sweater and sighed. "I have to get going... I—" she jumped slightly, startled, as Monsignor Pee-Paw leaped onto the kitchen table beside her and rubbed his face on her arm. "Well, hello, my handsome man," she said, her voice changing to mirthful. She raised her arm and stroked the cat's head and back, and Monsignor began to purr loudly. "I've missed you so much." She turned her body back to face the table again and leaned her head forward so that the cat could sniff and rub his cheek with hers.

I looked at the back of Annabel's head for a long while. No one would ever love Annabel that way I loved her, right then, in that moment. I reached my hand around her head and grabbed her by the jaw, then placed my other hand on the base of her skull.

"Bradley, wha—" she began, and as quickly and forcefully as I could, I turned her head to the right like I was unscrewing the top of a heavy metal jar. I felt a sickening crack at the top of her spine, and her head went instantly limp and bobbed in my hands. I moved my fingers over to her jugular vein and felt for a pulse. Nothing.

"Oh, Annabel, my darling," I said, wrapping my arms around her head and shoulders and hugging her against me. "Now we *can* be together all the time. Don't you understand? I never would have let them tear us apart." Monsignor Pee-Paw sniffed Annabel's forehead, opened his mouth slightly, and looked blankly at me.

I scooped Annabel's body into my arms and carried her into my bedroom: a bridegroom bringing his bride across the threshold. I had to juggle her a bit to evenly distribute her weight since her head had lolled to the side awkwardly, making me a bit nauseous. I draped her delicately on the bed, resting her head on a pillow. I finger-combed her hair so that it resembled a veil spilling beautifully to the side, and I adjusted her arms and legs so that she could sleep in the most natural and comfortable pose possible.

I mentioned how beautiful Annabel could look in an instant, right? This was one of those moments. I stood over the bed, looking down at her, allowing my eyes to take in every pore of her skin, every curve of her body. She had become a sleeping Botticelli maiden, a drowned Ophelia, my *Belle Dame sans Merci*, as Keats would say. In her beautiful stillness, she had achieved perfection. It was then that I knew, just as one always knows, that it was finally time for Annabel and me to consummate our love, and as I climbed onto the bed next to her and began to kiss her cheek, I felt my eyes well with tears of joy.

The next morning I awoke still entwined with my bride, my arm strewn over her naked breasts and my face buried next to her ear. I didn't want to wake Annabel, so I slowly brought my hand back toward my chest and pulled my face back from hers. In the morning sun, her skin looked positively radiant—glowing with a silk-like sheen. Annabel sleeps like a log, I discovered. Her body was rigid as a mannequin and did not move an inch as I climbed out from the bed.

Her purse was still in the kitchen, and I fumbled through it to locate her cell phone. She had switched her ringer off, and the screen showed four missed calls: three from Chris and one from her mother. No one had left a voice message, but both Chris and her mother had followed up with text messages. I read Chris' first.

Bel- I thought you were going to Nathan's tonight? What happened? Did you decide to drive to your parents early after all? Text me. C

Why would he call her Bel? Her name was *Annabel*. What kind of lunatic goes around making up new names for people? Chris had made me even more irritated with him, but he had given me an idea. I read her mother's message next.

I called, no emergency. Just seeing if you're driving down next week. Hope to see you, sweetheart. Love you. Mom

I texted her mother back.

Hi Mom. Sorry— I was out with Chris. I tried to get the time off from work, but the school won't allow it. I'll have to come down in the summer for a week instead. I miss and love you too. Annabel.

I texted Chris back.

C- sorry, got caught up packing. Decided to head to D.C. after all. Going to stay for a week or so. I figure, I've earned it. I'll email sub plans to Bradley and he'll bring them down. Have a good Easter and I'll see you in a fortnight.

I didn't know why I used the term *fortnight*, but the word just came to me, like a whisper from a muse, so I went with it. I shut off Annabel's phone completely, placed it back in her purse, and brought the bag into the bedroom to hide in my closet. I had to find the phone number for the absentee line and get busy making substitute lesson plans for her classes, but the sight of Annabel naked, lying prone on top of my bedspread, made me pause. I dropped her purse onto the floor

- 82 -

and climbed back onto the bed next to her, smelling her neck and hair. The tiniest hint of vanilla cake still remained, and I nuzzled my face against her nipples and smiled. I hadn't ever remembered being so happy.

It's now been two weeks since Annabel and I began living together, and I have to say, the transition was easier than people make it seem. We've faced only two hurdles. The first was when Annabel's body began to soften and leak. I awoke one morning to find the bedspread around her soaked with a putrid watery substance—and even before that, her nose and mouth and, well, *other* orifices had alternately leaked blood and other bodily fluids. But every couple faces challenges, and at least ours had an easy solution: I now stuff piles of paper towels under and around Annabel to soak up anything liquid, and I've plugged one of those oil-filled air fresheners into every outlet in my bedroom: I think I have three of them going at once now. They don't completely cover up the smell of rot, but they distract from it enough. It's kind of like when a lover becomes so sweaty, you begin to smell a bit of body odor every now and then as you're romping around the mattress: it's all part of the experience, and quite frankly, if your love isn't strong enough to withstand a fetid odor now and again, well, I guess it wasn't very strong to begin with.

The second hurdle occurred when I came home from work yesterday. I had accidentally left the bedroom door open while I was away, and I entered the room to find Monsignor Pee-Paw sitting on Annabel's bare stomach, bending down and licking her chest. It wasn't until I got a little closer that I saw what he had done. All of the flesh from her right breast was missing, the edges of the gaping wound speckled with tiny fang marks. Mastectomy by feline. I told you I have to get better about remembering to feed that guy.

I bring the crystal vase of daisies into the bedroom

and position it on the nightstand next to Annabel's head. Sitting on the edge of the mattress nearest to her, I take her hand gently in mine and bring it to my lips. "You are my life and my bride, Annabel," I say, and kiss her cold, loose skin. "I am in love with you, and you are in love with me."

She says nothing back because she knows: it's true.

Open House

Bill tore six slices of the precooked bacon from its plastic package and slapped them onto a paper towel. He placed the towel on a plate, put the plate in the microwave, and set the timer for two minutes. He liked his bacon crispy. "I like my bacon the way I like my women," he often told people with a wink. "Lean and salty... and a little overdone, if you know what I mean."

No one knew what he meant. But, people nodded and smiled accordingly. That's what people did around Bill: he had that kind of charisma. He could look you in the eye while he reached into your abdomen and took out an organ or two, and more than likely, you'd simply thank him for leaving you a kidney. Melinda suspected that about her husband when she first met Bill, she knew it when they married in a city park three years ago (no family in attendance—it was better that way: more intimate), and she blindly trusted it every time they walked into a new school auditorium amid the stale percolator coffee, over-baked PTO cookies, and sad brochures pleading with parents of potential students to apply.

Melinda, or Linda, as Bill called her, sat in a chair at the wooden kitchen table, the skin on the back of her thighs catching on one of the rips in the plastic-upholstered seat cushion. If she kept shifting, her skin would look like a road map, crooked interstates crisscrossing with blue rivers from the back of her knee to the curved ridge of her ass, and Bill would not like that at all: no *sir-ee*. So, she kept the lower half of her body very still as she stirred her coffee over and over, breathing in the sugary scent of the hazelnut creamer she had drowned it in.

Bill brought the plate of towel-wrapped bacon to the table, his last few steps quicker than the first, as the plate had gotten hotter than he had anticipated and holding it began to singe his fingertips. He snapped his hand back toward his body and rubbed his fingers quickly back and forth across his chest like a mad third-base coach instructing his pitcher not to throw the curve.

"Are you okay, baby?" asked Linda. "Do you want me to get some ice?"

Bill stopped the maniacal rubbing. "Nah, it's fine." He flipped open the paper towel, shoved a slice in his mouth like a cigarette, and began to roll it about with his tongue. Bill did the oddest things with food, Linda noticed. She was always afraid people were staring at them in restaurants, so they rarely ate out. "Hey, see what else is on," he said, pointing to the TV with his first and middle fingers welded together into a gun barrel shape. "We've seen this *Law & Order*, like, fifteen times."

The couple had two television sets in the house. One was in the kitchen, kitty-cornering the countertop next to the coffeemaker. The other was in the bedroom. "The living room is for sitting and visiting," Bill had said when he moved in a few months before their trip to the park, and Linda, of course, agreed. It was nice spending evenings in the parlor with Bill. Some nights, they'd each read books and bask in the silent hum that blanketed the house, but most nights, they spent hours just talking. Linda could listen to Bill talk all night. She thought that was pretty impressive: three years married and not once tired of his company.

Linda held the remote even with the set and clicked the channel button a few times. "Wait—stop: hold up. What's that?" Bill said, holding his hand in the air, palm facing his wife like a traffic cop. Linda watched the screen. It was a commercial for an open house at one of the local Catholic elementary schools.

Give your child the best educational opportunities available!
Choose Saint Benedict Joseph Labre Elementary.
Open House this Friday, October 30 at 6 pm.
See what the gift of a Catholic education
can do for your child!

Bill pulled the rest of the bacon slice into his mouth and chewed. Linda could hear the crunching of the driest pieces echo in his mouth. "Shall we go? It might be a good opportunity for Baby Jessica." When he smiled after he said this, Linda could see a piece of dark red bacon stuck in one of his teeth.

Bill and Linda did not have any children. They hadn't even tried for them. Sure: there was that one time that Linda thought she might be pregnant. Her breasts ached and her period was a full week tardy, so she drove to Walgreens while Bill was at work, bought a test, and smuggled it home, being careful not to let the neighbors see the bright blue and pink box practically glowing through the thin plastic pharmacy bag. She unwrapped the collection stick, placed it gently on the bathroom sink, and prepared to collect a cup of her urine for screening, but when she pulled down her pants to go, she found her panties stained with deep red blood. Her period had come after all—it had been playing a game of chicken with Linda and finally gave in. Of course, she had seen women on a number of daytime talk shows who claimed to have never known they were pregnant for months and months—they had even gotten regular periods—so she tested her urine just in case. Negative, but a close call just the same. If they had children, they'd never be able to play Baby Jessica.

Linda had dropped out of college in the beginning of her junior year, but as a sophomore, she had taken American Lit II in order to fulfill the Humanities requirement. It was in that class that she read Edward Albee's play, *Who's Afraid of Virginia Woolf.* Truth be told, she was *supposed* to have read it, but it had been just as easy to rent the movie featuring Elizabeth Taylor and her real-life on-again, off-again husband Richard Burton. The two main characters speak of their absent son throughout the play as they use him in frequent attempts to goad one another into anger. At the end—spoiler alert—the audience learns that there is no son: George and Martha made him up to disguise their own shared regret at not being able to have children.

Bill and Linda didn't use an imaginary child as a weapon in their domestic spats. They didn't suffer from shared psychosis either; Linda had learned about that phenomenon in her Psych 101 class, and they weren't imagining a child who wasn't there. No, Baby Jessica wasn't a real person at all. She was their code word for the game. Bill had come up with the moniker after watching some Reagan-era nostalgic news program: in 1987, an 18-month-old child in Texas became stuck in a well, and the cable news channels went berserk covering the rescue attempts. Baby Jessica, as she was known, was finally rescued, suffering only injuries to her foot. "Those goddamn news people couldn't stop talking about the kid. I mean, I know there are slow news days, but damn: gimme something better than some recycled Lassie script," he pointed out. "But you know what I think? I think the news was trying to distract America from all the terrible crap going on in the world. Oil tankers blowing up, people getting cancer and AIDS, the economy nose-diving... give the people a kid in peril and a cherry reunion at the end, and *poof*! All their worries, gone."

That's what Baby Jessica was to Bill and Linda: a distraction from their boring lives. A purging of their anxieties and regrets. For the last three years, they had played Baby Jessica every Halloween, and every year, they had walked away scot-free. And Bill was always extra passionate with Linda afterward: making love to her for hours, then curling up next to her in their queen-sized bed, nuzzling his face in the crook of her neck. "I love you, pretty girl Linda," he whispered to her last Halloween. He rarely told her he loved her. It had been a special evening.

Bill and Linda shook their rain-soaked umbrellas in the entryway of the Catholic school's gymnasium. Linda didn't want to carry the umbrella all night, but she didn't want to risk it getting stolen at the makeshift coat check, either. Bill hated when her hair frizzed and her mascara ran. He said it made her look like a dead hooker. She pulled the umbrella strap tight around the base and latched it, then wiped her damp palms on the bottom of her cardigan sweater.

Like a typical salesclerk, a stout woman with short-cropped salt and pepper hair wearing a navy skirted suit approached Bill and Linda within a minute of their arrival. "Well, hello! Welcome to Saint Benedict's. I'm Sister Monica." She grasped Linda's still slightly wet hand in hers and shook it up and down. "I'm the headmaster. And who is your little angel?"

Linda pulled her hand away as if she'd been bitten, then instantly regretted it. She was always nervous in social situations, and given what she and Bill planned to do, it was likely their every move could be scrutinized and their plan foiled before it had even begun. She had to act normal. What would a normal mother inquiring about parochial school for her child do? "Her name is Jessica. She's at home with a sitter because we weren't sure how late we'd be here," Linda said quickly, making sure to smile with all of her teeth. She knew she looked more sincere that way. "Do you mind if we look around?"

For just a moment, Sister Monica glanced at the space just behind Linda and Bill, then her eyes searched Linda's face and she brandished a tight-lipped smile. "Oh my goodness:

please *do* look around. We have a number of tables set up by the children to showcase all of the activities and opportunities available for little Jessica." The headmaster seemed to spot the person she had been looking for, because she placed a hand on Linda's upper arm to show that their conversation had come to an end; then she excused herself and moved on to another arriving couple.

"Well, that was a quick sales pitch," Bill said under his breath. He nodded at the display tables. "Let's take a look, shall we?"

The two wandered from stand to stand, eyeing the sports, clubs, and specialized classes the private school boasted. Three to five children positioned themselves behind each display, some sitting painfully in worn, orange plastic chairs; others shifting from one foot to another in a nervous dance recital. Many were talking animatedly with their classmates; most appeared sallow, almost sickly, under the harsh fluorescent lights. Linda perused each activity: soccer teams, baseball teams, basketball teams; choral groups, a hiking club, even a knitting and sewing club. *What eight-year-old knits?* thought Linda.

Toward the middle of the gym was a table staffed by three children, all of whom looked to be about nine or ten years old. Linda and Bill checked the sign propped at the front of their display: "Baking and Cooking Club." Two of the children stood erect at one corner, facing each other: a boy and a girl. The girl was short with round brown eyes and a mop of curly brown hair pinned back with a pink ribbon barrette. The boy was tan—strange for the middle of the autumn—with hazel eyes and a willowy build. He wore a tall baker's hat, obviously a wayward piece from a child's dress-up set, jauntily over his dirty blond locks. They were playing some sort of game where the boy held his palms upright in front of him and tried to pull them away before the girl could successfully slap them. The girl kept making contact with the boy's hands and laughing hysterically each time the sound of skin cracking echoed across the room.

Next to those two, however, was another child. A boy. This boy was sitting in a rickety wooden chair, his shoulders slightly hunched, his eyes staring down at the table in front of him. He was a heavyset child with dark hair, ruddy skin, and eyes that were slightly rimmed with the redness of fatigue. A cowlick stuck out defiantly by the back of his crown. He looked like he was willing himself to disappear, silently begging the staunch white tablecloth displaying cookie cutters and awkwardly posed photographs to rise up like an apparition and swallow him whole. Bill looked at Linda. This was the one.

Linda walked nonchalantly to the edge of the table. She placed a finger on the edge of her mouth as if deep in thought. "Say, what have you baked this year in your club?" she asked the trio, letting her eyes dance on each one of their faces.

The young couple continued their game as if they did not hear her. The girl slapped the boy playfully on the hip, and the boy yanked off his hat and threw it at her, softball pitch-style. Tufts of sandy locks stood at strange angles on top of his head. The girl shrieked with pleasure, caught the hat in her hands, and said, "Now it's mine!" and ran off into the growing crowd of the gymnasium. The boy followed, laughing a nervous boy laugh.

The sitting boy did not move. He didn't even flinch.

Linda paused and looked at the boy sitting in front of her. She peered down at the spot of floor still visible under the edge of the tablecloth. Next to the boy's worn, grey sneakers were three crumpled wrappers: two from Little Debbie chocolate snack cakes and the last from an Almond Joy candy bar.

"Do you bake at home?" she asked the boy. His body and eyes did not move, but Linda saw him swallow and pinch his lips together.

"Sometimes." His voice was small, almost a whisper. If his classmates hadn't run off, the cacophony of their game and giggles might have drowned him out completely.

Bill fingered a star-shaped cookie cutter. "I love sugar cookies: I mean *love* them. Mrs. Brady just baked a whole bunch for the party tomorrow night, too." Linda flinched slightly at the name "Brady." They had forgotten to agree on a fake last name before arriving. It was always something ironic, some adaptation of a utopian television family. Last year they were the Bradfords; the year before that, the Waltons. Linda always suggested the Huxtables in honor of her favorite show as a kid, but with that whole Cosby mess in the news, Bill said they needed to be less conspicuous. Bill always made the big decisions.

Linda held out her hand as if introducing herself at a job interview. "I'm Mrs. Brady, and our daughter is about your age. Her name is Jessica. What's your name?"

The boy was silent for a beat, then he lifted his head to look at Linda. "Sam." His eyes were bright: blue, or maybe green. It was hard to tell. He ignored Linda's hand, so she pulled it back and put it in her pants pocket.

"Well, Sam, we could really use a dessert expert at our Halloween party tomorrow. Are you trick-or-treating this year?" Linda asked, keeping the cheer in her voice. "What are you dressing up as?"

Sam blushed at the word *expert*. "I am a dessert expert. I help my mom bake cookies and cakes and brownies all the time." He smiled slightly but shyly. "I'm going as Batman."

"Reeeaaaallllly?!" Bill said, dragging out the response into multiple syllables like a cartoon character.

"That's so cool! Jessica's party is superhero-themed! She's going as Wonder Woman, of course. What other superheroes do you like, besides Batman, of course?"

Sam's posture relaxed, and his smile spread like warm peanut butter on toast. "Um, I like Superman, too. And The Flash. Spider-Man's alright, I guess. But I like Batman the best. I play the Lego Batman game on my Xbox all the time."

Linda smiled. Of course the kid had an Xbox. He probably spent all day Saturday and Sunday with his round butt glued to the couch, his eyes cemented to the TV screen, a game controller in one hand and a fistful of Oreos in the other. She turned her head slowly and scanned the room. Where were this kid's parents? Didn't they come to support their son's extra-curricular activity?

"You know, I just tried my hand at baking these chocolate-covered coconut macaroons, but not everyone likes coconut. I hope people will eat them at the party," Linda said. She painted a worried expression on her face for good measure. She could see Bill smiling his sideways grin out of the corner of her eye.

Sam practically sprang from his seat. "Oh, em, gee: I *love* coconut!"

"Well," Bill said, leaning forward conspiratorially, "I know Jessica doesn't have many friends coming to her party. Jess has been homeschooled for the past three years, and she doesn't know many kids. They are going to trick-or-treat together around our neighborhood later afterwards... lots of houses on our street give out the good stuff: you know, like the full-sized candy bars. 'You know what I mean?" He winked at Sam.

Sam nodded his head so fast, Linda thought it might come unhooked and roll onto the table.

Linda searched the gymnasium purposefully with her eyes. She held her hand up to her forehead as if she were blocking out the sun to focus her view. "Where are your mom and dad? I'll go introduce myself and ask their permission... if you'd like to come, that is."

Bill and Linda held their breath. This would be the make-or-break moment. If Sam declined, they'd have to start all over with another awkward kid. Plus, they ran the risk that the slapping game stablemates would return soon and want to attend as well. They had to close the deal and get outta Dodge.

Sam stood up. Linda could now see all of his pudgy frame. He balled his fists and held up his arms in a Strong Man pose and jumped up and down twice. The skin on the sides of his torso bounced visibly up and down inside of his t-shirt. "Yeah! I want to go!" He beamed at Linda. "My mom isn't here. She's gonna pick me up at eight o'clock."

Bill reached into Linda's jacket pocket and took out the small notepad and pen he had placed there for just this reason. "Okay, let me write Jessica's name and our address and phone number on this paper. You show it to your mom and tell her she can call us tonight or tomorrow if she wants. The party starts at four o'clock sharp, so don't be late!" He scribbled furiously and handed a small slip of paper to Sam.

"And make sure you wear your Batman costume: there are prizes for the coolest costumes," Linda added. She watched the boy carefully fold the paper once, then slip it in his pants pocket. Bill folded his arm around Linda's waist, and the two walked slowly and deliberately toward the door, trying their very best to muffle the smiles on their faces.

It was three in the afternoon on Saturday: Halloween, at last. Linda had been certain to decorate the living room for a kids' party in case Sam's mother wanted to come inside and look around. That had happened last year: young Bethany's father, his chest puffy and broad, accompanied his daughter to the door, and he must have suspected something because he asked to use their bathroom even though he didn't reek of booze, didn't appear sick, and seemed to be old enough to hold his bladder until he returned home. Linda had opened her door wide, spread her arm out like a professional greeter welcoming a member of royalty, and ushered the pair inside. *Yes, of course you can use our bathroom: it's right there—first door on the right in the hallway leading to the kitchen. Why, no, my husband isn't home: you just missed him. He took Jess to the party store to pick up streamers. Would you like to sit down?*

Linda had even invited the man to stay for the party. She felt her heart race as she said it, knowing it was a bluff from which she would have no way of recovering if the father took her up on the offer. As she placed apple after apple into the water in the wide washing bucket, she rambled on about the weather and the upcoming town election and had focused on keeping her toothy smile wide and genuine. After an awkward moment or two, Bethany's dad stood up, tousled his daughter's strawberry blonde hair piled daintily within the constraints of a plastic princess crown, and walked toward the door. He even thanked Linda for inviting his child: their family had recently moved to town, and the poor, introverted girl hadn't made many friends.

"We're going to have a super time!" Linda had said enthusiastically, more to herself than to the child or her parent. Later, when she drove Bethany home, she was *so sorry* to report that the girl had fallen down the cellar stairs when the children were playing hide-and-seek. A few scrapes and minor bruises, nothing broken. A few days rest and she'd be good as new. Bethany was too sleepy to argue, and her pillowcase overflowing with candy must have served as adequate hush money, because Linda never heard from the father again.

Linda secured the last delicate orange streamer to the crown molding around the doorway that separated the living room from the dining room. She had hung furry plastic spiders from the ceiling, draped black cloth over the end tables, and put out bowls of candy corn. The cookies cut in the shapes of cats and topped with black-colored sugar were spread across the wide, silver serving tray, each overlapping the next like tiny Rockettes performing a final number. She had stuffed an old pillowcase with the contents of three full bags of fun-sized candy and poured a fourth bag containing Almond Joys and Mounds bars into a bowl by the front door, as she had run out of time to make the macaroons.

If Sam's mother questioned why Sam was the only child there, Linda was prepared to affix her best sympathetic countenance and deliver her prepared response. She practiced while she straightened the chairs and brushed imaginary lint off of the sofa. "Gee, you're the first one here: the party doesn't start until five," Linda announced to the empty parlor. "Jess and her dad made a quick trip to Shop & Save. We forgot the Fritos: can you believe that? ...What's that? I said it started at four? Oh, gosh, I don't think so, but that's okay: Sam, you can help me set up the drinks and test-drive the cookies: what do you think about that?"

She nudged a sugar cookie that had shaken free of the chorus line and touched the edge of the tray lightly with her finger. Arranging party snacks reminded Linda of the open house-style housewarming she had held when she first moved in. She had invited all of her co-workers at the dental office, as well as her mother, aunts, uncles, and cousins. All day, she ran from room to room, offering trays of tapas and crudités, spinning her sweaty head from guest to guest until she was dizzy. Her mother had told her that an open-house style housewarming was the classiest and most welcoming type of new home party, and that Linda was too white trash to ever be able to pull off such a thing. She hadn't warned her that because guests could come and go as they pleased, she would have to have fresh food and drinks available all afternoon if she was going to be an appropriate hostess. Linda's feet ached for days following the party, and she never wanted to see a mini quiche again for as long as she lived. As she ran frantically over her newly refinished hardwood floors, she had spied her mother leaning against the walnut sideboard, balancing a wine glass stem between two delicate, meticulously manicured fingertips, shooting her glares of disappointment and disgust. Thank goodness at least Bill accepted her, white trash warts and all.

She and Bill hadn't had a reception after the wedding. They had simply retired to the cozy craftsman-style bungalow, drank champagne, and fed each other the cake Linda had procured from the bakery down the road earlier in the day. There was so much less stress that way, and Linda had Bill all to herself: no sharing him with family or friends. She got such a limited amount of Bill as it was—he held his feelings so close to the vest—that she cherished her time alone with him on holidays and at special events.

The doorbell rang. Linda glanced at her watch. Quarter to four. Was he early? She straightened her blouse, smoothed her hair with her hands, and practiced her expressions. *Big, toothy grin of joy. Furrowed brow of motherly concern. Wide eyes of confusion and astonishment.* Her face clicked through the emotional flip chart she knew people expected of upstanding mothers and wives. She stretched her jaw, cocking it to and fro, then wiped the slate clean and swung open the front door.

Sam stood, round and sweaty, on the top cement step, his hand still hovering over the doorbell. A brown, beaten-up Chevrolet of 1980s vintage idled in the street near the curb. Linda leaned down and tried to spy the driver, but all she could make out was an outline of fuzzy hair and a faux-fur trimmed jacket hood. She pantomimed saying hello, then shooed Sam into the house with her hand on his shoulder. The car sped off without so much as a honk or a shadowy wave. Sam did not look back.

"Well, hey! You're a little early, Sam, but come on in and make yourself at home," Linda sang. She pointed to the couch against the picture window. "Have a seat. Would you like something to drink?"

Sam pushed up the black mask that had been covering his face from his nose to his forehead with his wrist. "Um, do you have any root beer?"

Linda thought for a moment. "Let me take a look! I'll be right back." She spun on her heels and walked briskly to the kitchen. She would have to work fast: she hadn't anticipated the boy being *this* eager to arrive. Grabbing her rolling pin from the counter with one hand, she pulled open the cabinet above the sink with the other and grabbed the thin, caramel-colored pill bottle. She shook out one of the mint-green tablets and quickly crushed it into powder with the rolling pin: Sam was a hefty kid, Linda thought, but a single 7.5 mg pill should be enough. She peered into the refrigerator, spied one lonely can of Barq's in the back, and put in on the counter.

"Excuse me," said a tiny voice behind her as she poured the soda into a glass. She turned quickly, keeping her body pressed against the counter to hide the tiny pile of green powder. She was frozen, unsure of what to say next.

"Well, Sam: it's nice to see you again," said Bill, suddenly appearing in the doorway to the butler's pantry. He held his arm above his head and pressed his elbow against the door frame. "What say you and I hang out in the parlor until drinks are served, yeah?" He shuffled up next to Sam and shooed him back into the front room like a shepherd. Linda brushed the green powder to the edge of the countertop, held the lip of the glass of root beer below, and dumped the drug into the fizzy drink; the bubbles raced to the top to meet it. She ran a spoon through the liquid a handful of times. She didn't want to over-stir, or the drink would get flat and the boy wouldn't finish it.

Back in the living room, Sam was again sitting on the sofa, his mask still pushed astray. He had moved the bowl of candy corn from the end table to the cushion next to him. "Here you are!" Linda handed him the glass of brown liquid, and the boy took it from her excitedly and began to gulp. He had imbibed half of the drink before removing it from his mouth to take a breath. Sam held the glass in front of him, searching the spaces nearby for a flat surface to rest the glass. Seeing none, he looked at Linda.

As if reading his mind, she replied, "Drink up! There's plenty more where that came from!" and like a trained seal, Sam emptied the solution into his stomach, let out a satisfied *Ahhhhh*!, and wiped his mouth with the back of his free hand. He pulled his mask back down over his eyes and nose and held the glass up in Linda's direction.

Linda felt an instant wave of irritation. Did he expect her to be his maid? To wait on him hand and foot? She wondered if his mother did. He certainly lacked for exercise. Her own mother never would have brought her a soda, let alone stood by like a lady-in-waiting. She snatched the empty glass from his hand and placed it on the dining room table next to the cookie tray.

"So, Bruce Wayne, are you limber enough for the party games we are going to play?" Bill asked Sam, the question dripping with honeyed maleficence. Most children's radar would have alarmed immediately at his tone, and Linda put her hand on her forehead as if to push the concern out of her mind. "How 'bout we fix you another drink, and then we'll start to practice the candy corn toss," Bill continued. "By the time the other kids get here, you'll be a master!"

"Uh... we're out of root beer, though: would you like a Coke?" Linda asked. She knew this was Bill's signal to give the child another dose. At the dental practice, a full-grown adult was prescribed one tablet of Midazolam for anxiety before a complicated procedure, and even then, the patient had to be driven to and from the appointment because of the sedative properties. Sam was a child, but he was a hefty child. A full fifteen milligrams might knock him out completely. She glanced at her husband. He cocked his head to the side and raised an eyebrow at her. *You're not wimping out on me, are you, pretty girl?* She shook her head slightly to show him she was not.

Sam nodded his head furiously again. His face was slightly pink, like he'd been running. The costume was heavy and thick, and Linda had turned the heat up to 75 degrees, even though it was still the season for light jackets. She returned to the kitchen, crushed another pill, but swept only half of it into the soda. The rest she brushed into the sink and washed down the drain.

Back in the living room, Sam was tossing candy corn into the air and trying to catch the pieces in his mouth. His head was tipped perpetually backwards, his mouth agape like a big fish scooping minnows from the air. Linda stood and watched him for a moment, then looked at Bill. His eyes were wide as saucers and wet; it was the same look he often gave when she presented him one of her gourmet dinners, a dish she had taken hours to prepare just for his pleasure.

Two pieces sailed into the boy's mouth without his making much of an effort. Sam's head dropped and he looked at Linda. "Here you go," she offered, holding the glass of cola toward him. He walked the three steps to meet her and accepted the drink without a word. As she watched him guzzle, Linda's worry button began to buzz. *Maybe we should have waited longer to see how he's reacting to the first pill. Maybe this is too much medication after all.* As the last drop slid effortlessly from the glass into Sam's mouth, Linda grabbed the tray of cookies from the table and thrust it in front of him. "Cookie?"

Sam stuck his hand out to grab one when Bill leaped to his feet and pushed Linda and the tray back toward the dining room. "Cookies later. Let's practice for pin-the-tail," he said. He pulled an old black bandana from his back pocket and pulled it through a loose fist on his other hand, appearing to caress the cotton fabric with his fingertips. "C'mere, Sammy. Let's practice balancing and focus."

Before Sam could protest, Bill tied the kerchief over the boy's eyes, placed his hands on Sam's shoulders, and with some force, spun Sam's body clockwise once, twice, three times. He gave Sam's collarbone a final squeeze and pushed the boy backwards softly. Sam teetered for a moment, then straightened. He attempted to walk forward. His body, still trapped in the centrifugal force, leaned right, then left, then right again. Sam took a tentative step forward with one foot but seemed unable to follow with the other, his body frozen in a strange half-warrior yoga pose.

"Uh... I'm dizzy," Sam said in a tiny voice. He raised his hand to push the blindfold from his eyes, but Bill jumped forward and held his arm.

"Oh, no you don't!" he sang in an unnaturally chipper tone. "Not yet!" He clutched Sam's shoulders again, this time harder. He spun Sam counterclockwise, and the boy's torso twisted ahead of its appendages, causing Sam to hold his arms out like a bird to keep from falling. As he tilted forward, Bill pushed him hard, sending the boy backwards and almost falling again. Bill began to circle the boy, running faster and faster around the boy, pushing him this way and that, until

Sam looked like an animatronic rag doll. After a minute or two of this, Bill exerted one final shove, and Sam fell down into a sitting position on the brown carpet.

"Oh my goodness! Are you alright, Sam?" Linda said, pulling the handkerchief from his head and holding out her hand to help him up.

Sam pushed himself into a squatting position, then lost his balance and tipped sideways. On the second try, he managed to push himself back up to standing. He pulled his Batman mask from his head and dropped it onto the floor. "Yeah... dizzy. I feel dizzy."

"Stand right there, buddy," said Bill. "Get your balance back. Hey, how about we catch candy corn again? You stand right there: I'll throw them into your mouth!"

Bill pitched his hand into the bowl and pulled out a handful of candies. He held one kernel between two fingers of his opposite hand even with his ear. "Okay, buddy. Open up!"

Sam stood staring at Linda for a moment. Then he opened his mouth an inch.

"Wider," said Bill.

Sam opened his mouth a tiny bit more.

"Wider!" roared Bill.

Sam opened his mouth like he was preparing for a tonsil exam. Bill gently tossed the candy corn into the boy's mouth. Sam chewed it and swallowed but did not open his mouth again.

"Again," Bill instructed.

Sam opened his mouth an inch, heard Bill suck in a forceful breath, and opened his mouth as wide as he could manage. Bill lobbed another candy into it, then backed up five paces. "How about from here? Hey: here's an idea. Let's play horse. Linda, why don't you see if YOU can make all of my trick shots, huh?" He spun his arm backwards like a big-league pitcher preparing for a fastball. "Open up, Sammy. Don't make me ask you again."

Sam closed his eyes so tight that his lids seem to sink and disappear into his face. He put his hands over his ears as if to shield them, and opened his mouth into an O-shape. *This is what Munch's painting looks like blinking*, Linda thought. Bill began to run around the room, first throwing, then pelting the boy with candy corn. The pieces popped and binged off of the boy's white, soft flesh like an orange and yellow hailstorm.

When Bill had run out of candy to throw, Sam tried to walk toward the couch during the reprieve. His pace was wobbly, drunk-like. "I don't feel so good," he said, slurring his words.

Linda placed an arm around him and helped him to the sofa. "Lie down, Sam: it's okay. Let me get you some ginger ale and crackers, okay? You probably just had too much sugar, sweetheart," she cooed. Bill backed up against the doorframe and clicked his teeth—a tiny pout as the pause button was hit on his fun.

Linda walked with purpose back to the kitchen and poured a small glass of ginger ale—sans powder—and looked quickly for some saltines. Finding none, she returned to the living room with only the soda. Sam was half-sitting, half-leaning on the sofa, his eyes heavy and half-closed. "Okay, sweetie," she pleaded in her kindest voice possible. "Drink this up now. Take some deep breaths." She placed the glass in Sam's sweaty hand.

Sam's eyes rolled a bit in his head like wet marbles. He clutched the glass weakly and brought it shakily to his lips. Just as the brim tickled his mouth, his body lurched forward in a spasm. Ochre vomit spewed onto his black shirt. His body convulsed twice more, sending two sprays of the putrid-smelling sick onto Linda, who had to close her eyes and inhale slowly through her mouth to not begin retching herself.

Bill patted Sam's back forcefully, like he was burping a plastic doll. "Well now, that's unfortunate. More room for cookies though, huh?" He shot a glance up at his wife. "Get the boy a wet towel, would you, Linda? For God's sake, the kid's covered in throw up."

Linda retrieved an old hand towel from the linen closet and dipped it in the tub filled with apples and cool water. She dabbed Sam's face carefully, watching his glassy eyes follow her facial expressions suspiciously. "I think I want to go home now," he mumbled drunkenly. "I don't want a cookie."

Linda peeled Sam's soiled top from his round, sweaty body, being careful not to shake any of the vomit onto the floor. Underneath, he wore a ribbed white tank top, the kind Marlon Brando wore in *A Streetcar Named Desire*. As if reading her mind, Bill burst out laughing. "Stella!!" he yelled. "Stelllll aaaah!" He guffawed and rubbed his stomach.

Linda took two steps backward. "I'm going to rinse off your shirt in the sink, Sam." She paused and looked at Sam straight in the eye. "You drink that ginger ale and Bill will drive you home, okay? Do what Bill says and everything will be okay."

She brought the shirt to the guest bathroom and ran it under warm water, watching the light brown chunky mess pause momentarily at the drain, then disappear. Never had a child gotten sick before. She wondered if this would affect the amnesic properties of the Midazolam. She and Bill had to be more careful. She was stupid to give him so much of the drug without food.

She squeezed the shirt, twisting it into a long, wet log and wringing it three times. Once it was no longer dripping, she returned to the parlor.

Bill was standing behind Sam, who was bent in a wobbly right angle, his head almost completely submerged in the tub of apples. Bill was holding his shoulders and Sam was flailing his arms about wildly. Linda thought she could hear a muffled, underwater scream.

"Bill! What are you doing? Stop! Stop! You're going to kill him!" Linda shrieked, dropping the shirt in a wet plop on the carpet. She stood next to her husband, half covering her face with her hands. "Oh my god, Bill: please—please let him up!"

Bill grabbed the top of Sam's tank top by the straps and pulled. Sam sputtered and gasped for air, his mouth stretched wide and angled toward the ceiling. "We're just bobbing for apples, Linda! What's the problem? Sammy here almost got a good one, too: didn't ya, Sammy?" He pushed Sam's face back into the water and held his palm firm against the top of Sam's neck. Water splashed from the bucket and onto Bill's t-shirt, soaking it to near translucence.

Linda pushed her husband hard: pushed him with all the force she could muster. Bill was a big guy—much bigger than Linda, and almost always much stronger. This time, she was able to gain the upper hand. She pulled Sam backward and away from the tub. He coughed violently, spraying Linda's face with spit and drool. "Are you alright?" Linda said, smoothing Sam's wet hair against his forehead over and over. "You slipped and fell forward... Oh my goodness: you're soaked: Let me get you a towel: hold on, Sam... just hold tight." She ran to the linen closet again and sorted through the piles of towels like a madwoman. She wanted to give Sam the cleanest, softest towel. She spied a fluffy yellow one, pulled it from the pile, and ran back to the living room.

"Sam, here is—" She stopped short. Sam was not in the living room. "Sam?" she called, walking cautiously through the dining room and into the kitchen. No Sam. "Sam?" He was not in the house. She stupidly opened a cabinet. Did she expect to find him hiding inside? She closed the door and leaned her back against the counter, crossing her arms in front of her chest. She supposed it was time to clean up.

She dumped the tub of water into the kitchen sink and laid the wet apples on the counter to dry. She rinsed the empty glasses of root beer and coke and ginger ale and stacked them neatly in the dishwasher. She removed the tablecloths from the end tables, dumped the remaining bowls of candy corn into the trash, and picked Sam's folded, wet Batman costume from the floor. She was nibbling the tail of a sugar cookie when the doorbell rang.

Although Linda wasn't entirely surprised to see a police officer standing on her stoop, she pasted her best bewildered expression across her face and smiled prettily at him. *Think: wide eyes of confusion and astonishment.* She remembered to show all of her teeth. She glanced over at the squad car parked against the curb, the same place Sam's mother had peeled away from after leaving her sad, doughy son in Linda's care just a few hours earlier. Sam's pale face stared at her from the back seat.

"Ma'am, we picked up a boy walking through the neighborhood who told us some very disturbing things about a party you are having here," the officer said. His steely grey eyes met hers and did not move. "'Mind if I take a look around?"

Linda stepped backwards into her foyer. "Oh my goodness: no, of course not! Come right in," she said.

The policeman stepped cautiously into the house. He followed Linda into the living room, looking at everything from ceiling to floor, seeming to memorize it. "So, what can I answer for you?" Linda asked, sitting daintily on the edge of the sofa.

The officer did not make a move to join her. "The boy tells us that you fed him things to make him sick. He says you assaulted him and tried to drown him in a tub of apples."

Linda laughed nervously, but the cop was not smiling. "Well, that seems like an odd story. Are you sure it was *this* house he visited?" *Smile. Teeth.* She cleared her throat.

"The boy was wearing an undershirt when we saw him walking one block over," he continued. "'Says you took his clothes."

Linda laughed again. "Well, isn't that funny?"

The officer did not think it was funny. In fact, he was very stern as he walked toward the dining room table and picked up the wadded-up, wet shirt Linda had placed next to the cookie tray. "What is this, ma'am?"

Linda could no longer evoke a laugh. "My husband... my husband may know what is going on..." she began. She looked frantically about the room. Where was Bill when she needed him?

"Your husband?" repeated the officer. "Is his name Bill, by any chance?"

"Why, yes," Linda said. Her face felt hot. She wiped her palms on her still-soaked t-shirt in an attempt to cool herself. "How did you know that?"

The officer took two steps closer to Linda. "I need you to come with me, ma'am. We have some questions for you at the station."

As if in a dream, Linda rose to her feet and followed the policeman outside and to his squad car. Sam had exited the vehicle and was standing next to a blonde policewoman on her lawn. As she passed by Sam, she saw the cop place her hand on Sam's upper arm, as if ready to pull him back if Linda made any unsightly movements. "She... she kept talking to some guy who wasn't there," Linda heard Sam say. "But it was just her. No one else was there."

The gray-eyed policeman opened the back door of the squad car and motioned for Linda to climb inside. As she did, she heard Sam's tiny voice squeak, "Can I just go home now? I just want to go home."

The officer closed the car door, and Linda wiped the humid glass and peered out toward her tiny bungalow. Baby Jessica was ruined. Bill would be mad when she came home tonight. She was sure of it.

Interlopers

She was starting to look like a hag. Her mother had always warned her not to let her looks go, but no, Carol Shattuck had turned her head for just a moment and *whoosh*, there went her tight skin, her bright eyes, and her shining chestnut brown hair, like a crisp dollar bill out of an open car window. Somewhere in the back of her mind loomed the fragmentary bits of a Slavic fairy tale her grandfather used to tell her: something about a skeletal witch with fearsome teeth of iron who lived in the woods. At forty-six years old, she imagined she resembled the protagonist, now that the thin skin hovering below her hazel eyes puffed and darkened like rotting fruit each morning and the hair at her temples sprouted new silver strands seemingly overnight. She had become the type of woman who stocked up on root touch-up color and teeth whitening strips like a doomsday prepper hoarding canned goods and freeze-dried meat. She patted eye cream and concealer next to her nose like a geisha preparing for a dance. She slapped her cheeks in the hope of puffing them slightly to mask their hollowness. She avoided bright lights like a vampire.

Carol speeded along Balboa Street, multitasking as she did each evening rush hour, simultaneously spraying face moistener, back-combing her hair, and clicking through news radio for something palatable. NPR was interviewing a refugee from Guatemala who had taken sanctuary in a Unitarian Church in Oakland. Carol hit the SEEK button again. She was so tired of hearing about the plight of America's flotsam and jetsam. She and Harrison paid taxes through the wazoo each year. They had sweated their ways through law school: he at UCLA and she at Loyola, and yes, they were both fortunate enough to have parents who were well off enough to pay for their college and post-grad work, but Carol didn't think she should feel guilty about that. She couldn't recall there being an array of exit doors on her mother's birth canal for her to choose from—door number one, affluence and pedigree; door number two, poverty and a cycle of ignorance—she had landed where she was supposed to land. It was just others' bad luck that they had drawn the shorter straws.

Her cell phone rang, an obnoxious, sing-songy tune that her carrier had programmed. It was free advertising for them, since Carol had neither the patience nor the technological skill to change it. She palmed the steering wheel with her left hand while feeling blindly inside of her Chanel calfskin handbag for the phone with her right. Out of the corner of her eye, she saw the crowds of people congregating around Golden Gate Park. She knew some of them were students leaving late afternoon classes at the University of San Francisco. Others were stay-at-home moms cutting through the park on their way home from a day at the zoo with their little ones. Carol remembered what it was like in those days. She had reduced her caseload to part-time when her two boys were little; it was only in the past decade, since they had morphed into teenagers, that she threw herself face-first back into long hours at the firm. She liked contract law. It was all about the degree of nebulousness one could locate and eviscerate. As a child, much to the chagrin of her debutante mother, Carol loved construction sets. She excelled in building the best mousetrap, constructing the most intricate Rube Goldberg machines, and she always left her competition in the dust. She could see every possible opportunity for escape and plugged holes and patched mistakes long before completion. Contract law required the same set of skills, only in reverse. Carol looked for loopholes and she threaded her needle within them before opposing counsel could spot them first. The best contracts, she quickly learned, were short and rigid: no wiggle room allowed.

Recently, an old friend from Loyola called her up to ask for a favor. Sally Kruger, a former family law attorney, had signed a contract with a small New England publishing company to write her biography; such a publication might resuscitate her relevance on the hired speaker circuit. She had always wanted to write memoirs of her own, Sally explained, but she had neither the talent nor the time to put the darn thing together. After being abandoned by two writers at previous companies, the third time had been the charm: the family-owned publisher had hired an ingénue who swallowed up the task like a hungry zoo animal. Not only had this hired writer written a beautiful book, but she had met her completion deadline with two months to spare. The book was done, Sally told Carol, but why should the writer get any credit for authorship? After all, it was *her* life on those pages: shouldn't SHE be considered the author? Carol had said she'd get back to her: she would have to take a look at Sally's contract with the publisher. Although she didn't vocalize it, Carol assumed it would be a slam-dunk case. A small, relatively new, family-owned company meant nervous parents juggling their children's welfare against a shoestring business budget. And they likely didn't have a shark-bite lawyer like her on staff.

Carol's hand finally grasped the soft-sided case of her phone and pulled it to the top of her bag. She glanced down to read the caller ID: it was Sally Kruger. Reluctantly, she tapped the green ANSWER button and cradled the phone next to her ear.

"Hey, Sally—I am just on my way home. Can I call you when I get there?" Carol asked brusquely. Sally could be needy, and when she was needy, she talked. And talked. And talked more still. One evening around Thanksgiving, Carol grew so tired of squeaking a word in edgewise that she simply placed the phone, screen-side down, on her bedroom dresser and returned to her family who had gathered in the living room. When she returned more than six hours later, Sally was no longer on the line. The women never spoke of the incident, but Carol couldn't help but wonder how long she had stayed on the phone, yakking away indefatigably.

"Of course, Carol..." Sally's voice quivered a bit, like she was in a vibrating train car. "But listen: I had to tell you this—I am starting to wonder if perhaps the publisher hired this girl for unsavory reasons of his own benefit, if you know what I mean. I finally got a good look at her. All big hair and tits."

Carol balanced the steering wheel between her knees and quickly rubbed droplets of argan oil across her damp face, making it glow. She pulled her Clarins firming cream from her bag, unscrewed the top with one flick of her wrist, and scooped a small amount and smoothed it over her neck. Tossing all of her beauty arsenal back into her bag, she shifted her phone to her left hand and held it to her ear. "What are you saying? She slept her way into the job?"

Sally laughed, a vibrating laugh as if someone was shaking her up and down like a bottle of salad dressing. "I mean, I don't *KNOW* that, but I mean, come on—pretty girl, married man, no published books under her belt—why else would he hire her?"

Carol grabbed the rear-view mirror with her right hand and swiveled it so that she had a full view of her face and neck. She leaned in more closely, stroking and patting her ring finger slowly under each eye to try to reduce the swelling—it was a trick she'd learned from her aesthetician. "Mmmmm," she said into the phone. "You have no proof, and besides, the girl wrote a solid manuscript, according to you.

Whether she did it with her mind or her vagina shouldn't be relevant."

"Oh, but it is," Sally hissed, "if the implication is pressed upon the family. I can't imagine his wife being too thrilled to fight with an accusation of adultery looming overhead."

Carol rubbed her fingertip along her lips, trying to transfer any oil that remained on her fingers onto them. She was almost at Arguello Boulevard, almost away from the park and its hippies and homeless drifting like helium balloons from Haight-Ashbury. Soon she'd be passing through the Hayes and the Tenderloin and the Tendernob, as it was now called, and arriving at her spacious, contemporary home in prestigious Nob Hill with just enough time to change into a little black dress and go to dinner with Harrison.

She was readjusting the rear-view mirror back to its previous position and didn't see the two women in the crosswalk until their bodies ricocheted off the hood of her Mercedes with a sickening thump. Even though she slammed on the brakes, Carol felt the front axle teeter over their prone bodies one by one. She sat still in her car, a mouse frozen in a trap. She could still hear Sally's voice talking to her through the phone on the floor near her feet.

2 of 3: Red Sun

Carol wasn't getting out of the car. She knew the women were trapped below her—she could almost feel the heat of their bodies rising up through her floorboards and grasping at her calves. All around her, people were screaming and running toward her vehicle. People banged on her windows, yelled obscenities, asked *What the fuck is wrong with you?!* and pleaded *Call the police! Call an ambulance!*

Quick! But Carol moved only inches, enough movement to reach down and retrieve the cell phone from her floor mat, click the red END CALL button to silence Sally's incessant yapping, and dial Harrison's cell phone number. She told her husband he had to come get her. Like a small child, she cried without tears into the receiver. *Please come get me, Harrison. I'm at the corner of Golden Gate Park. By the Conservatory of Flowers. Please hurry.*

There was a quick, granite-like rap at the driver's side window. Carol turned her head slowly. A middle-aged policeman in full uniform was bent down, looking at her through the glass. "Ma'am? Would you step out of the vehicle, please?"

Without opening the door or the window, Carol responded. "No, officer. I'm staying in my car," she said.

The officer looked at her for a long while. "Would you turn off your vehicle, please, ma'am?"

Carol placed the floor shifter into PARK and turned off the engine, but she remained in her seat. The crowd had doubled, and a handful of other policemen were mingling around the dozens of onlookers, trying to keep the curious and the quick-tempered away from the scene. "Ma'am," began the officer at her window. "Would you roll down your window, please?"

As she pressed the button and the clear barrier between her and the world dropped slowly away, a noisy ambulance pulled up beside her, its siren echoing about her grey leather interior. Two EMTs in deep blue uniforms hopped out of the cab and disappeared around the back of the truck. When they resurfaced, they were carrying a stretcher.

"Okay, ma'am, I'm going to ask you again. Please exit the vehicle." Carol stared at his bright silvery badge. His number was 230. She didn't know his name, but she could remember his badge number in case it came up later.

"I'm not getting out of my car, and I'm not speaking to you anymore without my lawyer present. He's on his way," Carol said. "Now, if you'll excuse me." She pressed the button on the window control again, and the clear barrier returned. From her vantage point, she could see the EMTs squatting on the ground, debating how they should proceed in pulling the women out from under the car. One or both may have been pinned. After what seemed like an eternity, her phone rang. It was Harrison.

"Honey?" he said softly but firmly. "Honey, I need you to listen to me very carefully. Slide over to the passenger side. Take anything of value from the car, including the registration and stereo faceplate. Have it in your hand and ready to carry with you when I come to your door…" Harrison paused. Carol knew he would know what to do. Twenty-four years defending white collar criminals had made facilitating these kinds of squeamish situations a piece of cake. "I'm parked right behind you, honey. About twenty feet back. I'm coming over now."

Carol slid over to the right side as she was told and gathered her belongings in her Coach bag. She turned her head and peered at the crowd, trying to spy her husband's broad shoulders and receding hairline, but the glare of the dipping sun made it all but impossible for her to see anything but a red and orange and yellow blur. She glanced at her face in the rearview mirror. Her cheeks were flushed, but it made her seem younger somehow. She ran her fingers along her upper lash lines, trying to curl them backwards. Instinctively, she fished her hand through her purse in search of a comb. Harrison's baritone courtroom voice boomed from outside the barrier.

"I'm her lawyer. Do you have any reason to arrest her? Do you have any reason to impound the vehicle?" he said.

Officer 230 responded, but in a mushy, muffled tone that Carol could not understand.

Harrison rapped softly on the driver's side window, and Carol pushed the button on the door to lower the glass slightly. "Hand me the registration and your license, Carol," Harrison said evenly. She did as she was told, and her husband made an upward hand motion to tell her to close the window again. She did. Officer 230 brought her license and registration back to his squad car. After a long moment, he returned and spoke again to Harrison in the same muffled volume. Harrison turned to his wife and motioned for her to get out of the car.

Carol opened the door slowly and crawled out like a cat burglar trying to avoid laser sensors. Immediately, the crowd began to shout at her. Angry words. Incendiary threats. Shames. Harrison draped his arm around her shoulder and escorted her briskly back to his black SUV, the sprinkling of beat cops serving as makeshift fences between the mob and Carol. She climbed into the passenger side seat, shielded from public view by the tinted glass, and her eyes drifted over toward her Mercedes. The first stretcher was being carried into the ambulance. It was draped by a bright white sheet.

3 of 3: Black Midnight

Carol sat quietly next to her attorney, one Harrison had hired—the best in the business, next to him, of course—and stared straight into space. In the seats immediately behind their mother, Carol's sons, Ray and Theo, sat dressed impeccably in Ralph Lauren shirts and freshly pressed slacks, their shoulders always back and their expressions free of worry or malice. Their father, a mirror image of them, accompanied them every day.

Carol had opted for a judge's ruling in lieu of a jury trial. Who knew what the jury could be comprised of? *Peers* was a term more rubbery than Silly Putty from what she had seen in courtrooms lately, especially in a city as heterogeneous as San Francisco. A wealthy, white, straight, cis-gender wife and mother would never get a fair shake from an unemployed gay man or—God forbid—a Hispanic woman with fifteen kids and a fat welfare check coming each month. No, a judge would see the incident for what it was: an accident, pure and simple. One of the women had died at the scene, but the other held on for forty-eight more hours; so, Carol was charged with two misdemeanor manslaughter counts two weeks later. When it came down to it, argued Carol first to her husband and then to the guests of the dinner party they held the following Saturday, the women weren't supposed to be there in the first place. They weren't supposed to be in the country at all.

Their names were Marina and Lila Vasilisa, ages 60 and 62, respectively. They were sisters-in-law and undocumented Russian immigrants living in the Richmond section of the city with Marina's Green-Carded children, Viktor and Ilonya, both in their late thirties. During the day, the women worked under the table for measly wages at a bakery on 22nd Street, and each evening, the women would walk, hand in hand, from their apartment on Geary down to the park to watch the sunset. Some nights, they would wander into the Botanical Gardens if they were open late for a wedding or function and inhale the rainbows of orchids and lilies while taking great care not to disturb or free the butterflies in the conservatory. They always obeyed the rules.

When Carol had struck them, driving fifteen miles over the speed limit, her eyes had been on her reflection instead of the road. Innumerable witnesses testified that they saw Carol holding a cell phone while driving, supporting the theory that what had occurred was not an accident but a crime by negligence. Carol had not consented to a breathalyzer at the scene—but to be fair, she hadn't been asked to take one either. Instead of coming down to the station and giving a formal statement, Carol emailed one to the police… ten days after Lila died. In her email, she insisted she had not been on her phone but rather had been alert and attentive. The sunset reflecting in her rear-view mirror had alternately blinded her, forcing her to keep adjusting her instruments. She had refused to leave the vehicle because she "became overwhelmed with a gripping fear that the people who had been hit would die. I simply could not force myself to get out." She had been frozen with sympathy and fear for the women's families. As a mother and wife, she simply could not imagine the agony Marina's children must be feeling.

Carol was found guilty, but initial sentence recommendations stated that she should receive only fifty hours of community service, most of which would be taken up by delivering weekly speeches on the dangers of distracted driving to traffic school attendees. When Viktor Vasilisa heard this, he could not contain himself.

"How could you do this?!" he yelled from the gallery. "If my mother and aunt had been citizens, you would have judged Mrs. Shattuck much more harshly. America is the land of equality—an eye for an eye! Is my mother's life worth only fifty hours?"

The judge pounded his gavel and called for order, and the bailiff slid quietly toward the prosecution's side of the courtroom, but Viktor was finished. He said something to his sister in Russian, and the two of them, along with the women's bakery co-workers and neighbors, walked somberly down the aisle toward the exit.

"Defendant must appear for sentencing three weeks from today. Bail is continued." The judge struck his gavel one additional time, and Carol turned to face her family. They joined together in a silent, smiling group embrace.

Three weeks later, Carol received her initial sentence. In lieu of paltry community service, she would serve 120 days of house arrest and was forced to wear an ankle bracelet. In addition, she was forbidden to drive a car at any time during those four months. If she failed to comply with those parameters at any point, she would serve ninety days in jail. As the judge read his ruling, Carol dabbed at the skin under her eyes with a linen handkerchief while Harrison, who sat next to her, patted her softly on her knee. For Viktor and Ilonya, it was not justice, but it was something. Most important to Carol, she could continue to practice law, and her confinement would be completed in time to see Ray compete in his final track meet in June. He had been training since the new year began, and his running endurance had been attracting big name college recruiters to meets almost every week.

Each morning, Carol placed a checkmark on the calendar and counted the days she'd completed. It was June 1st, and the weather outside was glorious: the kind of day that was neither too humid nor even slightly chilly. Carol marked the day on the kitchen calendar: 97 down, 23 to go. She would make rosemary chicken for dinner that evening, she decided. Being homebound had forced her to learn many new ways of cooking, and as a silver lining she had built quite a repertoire of recipes. She walked into the sunroom and over to the herb garden she'd started that spring and pinched a handful of rosemary from one of the plants. Back in the kitchen, she placed the fresh herbs in her mortar and worked at them with her marble pestle, a gift from Harrison on the day of her sentencing.

She heard her phone's odious ring clamor for her

attention from the other room. She rested her pestle, wiped her hands on a towel, and followed the sound into the bedroom. Her phone was face down on her dresser, which reminded Carol of Sally. She hadn't heard from her in a few days, but she did not have the desire nor the patience to placate her in that moment. In that moment, she simply wanted to smell the fresh herbs on her hands and watch through her window as the sun tickled her lawn; she wanted to work in silence at home, something she had not only become accustomed but had taken a real shine to.

The phone continued to ring. She would have to face the consequences. She turned the phone over, but instead of seeing Sally's name in the caller ID, she saw Theo's. She pressed the green ANSWER button and said, "Hello?"

Theo's voice was at once loud and stifled. He was speaking so quickly that Carol had to ask him to repeat what he was saying over and over. It was only later that she understood that it wasn't that he had been speaking unclearly: it was that Carol's brain could not comprehend the irony that befell her.

"It's Ray, Mom," Theo said, sobbing. "He was hit by a car crossing to the Presidio." He paused, choking on tears. "He's dead, Mom. And the driver just took off—no one even knows what the car looks like."

Carol held the phone with her left hand and sunk to her knees on the hardwood floor. It had been almost a year since Carol had callously killed two innocent women, but finally, she had received her sentence.

The Munchies

Don't ever have children.

I know you *think* you want them—all of your friends are doing it, so why don't you?! You stay home sick one afternoon, and every commercial on television features a youthful family of four: two pretty parents swinging two adorable munchkins around a green-lawned backyard. In these commercials, the sun is always shining, the dog is always clean and running obediently alongside the children, and the steam from the hotdogs on the grill is always smoky and delicious-looking. That's not a hotdog you smell: it's domestic bliss, my childless friend! Come and join the utopia!

If you believe that, I have a windowless van full of candy and puppies I'd like to give you a ride in. Climb inside and take a gander. While you're in here, does this paper bag smell like ether?

Here's the 4-1-1. That sun? It causes melanoma. That dog? It ate the remains of your chili-cheese burrito and has a wicked case of explosive diarrhea. And those hotdogs? They're really tofu, and no matter what that hot vegan barista tries to tell you, tofu dogs taste like shit. Once you climb into that windowless van, you might as well start binge-eating the Skittles, because there's no getting out. At least not for the next eighteen years.

I always wanted a family. I know it's not a manly thing to admit, but it's true. When I was a kid and I imagined what it would be like to be an adult, I saw myself with a house and a wife and two or three rug-rats. I never imagined the future beyond that still photograph, though. I don't know what I thought me and the wife and the kiddos would be doing all day: maybe tossing a softball back and forth, maybe riding a five-way tandem bicycle down a tree-lined street, maybe sitting side by side by side by side in a movie theater, passing a king-sized box of Junior Mints up and down the row. Having a family is just a thing you do, right? Your parents did it. Your parents' parents did it. How could you live your life without children?

It's possible—trust me. I almost had that life. Lila and I met on spring break at a resort my freshman year of college. She was dark-skinned and gorgeous, and I was a pale, introverted goofball. When she approached and offered to buy me a drink, I could only stammer out a weak "Sure" while doing everything in my power not to stare at her enormous breasts held back by a triangle string bikini top I assumed must have been made of steel. After a few rounds of Mai Tais, I had loosened up enough to tell her my name and turn on the ol' Michael charm. It turned out she was three years older than me and would be graduating three months later. We spent the rest of the week practically attached at the hip, and after keeping in touch almost daily by phone and Skype, six months after we met, she moved to Austin to be with me. Three days after I finished my degree, we married and moved to Rhode Island to be near my family.

They say that before you make the leap to marital bliss, you need to have two serious talks. The first should be about finances. You don't want to jump onto a moving train only to discover three months in that the caboose is filled to the brim with fifty thousand dollars of unsecured credit card debt and a wicked gambling addiction. The second should be about expectations for home and family. Lila and I lived together for three years before we tied the knot. We knew each other's spending habits as well as our own.

We never had the second talk.

On our five-year anniversary, we traveled back to the cheap resort where we first met. We sat at the same bar where she had offered to buy me that drink, and we walked hand in hand along the same beach where we first made love. As we huddled together on the sand and watched the sun dip slowly toward the water, I nudged her ankle with my big toe.

"Ew, Michael—quit it!" she laughed. She had always had this weird aversion to feet, never wanting to touch mine or really even see them if she could help it. I guess everyone has something that disgusts them.

I admired the sunset reflecting off of her tightly curled hair and felt my heart throb. "I guess this means I'll be the one taking the kids shoe-shopping, huh?" I laughed, picking up an errant piece of light green sea glass from the sand and slipping it into my shorts pocket. We'd collected sea glass since our first week together and over the years had amassed quite a collection; I planned to assemble all of the pieces into some sort of memory box when I had the time. When I looked back up at Lila, I saw she wasn't smiling. In fact, she was staring blankly at the water.

"Speaking of which…" I continued. "How about we start that family tonight?" I pushed my shoulder into her arm and waited for her smile. It never came. After a moment, she looked at me.

"Michael, I don't want to have kids," she said. "I thought you knew that."

I was dumbfounded. This was news to me. "What? What do you mean?" I asked. How could someone NOT want to have children? What was the point of getting married if you didn't want to have a family? What was the point of growing up and becoming an adult? I didn't know anyone over the age of thirty who didn't have kids. Even my aunt and uncle, after years of being unable to conceive, adopted two children from some foreign country on the other side of the world. I tried to imagine the two of us in our forties, childless. We'd be that sad couple in the mall at Christmas, buying expensive electronics, drunk at the Ruby Tuesdays before noon. I couldn't let that happen.

"I can't imagine us *not* having kids. You are so beautiful and smart, and we have everything—everything we could give children. We are healthy and financially stable, and you *love* kids," I said. "I mean... don't you?"

Lila looked down at her fingernails. "I mean, sure, I like them fine. I just don't want any of my own."

We were quiet for a moment. Then Lila playfully pulled at my t-shirt, stood up, and brushed the sand from the back of her thighs. "Come on, M. Let's go get a drink before the sun completely sets." She offered her hand to pull me up but made a concerted effort to keep her bare feet away from mine. I accepted her hand and we walked back to the hotel.

Everything would have been different had I just let sleeping dogs lie, but I just couldn't let it go. Six months later, we were both at home in the middle of the week; a blizzard had paralyzed most of the East Coast, and most of the businesses in the town were closed. We had enough milk and bread to feed a football team.

I wandered into the living room, still in my pajamas at eleven in the morning, and sprawled out on the couch to watch TV. As I flipped through the channels, a commercial caught my eye. In it, a man was sitting on a high-back sofa with his arm around a small boy. The boy was sniffling and must have been sick, and he kept drifting in and out of consciousness as the pair watched a silly cartoon. Each time the boy closed his eyes for more than a second, the dad hit the remote control and switched the channel to a football game. When the boy opened his eyes again, the father hit the remote and switched the screen back to the cartoon. "Anyone can be a father," said a voiceover at the end. "It takes a real man to be a dad."

I put down the remote and wiped the tear that had fallen silently down the edge of my cheek. I was meant to be a father. I was going to be a dad. For the next two months, I pestered Lila. I wish I could use a nicer word than that to describe my baby campaign, but pester just about sums it up. Every day without fail, I begged her to change her mind. Finally, I wore her down.

Sure, I know what they say: the minute you start trying to get pregnant, you can't. You're so focused on the end goal, your bodies just shut down and plug up. Not us. Within one month of agreeing to stop taking her birth control pills, Lila woke me up early on a Sunday morning. She was holding a pregnancy test stick, and the results window practically glowed with two bright pink "plus" signs. I leaped from the bed and bear-hugged my wife. I hadn't been this happy since the day I slipped the wedding band onto Lila's finger.

Finally, I unlatched myself from her soft body and pulled back to look at Lila's face. "We are going to be parents!" I said excitedly. Lila smiled. It was a tight-lipped smile, but she smiled. She raised her hand and touched her face, then stuck her index finger in her mouth. She was nervous, I could tell. *Once she realizes we are in this together, she will relax*, I told myself. *It will all be perfect*, I told myself.

I couldn't have been more wrong.

Lila had terrible morning sickness for the first few months, even having to be hospitalized for dehydration at one point. She barely ate, and when she did, it came right back up more often than not. We had agreed not to tell anyone about the baby until we had reached the 12-week safe mark, but when that day arrived, I made certain to invite my parents and aunt and uncle and brother over for dinner. By coincidence, it was also our six-year anniversary. By then, Lila was digesting most of her meals, but her nutrition mimicked that of an Atkins diet: meat and a few random vegetables with almost no starch or bread. It made her nauseous, she said, and I didn't argue.

When the dinner plates had been cleared, and Lila stood up to prepare the coffee, I motioned for my wife to sit. "Lila and I have some news we want to share," I said, hardly able to contain the grin that was forcing its way out of every muscle on my face. "We're pregnant!" Everyone *oooed* and *ahhhed*, and my mom stood up and hugged Lila for a long minute.

"When is the big day?" my uncle asked.

"He or she—we don't want to know the gender—is due on Christmas—can you believe the kid's bad luck?" I laughed and smiled at Lila. She was holding her hands in front of her belly, her fingers closed into fists.

My brother counted his fingers. "That's only six months away. You're already three months pregnant? But you look like you've *lost* weight," he said to my wife. "You're like Mia Farrow in *Rosemary's Baby*!"

Lila laughed. "I'm sure little Andy or Jennie will appreciate the Christmas irony then," she said. I watched her disappear into the kitchen. *I have a quick-tongued wife*, I thought. *Our kids are going to be smart as whips*. I got up from the table and went to help Lila with the coffee and dessert.

That night, I lay in bed watching reruns of a zombie drama on television. Lila was fast asleep beside me, her whole body minus her neck and head tucked securely under the covers—she could sleep anywhere, anytime. I envied that about her. I savored the opportunity to look at my beautiful wife without feeling her self-consciousness. Her deep brown skin was still smooth, though the first hints of crow's feet were forming around her eyes, and my brother was right: she looked thin, thinner than she had in a long time. The morning sickness had really taken its toll.

At her appointment earlier that week, when the doctor had difficulty locating the baby's heartbeat, I felt my stomach lurch and fall to the deepest recesses of my abdomen. Then he moved the paddle downward and a skipping sound, like a horse galloping, echoed from the speaker. "Good, strong beat," said the doctor. "Just what we like to hear."

I felt my shoulders relax back down into my torso and my intestines unclench. I smiled at Lila and reached for her hand. It wasn't until I held it that I saw the bandages wrapped around her thumb and forefinger. "What happened to your fingers?" I asked her, as the doctor packed up his machine and made a few notes on the exam room computer.

"It's nothing," she whispered, and pulled her hand away and hid it with her other hand beneath the sheet. She stared up at the watercolor picture taped to the ceiling above her and didn't look at me even when I told her I'd meet her in the waiting room after she got dressed.

A small snore drifted from between her parted lips, and I tenderly stroked her forehead and cheek. Her chest moved up and down slowly and rhythmically, and I let my eyes float down the waves of her blanketed body. Her tummy was still flat, but I wondered if I could feel anything inside; the beginning of the second trimester was too early for a kick, I knew, but the doctor had said something about a quickening, a bubbling butterfly feeling that was possible in the fourth month.

I slowly pushed the covers down Lila's body. She was wearing her usual sleep clothes, an old white tank top and cotton boxer shorts. When I could finally see the top of her shorts, I let go of the covers. I stealthily pinched the bottom of her tank top and pulled it to the underside of her breasts, exposing her stomach. Then, ever so gently, I laid my hand on her tummy, pressing my palm against her belly button, and waited. Nothing. Disappointed, I began to pull the covers back up, but it was then that I saw it.

Her left arm was slightly bent, and her hand was

spread open against the top of her hip so that her thumb rested on her torso and her index finger pointed to the foot of the bed. There were no bandages on her fingers anymore. Instead, where the bandages had been, where *skin* had been previously, was raw, torn flesh. The top corner of her thumbnail had been ripped off, and the skin and muscles beneath it were simply missing, like a dog or even a small shark had taken a big bite. The edges of the wound were jagged and deep red in color, and they were covered in deep brown scabs. I looked closer and saw something white peeking out from the remaining muscle. It was bone.

My stomach flinched and I felt hot bile rise in my throat. I closed my eyes and took a deep breath. This couldn't be real: could it? I looked again. Her index finger had a similar injury, except the entire nail was intact but almost all of the flesh was missing from the top knuckle and above. I was reminded, sickly, of the last time I had ribs at the local barbecue joint. Like her thumb, the scant remaining muscle was marbled like a raw steak and dotted with hard, brown scabs.

I sat in bed, staring for what seemed like hours at my wife's mangled fingertips. Had she been attacked by an animal? Had there been some sort of kitchen accident? Why didn't she tell me about it? Then, I considered something much more disturbing. Had she done this to *herself*?

I covered Lila back up, hoping, in a moment of wishful thinking, that I was having a terrible nightmare and that the next time I saw my wife's hands, they'd be normal again. I shook Lila by the shoulder urgently. She awoke with a start, blinking her eyes rapidly and looking genuinely alarmed. "What? What? What's going on? What's the matter?" she asked.

"Lila… Lila… what happened? What happened to your fingers?" I asked. Why beat around the bush, right? If she lifts up her hands and they are perfectly normal, I will look like an idiot: who cares?

Lila frowned, still halfway asleep. "What?" she asked, confused. Then, her face changed. She realized what I was asking her and glanced down at the blanket covering her hands. "What do you mean?"

I pulled the covers back dramatically, like a magician pulling a tablecloth away to reveal a trick. Once again, her mangled, raw flesh was exposed. I looked for the first time at her right hand and saw the same grotesque injuries were there on her middle and ring fingers. Her ring finger had no trace of a nail or any flesh on the first knuckle at all: there was only a peek of bone dotted here and there with a wisp of red, stringy sinew.

I shuddered uncontrollably and knew I would not be able to calm my stomach that time. Dry heaving, I bolted from the room and into the master bathroom and watched as the remnants of our spinach lasagna covered the white porcelain inside of the toilet bowl. *This is what Lila's fingers would look like if you put them in the food processor with a sprig of parsley*, I thought. The image made me vomit again. I stayed hovering over the toilet until I felt the world stop spinning and I had spit the last mouthful of bile into the red-tinted water. I reached up to the metal handle and flushed.

When I returned to the bedroom, Lila was sitting up with a pillow propped behind her back. At some point when I was in the bathroom, she had retrieved a box of bandages and had reapplied fresh ones over all of her wounds.

I sat on the bed and turned my body to face her. "What is going on? What happened? I don't… I don't understand." A sense of unreality, of being outside of myself, washed over me, like when Lila and I had tried psychedelic mushrooms. I vowed never to experiment with drugs again, but I would watch Lila's face melt like a Dalí clock five hundred more times if it meant I would never have to look at her mutilated fingers again.

Lila looked down at her lap and inhaled deeply. "I don't know… I don't know why it started or what is happening… but ever since I found out I was pregnant, I… I have this urge to chew on my flesh." She swallowed hard and started to cry. "I know I sound like a crazy person. I know it! I just… I don't know. I can't control it."

I watched her face. She was scared. On instinct, I reached out to hold her hand and then thought better of it. "Did you… did you tell your doctor about it?"

She met my eyes. "Are you kidding? They'll lock me in a psych unit, put me in one of those straitjackets or strap me to a bed or something." She began to cry again. "Do you want that to happen to me? Do you want your pregnant wife to be strapped to a hospital bed?"

"No—no, of course not," I said. "But this… this isn't healthy. I think that's an understatement." I paused. "Maybe it's some sort of vitamin deficiency? You know, I read once that that's where the vampire myth originated—that there were these people who suffered from this extreme iron deficiency and craved blood because of it. Maybe you're anemic?"

"They test for that stuff at my appointments," Lila said. "And I tried eating steak, even raw steak, even though I'm not supposed to eat raw stuff because of Listeria or whatever." She looked down at her hands pensively. "It's not the actual swallowing of the flesh. It's… it's the chewing. It's like," she paused. "You're not going to like this analogy, but it's like I'm high and have the munchies."

I sighed and stared at her bandaged hands. We were both quiet. "Please," she whispered. "Please don't say anything to anyone. I promise I'll try harder. Maybe this will pass, like the morning sickness."

I gently took her hand and put it in my palm. "How about this? The next time you have a craving, I want you to take my hand. Bite me instead. I know you, Lila: you won't be able to hurt me."

Lila smiled. "I can't bite you."

"I know," I said. "That's the point. It's worth a shot, right?"

She smiled and leaned over to kiss me on the cheek. "Okay, M. I will do that." She sat forward and readjusted the pillow so that she could lie prostrate again. "Goodnight, baby," she said, and closed her eyes, her face tilted toward me.

"Goodnight," I said.

On the television screen, a grey-skinned zombie shuffled up behind a sandy-haired man and began to gnaw on his neck. I clicked the *off* button on the remote just as the monster tore away a mouthful of flesh.

It all seemed like a faraway nightmare for a few weeks after that. The bandages remained on Lila's fingers—I mean, there was no putting back a third of a finger, and there was no way to explain away such an injury without rousing suspicion—so I stocked up on bandages at Costco. Soon, Lila's belly began to grow. The day after her 20-week doctor's visit, she took my hand and placed it on her rounding abdomen. "Can you feel it? The tickling? It's like soda bubbles bouncing off the insides of my uterus," she said excitedly. I tried my very best to feel what she was describing and was disappointed when I could not.

"Hey, I have an idea," I said. "Let's go to the movies—you know, that new Marvel one is out. I heard that if there's a lot of sound, sometimes the baby will get active and move around a bit."

Lila agreed, and we went to the 1:30 matinee. The movie had been out for almost a month, and we were the only ones in the theater. Had we still been newlyweds, we would have sat in the back row. It had been our secret rendezvous for the first years of our relationship: Lila would wear a skirt, and we'd sit in the back row so that no one was behind us. Once the movie got going, I'd unbutton my pants and she'd climb on top of me, still facing the screen, and I'd slide myself inside of her. If the movie was really good, no one would even think about turning around or venturing out for snacks.

There was nothing preventing us from trying it now, except the idea of grabbing hold of her pregnant belly made me nervous. She wasn't even supposed to wear high-heeled shoes now, never mind balanced precariously on her husband in a skirt in a dark theater. Besides, she was wearing jeans.

I bought an extra-large popcorn and a liter of Sprite. We always shared the snacks, at times fighting over who was hogging the popcorn. Halfway through the film, though, I noticed she hadn't touched the popcorn at all.

"Do you want some?" I whispered. On the screen, Chris Pratt squinted and made a witty remark. Lila shook her head. I looked down at her lap. She was gripping her hands together like a nervous flyer on a turbulent cross-country flight. I reached my arm over and placed my hand on hers, and she unclenched her fists and wrapped one of her hands over mine.

I used my free hand to shovel popcorn into my mouth again. The movie was good—better than I had thought it would be—and I started to wonder why we hadn't gone to see it when it was first released. I had been swamped at work, and there were a bunch of weekends when we had family things booked back to back, and—

A sharp pain, like I had been pricked with a needle, shot through my hand. I instinctively tried to pull my hand back but was met with resistance. I looked over at Lila. She was holding my hand with both of hers. My index finger was in her mouth. She turned her head to face me, the reflected glow of the screen illuminating her face in purple, making her look like a wide-eyed corpse. Her mouth was slightly open, and her teeth were planted firmly on the ragged edge of my cuticle. An explosion on screen shook the walls with sound, and as if on cue, Lila jerked her head away, tearing a long strip of skin from my finger. I screamed, but the sound drowned away in the swelling of music and gunshot sound effects. She spit the piece of flesh out, pushed my hand back toward me, and buried her face in her hands. I could tell she was sobbing.

"It's okay," I said. "It's okay. It's all going to be okay."

I wrapped the pile of napkins around my gaping finger, red blood soaking through the rough brown paper. I was starting to doubt it would be okay.

That evening, I made homemade chili: Lila's favorite. We sat silent at the kitchen table, but Lila barely touched her food. When I got up to refill my bowl, she pushed hers across the table at me. "I'm not hungry," she said. "You eat mine."

I thought about what to say to her, then realized there really wasn't anything I could say. I simply dug my spoon into her bowl of chili and ate. The whole time, I could not stop looking at the bandages wrapped around my index finger.

Lila went to bed early that night. "I think I'm just overwhelmed," she said. "Feeling the baby and everything… it's a lot. Maybe I'm starting to get stressed out. I should try to sleep more, I think," she said. She leaned down to kiss me, and for the first time since I first spied her at that beachfront bar in the tiny string bikini top, I felt fear. I closed my eyes and prepared for her to bite my face. Instead, I felt her kiss on my cheek and nothing more. When I opened my eyes again, she was gone.

Three hours later, I brushed my teeth, splashed water on my face and blotted it with a towel, and walked into the bedroom. Lila was fast asleep, her lips slightly open, her whole body covered save for her neck and head. The news played softly on the television. We never turned on the sleep timer: after living above a bar on Austin's Dirty Sixth for three years, we couldn't sleep unless it was a little bit noisy.

I slid under the covers and turned my head to look at my wife. She was so beautiful. I had to believe this would pass. Four and a half more months, and it would all be over, and we'd be a family. I'd be a dad. She'd be a mom. It would be perfect again.

When I woke suddenly two hours later, I was confused. On the television was an infomercial for a miraculous copper pan of some sort. As my eyes adjusted, I could see the host marveling at the nonstick capability as a perfectly cooked fried egg slid slickly onto a waiting plate. Something was wrong. Lila's knees were pressed against my chest. Her feet dangled near my neck.

"Lila?" I called groggily. "Lila, what are you doing?" My wife was lying on her side, her head next to my feet. "Lila?" I said loudly, but she did not respond. The light of the television flashed brightly for a moment, making her eyes glow like a cat's. That meant her eyes were open. She must have been awake—but why wasn't she answering me?

I reached sideways and felt for the lamp on the nightstand. Clicking it on, I could not believe what I was seeing. The blankets at the end of the bed had been pulled up and folded onto my knees, exposing my bare calves and feet. Lila had wrapped her hands around my right ankle.

"Lila?" I called. She turned her head slightly to look at me. Her mouth was slightly open, and a river of drool spilled from one side. I had no time to react before she jerked forward and clamped her mouth down onto my big toe, piercing the flesh with her teeth. A stabbing pain shot through my body as I watched my wife bite down with all of her might and rip my toe from its foot. Bright red blood poured from the gaping wound and splashed onto her face.

"Lila, no!" I screamed, but it was too late. She spat the appendage from her mouth and returned her teeth to my second toe. The room went hot and white.

"Simply amazing!" proclaimed the infomercial host.

Amazing.

Don't ever have children.

I know you think you want them—all of your friends are doing it. Your parents and your in-laws are asking, *what's the hold up, kids?* Your great aunt pours herself another glass of wine at Thanksgiving and nudges your shoulder. *Tick-tock goes the biological clock*, she whispers.

You'll just have to trust me on this.

Yeah, he IS pretty cute, this little guy here. We named him Andy after all. At the end of this month, he'll be a terrible two. It's hard to believe so much time has passed. Yeah, he does like his dolls. Progressive parenting, you know? We don't gender-fy our son's toys, thank you. If you're looking for a birthday gift idea, he could use a few more dolls, actually. He's chewed the hands off of every one we've given him. Teething: what can you do?

Anyone can be a father. It takes a real man to be a dad.

Now hand me my crutches, would you? Lila's pregnant again, and we're clean out of bandages.

Stiff as a Board

"Jesus, mother-fucking fuck!" Karen slammed her sizzling finger against the ironing board. She had been so mesmerized watching the studio lights dance off the glitter in the judge's eyeshadow on the softly-lit courtroom drama on the T.V., she hadn't seen how close to her hand she had pressed the hot iron. All it took was an overenthusiastic swoop, and her digit angrily throbbed a rhythmic response.

"Ouch, FUCK!" She stuffed her finger in her mouth like a five-year-old. She knew she should be running it under cold water... or was it hot water? Feed a cold? Starve a fever?

Darien cackled wildly and stuffed a fistful of Cracker Jack in his mouth, the crumbs drifting downward into the crevices between couch cushions, immediately collecting dust and dirt and hair and filth. It was as if he hadn't heard her yelp and accompanying cuss words; more likely, he *had* heard her—loud and clear—but was actively ignoring her, as he often did these days. Karen and Darien had been married for seven years. Met at 22, moved in at 23, married at 25: the three M's of courtship. *More like the Sphinx's riddle,* Karen thought. What walks on four legs in the morning, two legs at noon, and three legs at night? Answer: Karen's marriage, now in its final life stage, hobbling along, creaky and old and too weak to make much of a fuss.

She was 32 now, and having donated the best years of her thighs and ass to a man who guffawed at the antics of reality court television, she was miserable. It seemed she had fallen into some sort of Sisyphean bear trap. Tuesday through Saturday, she manned the concierge at Alewife Park's posh condo co-op, an ostentatious skyscraper of postmodern uber-apartments sporting the latest digital advancements and all the conveniences of a personal assistant. Residents could monitor their lights, adjust their central air, program their DVRs, and even set their coffeemakers from their comfy swivel chairs in offices packed deep in the Prudential Building, and on the way up from the attached, heated parking garage, grab a fresh caramel macchiato (*no whip, please*) and instruct the mousy girl at the front desk to make dinner reservations (*don't let them push us to ten o'clock—that's much too late to be drinking Sambuca flambé, dear*).

Each day, Karen wore a smart grey suit, crisp white blouse peeking out beneath, and minimal makeup (*we don't manage a brothel here, love—reel that rouge in*) and plastered on a bright smile for her manager and tenants. She owned three of the exact same quiet, grey pant suits and five of the same crisp, white blouses, and each Sunday she washed the whole lot, hanging it to dry on lines strewn across her dark basement. She wouldn't dare throw any of the pieces in the dryer for fear they would shrink or disfigure, and when she woke up each Monday, the first thing she'd do is pull the rickety ironing board down from its hanger on the backside of the front room's closet door, fill the reservoir of her Maytag iron with tap water, and press her work clothes until they appeared new, or at least newly dry-cleaned.

Darien, on the other hand, spent most weekday mornings on the couch. They had met at an alumni job fair at Northeastern: she, sporting a useless Media and Screen Studies degree while he lounged comfortably on the cushion of a combined Pharmacy/Biochemistry bachelor's. Did he really need help finding a job? she asked him incredulously at their first meeting.

"Nah," he answered nonchalantly. "I'm good. I just missed the food." Karen stared at the mountain of rolls, salads, and assorted tapas balanced precariously on the Styrofoam plate he held in his hand. She didn't know what to say.

Darien worked part-time as a pharmaceutical rep: part-time, because he spent the other half of his workdays peddling the pills he managed to skim off the top of his sample bags as well as generous bags of premium weed he procured from some nebulous pipeline of pot farms in Maine. Mostly, he just couch-surfed and ate like he was still 22 years old, his belly rounding a little more with every passing year. Sometimes, Karen would catch herself staring blankly at him. She swore she could hear the hair growing in his shapeless, matted beard, could smell the build-up of pot smoke and French press coffee wafting from his mop of black hair that now curled here and there around his ears, grazing his jawline like a garden snake.

Darien dropped his sales suits at the cleaners every week and retrieved them like clockwork the following day, so Karen only needed to wash his casual and underclothing. They maintained separate bank accounts and separate cell phone plans; they paid bills like roommates, splitting everything, from groceries to mortgage payments, right down the middle. Incidentals—like dry cleaning—were luxuries each would choose to indulge or forgo. Karen was the practical one. She was the ant to his grasshopper. The one area where she refused to budge was life insurance: she made Darien open up a policy and she opened one as well, and as incentive, they each paid the premiums on the other's. Someday, she told herself, Darien would appreciate her pragmatism. Someday, he would see she was right to be wary.

"No, no, don't get up: I'm fine, thank you," Karen said, more to the air than to Darien. She waved her finger in the air, then abruptly brought her arm back to her side. The very movement of the wind against her blistering skin was surprisingly excruciating.

Darien raised an eyebrow at her and pulled his foot out from under his thigh. Without saying a word, he stood up from the couch and walked into the kitchen. Karen could hear him fumbling through the freezer. He returned with a paper towel wrapped around a freezer pack, took her hand gingerly in his, and pressed the makeshift icepack against her wound.

"Thanks, Dae." Karen smiled. He wasn't all bad all the time, was he?

Darien tilted Karen's hand in his, examining the fingertips poking out from under the towel. "Jesus, Karrie: your cuticles are a mess. Ever heard of hand lotion? What must the Howells think?" Darien called the residents of Alewife Park the Howells after the cartoonish millionaire and his wife from *Gilligan's Island*. They, too, were snooty and two-dimensional.

Darien picked at a hangnail on her ring finger. "Quit it!" Karen shooed him away. Her hands were a mess: dry and cracked like her mother's had been when they had lunch in Brookline Village last week. Of course, her mother was 60 years old and worked as a crossing guard and it was the middle of January.

Darien shrugged and returned his body to the husband-shaped divot in the sofa, a round peg snugly inserted into a round hole. He brushed the coffee table with his arm, reached beside the couch, and pulled out his sample suitcase. "Need anything for the pain?" he asked his wife.

Karen shook her head. Darien unzipped the case and removed two clear bottles of bright red capsules. Karen could see they each sported a clean yellow stripe drawn horizontally, not vertically, along the side. They reminded Karen of the Soviet flag, stitched out and reshaped like silly putty into bullet-like ovules. "Those are new," she said.

Darien unrolled a sheet of small, clear baggies and began divvying up the red and yellow pills, three per bag. A children's song from long ago muscled its way into Karen's consciousness. *Black sheep, black sheep, have you any wool?*

she absentmindedly sang in her head. *Yes sir, yes sir, twenty bags full!*

Noticing she had forgotten to switch off the iron, Karen placed her hand on the switch. It was only then that she noticed that the hangnail on her left hand had begun to bleed. Crimson capillary blood had dribbled onto the ironing board cover where she had been resting her hand, leaving a tiny smooch of red that was quickly drying to brown. She sucked on her finger until the bleeding stopped, then wandered into the bathroom to find first aid cream and Band-Aids to cover her wounds.

The next day, Karen was covertly flipping through a *Vogue* magazine that somehow had fallen out of a tenant's mailbox. *Upgrade Your Wardrobe for Spring!* the front cover shouted enthusiastically. Karen eyed the cuff on her suit. An almost unperceivable fray could be seen along the hem. She would have to replace her suits in a month or so, and the management company would not accept discount attire. She was still catching up on Christmas bills and had yet to pay the yearly premium on Darien's life insurance policy that was due next month, and now she'd have to budget a few hundred for her *Upgraded Wardrobe!* She pressed the pump on the drugstore almond-scented hand lotion she kept near the phone and rubbed her knuckles and nail beds. When her rubbing evolved into wringing, she winced after bending her blistered skin without thinking.

Goddammit, she thought, readjusting her bandage delicately so as not to disturb the wound further. *Why am I such a klutz?* She learned the hard way that morning that it was, in fact, cold water, not hot, that should be applied to a severe burn—if for no other reason than the opposite hurt like hell. She had spent most of her morning shower swinging her hand around wildly to shake off the searing pain.

The big sliding glass doors into the atrium slid open, bringing in a whoosh of ice-tinseled air that felt refreshing against Karen's face. Since it was early afternoon and most of her residents worked traditionally yuppie, daytime power-jobs, she would have few interactions with humans for the next few hours save for a handful of awkward exchanges with delivery men.

One of them, a rep from the company where the building purchased its bottled water, had dropped onerous hints to Karen about holiday tipping. She wanted to say to him, "Who do you think is responsible for tipping you: me? Come Christmas, I barely clear $500 in a building of 25 units," and it was true. Sure, there were a few kind and generous people: Mr. Adams in 6F with the Pomeranian and the Ficus she'd agree to water when he visited his mother in Palm Springs each May, or Mr. and Mrs. Salinas in 9A who were dark and beautiful and quiet and asked for nothing, yet left her an intricate, handmade card containing a hundred-dollar bill on her desk one gloomy afternoon following Thanksgiving. Many saw her as an indentured servant, a robot they ordered from Amazon that never needed charging. Most did not even wish her a happy holiday.

With the January gale came Mr. Farsley, a tidy man with an abrupt manner and a stiff gait. He was hauling at least five large paper sacks from an expensive store Karen had walked by on Newbury Street. She had never ventured in, not even to browse, as it seemed like the kind of joint that required a deposit or reservation to even enter. Karen placed Mr. Farsley as being in his late 50's, but he may have been even younger—it was hard to tell as she had never seen him smile. He stood 5'9" with a solid frame; dark grey hair sprinkled with streaks of pure white piled thick on his head like a dirty mop. His eyebrows were trimmed and accented his steel grey eyes, which Karen noted were glaring at her immediately upon arrival.

"Miss, some help here?" he called sternly. It was more of a command than a request.

Karen stumbled awkwardly out from behind the counter. "Of course, Mr. Farsley," she answered, hearing her voice crack. At this, Mr. Farsley stopped dead in his tracks and let go of the bags. They fell in a big brown pile in the middle of the blue Berber carpet.

Karen gathered the bags by their stiff paper handles and steeled her shoulders to brace the weight. Now unencumbered, Mr. Farsley patted his coat pockets as if to reassure himself of their contents, then readjusted his beige, cashmere scarf, throwing it dramatically over his shoulder before walking toward the elevator. He made no move to help Karen, who was half-trudging, half-waddling toward the doors, her damaged finger groaning under the pull of the bags.

They rose in silence up the ten levels to Mr. Farsley's floor. The elevator, new and pristine, slid soundlessly up like it was covered in cotton batting. Even the doors gave no hint of a creak or squeal; the only warning that it was time to disembark was the delicate *ding* as the number 10 changed from white to red on the panel in front of them. Karen followed Mr. Farsley obediently down the hall to the end unit, and she only paused for a moment before entering the apartment to deliver his purchases.

"Just put them over there," Mr. Farsley directed. He stood in the gleaming white kitchen and motioned toward the adjacent living room, a modern and tastefully decorated area with a white low back sofa, a yellow chaise lounge, and a Queen Anne chair—none of which appeared to have been sat in, ever. A heavy, pale yellow wool rug tied the furniture into a tidy grouping around a simple, glass-topped coffee table.

The first thing Karen always noticed when she entered one of her tenant's apartments was the smell. Everything smelled new. Expensive. Fragile. They were what a *Town & Country* magazine or the Pottery Barn catalog would smell like if they sported those tear-out perfume samples (*how tacky!*). Karen closed her eyes for a moment and took a deep breath. For just one sliver of a moment, she felt what it was like to live as one of her tenants. It felt rich. It felt extravagant. No—it felt *safe*.

When she opened her eyes, she was embarrassed to see Mr. Farsley looking quizzically in her direction. He started to speak, but instead he raised a hand to his forehead. She could see he was sweating profusely, even though the temperature was temperate and comfortable and he hadn't exerted himself one bit on the trip from the lobby.

"I... I... whew, I feel..." he began to say. Then, his face turned bright pink and his eyes bulged out from their sockets. His hand moved in a jerking motion to his right shoulder and his hand grasped his upper right arm. "I..." he struggled. Karen stared at him confused, as his mouth twisted into an ugly grimace, his eyes looked upwards, and his body toppled forward like a surfboard flopping into the water. He landed with a swishy thud, emitting a sickening crack when his nose smashed against the cold, hexagonal tile floor.

Karen felt the scene switch into slow motion; she was suddenly trapped in a twentieth century horror movie and someone had slowed the filmstrip down. When she crouched beside Mr. Farsley's body and shook it by the shoulder, there was no response. It took all of her strength to heave his meaty frame over onto its back, and when she did, Karen could see that there was no hope. Mr. Farsley's pupils were large and black. His mouth still showed traces of the painful scowl, and a mouthful of drool had pooled on the side of his face, leaving a snail's trail of wet desperation along his cheek and back behind his head.

As a last resort, Karen took Mr. Farsley's wrist in her fingers and felt for a pulse. There was nothing. Realizing she was holding hands with a dead man, she dropped his arm with a flinch, then replaced it by his side, trying to hold down the wave of vomit churning in her stomach. It was then that she saw them.

There were two red capsules with yellow stripes in a clear baggie on the floor next to Mr. Farsley's hip. The bag must have toppled out of his coat pocket when she flipped him over.

Two pills. Not three.

Mr. Farsley must have taken one.

And then he had a heart attack.

A million thoughts crossed her mind.

When Karen was a girl, she was invited to a sleepover at an older neighbor's house. The girl's name was Kristen. Kristen's parents had a very "hands-off" approach to parenting—that likely explained why she had ended up a pregnant dropout at the age of fourteen—but when Karen was eight and the girl was ten, the party was a thrilling endeavor that had been the highlight of her year. After the sun went down, they watched an assortment of risqué movies, ate greasy pizza on napkins, and shoveled sugary spoonfuls of cake into their mouths until they were nauseous. Then Karen and Kristen and the other girls—there were seven of them total—played Raise the Dead. They took turns lying very still on their backs while the other girls positioned themselves strategically around the body: two on each side, one at the head, and one at the feet. Using only the tips of their fingers, the girls lifted the dead weight of the seventh girl from the floor, chanting "light as a feather, stiff as a board" ominously, over and over, until they had lifted her as high as their waists.

When it was Karen's turn to be the body, she closed her eyes and tried to imagine herself weightless. She heard the girls' rhythmic voices sigh in unison, their tinny vocal cords doing their best to evoke the eerie melody of witches casting a spell. When she opened her eyes, she was shocked to find herself not just suspended in the air but hovering high above the girls' heads, their arms raised as far as they could muster. Karen flinched and buckled, her body flipping before she dove face-first into the plush, sea green carpet below.

Mr. Farsley was not going to rise up anytime soon. As a matter of fact, his body felt like it was harboring bricks of lead. Karen tried to move his body, but no matter how hard Karen pulled his hands above his head, the solid hunk of dead flesh would not budge. She needed help. For the first time in a long time, she was grateful she was married.

It took Darien four rings to pick up the phone.

"Sorry," he began. "I was on the line with Time Warner. I'm changing the cable package. Do you think we *need* ESPN, or—"

"Listen!" Karen interrupted. "I need you to come to Alewife. I need your help with something. Something happened, and I..." Karen stopped herself from explaining. You never knew who might be listening in since 9/11. She had read somewhere that the government had installed some sort of software on the cell towers that captured conversations as soon as key words such as *bomb*, or *dead*, or *jihad* were uttered. At the time, she had dismissed the idea as paranoid and delusional, something one of Darien's couch rot friends would have proposed after their living room was thick with smoke and reeked like a skunk on fire. Now she wasn't so sure.

"What? What are you saying?" Darien was yelling. The sound of a blender on *chop* cycle roared in the background. "I can't hear you."

Karen's eyes darted over to Mr. Farsley's kitchen counter. It was made of cool granite swirled to look like marble: waves of silver and ash folded into streaks of ivory and cadet blue like spun sugar into soft butter. On it were six unopened bottles of sparkling water, the kind Karen knew cost more than a glass of wine at a restaurant. Next to the bottles was a pair of black winter gloves. She didn't need to touch them to know they were made of leather: baby soft, Italian leather. Penthouse sofa leather, as her mother would say. Not shoe leather.

"Come to the apartment building. Now. Call my cell when you are in the lobby and I'll buzz you up," Karen said quickly.

Darien was silent for a moment. "Okay," was all he said, and Karen hung up.

They had to hide the body. The police could trace Mr. Farsley's death back to Darien, and even though she herself had nothing to do with the transaction, she would definitely be fired from her job, being the wife of the drug dealer who sold the poisonous pill. The two of them stood mirroring one another, their hands on their hips, staring at Mr. Farsley's camel coat-covered corpse on the floor, his tweedy pants, his freshly shined shoes. Karen knew her tenant had paid the man who maintained a chair in the Red Line T station to hand-shine his Ferragamo wingtips—all of the bachelors in the building did so on a regular basis, as if paying someone to kneel before them was an acceptable substitute for a subservient, willing life partner. Mr. Farsley never had a romantic partner that she knew of; come to think of it, he'd never had a visitor: not a family member, not a colleague, not a friend. Karen would know: all visitors to the building had to pass by her, and visitor cars had to be registered with the concierge desk if their owners wanted to avoid being towed.

Karen replayed the scene in the lobby in her mind. He hadn't even called her by name. She had worked there for years, carried Mr. Farsley's packages and grocery bags, dry cleaning and mail, week after week, and he couldn't even address her by name? Or even yet, ask her politely to help him?

She glanced at the expensive water bottles on the counter. He hadn't ever given her a holiday tip. Never wished her a good afternoon, or even acknowledged her presence when he wasn't in need of her service. She was a piece of meat to stab into and consume for sustenance when he needed her: that was all.

Darien had placed one of the leather gloves on his left hand and was pulling the right one on with relish. When they were both snugly in place, he clenched his fists a few times like he was squeezing something, then stretched his arms out in front of him and admired his new acquisition. "These are niiiice," he said, stretching the last word out like a cat awakening from an afternoon nap.

Karen started to admonish him for touching a tenant's belongings—she never would have allowed Darien to do something like that in the past—but she stopped herself. Maybe these gloves were her holiday tip this year. Yes, these were her overdue gratuity, but they wouldn't cover last year, would they? Karen would have to find something else to make up for that oversight. She scanned the living room. Seeing nothing of interest, she walked down the short hallway that connected the great room to the sprawling master bedroom and padded soundlessly inside.

The walls were a faded daffodil color, and long trains of shiny buttercream fabric circled and draped over black iron curtain rods, partially muting the mid-afternoon sunlight streaming through. The king-sized bed sported more pillows than Karen had, had had, or would ever have in her whole house. A brown sueded coverlet sprawled across the bed, the only dark spot in the whole residence. Karen and Darien's queen-sized mattress was so old, there were permanent body-shaped indentations where they slept, making their worn blue comforter look like rippling ocean water. There wasn't an indentation anywhere in Mr. Farsley's bed. Karen approached the mattress and was squatting to feel its firmness for herself when Darien appeared suddenly in the doorway, startling her.

"Kae, you should really call someone," he said. "I put the pills in my pocket. There's no way to trace them back to me. I appreciate the thought, but—"

"Do you think that's the only evidence tying you to his death?" Karen asked, more rhetorically than in anticipation of a response. "I mean, do you recognize him? Is he a regular client of yours? What about cell phone records? They are definitely going to do an autopsy: he isn't old enough to have died of natural causes." She stared at Darien. He was eying a watch on Mr. Farsley's dresser. They were both quiet. Then, she stood up.

"Help me pull his body onto this." She grabbed a large, fluffy white bathrobe from a silver-colored hook by the bed. It was the kind of robe posh spas gave their most pampered clients to wear while visiting, the kind you could take home from a nice hotel room, provided you didn't mind the additional hundred-dollar charge upon checkout. "Then we can drag him into the bathroom. Maybe put him in the tub for now?"

Darien picked up the watch and held it in his hand, moving his arm up and down slightly like he was trying to guess the jewelry's weight. He looked at Karen and stuffed the watch into a back jeans' pocket without an explanation. "Alrighty," he agreed.

It took them a bit to position the corpse firmly on the robe—he kept sliding off the side each time they dragged the robe a few feet—but once they had centered his lumpy frame, they were excited to find they could glide him along the hardwood rather easily. They would have made it all the way to the bathroom without incident had the arm of the robe not caught on the side of the thick yellow rug on the border of the living room area. When it caught, Karen and Darien were jerked backwards, and Darien toppled sideways onto Mr. Farsley, landing with his head less than a foot from the dead man's hip. As if to vocalize his protest at Darien's proximity, Mr. Farsley emitted a thunderous fart, his abdomen visually shrinking considerably as the sound echoed across the apartment.

Darien's expression changed from surprised to collected to horrified in a matter of twelve seconds. He pushed himself back to a standing position with one hand while cupping his other over his mouth and nose. "Jesus, Mary, and Joseph: do you smell that?!" he exclaimed, his voice muffled by a sweaty palm.

Karen didn't. And then she did. The stench was putrid: a potpourri of steamed broccoli, rotten eggs, and some sort of expensive cheese (*Camembert, perhaps? You know how well it accents the 1992 Sauvignon Blanc*) wafted from Mr. Farsley's nether regions like smoke from a campfire. Karen placed her own hand over her nose to keep from vomiting. "Come on, we have to finish," she chided, and pulled her side of the robe with her other hand.

But Mr. Farsley made it to the bathroom too late to save his dignity. Twice more they had heard the same wet rumbling coming from his abdomen, and when Karen turned to look upon reaching the tub, she saw the dark brown stain spreading outward from his buttocks on the tailored dress pants. "I don't think dry cleaning is going to cut it this time, Mr. Farsley," she stated out loud. "You might want to look into replacing those pants."

Darien replaced his hands on his hips. He was still wearing the gloves. "Kae, I don't know how we're going to get him in the tub. He's way too heavy."

Karen mirrored his stance again. "Yeah, you're right. He's just going to have to nap here on the floor." She looked about the room. When she located the thermostat, she turned it down to 40 degrees, and within minutes they were surrounded by the whispering sound of blowing air. "Each room can be programmed at different temperatures. As long as we keep the door closed, it will be like we've placed his body in a big refrigerator. No rot, no smell... well, *almost* no smell."

Karen shut off the light, and they exited the room and closed the door. She briefly contemplated turning the light back on; it seemed sad to leave a person alone in the dark. Darien walked immediately back into the bedroom. He opened and closed dresser drawers, pausing now and again to examine a piece of jewelry, an interesting tie, or a trinket he discovered. He pulled out a silvery Zippo lighter from the top left drawer, flicked it open and lit it with one hand. The flame appeared, orange and strong. Darien closed the lid to extinguish the fire and tossed the lighter carelessly onto the top of the dresser. He moved on to the smaller furniture. From the very bottom drawer of the nightstand, he pulled a long ivory envelope.

"So, what do you think this is—porn? A love letter from a favorite prostitute? A hunk of hair from a victim?" Darien joked, waving the envelope in the air between two gloved fingers.

"Oh, just open it," Karen said nervously. She had the eerie feeling she was being watched, and that the eyes were coming from behind the bathroom door.

Darien slid one finger under the seal and peeled the flap back. He peeked inside, then held the contents out with both hands like an acolyte to a messiah: stuffed in the envelope was money. A lot of money. Darien ran one finger along the top of the bills, revealing their denominations. Fifties. Hundreds. A few twenties. There were thousands of dollars in his hands. Mr. Farsley would finally be giving Karen her holiday bonus.

"We are getting out of here, now," Darien said, stuffing the bounty into the inside pocket of his coat. "And I'm keeping these gloves."

"What should we do about..." Karen tilted her head in the direction of the bathroom.

"We'll figure it out, Kae. I think we need to stop pushing our luck and get out of here now," Darien said. "Besides, your shift is almost up. You need to get back to the desk." He patted his coat and jeans pockets as if searching for keys. "I feel like we're forgetting something."

"The body in the bathroom, maybe?" Karen retorted. She walked back out to the kitchen and took a long look around the apartment, pretending to be a police detective. She gazed briefly with dismay at the slightly smudged, crimson puddle dirtying the tile floor; surely Mr. Farsley kept a box of cleaning materials somewhere in the apartment in the event the maid service was delayed for a dreadful accident, like an amphetamine-induced coronary, transpired. She fingered the key ring in her pocket. Worst-case scenario, she could borrow a mop and a bottle of bleach from the maintenance closet down the hall. Seeing nothing else out of place, she grabbed one of the bottled waters from the counter, unscrewed the cap, and took a long swig.

"Listen," said Darien. "He's not going anywhere. We wait. Something will come to us. We'll figure out what to do with him sooner or later. Just keep up on the upkeep of the apartment, and no one will be the wiser."

And so, Karen added Farsley maintenance to her daily routine. On her coffee breaks, she'd ride the gliding elevator back up to the tenth floor, pad soundlessly down to unit 1011, and let herself in. If anyone asked, Mr. Farsley was on vacation and had asked her to water his plants while he was away. *They are very temperamental*, she imagined herself mimicking him, accompanied by a flippant eye roll to punctuate her projected annoyance to anyone who might inquire. *You know how tenants like Mr. Farsley are: very picky.* She'd add a big smile to show how much she enjoyed helping others. *You're such a trooper, Karen!* they'd respond. *We are so lucky to have you!*

Karen stood in the middle of the thick yellow rug and looked around. She wondered how long she and Darien could keep this up; three weeks had passed since the tenant had taken a permanent belly flop. Was Mr. Farsley the type to pay ahead on his utilities and cellphone? How long would it be before the credit card companies began sending collection notices? At some point, they would have to get rid of his body.

Which reminded her.

It was the worst part of her daily visit, but she knew she had to check, or her imagination would gnaw at her that night. The one time she hadn't checked on Mr. Farsley, she had awoken screaming, convinced he was lying in wait in their kitchen pantry, ready to smash her skull with a can of kidney beans. Seeing his corpse lying face down on the cold tile floor somehow reassured Karen's psyche that he wouldn't be murdering her that evening with legume-filled weaponry.

She opened the door to the bathroom slowly. The last time she visited Mr. Farsley, she had been so carelessly forceful in her entrance that the door slammed against his softening flesh and left a slight dent in it. A wave of cold air slapped her face, reminding her of Mr. Farsley's last saunter through the complex's entrance. She slid her body through the opening between the door and the frame, switched on the light, and closed the door behind her.

Mr. Farsley was still there. The cold air had kept him mostly intact, but it was clear that he wasn't fresh anymore. The smell of rotten meat, mixed with grated cheese and something Karen couldn't put her finger on—bad breath, maybe?—filled the small space. So much for the array of lavender candles (*soy-based with lead-free wicks, of course! You DO know that candles are a chief cause of harmful indoor air quality, dear*) that lined the side of the sink. She picked up the oversized can of lemon-scented Lysol she had placed on top of the toilet for just this purpose and sprayed a quick burst into the air above them. A delicate shower of tiny citrus droplets rained down in front of her.

Karen sat on the closed toilet seat and stared down at Mr. Farsley. How long could she keep this up? Would she have to start cutting him up and smuggling the pieces into the garbage chute? The very thought of it made the bile rise in her throat. *You would zzzzz have the zzzzzzzzz,* Karen heard Mr. Farsley say. Wait: that was impossible... Mr. Farsley was dead. Wasn't he?

"What was that you said?" she asked Mr. Farsley.

Silence.

"I didn't hear you," Karen repeated, louder. "Say it again."

I said, you wouldn't have ballzzzzzzz. Mr. Farsley's slurred voice drifted up from under the grey mop on his head. *And besides, you zzzzzz zzz zzzzzz zzzzzzzzzzzzzzzzz.*

Karen jumped to her feet. "What??!!" she yelled. "What are you saying?!"

Silence.

Karen kicked the side of Mr. Farsley's body as if to rouse him, but more out of sheer frustration. His torso was bloated and seemed to have almost doubled in size. It felt like she was kicking the side of a futon mattress. She grabbed the door handle and intended to leave the room, but Mr. Farsley spoke again. This time, she could make nothing out. *ZZZZZZzzzzz zzzz zzzz zzzzzzzzzzzzz*, he moaned.

Karen was at the end of her rope. If he wanted something, the least he could do was speak clearly. She grabbed the right side of his body near the shoulder and pulled it backwards as hard as she could. The body flipped up and over, and Karen saw Mr. Farsley's face for the first time since he had fallen and died. He looked nothing like that man anymore. The skin on his face and neck was dark red and purple and puffed out in such an extreme way that his features were almost unrecognizable as human. Blood had dried and crusted all around the two holes where his nose had been, but the bones creating a nose shape had bent and folded into his skull like a broken ironing board. The sockets where his eyes had once been were presented empty and wet. Out of his mouth oozed a thick, dark liquid. Karen didn't think it was blood, but she didn't want to consider what it could be.

He was neither light as a feather nor stiff as a board.

Pleeeeeeezzzzzzzzz, the bloody purplish mass that was once Mr. Farsley begged. *Pleeeezzzz the zzzzzzzz zzzzzzzzz*.

Karen's mind was swimming. She felt feverish. "What? What? Say it again," she begged. She leaned closer to the corpse, holding her nose to keep from collapsing from the putrid smell. She held her ear next to its mouth. With one fetid breath, Mr. Farsley made a final plea.

Ziiiiippppppppo.

There were no sprinklers in the bathroom: she finally had a solution. Karen sprinted to the bedroom and retrieved the silver object from the top of the dresser. She brought it back to Mr. Farsley, placed it in his hand, and covering his blackened fingers with her own, opened the top of the Zippo, and lit the flame. Then she gently let his hand drop to the flooring, and the lighter fell sideways and onto his camel coat, where the fire paused only momentarily before greedily licking the fabric and excitedly beginning to spread.

Karen backed out of the room, leaving the door ajar. She walked purposefully back to the front door, opened it, and walked calmly to the elevator. Fifteen minutes later, when she saw the fire alarm signal for floor ten light up on her switchboard at the concierge desk, she picked up the telephone and called 911.

The fire had contained itself to a backroom of one apartment, but that area had been destroyed beyond inhabitable conditions. It appeared that the resident had been lighting a candle when he experienced a massive coronary. Unfortunately, an aerosol can in the bathroom had caught fire and exploded, compromising some of the evidence. Karen saw the fire marshal shake his head apologetically at her boss, pack away his clipboard, and join the rest of the emergency crew as they exited Alewife Park's lobby, the sliding glass door shushing a silent farewell behind them.

On the following Monday, Karen pulled her ironing board from its home on the back of the closet door and stretched its stiff legs to the floor, wincing a bit against the metallic creaking sound this motion created. Darien was lying prone in his usual spot, tossing peanuts into his mouth like a kid at a carnival game; a sprinkling of forgotten shells lay strewn about his lap and on the floor by his feet. He was laughing at some satirical adult cartoon on the gigantic flat-screen television that he had purchased with their Farsley money without consulting her. Sometimes, he'd laugh so heartily, his mouth would gape open and she could count the cavity fillings on his molars and wisdom teeth. He had not acknowledged her since she had cleared the breakfast plates away an hour ago.

Karen plugged in the iron and glanced at her now-healed finger without thinking. Not a trace of her previous burn remained: she had cleaned and cared for the accidental injury well enough to cover her mistake. Then she looked at her husband a long time, smiled, and made a mental note to put her check to the life insurance company in the mail tomorrow.

Just a Taste

Grandpa winced a bit as he lowered his body to sit on the edge of the queen-sized bed. His lower back emitted an audible crackle and his face crinkled into a slight grimace, but only for a moment, and then he was back to being Pappy again, the man who jollily tucked his grandchildren in each and every night that they stayed with him over school vacations and holiday weekends. That Patriots' Day weekend, Brian and Darlene, ages five and seven, respectively, would be staying with him and Gramma until their weary father drove the four-hour trip to retrieve them Monday evening.

All of Pappy's grandchildren looked forward to their weekends away with their grandparents. Every dinner was preceded by a prayer of thanks where all who attended joined hands and proclaimed out loud what they most enjoyed about their day, and every bout of sleep was preceded by one of Pappy's colorful stories. The children were never certain if what their grandfather told them was real or make-believe, but they listened intently to every thread he wove. The scary stories were the best ones, although the children were sworn to secrecy and forbidden from repeating any of them to their parents.

"What kind of tale would you like this evening?" Grandpa said, shifting slightly to grind his bony frame into the soft mattress. His stories were often long and winding, and he needed to nestle in and get comfortable before beginning.

Darlene's eyes grew wide with excitement. "Tell us again about the wolf who lives in the woods, Pappy. The one who eats the hunters."

"No, no," protested Brian. "We already heard that one. Tell us a new one, Pappy."

Grandpa put his hand under his chin and pretended to

be lost in thought. "Hmmm... now let's see. A new story, huh?"

"A *true* one," insisted Darlene. "A hundred percent true story. That you saw with your own eyes."

Brian considered this. "Yeah," he agreed. "One you *know* is true. Like, for a *fact*."

Grandpa gazed at the wood-paneled wall of the cabin's second bedroom and allowed his eyes to dance along the windowsill. White flakes drifted softly against the black sky; it was beginning to snow. Snow in April in Maine. He chuckled to himself. It seemed like New England calendars were half winter, half summer these days, with maybe an hour or two of spring and autumn sprinkled in. You could miss the change of seasons if you overslept one morning. It made him think of one story he hadn't told any of his grandchildren, a very special story that he had never told a soul.

"Alright, my loves," he began. "This is a story that is absolutely true. You must never repeat it for as long as you live, though—not to anyone, not even Gramma. Do you promise?"

The children nodded their heads furiously in unison.

Grandpa looked at the window once more and took a deep breath. And then he began.

Sarah Arthur was a quiet woman. Her pale skin seemed to blend with her wispy, platinum blonde hair like one smooth canvas dotted only by the tiniest splattering of freckles. Such a complexion would be expected to redden at the drop of the hat, but Sarah's alabaster countenance remained fixed in its milky whiteness, no matter the temperature, weather, or conversation. She was born in Brady Lake, Ohio, a summer resort town southeast of Cleveland, smack in the middle of 1950, and when it came time for girls her age to marry, join the hippie exodus headed west, or go to college, Sarah chose the least of three evils, or at least the one that allowed her to interact with people the slightest: she went to college, commuting to neighboring Kent State University, ironically, as a double major in communication studies and psychology.

At the age of twenty, she was walking across campus on her way to her afternoon classes when a group of protesters began to shout, "Pigs off campus!" She turned just in time to avoid being struck by a wayward canister of tear gas thrown by a National Guardsman running toward the crowd. Fascinated by the gathering ruckus, she climbed the steps of Taylor Hall, placed her books gently on the marble ground, and pressed her back against the cool cement structure to watch.

When the gunshots rang out, she saw a classmate from one of her honors classes get shot in the arm and chest and tumble backward; Sarah could not remember the girl's name. "They're fucking shooting! They fucking killed somebody!" yelled a shaggy-haired boy who appeared in the doorway just to the left of Sarah. He saw her standing there, seemingly frozen, and shook her upper arm. "What are you doing? Run! Get the fuck inside!" he yelled. Sarah was irritated. How dare this boy, this unkempt radical, touch her and tell her what to do. She jerked her body away from him and then, in one quick movement, grabbed the boy by the shoulders and push-pulled him sideways toward the steps. Taken off guard, the boy stumbled forward and fell face-first down the stairs just as a panicked mob ran unchecked in the opposite direction, stomping and crushing the boy in their wake. When the crowd thinned, Sarah calmly stooped to retrieve her disheveled stack of textbooks, stopping only briefly to glance at the boy's bloody, broken body before walking curtly into the building.

She told this exact story, uncensored, to Mads Sorenson, a boy she had just begun dating, later that evening at Major's Bar. In response, Mads took a long pull on the tobacco pipe he'd inherited from his grandfather and grabbed Sarah's hand. "I'm going to call you Sadie from now on, my love," he said, blowing a stream of smoke at the ceiling. "Because you are one sadistic bitch, and I adore you for it." Sadie smiled one of her infrequent smiles and looked down at her hands modestly. They were married twelve months later.

Mads was originally from Lunenburg, a small town in Massachusetts squeezed tight along the New Hampshire border, and after a small service with Sadie's parents and neighbors, the newlyweds packed up what little belongings they owned and drove to New England to live in the farmhouse on the nearly one hundred acres Mads's parents had left to him. They purchased a convenience store on the edge of Marshal's Pond, and within two years of wedded bliss Sadie found herself pregnant with their first child. As her stomach rounded, the bills began to mound. The store wasn't as lucrative of an investment as they had hoped.

Sadie sat in the wooden rocking chair by the fireplace and scratched the underside of her belly. She had developed the itch in the middle of her second trimester, and with only a month left before her due date, the constant prickling had only maddened her more and more each day. What frustrated her most was the absurd contortion she had to achieve to reach the culprit; it seemed like her whole body had swelled into a clumsy, plodding mass. When she stepped on the scale at her obstetrician's appointment, she looked the other way.

Mads sat at the large dining room table ten feet from his wife, tapping his fingers on a calculator and scrunching his face into a perplexed expression. "I just don't understand why things aren't balancing. Our inventory records are way off," he said. "According to these numbers, we're missing multiple boxes of canned and paper goods. Where could they have gone?"

Sadie stopped scratching and took a deep breath. Sometimes her husband was so dense, she had to stop herself from calling him an idiot despite her gut reaction to do so. Just a month previous, her hands had shot out on impulse to choke Mads, and when she realized what she was doing, she compensated by smoothing his shirt collar and kissing him on the cheek instead. "What about those kids you hired to work in the evenings?" she asked. "Maybe they've been pilfering more than a stray candy bar or two."

Mads's fingers stopped clicking. He patted his shirt pocket, feeling for his pipe, and looked at his wife for a long second. "How could I know for sure?"

Sadie commenced scratching again. "Leave out new inventory. Mark it. See if it disappears, then check the receipts after each shift."

Mads looked back at the stack of papers on the table. "And if the kids ARE robbing us blind?"

Sadie took another deep breath. "Oh, I'm sure we'll think of something, darling."

Mads did as his wife had suggested, and sure enough, after meticulously counting and recounting their items after each and every shift, he discovered that two young men, slacker roommates on the five- or six-year plan at nearby Fitchburg State College named Pete and Burt who worked the Saturday and Sunday late nights, were stealing. Mads even parked in the shadows one evening and watched his employees through a pair of binoculars Sadie had given him to aid in his bird-watching—a favorite pastime since he was a child—and witnessed the two fill duffel bags with boxes of macaroni and cheese, cases of soup, and rolls of toilet paper before tossing their booty into the back of a wood-paneled Pinto station wagon in the parking lot. He returned home furious and reported to Sadie what he had seen.

"Oh, Mads," she said, not looking up from the book she was reading in the rocking chair by the fire. "You've always been entirely too trusting. People will usually take advantage of a situation when given the opportunity." She scratched her stomach through the crocheted poncho she wore almost daily: her pregnancy uniform, since nearly everything else no longer fit and she refused to buy maternity clothes. Why waste money on something she would only wear for a few months of her life?

The next evening, while her husband dozed in front of the television, she wrapped a woolen scarf around her neck, stuffed her swollen hands into a pair of leather work gloves, grabbed the keys to the store, and drove to Marshal's Pond. When she arrived, Pete and Burt were sitting on stools behind the counter, puffing on cigarettes and playing a game of pitch.

"Hello, boys," she said cheerily as she entered.

Pete's feet whipped backward from their place on the edge of the counter and he visibly straightened his shoulders. "Hi, Mrs. Sorenson," he said. "Can we help you with anything? I mean, in your condition…"

She waved her hand dismissively and headed toward the household goods aisle. "Don't be silly. I'm just picking up a few things for Mads before closing. Don't bother yourselves at all." She walked immediately to her targeted items, picked them up, and walked to the backroom of the store. She locked the deadbolt and with some effort, slid the double pedestal metal desk partially in front of the exit door. As she slowly returned to the front counter, she unscrewed the tops of the lighter fluid canisters she had taken from the shelf and poured an even river behind her as she strolled.

Burt was lighting another cigarette with his previous one. Seeing this, Sadie tossed a box of kitchen matches she had picked up onto the shelf of impulse-buy items. "You boys have a good night," she said. When the tip of Burt's new cigarette glowed orange, she reached over and gently took the old smoldering one from his hand. "Let me dispose of this— we can't be too careful." She pulled her scarf closer to her neck and walked to the front door, dumping the remaining contents from the fluid bottle inconspicuously onto the linoleum. She pushed the front door open, tossed Burt's burning stump into the middle of the tributaries, and quickly pulled the door closed behind her. She locked the door carefully and tightly, then walked to her car. As the flicker of orange flames danced in the distance behind her, she tossed the empty canisters and her leather gloves out of her car window and into the pond.

When she arrived home, Mads's snoring was competing with Alan Alda's questioning of contestant number three on *To Tell the Truth* as the celebrities and audience attempted to determine if he was the real convict Ed Edwards. Sadie leaned down and tried to kiss her husband tenderly on the forehead, but as she did, she felt a sharp cramping in the middle of her abdomen. She braced the back frame of the couch to steady herself and took a series of short, halting breaths. The next morning, as she lay quietly in her hospital bed, staring down at her feet for the first time in months, Mads came into the room, bringing a bouquet of bright, cheery flowers. Together, they celebrated the arrival of their first baby girl, but his joy was tempered with sadness: while the couple had been rushing to the hospital, a terrible fire had destroyed their store and claimed the lives of the two employees working at the time. A week later, Sadie filed their insurance claim. They did not rebuild.

The Sorensons were not cut out to be business owners, but perhaps, Mads suggested, he could work the land to raise and sell food: his parents had been farmers, after all.

Sadie longed for a life outside of the home and accepted a part-time job as a library assistant at the branch in neighboring Leominster. In the beginning, it seemed to be the ideal arrangement: Mads worked the farm from sunrise to noon, and Sadie worked in the library from midday to dinner, and each would parent while the other was away. By late summer of 1977, the couple had produced three children, all under the age of five. Their hands were no longer full: they were overflowing.

Sadie stood in front of the stove, forcing the metal masher through the hot potatoes, creaming with it pats of butter and heavy shakes of salt and pepper. Her second child, another girl, wrapped her arms and legs around her mother's lower leg like a monkey. When she moved sideways to grab more butter from the dish, Sadie had to slide her leg rather than pick it up, and this was forming a stitch in her thigh. She tried shaking the girl loose to no avail. "Mads, it won't cost but a day's profit each week to hire a part-time assistant," she said, more to the stove than to her husband, who was sitting at the kitchen table with his forehead touching his dinner plate. "You are exhausted. I am exhausted. We need help."

Mads groaned. "You're right, Say. I will post an ad on the community board at the Market Basket in the morning."

Sadie shook her leg as hard as she could, and her daughter's head hit the oven door, making a loud metallic bang. "Ow, Mommy!" she wailed and unhooked herself long enough for Sadie to move her leg out of reach.

"Make sure it's for the latter half of the morning into the early half of the afternoon," Sadie reminded. "If he's willing, we could let a room in exchange for longer hours."

Mads lifted his head and sat back in his chair.

Within a week, Peter Gunness, an enormous man whose speech volume was incongruous to his physical size, had moved the worn contents of a shabby suitcase and hobo shaving kit into the Sorensons' guest room at the end of the hall. The children took to him immediately, likely due to his gentle giant appearance, kind nature, and most of all, willingness to transform himself into a hulking farm animal and offer rides around the spacious house to one, two, or even all three of the girls at once. Although she knew that she should be overjoyed with the bond Peter was forming with her children, Sadie could not help but feel irritated by Peter's very presence. There was something about the sluggish speed at which he answered questions, the meandering manner in which he told stories, and the disgusting habit of opening his mouth wide, especially when it was filled with half-eaten food, to guffaw at her eldest daughter's pedestrian jokes. Peter was a hard worker—there was no denying that—but he was a slow worker, and the farm production had barely increased; calculating the increased cost for the additional food (Peter ate meals in proportion to his size), they were losing money.

As Sadie stood at the kitchen sink one evening cleaning the evening's dinner plates, Peter played a game of Hungry Hungry Hippos with the girls at the table. The incessant banging of the plastic heads attempting to gobble marbles was almost too much for Sadie to bear; she paused for a moment and took a series of deep breaths to steady herself as she stared at soapy dinner knife in her rubber-gloved palm.

"Peter," she began, shutting off the water and turning to face the table behind her. "Do you have any family that you keep in contact with? Parents? Siblings? Distant cousins even?"

Peter continued to slam his mammoth fist onto the lever to make his hippopotamus mouth open and close. Sadie was about to repeat her question when he looked up. "No, ma'am. My parents died a long time ago, and I never had no brothers or sisters. Didn't know my cousins neither. Made Christmas mighty lonely, to tell the truth." He stopped hitting the lever and stared into space, lost in thought. His eyes grew wet, and fearing he'd begin to cry, Sadie spoke quickly.

"I only ask because the insurance salesman dropped by recently to update our policies—you know, with three little ones, we want to keep on top of things just in case—and I realized, we don't know anything about your kin. What if something were to happen? Is there someone you'd want us to contact?" she asked matter-of-factly and wiped her rubber-gloved hands on the front of her apron. "Who is the beneficiary on your life insurance policy? You *do* have one, don't you?" She stressed the word *do* to give the impression that everyone had a life insurance policy, that it was as expected as obtaining one's driver's license.

Peter looked at her blankly, then scrunched up his mouth in a sideways smirk Sadie had come to know as his "thinking face." He was silent for a moment. In the meantime, bored with their ear-splitting marble game, the girls slid down from their seats at the table and ran into the living room to watch *The Muppet Show* as they did every week. Peter picked up a marble and rolled it between his thumb and forefinger. "I don't have anyone to contact, Miss Sadie. No one." He looked at the marble, lost in thought. Finally, he added, "I never got insurance. I guess I have to do that, huh?"

Sadie pasted on the nurturing expression she had added to her suitcase of masks since becoming a new mother. When one of the girls scraped a knee or felt feverish, she slid into this countenance as easily as she put on an overcoat. She learned quickly that the earlier in the incident she wore it, the less time she had to spend inhabiting it. "Oh, Peter. You have *us*, silly." She rested a hand on his shoulder, making it slightly damp in the process. "We're your family." She smiled warmly, and Peter blushed and looked down at the table, but

Sadie could see he was grinning. "It's settled," she said. "I'll call the insurance man tomorrow and have him swing by one night this week."

Two days later, Sadie, Peter, and Mr. Grimaldi sat at the very same table—the Hungry Hunrgy Hippos game nowhere in sight—while Mads entertained the children in the living room. "That's an awfully large policy for someone with no dependents, Mr. Gunness," Mr. Grimaldi said. He shot a sideways frown in Sadie's direction. It had been her idea for Peter to take out the highest policy he could that did not require a medical exam, though it had been Peter's idea to list Sadie and Mads as his sole beneficiaries; this was only after Mr. Grimaldi explained to him that including the three girls as well would be pointless, as Sadie and Mads would have legal control over their children's finances until they reached eighteen anyway. Sadie Sorenson had always rubbed Mr. Grimaldi the wrong way; there was something about the enthusiasm with which she had opened sizable policies on each of her toddler children that made his spine stiffen. Each time he shot a surreptitious glance at Sadie when she wasn't looking, he wondered what Mads saw in the waif-like body, empty coloring, and icy mien. She reminded Mr. Grimaldi of a snowman whose sides had melted away in the midwinter sun, the coal mouth runny and fixed into a harsh sneer.

Peter simply smiled back at Mr. Grimaldi. He was more than happy to pay the full year's premiums in one lump; he had been storing his wages away for years, long before working for Sadie and Mads, although what he had been saving it for he hadn't known. Now he knew.

Mr. Grimaldi sighed and handed Peter his pen. "Okay, Mr. Gunness. Sign right here… and here… and one more: here."

When the business was complete, Sadie escorted him to the door. "It was lovely to see you, Mr. Grimaldi," she said, her pleasant neighbor mask still cemented in place from when she first heard the insurance salesman ring her doorbell two hours previous. "Thank you for being so kind as to come to the house. It's so difficult with the children, you know."

"It's my pleasure, Mrs. Sorenson," Mr, Grimaldi said, placing his fedora on his head and tipping it slightly as a gesture of gratitude. "And have a wonderful Thanksgiving."

"You as well." Sadie shut the door tight behind him and shut off the porch light. In the next room, Peter was clomping around on his hands and knees and braying like a donkey while the children squealed with laughter and delight. Thanksgiving was only a week away; Sadie would begin her research during her shift at the library the next day.

Thanksgiving morning, Mads awoke alone in the couple's double bed. He felt the indentation where his wife's body should have been; it was cold. Sadie had gotten up many hours before, determined to make this year's holiday feast the most delicious one yet. When everything was on the table, emitting streams of delicious steam, she called to her family and Peter who were relaxing in the living room in front of the television, watching Chicago and Detroit take turns tackling one another. One by one, the children and men sat in their assigned chairs.

Sadie sat in her place next to Mads. "Okay, everyone, hold hands," she instructed, and everyone did; her eldest nudged Peter, who sat with his hands in his lap, and he stretched out his arms to engulf one child's hand in each of his. "Now everyone say something he or she is thankful for," said Sadie. "I will start." She closed her eyes and took a deep breath, then opened them wide again. "I am thankful for my loving husband, my beautiful children, our warm and cozy home, and of course, for the addition of Peter into our family." With this, Peter's cheeks blushed pink, and he smiled and looked down at his plate.

When everyone had a chance to speak, Mads said, "Okay, dig in!" and the table was quiet but for the sounds of forks clinking and mouths chewing. After each bite of her turkey and stuffing, Sadie took a sip of wine from her glass. She noticed that Peter wasn't drinking from his glass, which was filled almost to the rim.

"Peter, drink your wine: it's Thanksgiving. It's bad luck if you leave any in your glass!" chided Sadie.

Peter wrapped his giant hand around the delicate stem and brought the glass to his lips. He took a small sip and made a face. "I don't care for wine, Miss Sadie. It's too sour or something."

Sadie wagged her finger playfully from across the table. "Now, now, Peter: we can't have you cursing this family because of a little taste bud stubbornness. Besides, the more you drink, the better it will taste."

Peter looked at her, looked at the wine in his glass, and reluctantly took another gulp. She was right: the more he drank, the less yucky it tasted. And he didn't want to be the one to bring the Sorensons bad luck, so he held his breath and swallowed the rest of his wine in one tip of his head.

Later that evening, as Sadie was wiping the last of the apple pie crumbs from the kitchen counter and drying the stemware carefully with a dry cloth, she pushed the door of the cabinet under the sink closed with her knee. Somehow, it had come ajar since she closed it earlier that morning when she was preparing the dishes and glasses to set the table. She couldn't have the children pulling the door open in curiosity: the box of rat poison was positioned immediately in front for her easy access.

From that day forward, Sadie made it her mission to sneak a teaspoon of that rat poison into Peter's food each day.

At times, it was more difficult than she anticipated: she had to make certain that Peter and only Peter received the plate with the white powder dissolved into the serving of squash, or macaroni and cheese, or lasagna. She panicked when the crystals clumped at first in the baked potato soup she'd slaved over all Saturday; her heart skipped a beat when Peter accidentally spilled his plate of baked ziti all over his lap; luckily, his table manners were so unrefined, he had no qualms about picking up every morsel from his clothing and sticking it into his mouth. Some of the meals were so tasty, he licked his plate, an action Sadie encouraged until she saw her children mimic him.

Although Peter's appetite remained steady at first, he was struck with debilitating nausea and vomiting almost every evening. He began to complain of pain in the soles of his feet and the palms of his hands, and therefore, the hands and knees animal rides were placed on moratorium, much to the disappointment of the children. After three weeks of regular rat poison supplements, Sadie noticed that Peter's hair was falling out in clumps. When she visited the washroom immediately after him, she recoiled in disgust at the sprinkling of thick black and grey hairs on the white porcelain sink: they reminded her of rat whiskers, and after that, each time she scooped the teaspoon of white powder into Peter's food, she imagined his face twitching and his nose crinkling like a nervous rodent.

The day before Christmas, Peter took to his bed with terrible stomach pains. It was just as well, as the library was closed for the holiday and all winter farm upkeep was on hold until the most recent snow accumulation had cleared. However, cabin fever ran amuck among the children, and by the time dinner was over, they were restless and cranky and driving Sadie crazy. When she banished them to their room to keep them out of her hair, the girls instead hovered nervously outside of Peter's bedroom, whispering worries to one another.

"Girls!" Sadie scolded. "Leave Peter alone. He doesn't feel well. Go and play quietly in your room, please, so he can rest."

The girls scattered, and Sadie took a peek at the ponderous lump wheezing audibly under the quilt. "I'll bring you a treat to soothe your stomach, Peter," she whispered, and walked silently down the hall to the kitchen. She removed the carton of peppermint stick ice cream from the freezer and spooned a large scoop into a dish. After topping the serving with a teaspoon of the rat poison, she added a second scoop and recapped the carton and replaced it in the freezer.

As she was placing a clean spoon in the dish, she heard the phone ring in the living room. When Mads did not answer after three rings, Sadie walked into the room and found him dozing in the recliner, his tobacco pipe still surreptitiously smoking in his hand. By the time she picked up the receiver, the caller had hung up. She smothered the tendril of smoke and placed her husband's pipe on the side table, then returned to the kitchen to find her eldest daughter shoveling ice cream ferociously into her mouth: the pile of dessert Sadie had prepared special for Peter was half gone. "Put that down!" Sadie shrieked, and the child was so startled that she tossed the utensil on the floor. It tinkled and clanged on the linoleum, and the girl began to cry. "No, no—it's okay, my love," Sadie said. "That dish was for Peter, to cheer him up. Mommy didn't mean to yell at you." She thought for a moment. No Peter would mean no live-in nanny, no one to tire the children out and play obnoxious marble games or give horsey rides. Every day would be a day trapped together, the incessant whines of little girls bouncing off of the farmhouse walls and piercing Sadie's eardrums. She would return to being a full-time parent of small children, and that was one job Sadie wanted no part of, despite the pantomime she had been playing for the past five years.

"On second thought," Sadie said to her daughter, "go ahead and finish the ice cream. Mommy will scoop more for Peter." She pulled more dishes from the cabinet and placed them on the counter. "And when you're done, go fetch your sisters. I bet they'd like a dish of ice cream, too." She made certain to churn one teaspoon of white powder into each of the three dishes of peppermint stick. As her daughters sat at the table, smacking their lips and complaining of brain freeze, Sadie dipped a clean spoon directly into the carton, scooped out a healthy mouthful, and smiled as the creamy coolness melted away on her tongue.

It was January 21st when Mads found Peter collapsed in the barn. He had ventured out to fetch an extra shovel in the odd chance the forecasters' prediction of only rain was incorrect. His intuition had been right on the money: Massachusetts was shrouded in 21 inches of snow over the span of 48 hours. The roads were nearly impassable, so the coroner did not arrive until two days later.

"Where's Peeta?" cried Sadie's youngest daughter after the second day of his absence. Peter's name had been one of the first words she had spoken, and for a split second, Sadie felt her heart break with regret at her child's mourning. Then she stroked her hand along the girl's forehead and felt the strands of hair release from their roots and fall onto the front of her footed pajamas, and the feeling was replaced by stony disgust.

"Go play with your sisters and Daddy in the living room," Sadie instructed. "Mommy will fix your cereal and you can have breakfast in a minute." She watched the tot teeter into the next room. As she poured the milk over the corn flakes sprinkled with white powder, she made a mental to-do list in her head. When the roads were sufficiently sanded, she'd drive into town to see Mr. Grimaldi and cash in Peter's policy; on the way home, she'd stop at the hardware store. The box of rat poison under the sink was almost empty.

In spectrometry and flame tests, the heavy metal thallium appears bright green; its name comes from the Greek word *thallos*, a reference to its color. Thallium is an effective poison that was included in insecticides and rodenticides until the late 1970s; although accidental thallium poisoning was rare, its use as a homicidal agent was well documented, prompting its removal. Because the substance was odorless and tasteless, and the poison's effects took weeks to build to toxic levels, victims were often unaware that they were being slowly but methodically murdered. Symptoms of thallium poisoning begin with mild abdominal upset but soon progress to violent stomach cramping and vomiting, extreme hair loss, and progressive neuropathy.

In the weeks that followed Peter's death, the Sorenson children grew thin and pale, even thinner and paler than they had been already. "Our home is one big Petri dish," Mads told the neighbors. "As soon as one girl recovers from the stomach flu, another one takes her place in the bathroom. Just can't seem to shake it away. It's darn lucky Say and I haven't gotten sick."

On Monday, February 5, Sadie showered early and went to work. To compensate for the lull in farm production income, she had volunteered to cover a few of the morning shifts at the library. When she arrived to unlock the front door, the orange tabby cat who frequented the facility was waiting for her.

Sadie bent down and scratched the cat's head. "Well, hello, Marmalade," she cooed. The tom had claimed the library's campus as his domain, and when Sadie worked alone, she often brought him inside with her for company. "Are you hunkering down for the storm?" The morning paper had predicted ten to twelve inches of snow over the next few days. Sadie's rusted yellow Volkswagen Bug skipped and slid in slippery weather conditions, but Mads's pickup had a plow blade attached from November through April and she had difficulty driving it even without the additional hindrance. She slipped her key in the lock and turned, then pushed the door open. Marmalade padded quickly ahead of her, and Sadie reached her right arm along the wall to switch on the lights.

As afternoon sunbeams crept along the carpet, the snowflakes outside began to multiply alarmingly fast. When the phone rang at two o'clock, Sadie knew it would be the evening shift librarian, a girl of about twenty-three who wore distractingly low-cut blouses and climbed the shelving ladders like she was shimmying up a stripper pole, calling to say she couldn't make it to work. It didn't matter: Sadie's supervisor Claire, the Reference librarian, had decided they would close the facility early before the roads got any worse. Before she left for the evening, Sadie filled a wide bowl with water and set it down behind the circulation desk. She shook off her wool cardigan and balled it into a nest on the floor near the heating grate. She scraped onto a paper plate the tuna fish and pieces of American cheese from her lunch sandwich, and as soon as Claire braved the storm, leaving her to lock up, Sadie put the plate on the floor next to the water bowl. She knew the fish would smell, but not for long: Marmalade began to gobble the dinner immediately. She scratched his orange head a few times before bundling her parka and putting on her gloves.

"Goodnight, my little man," she called from the doorway.

The roads were as treacherous as Sadie anticipated, so she held tight to the steering wheel and drove slowly along the long, rural roads toward home. At one point, the squalls became so furious, she could not see the road, and the space in front of her windshield became a dead zone. Sadie was reminded of *The Twilight Zone* episode where Billy Mumy played a boy who had the power to imagine anything and so he made it snow, and his family was too frightened to chastise him, despite his wish killing the town's badly needed vegetation.

Sadie breathed a sigh of relief when she felt the tires ease over the untouched blanket of snow in the farmhouse's driveway. She pulled the top of her coat close to her neck and draped her purse over her shoulder and opened the car door. The snow was almost spilling inside, and when she trudged as quickly as she could to the back porch, she found herself walking like a pirate, her legs spread wider than usual, in order not to trip and fall in the accumulation. "Phew!" she called once inside. The warm, dry air felt comforting, like a clean towel draped across her shoulders after a long bath.

Nobody met her at the door.

"Mads?" she called. "Girls?" She wandered down the long hallway and into the children's bedroom. Mads was squatted by her youngest daughter's bed, his forehead resting on the blanket. The child, now nearly bald, was greyish and still: even her chest remained fixed and unmoving. The two other girls huddled together in another bed. They stared at their mother, silent, as she approached.

"Mads?" Sadie said quietly. "Mads, what's going on?"

Her husband lifted his head. His face was red and his eyes were puffy, like he'd been crying. "She's gone, Say. She... she said she felt achy, and I thought it was just the flu, you know?" Mads's voice grew high-pitched and squeaky, like an adolescent boy's. "So, I told her to go to bed and I would bring her some soup in an hour." He stopped and looked down at his dead daughter. "And I... she..." His voice trailed off and he simply stared.

Sadie looked around the room. A bowl of chicken noodle soup sat on the dresser, untouched. "Oh, Mads..." she began. Her eldest daughter began to cry. Sadie walked over to the twin bed where the girls were huddled, but when she was within arm's reach, the child shrank back to dodge her touch. "Oh, my loves," Sadie began, slipping the nurturing mask onto her face, "It's alright... it will be okay, Mommy promises."

Sadie stared at her daughters and took a deep breath. Piles of wispy blonde hair lay like a halo of feathers on the pillow behind them.

Snow continued to accumulate across New England. Two days had passed since the toddler had died, and as the roads were again impassable, her tiny body lay untouched in the children's bedroom while the older daughters slept in Mads's and Sadie's marital bed. Mads slept in the recliner in the living room. Sadie was unable to sleep, not out of guilt, but rather, because her dead child was unfinished business, and Sadie did not care for open ends.

By Wednesday night, nearly two feet of heavy snow had piled beneath the Sorensons' windows, and Massachusetts' governor had declared a state of emergency. Thursday morning, the metal clanging of plow trucks echoed across the farm's fields, and the road was relatively clear at last. Mads removed the snow from the driveway and as a way to distract himself from the tragedy, spent most of the day shoveling winding, narrow paths from the house to the barn to the shed to the edge of the woods and back again. Exhausted and frail but finally unencumbered by the weather, the two children trudged outside and wandered to and fro through the paths, their bodies completely disappearing in the sheer height of the snow on either side.

The coroner retrieved the youngest child's body before noon; Sadie remained in the house to complete the necessary paperwork and answer questions. The morgue worker made notes on his form, occasionally stopping to clarify a fact or two; as he did so, Sadie watched her two remaining children out the window. Now and again, one of their heads would appear when the path aligned itself with her restricted view, then it would vanish, swallowed again by the white desert. "I'm sorry: what was that?" Sadie asked the questioner in the dark navy jumpsuit.

"I asked how long the child had been exhibiting symptoms," the man repeated.

Sadie thought for a moment. "Just before Christmas, I'd say. But she wasn't sick *all* of the time. I would have taken her to the doctor if she had been. Just kept rebounding. This last bout took both of us by surprise," she paused to give the impression she was lost in grief, then blinked her eyes quickly and continued. "Who dies of the flu these days? I mean, for goodness' sake."

The man's face registered no emotion, and Sadie reminded herself that this was his job: he dealt with the survivors of family tragedies all day and had likely learned to compartmentalize any sympathy long ago. She watched the stretcher carrying the tiny black bag as it was pushed through the kitchen and out of the front door. The man placed his paperwork neatly in a small briefcase, curtly shook Sadie's hand and offered rigid condolences, and followed the stretcher outside.

After glancing briefly at the cabinet below the sink and considering what she could make for dinner that evening that the girls would enjoy, Sadie looked out of the window again. The girls were half-heartedly playing, trying to scale the mountains of driveway snow Mads had created with his plow. Mads, for his part, was standing aimlessly by the entrance of the barn, staring into nothingness. Sadie put on her coat and boots and followed the path to stand beside him.

She placed a mittened hand on her husband's broad shoulder. "Thank you for doing all of this shoveling, but please, don't overdo it. You'll hurt yourself," she said softly, and she meant it. Sadie had loved no one in her life, not really, but Mads had been one person closest to melting her heart. He was her touchstone. Despite her fierce independence, without Mads, Sadie would be lost. Deep down, she knew that he knew what she was capable of, had known what she had done, but he loved her above everything. She would never know that unconditional acceptance from anyone else.

"Why don't you let me do some of the work?" she said. "Go inside and take a nice, hot shower."

Mads sniffed and crinkled his mouth. "There's just the chopping of the wood for the fireplace left. I can manage," he said.

Sadie gripped his upper arm. "Hey, I have an idea," she replied. "Why don't you show me how to chop the wood? You keep saying you're going to teach me to use the ax: how about right now?" It was true: she had been asking about using the ax. She had little to no arm strength, and truth be told, she'd prefer that her husband do the manual labor around the farm, but she also didn't like feeling helpless. If they needed wood and Mads was unavailable, she wanted to be able to retrieve it herself.

Mads smiled slightly. "My wife: ever the independent warrior woman." He put his hand on the back of Sadie's arm and guided her toward the barn door. When her husband was inside, Sadie took a quick look backward. She watched her daughters long enough to see her eldest child, who had managed to climb onto a five-foot bank, sink suddenly into the snow. Her face flashed an expression of horror as her body slid effortlessly into the white mountain, the cold engulfing her like a tomb. In a split second, she was simply gone; even the top of her pink hat was swallowed by the bank.

As her middle child began to climb the same pile in a fruitless effort to save her sister, Sadie silently followed Mads inside the barn and closed the door behind her. The wind and winter clothing muffled any remaining screams of help from the outside.

Valentine's Day of 1978 came and went without a box of chocolates or a bundle of red roses in the Sorenson house, although there were plenty of gaudy flower arrangements and baskets of comfort food strewn about the kitchen. Sadie and Mads were too busy finalizing the memorials for their three children to acknowledge the holiday. They maintained their physical strength by consuming the neighbors' casseroles and sympathetic nods.

When the two older girls disappeared without a trace on the day their sister's body was taken by the coroner, the parents assumed that they had run away in a confused expression of grief, but they were certain that their children would return within an hour or so. There were only so many places they could have run: after all, the woods and fields were blanketed with several feet of snow, and there were no footprints belying their movements in the untouched whiteness. They must have walked to a neighbor's shed or retreated to the basement of the farmhouse. However, when a thorough search of the home and inquiries to every person within a mile's radius proved unsuccessful, Mads and Sadie became concerned.

A week later, as the blizzard's havoc finally began to melt, a postman spotted a pink pom-pom sticking out of the snow a few feet from the driveway. Upon closer inspection, he found a diminutive yellow mitten poking out like a crocus a few feet beside it. When his daughters' tiny frozen bodies were unearthed an hour later, Mads collapsed. He was still wearing the bandage across his forehead when he signed the final paperwork at the morgue.

Sadie stayed at home. There were whispers in the town, talk of blame and poor parenting; after all, accidents happened, illnesses struck, but to lose three children in the span of a week was just plain neglect, and that it had happened just a month following their farmhand's demise was plain suspicious. Sadie was tired of walking in public with her face pointed at the ground, and her mother in mourning mask was becoming worn and frayed from overuse. Mads, for his part, had transformed overnight into a walking zombie, and Sadie caught him staring blankly at her while he chewed the stem of his pipe more than once over the span of a few days. She thought she recognized a glint of accusation in his eyes, but she wasn't certain. It was better if they went about their business separately for a while, at least until her husband acclimated to the silence in the house.

Sadie was practicing her new-found ax-wielding skills in the barn. Certainly, she had great difficulty swinging the massive instrument onto the cords of wood, but the task took her mind off of things, and since the library expected that she would take a week in bereavement leave, she was trapped at the farm for at least a few more days. She thought she might as well get the domestic chores done.

She had amassed a small pile of kindling for the fireplace when the door of the barn swung open and Mr. Grimaldi walked inside. He was wearing a thin flannel jacket, something too lightweight for the weather, but Sadie supposed he wasn't used to being outside for very long. He lived in neighboring Fitchburg, a bustling metropolis compared to Lunenburg, and worked in a cozy, heated office all day.

He blew into his gloved hands and rubbed them together quickly, and as he spoke, he bounced a little on his knees like a nervous child. "Morning, Mrs. Sorenson," he shivered. "I hope I'm not disturbing you. I thought I might find your husband here."

Sadie rested the ax on her shoulder. Mads always reminded her of Paul Bunyan when he struck that pose, and Sadie imagined that she looked formidable when she mimicked it. "Well, hello, Mr. Grimaldi. What brings you all this way in the cold?" She was the pleasant neighbor once again. "Can I offer you a cup of coffee or hot tea to warm you?"

Mr. Grimaldi glanced around nervously and continued to rub his hands and bounce. "In a moment, sure: that would be lovely." He shifted his weight between his feet like he was steadying himself. "Is your husband home, by any chance?"

Sadie's smile remained cemented across her mouth. "Why, no, he's not. He's in town doing some business," she said. "Perhaps I can help you with something?"

Another visible shift. "Well, yes, Mrs. Sorenson, perhaps you can." He paused. "I'm so sorry to approach you in this very difficult time, but the insurance company has some questions about your girls... and about Mr. Gunness, too."

Sadie clenched her jaw. "I understand. You have a job to do," she answered. "What kinds of questions?"

Mr. Grimaldi swallowed and looked nervous again. "Well... the thing is, with the... tragedies so close together, and the strange symptoms shared by both Mr. Gunness and your little one... well, they are ruling the cases suspicious and are refusing to pay your claims until there is a formal investigation by law enforcement."

Sadie stared at the man for a long minute. "I'm sorry: the *insurance carrier* is refusing?"

Mr. Grimaldi swallowed again. "No, we as the policy

administrators have placed the cases on hold. Just until any confusion is resolved."

"Confusion?" Sadie repeated. "Who is confused? And by what? My farmhand and youngest daughter died of the flu. Even Dr. Haskell said so." Dr. Haskell was the Sorensons' family physician, a kind but elderly man who still made house calls and referred to girlfriends as "dames" and wives as "the little women." Sadie tolerated him because he was no frills and retained the same price structure from when he first opened his practice after World War II; without health insurance, they could not afford big city medicine.

"Dr. Haskell is not a medical examiner," said Mr. Grimaldi, "and to be honest, ma'am, the coincidence of Peter having opened such a large policy so close to his demise is... well, strange, to say the least."

Sadie was silent again. Then she asked, "Are you the one who placed their cases on hold?"

The two stared at one another for a long minute. "Mrs. Sorenson, on second thought, I think I'd better come back when your husband is home. I think this is a conversation we should be having all together." He grabbed the brim of his hat and pulled it down quickly to bid her farewell, then turned to exit the barn from the same door he had entered.

Although he heard Sadie's footsteps as she walked swiftly behind him, he did not turn or move quickly enough to duck the path of the ax as it planted itself square between his shoulder blades. He arched his back in an unintentional reflex, and Sadie pulled the handle with both hands and wrenched the blade from his flesh. Mr. Grimaldi turned sideways and Sadie hit him again: this time, at his waist, just above the pocket of his flannel coat. The blade chopped the tip of his elbow off in the process, and a tiny yarmulke of green plaid fell into the wood shavings that covered the barn floor.

Mr. Grimaldi tried to speak but could not find his voice. Instead, he collapsed onto his back on the ground. A thick puddle of deep red blood began to pool beneath him; it felt warm against the cold earth. He watched as Sadie straddled her feet on either side of his knees, brought the ax high behind her shoulder, and swung it around and into his chest, crushing his ribcage.

"I suppose you should have accepted that cup of tea after all, eh, Mr. Grimaldi?" Sadie said. She laughed a little and pulled on the handle to remove the weapon from his torso. Mr. Grimaldi coughed and sputtered, and bright red blood spat from his mouth and dribbled down the side of his face. The blade caught on his ribs and would not budge. Sadie tugged and twisted the handle, but the ax was firmly lodged in his body. She even stepped on his stomach to gain some traction and pulled but found it was a useless endeavor. Finally, she left the implement sticking out of the insurance salesman's body like an explorer's flag and decided to return to the house to clean herself up.

When she reached the barn door, it opened, and there stood Mads, chewing his pipe. He stared at his wife for a long minute, confused by the splattering of blood across her face and jacket. Then he glanced over her shoulder and saw the tableau of Mr. Grimaldi with the ax and understood. "Are you alright, my love?" was the first thing he said, resting his hand on his wife's upper arm, the only clean stretch of clothing on her that was within immediate reach.

Sadie smiled one of her infrequent smiles and looked down at the floor. "Yes, Mads," she answered. "I'm okay. He... he..." she began. For the first time in a long while, she didn't know what to say. Without her suitcase of masks, her script was blank.

"Shhhh," Mads whispered, soothing her. "I think this place was due for a remodeling anyway." He walked over to

Mr. Grimaldi and fished his hands carefully within the pockets of the man's coat. He removed a set of keys and a wallet, slipped them into his own pocket, then brought out the tiny box of wooden matches he used to light his pipe. He struck one of the matches against the box's flint and tossed it onto the ground in the dry sawdust next to a nearby bale of hay, then turned quickly and marched out of the barn, pulling his wife along with him. He handed Sadie Mr. Grimaldi's keys, and the two of them walked side by side to the truck and visiting car in the driveway. Sadie got into Mr. Grimaldi's sedan and Mads got into his truck just as thick smoke began to pour from between the slats of the battened windows of the barn. As the two of them drove to Marshal's Pond to dispose of the vehicle, the sky began to shake a sprinkle of fresh snowflakes onto northern Massachusetts.

Mr. Grimaldi appeared to have simply disappeared without a trace. Without a body, his family was unable to cash in his policy for seven years. Two towns away, with the combined insurance money from Peter, the children, and the near-total destruction of the barn and farmhouse, the Sorensons did not rebuild. Instead, they relocated north and started anew, and Lunenburg never heard from them again.

Darlene and Brian's eyes grew wide as their grandfather became suddenly silent and appeared to have finished his story. "But Pappy," said Darlene. "Did they ever have more kids? Did they ever get caught?"

Grandpa scratched his sandpaper stubble and stared at the window. The snow was beginning to pile up. He would have to jump-start the blower again to clear the walkway once the wind died down. The mail carrier wouldn't deliver on the rural routes after a heavy storm, but he liked to keep the grounds tidy in case of visitors. He inhaled deeply, then coughed a bit to shake the tickle from the back of his throat. "Yes, as a matter of fact, they did have more children. Foster kids. Sadie and Mads took in a few of them over the years, and two even stayed past their eighteenth birthdays. They consider Sadie and Mads their parents even to this day."

Brian cleared his throat. "But the police never got them?"

Grandpa laughed. "No, I think Sadie was too smart for them. Mads, too. They never cashed in on another insurance claim. I guess they knew when not to push their luck." He leaned down and pulled the covers up to his grandchildren's necks. "Now, the two of you stay snuggled in this bed until morning: you hear me? No use getting up and battling the cold. Maybe I can get your Gramma to make some of her chocolate chip pancakes special for you tomorrow. Would you like that?"

The children nodded in unison, and he reached over and stroked each of their foreheads lovingly and stood up slowly from the bed. His spine and knees snapped and popped, and Grandpa winced as he hobbled steadily to the doorway. "Goodnight," he called and flipped down the light switch. The children's voices echoing his farewell caroled happily in the darkness.

He wandered into the big kitchen, dark save for a lonely light above the stove. A brightness flashed on the edge of his peripheral vision and he turned to see the refrigerator light illuminate the room and cast a bluish light on his wife's heavy terrycloth bathrobe. "Fancy meeting you here," he said.

His wife's alabaster skin glowed in the moonlight that beamed through the window beside her. "I was just getting some dessert," she said, pulling a carton of peppermint stick from the icebox and sliding off the cover. "Would you like some, Mads?"

He walked slowly over to her and took the clean

teaspoon from Sadie's hand. "Just a taste, my love," he replied, and kissed her forehead lovingly. He stuck the utensil in the middle of the smooth, white ice cream. "Just a taste."

Petrichor

Carbon monoxide: the silent killer! screamed the bright yellow label punctuated with thick, red lettering. Amanda let her fingers graze the boxes of sensors stacked officiously next to the smoke detectors and radon gas monitors in the domestic panic aisle of the Ace Hardware store down the street from her house. She had done her homework. Any CO reading over 35 parts per million was dangerous. Common household items that were sneaky sources of carbon monoxide included gas dryers, gas and oil furnaces, and automobile exhaust pipes. Just last week, the entire dinner rush of a seafood restaurant on the North Shore had to be evacuated after patrons complained of dizziness and a server passed out; the reading there was 300 parts per million. There was a leak in the water heater's flue pipe, and the gas that was supposed to be funneled outside leaked into the bottom floor of the crowded eatery, filling the space with the invisible, odorless gas.

The restaurant didn't have a carbon monoxide detector; state law doesn't mandate them for areas where people don't sleep. Amanda picked up the box for the type of detector she knew her father had installed on the wall at the top of the basement stairs. That model plugged into the wall outlet but was backed up with a 9-volt battery. She replaced the box on the shelf, wandered over to the candy display at the front of the store, and selected a package of Chuckles. She fished two dollars from her pocket and brought the sugared gummy candy to the register to pay.

Twelve years earlier
"If you tell the truth, I promise I won't punish you for writing on the desk." Dave stood with his hands on his hips,

hovering like a giant in a fairy tale above Amanda's 6-year-old frame.

Amanda teetered between two sneaker-soled feet, chewing absentmindedly on a hangnail on her right thumb. "I didn't write on the desk," she insisted, but her voice was low, almost a whisper, and she stared at the ground, unable to meet her father's eyes.

Dave folded his arms in front of his chest. "Then who did?" he asked.

On the other side of the bedroom she shared with her younger sister, Andrea, her 4-year-old sibling sorted out the red and white Lego blocks; she was constructing a building of some sort: a hospital maybe? Amanda didn't know. "Drea did," Amanda said, looking at her father in the eye for the first time since he had discovered the writing on the antique mahogany desk the two sisters shared. On the bottom left corner, in letters about the size of Amanda's palm, was one word written in shaky cursive. *Love*. It was the first word Amanda had learned to write in cursive, and she had practiced looping the languid capital L over and over that afternoon: in chalk on the driveway, in waxy crayon on the inside cover of her spelling workbook, even in black magic marker on the sheets of white lined paper her first-grade teacher, Mrs. Cantor, had passed out to the children earlier that day. But she had run out of driveway space, and workbook space, and lined paper, and well, the desk had been so empty, so plain…

Amanda crossed her arms and scowled. "Drea did it," she repeated.

Dave tapped his foot twice. "Amanda, I'm going to say it again. If you tell the truth, I won't punish you for writing on the desk." He paused and squatted down to face his daughter. "Now, tell Daddy the truth. Did you write on the desk?"

Amanda let her arms fall to her sides. "You won't

punish me if I tell the truth?"

"I promise: I won't punish you for writing on the desk," Dave answered carefully.

Amanda took a deep breath. "I wrote on the desk, Daddy. It was me. I'm sorry."

Dave stood back up and looked at the permanent Sharpie squiggles on his mother's old dressing table which the girls had repurposed. Then he grabbed Amanda by the arm, hard, and shook her. "You're a very bad girl, Amanda," he said, pulling her toward himself. With his other hand, he slapped his daughter on the buttocks and back, two, three, four times.

Amanda cried out in pain. "You said—" she sobbed. "You said you wouldn't punish me if I told the truth!" Her face was red and splotchy and wet. Snot dribbled down her cheeks.

"I told you I wouldn't punish you for *writing on the desk*," Dave said. "I never said I wouldn't punish you for lying." He punctuated this last rationalization with a shake of Amanda's tiny arm, then let go of his daughter. She sank to the ground and began to cry again. "And you're cleaning that magic marker off that desk. I don't care if it takes all day." He took a long last look at his eldest daughter, then turned and left the room without another word.

The next day was Saturday, and although it was rainy, Amanda was excited to get up and start the morning. Andrea had decided to construct a whole town out of Lego bricks, but she needed Amanda's help. Together, they dumped the big box of plastic bricks onto the soft, green carpet of their bedroom and began the assembly process. Amanda had just completed the basement foundation of what would be a small blue house when their father appeared in the doorway with a small bucket and handful of rags.

"Amanda," he said sternly. "No playing until you

wash that word off of the desktop." He dropped the bucket next to her on the floor and tossed the piles of rags into her lap.

A fetid, sour smell wafted up from the plastic pail. "Pee-yooo!" said Andrea, holding her nose between her thumb and forefinger. She held a Lego axel and two tiny wheels in her other hand. "Stinky!"

Dave snatched a rag from his daughter's thigh and pushed it into the clear liquid. "It's just water and vinegar. You'll have to scrub really hard, Amanda. You are really going to have to use some elbow grease to get that marker out. Now get to work, and I don't want to see you stop until that writing is completely gone."

Amanda put down the tiny blue brick she held in her hand and sighed. "Okay, Daddy." She stood up and carried the bucket closer to the desk, then reached into the foul-smelling water to grab the submerged rag, squeezed most of the liquid out of it, and began to rub the loopy black letters over and over, pressing down as hard as she could.

Dave began to walk out of the room, but when he was an inch from the door, he turned. "Do not stop until the marker is *completely* gone. Do you understand me? *All of it.*"

Amanda did not look up but nodded to show her father she understood. He quietly left the room and walked back downstairs, and Andrea continued to sort through the multicolored blocks, assembling Seussical structures for the next hour as her older sister rubbed and dipped and rang and rubbed and rubbed and rubbed and rinsed and rubbed and dipped and rubbed and rubbed... until finally, Amanda's shoulder seized with pain and she could not move her hands over the same stubborn mark any longer. The vinegar mixture had done nothing to the word—it remained in place like a petulant child refusing to budge.

Amanda collapsed dramatically onto the floor next to

her sister and watched her construct another building. After a short while, she picked up the bricks and joined her, and the two played quietly together, so engrossed in their project that they neglected to stop for lunch, so by four-thirty, their stomachs rumbled with hunger.

Dave returned to the girls' bedroom, but when he saw Amanda on the carpet next to her sister, he stopped short. He turned and examined the desktop. "Amanda, why aren't you scrubbing this desk like I asked?" he said.

Amanda clicked two yellow 8-prong bricks together with a satisfying snap. "I tried, Daddy. It won't come off. I scrubbed and scrubbed and my arms hurt, so I stopped." She examined her police station in progress and wondered if she had enough Legos to add a garage for the cruiser she planned to build. She didn't see her father move toward her, and when he grabbed her tightly around the neck and yanked her to her feet, she found herself gasping for breath, not only because of the choke but because she was so startled.

As suddenly as he had grabbed her, Dave released his grip on his daughter and brushed his palms on the hips of his jeans. "No. You're not going to spoil my dinner, Amanda. I'm going to enjoy my dinner tonight: you're not going to ruin it like usual." He began to walk toward the door. "Dinner is in an hour. Make sure you come downstairs and set the table before that."

Amanda and Drea set the table without speaking. Forks laid neatly across napkins folded on the diagonal, knives and spoons to the right of the plates, small, squat glasses filled to the brim with plain, white milk for the girls. Their mother, Pauline, had made one of her family's favorites: meatloaf with pan fried onions and green peppers drizzled over mashed potatoes. For a moment, no one spoke: they were all too busy stuffing their mouths with hot comfort food. Then, Andrea began to tell her parents all about the tiny city she and

Amanda had constructed that day: the police station and the hospital, the rows of tiny houses and the city park, even an ice cream parlor. Amanda added her own details to the replay, explaining how they had added chimneys to the houses after forgetting to do so initially: after all, how could Santa visit without a chimney? From across the table, Amanda's father smiled at her.

When the last bite of meatloaf and potato was scraped from plates, Amanda tilted her head back as far as she could to drain the last drop of milk from her glass. She replaced the cup on the table and wiped her mouth with her napkin.

"Are you done eating, Amanda?" Dave said, still smiling at her from across the table.

"Yes, Daddy," she answered.

"Then go to your room and clean up the Legos from the floor," he said. "I'll be right there."

Daddy must want to see the city we created, Amanda thought. They had worked on it so hard all day, she was excited to show him what they had accomplished—all from their imagination. Amanda raced up the stairs and scooped the unused bricks into the storage box, then made some last-minute adjustments to the town structures before her father could see them. She was adjusting the edge of a roof piece on the hospital when Dave appeared in the doorway.

"Daddy, look what we made!" Amanda said excitedly, but it was only then that she saw her father's expression. He was not smiling. In fact, his face had no expression; his eyes were dead. He closed the bedroom door behind him, walked over to one of the girls' beds, and sat down.

"Come over here, Amanda," he said, his tone flat and even.

Amanda was confused. Didn't he want to see their Lego town? Hadn't he been smiling at her the whole time they had eaten dinner? "Why?" Amanda asked, her voice very tiny. Something was not right.

Dave stared at his daughter. "I'm tired of getting upset before dinner and not being able to enjoy a meal," he explained matter-of-factly, "so I decided tonight, I was going to wait until after dinner to do this—and I'm glad I did. I had a nice dinner. You didn't ruin it."

Amanda felt the insides of her stomach turn cold and slide down to the pit of her pelvis.

"Now get over here. *Now*."

Amanda began to cry. "No… Daddy, please. I tried to scrub the marker off. I tried so hard and it didn't come off. I scrubbed it and scrubbed it." She wrapped her arms around her shoulders, hugging herself.

Dave's voice dropped an octave and flattened. "Get over here, now, or I swear to God, Amanda, I will grab you by the throat and pull you over here myself."

Amanda walked slowly over to her father, crying harder with each step. When she was within arm's reach of him, Dave said, "I'll give you something to cry about." He pulled his daughter over his knees and spanked her hard, over and over, until Amanda began to scream and the stinging had turned to numbness. When he stopped, she crumpled onto the floor and sobbed until her head pounded and felt like it would explode.

Dave walked to the bedroom door and opened it. "I'm glad I didn't let you ruin my dinner," he said and walked back downstairs.

That night, Amanda lay in bed, staring at the ghost boxes of light that sailed across her ceiling each time a car drove by outside. She could hear a faint scratching, perhaps a scurrying, in the attic above her head. When her parents had bought the house, they discovered that they had no access to space between the second floor and roof: the previous owner had sealed the tiny square in the hallway ceiling with plaster. Two years later, when Amanda was born, they hired a contractor to build a one-story addition between their two-story house and the detached two-car garage, sandwiching between them a new, large master suite and three-season porch. Amanda, and eventually, Andrea, were assigned the large, second floor bedroom overlooking the addition. The other bedroom was kept as guest quarters.

Now, as she isolated the sound of the tiny attic creature from the sounds of the wind outside the windows and of her sister delicately snoring in her own bed three feet away, Amanda wondered how this squirrel, or mouse, or maybe baby raccoon had managed to force its way into their sealed space.

But mostly, she wondered how it would ever find its way back out.

Four years later

When Amanda was ten, she decided to quit playing soccer. She decided to quit going to dance lessons, and she decided to quit joining in with the neighborhood boys in their makeshift games of kickball or badminton. Her thighs had begun to round, and they stuck out from her hips instead of staying obedient in long, lean lines, and she found herself, so overcome with self-consciousness, tripping over her two feet just walking down the street to the park. It was easier—safer—to simply stay planted in her own backyard or her own room and to read a book alone.

Her neighborhood was filled with children with ages ranging from four to fourteen. The house next door boasted three children: two girls and a boy, and the youngest child, Greg, was four years older than Amanda. Every once in a while, Greg and Amanda would cross paths at a block picnic or birthday party, or the two would be shoved together in the back of a station wagon when the families carpooled to a soccer tournament or catechism class, but for the most part, they kept their distance, so what happened that week in early April was completely unexpected, at least for Amanda.

As she sat at her desk in her bedroom, tracing her finger over and over the faded letters *L-o-v-e*, Amanda procrastinated doing her math homework, choosing instead to daydream as she watched the cherry-red cardinal dart from feeder to feeder in the neighbor's backyard. It was one of those early spring days, when the sun and temperature felt like early June but the half-dead grass and stick-figure trees revealed Mother Nature's true identity. Amanda looked back at her worksheet.

Kathie baked 10 cupcakes. She decorated 6 of the cupcakes with rainbow sprinkles and the rest with chopped nuts. What fraction of the cupcakes had nuts on them? Express your answer in the simplest form.

Amanda didn't care about Kathie or the likelihood of the baker being slapped with a potential lawsuit for her choice of allergen-laced embellishment; why did math word problems always have to involve food? If it wasn't cupcakes, it was apples. Or slices of pie. Or puppies, which weren't food items, per se, but they sure did eat a lot. It was only three o'clock: her parents wouldn't be home from work for another two hours, and that meant dinner wouldn't be ready until at least six. She mulled over the idea of rummaging through the kitchen cabinets for hidden cookies or Goldfish crackers.

Then, out of the corner of her eye, she saw it. Next door, from an upper window, something white and cloth-like sailed downward onto the wooden back deck below. Amanda got up from her chair and stood by the window to get a better look. A moment later, Greg walked out onto the deck, stark naked, and bent over to retrieve his underwear. Horrified,

Amanda stepped back, but her movement was not quick enough to avoid detection by Greg, who met her eyes as he spun to walk back into the house. Amanda stood frozen: she had never seen a naked boy before—not even by accident, and her friend Ann Marie's brother was always traipsing around the house in only a pair of ratty sweat shorts. Greg and Amanda both stood motionless for a long minute, staring at each other like a deer and predator, and then Greg continued on into the house, letting the screen door slam loudly behind him.

From deep inside the house, the phone rang. Neither Amanda nor Andrea were old enough to have their own extension on the second floor, so Amanda had to run down the stairs to the kitchen in order to pick up the receiver on the fourth ring. "Hello?" Amanda said, slightly out of breath.

"I know you saw me," said the voice on the phone. It was breathy and slightly wet. To Amanda, it sounded… sweaty, if voices could sweat.

"Uh… what?" she stammered. She looked around the kitchen, suddenly self-conscious.

Greg let out an audible, somewhat exasperated exhale. "I know you saw me, and you can't tell anyone," he said, slightly menacing. "Do you understand?"

Amanda bit her lip. "Yes. I understand," she answered.

"Good," Greg said, and hung up the phone.

As promised, Amanda didn't tell anyone what she had seen, and she avoided her parents' eyes as she picked at the spaghetti and meatballs her mother served that evening for dinner. For some reason, she felt dirty, like what Greg had done was an unclean crime and she had been a co-conspirator. It swallowed her appetite and replaced it with a slightly sick feeling in her stomach, like she had sipped sour milk.

The very next day, Amanda walked the three-block

route from the bus stop back to her house, clutching her heavy textbooks close to her chest and concentrating hard in order to not catch the lip of her shoe on an uneven part of the sidewalk. As she passed Greg's house, she heard a hiss coming from across the side yard. Greg, home from high school already, peered out from behind his family's shed, which abutted Amanda's family's garage. "Psssst," he repeated. "Amanda, c'mere."

Amanda stopped and looked around. The neighborhood was asleep, tucked in safely at work or after school activities. She walked cautiously across the stunted, brown grass toward the shed. "What do you want?" she asked.

Greg ducked back behind the shed, out of sight. As she walked behind the narrow structure, she found herself pulled off balance and yanked into the darkness of the tiny house, her school books spilling about on the lawn outside. Greg grabbed the metal door and pulled it closed, cloaking them in darkness. As Amanda's eyes adjusted to the sliver of light peeking through the hinge of the doorway, she realized that Greg had boxed her in. She pushed backwards to avoid touching him and felt the dirty metal walls soiling the back of her grey sweatshirt and jean shorts.

"What are you doing?" she asked, louder than she intended.

Greg pushed forward, his knees resting on the front of her thighs. She could feel his breath on her forehead; it smelled sour, acrid, like a wet dog. "Shhhh," Greg whispered, fumbling with something around his waist.

The tiny, cramped space shrank even smaller, and suddenly the air seemed heavy and damp. Amanda pushed against Greg's chest with her hands, but his body remained fixed, a wide tree trunk. "I want to get out of here!" she said insistently. "Let me out!" But Greg only grunted back, then held his forearm perpendicular to Amanda's throat and pressed it there, trapping her against the shed wall. He grunted again and moved in a shuddering manner, and Amanda wondered if he was crying or, in some bizarre way, laughing silently like a cartoon. This continued for a minute, and then Amanda felt Greg's arm go limp and something wet and sticky dripped onto on her thigh. She wiped the warm, thick substance with her palm, and having nowhere to wipe her hand, brushed as much of it as she could onto the side of her jean shorts. She looked at Greg and could faintly make out the outline of his face, beads of sweat dotting his skin like freckles.

He moved slightly sideways, enough for Amanda to squeeze past him toward the door. "Tell anyone about this and you're dead," he growled. When the sunlight hit both of their faces, Amanda did not turn to see his expression. She hurriedly gathered up her schoolbooks from the lawn, tucked her hair behind her ears, and ran shakily behind the garage to her back door. She told no one about what had transpired, but from then on, she walked the extra five minutes around the block on her way home from school so that she never had to pass Greg's house again.

Six years after that

In the ten years since she'd first learned to write in cursive, Amanda mastered another art of communication: interpreting social cues. She became so adept at noticing when others shifted, even only slightly, in their psychological comfort zones that friends often commented that she seemed to be the most sympathetic person they'd ever met. At sixteen, when most teenagers were catatonic within their own heads, Amanda was more in tune with the outside world than with her own.

The alarm didn't register in her head like a barometric pressure sensor predicting woe for tornado alley; no, it originated in her stomach. When her father sat down for dinner, she didn't need to meet his eyes before her gut told her what kind of meal they were all about to experience. Perhaps it was the way he sat down, or the abruptness with which he shuffled his chair closer to the table, but whatever it was, Amanda knew what was set to befall her before the first bite of food entered her mouth. It was out of her control, and missing dinner was not an option in their family. Like a soldier resigning himself to the battlefield each morning, Amanda sat in her assigned seat across from her father each evening at six o'clock, waiting for the bombing to begin.

Dave had long since given up his Zen-approach to corporal punishment as dessert fodder only, and he knew that a sixteen-year-old was too old to spank, but he was just as happy to remind the women in his household who wore the pants in other ways. He could not, *would not*, tolerate any female's psychic castration of him. Geraldine Ferraro may have made it all the way to the VP ticket five years earlier, but goddammit, she had certainly demolished Mondale's chances of ever winning with that bitch mouth of hers disparaging her husband every which way. His daughters would learn to never laugh at men, period. They committed this rule to memory hard and fast early on, often sitting at the table with their heads propped in their hands, their nail-polished fists placed strategically below their cheekbones so that they pushed their mouths down into frowny-face masks. Any twitch of a smile could be considered mockery or insubordination, and the girls knew better than to risk the consequences.

The first time he choked his daughter, it was by pure primal instinct. She had it coming, with that smart mouth of hers. There was something in her face, something that told him that she believed she was better than him, that he could not control her, and he had to put a stop to it right that instant. He jumped up from the table with such force that his heavy wooden chair fell backwards and clattered onto the floor in a raucous commotion, startling both his wife and his daughters. He stomped around to Amanda's side of the table and stretched his meaty hand around her throat, surprised at how much flesh he was able to grip. He watched with satisfaction as her face changed immediately from smarmy to terrified, and as she gasped for air and flailed her arms about, Dave held her tighter, even pulling her slightly from her seat, until Pauline, in her even voice, said, "David, stop it. Sit down and finish your dinner," and he let go.

He returned to his seat and watched Amanda's face as it continued to blush red and her neck splotched with nervous hives, and he knew he had won. From then on, his daughters would give him the respect he deserved.

It was the same nightmare for Amanda every day, only it wasn't a dream. This time, she was standing in the dining room, her father standing next to the French doors to the living room, the windows dark with evening sky. Her father was running toward her, his hands stretching toward her neck, his eyes wild. He was screaming something at her, but she couldn't hear him: her mind had fallen back inside her body as it often did those days, covering itself with a heavy blanket of self-preservation. She was frozen in place for just a moment, and then a voice inside of her pushed her, hard. *Run*, it said. *Run*.

Amanda turned and ran the opposite way around the table, taking her father off guard. As they stood in a stalemate, staring at one another from across the broad tabletop, Dave began to pant slightly. He was in his forties now, no longer a young man, and although she had gotten rounder, fuller, over the past year or so, his daughter was still a spry teenager with young lungs. Her eyes darted back and forth like a trapped animal. "So help me God, when I get my hands on you…"

Dave bellowed, hoping his threat would cause her to surrender and shelter in place, but Amanda took the opportunity to turn and run through the open door leading to the kitchen, and Dave followed behind at her heels.

Everything seemed to move in slow motion: her stockinged feet hitting the linoleum, her father's voice, the murmur of the television in an adjoining room—it was all capsulized in an old eight-millimeter film reel being fed ever so slowly through a broken-down projector.

Step.

She reached the kitchen, pitch black but for the tiny light over the oven.

Step.

Her father was behind her. She could feel his rage, sense it growing with every passing second.

Step.

The den. She could see the entrance to the den from her place in the kitchen.

Step.

Her mother was sitting in the brown recliner in the den, staring blankly at the television.

Step.

Mom, please help: please help me.

Step.

She felt the displacement of air as her father's hand reached out and swiped the space an inch behind her back.

Step.

The den was two steps away. Why wasn't her mother looking at her?

Step.

"Mom!" Amanda screamed with panic. "Mom! Please help! Please help me!" She flung herself at the brown recliner, but her mother pulled her arm away and did not look away from the television. "Mom!" Amanda screamed at her mother, pleading with her through tears. "Please!"

She felt her father's hands on her back, grasping at her waist. Again, her mother recoiled and would not meet Amanda's eyes, so Amanda grabbed the closest palpable object: the back of the recliner. She clutched the scratchy woolen fabric with both hands and shut her eyes tight. She felt her father pull hard on her waist, almost forcing her pants down, but this was no time for modesty; she dug her fingernails into the rough upholstery and held on for dear life.

Her body was horizontal in the air, and as her father grasped and tore at her torso with all of his might, she felt her nails ripping through the fabric, breaking it in some places. Dave let go of his daughter's waist and focused on peeling her claws from the chair back. He grabbed her wrists and forced them backward, not caring if he sprained or broke her hands or forearms, and finally, he dislodged her from the recliner where his wife sat silently and tossed Amanda on the nearby couch like a rag doll. Before she could move again, he wrapped both of his hands around her throat.

Her eyes were open now, and she stared at the ceiling above, imagined its textured roughness. Her father was bent over her, squeezing both of his hands around her neck and shaking her back and forth. She put her hands over his out of instinct to try to free herself, but he would not let go. She tried to take a breath, just one breath, but found she could not. It was like the sensation she had felt when she had accidentally inhaled a cube of cheese at the family Christmas party last winter: one second, she could breathe, and the next, her lungs were useless: a bottle with the cork shoved tightly inside. The lights in the room dimmed and grey clouds floated by her vision. She looked downward and saw the back of Pauline's head; her mother was still watching TV like nothing was going on. Amanda sank as far back into herself as she could bend, and the room turned dark and cold.

When she awoke on the couch some time later, her father was nowhere in the room. Her throat was raw, like she had thrown up acidy bile, and tender. Pauline was still sitting in the brown recliner, watching television. Amanda silently sat up, carefully stood, and quietly walked down the hallway and up the stairs to her room. She climbed into bed without bothering to brush her teeth or wash her face, but she did remove her pants and underwear and shove them to the bottom of the hamper. They were soaked in urine.

Dave, emboldened by his wife's lack of interference in his novel approach to herding his daughters' behaviors, bragged to friends and relatives alike that "any smart word" from one of his kids would be met with a chokehold. "So, I just grabbed her by the throat," Dave explained to twenty relatives at Easter dinner, "and it was the end of *that* issue, I'll tell you that!" He guffawed and made a pantomime of strangling someone with gusto; Amanda concentrated on cutting her ham into tinier pieces.

The next week, Amanda sat in the passenger seat of the beat-up Malibu parked in front of her house and stared up at the home's roofline delineated by moonlight. Eddie stretched back in his seat, simultaneously wrapping his right arm around Amanda's shoulders, making her jump. She could no longer stand being surprised by touch: someone sneaking behind her to place their palms over her eyes to play "guess who" would make her stomach drop into her thighs, and she couldn't bear to wear turtlenecks or any jewelry tight around her neck. Once a gregarious child, she now turned beet red anytime she spoke up, and hives crawled over her neck and chest each time she found herself in a confrontation or even a friendly debate. It wasn't just her fight or flight trigger finger that itched; it was her whole hand.

When Amanda pulled away instinctively from his

forearm, Eddie clucked his tongue and shimmied closer along the bench seat toward her. "What's the matter?" he cooed, rubbing her thigh. "You're so jumpy."

Amanda gathered her purse from the floor and placed her hand on the door handle. "Nothing. Thanks for the movie," she said, and she meant it. Everything was as it had been for the past four years. Everything, that is, except for the roofline. From her vantage point on the street, it appeared to be sagging on the right side—the side over her bedroom.

She opened the car door and stuck one leg out. "Are you going to walk me to the door?" she asked coyly, but her date was already turned back toward the windshield, his hands at ten and two on the steering wheel.

"Nah, I'll call ya later," Eddie said, and Amanda paused only a moment before climbing the rest of the way out of the car, shutting the door, and walking the twelve steps across the lawn to the door of the three-season porch. She did not turn back to wave goodbye, and Eddie did not wait to see if she got inside safely.

That night, she lay in bed, staring at the ceiling as she often did when she could not sleep. When everything was silent, she heard it: not scratching or scurrying, but tiny footsteps tip-tapping around the attic. It seemed to be pacing back and forth in the space above Amanda's head, and she could have sworn she saw the faintest sprinkling of ceiling dust drift toward her bedspread, shaken downward by the sheer weight of the animal's plodding. The hapless creature, trapped since her childhood, had grown.

And two more years still

It was the close of the final month in Amanda's senior year of high school. She had applied to all of the local colleges per her parents' instruction, but on the sly, she had mailed with crossed fingers an additional application to a semi-prestigious school two hours away. One afternoon, she found a fat envelope waiting for her in the mailbox, and upon its discovery, brought the package to her room and tore it open, barely able to take a breath. She had been accepted, and moreover, the school had granted her a half-time scholarship, enough funding to almost bridge the gap between attending their school as a dorm resident and commuting to a local college: her parents couldn't deny her this opportunity.

She heard voices outside on her driveway, and believing it was her mother, she raced down the stairs, letter in hand, to share the good news. She stopped short, however, when she saw that it was Greg and his friends playing with the garden hose on their edge of his property instead.

"Hey, Amanda," called one of Greg's pals. Amanda thought his name was Kyle. Or Kane. Maybe Ken. "Hey, c'mere." He leaned forward and said something to Greg in his ear.

Amanda hovered on the cement steps in front of her screened porch. "What is it?" she called back. There were three of them, standing at the edge of the flower beds. Greg began to casually spray the daffodils and their yellow heads bobbed back and forth like a dance troupe.

The third boy whose name Amanda definitely didn't know picked up a small stone from the grass and tossed it back into the lawn like he was trying to skip it on water. "Come on over: we want to ask you something," he said. He was smiling an easy smile. A trustworthy smile.

Amanda folded her acceptance letter in half and tucked it into the back pocket of her shorts. She walked slowly down the driveway and over to the neighbor's property line. When she was just a few feet away from the boys, she stopped and put her hands on her hips. She could feel something was off, but she couldn't place how. "What did you want to ask?"

The rock thrower looked toward the sky and wiped

his brow dramatically. "Wow, it's hot out here. It hasn't rained in like… two weeks, yeah?" He looked at Amanda and then bent down to grab another stone. Before looking back at her again, he said, "Do you know if we'll have any relief soon?"

She was too busy watching the nameless boy that she didn't see Greg raise the hose nozzle toward her. He squeezed the trigger hard, and water shot out and all over Amanda, soaking her t-shirt to virtual translucence. She crossed her arms over her chest and turned her torso in an attempt to shield herself, and the three roared with laughter. Greg turned off the water.

"We wanted to know if I still made you wet," Greg said, an odious smile plastered across his mouth. "Like that afternoon in the shed." The three men burst out laughing, and Amanda walked as fast as she could back to the house, clutching her shoulders.

"I guess the answer's *yes*," said KyleKaneKen, cackling with amusement.

Amanda pulled open the screen door and ran inside before it had a chance to close behind her.

Now that her two daughters had busy social lives and part-time jobs of their own, Pauline began to branch out and plan activities for herself. She joined the neighborhood book club and the town's film club, and on the first weekend of every month, she traveled to the casino with her sisters for an overnight, leaving Amanda and Andrea alone with their father.

It was the first Saturday evening in June, and Amanda had taken to counting down the days until she could leave for college, placing big X's on the calendar next to her bed. Their mother having left that morning, it was up to Amanda and her sister to prepare and serve dinner. Amanda pulled the pan of breaded chicken breasts out of the sweltering oven and rested it on one of the cold burners on the stove. She ran the masher through the potatoes one last time and tossed the string beans in healthy pats of butter and a sprinkling of minced garlic. Dave said nothing as she retrieved his plate, carefully placed with tongs two crispy, golden breasts next to large mounds of the side dishes, and slid the plate in front of her father again, the steam fogging up his glasses. After she had served her sister and herself, Amanda sat back down in the seat across from her father and began to cut into her piece of chicken.

"Well, this looks delicious, girls," Dave said. Amanda smiled in spite of herself. For once, her father was pleased with her. "There's nothing I like better than a pair of juicy, tender breasts," he continued. His tone was conspiratorial, like a character in a spy movie, and it made Amanda feel dirty, although she could not place why. Amanda looked up and saw that he was staring right at her. She nodded and looked back down at her plate, concentrating on cutting each piece into tinier and tinier bites. Her father began to chew his food, and as he did, he began to moan slightly. "So good," he said, and when she finally looked up at him, he winked at Amanda.

When everyone had eaten and Andrea was running soapy water into the baking dish in the sink, Amanda took it upon herself to stack the dirty plates together, piling the used silverware on top. She leaned toward her father to collect his dish, and he turned his head toward her and sniffed audibly into the air. "Jeez, Mandy," he said. "You go running today? You're a little ripe."

Amanda blushed, mortified. She hadn't exercised that day, hadn't sweat under her arms at all. She leaned her face toward her armpit and smelled herself. "What? I don't smell anything," she said.

Dave laughed his hearty guffaw that Amanda had grown steadily to hate. "No, Mandy: I'm not talking about your underarms. Hasn't your mother ever suggested you eat more yogurt? You know, for your women's health." Amanda wanted to sink into the floor, but she stood, paralyzed, while her father continued. "You know, it's supposed to keep away all that rancid yeast. You should try it." He raised an eyebrow at her. "Really."

Confounded by how to react, Amanda simply stood there for a long minute. Then she nodded her head, piled the rest of the dirty dinnerware into her arms, and carried it to the sink without a word.

Before she climbed in bed, she washed her face until her skin was red and shiny and raw like the surface of an apple that had been rubbed over and over. She would never be clean enough again.

Hours later, something woke her in the middle of night.

Her window was open, and Amanda lay in bed, listening, to see if whatever had aroused her would repeat itself. Hearing nothing, she climbed out of bed and walked over to the open window. She shoved her flip-flops into the back pocket of her pajama shorts, and as silent as a cat burglar, she slid the screen upwards and contorted her body to climb out onto the roof above the three-season porch. Because her parents' bedroom was below the other side of the roof expanse, she restricted her movement to in front of the pitch, still keeping her footfalls extra light to avoid any detection. Carefully, she placed bare foot after bare foot on the rough grey shingles, being cautious not to slip on the hint of dew that had already begun to form like icing.

Once she had made it to the edge of the roof where the roofline began to climb upwards again to trace the outline of the garage, she stretched her foot down to touch the top of the wooden lattice decorating the front of the porch. She tested the structure for sturdiness, gradually adding more of her weight to it until she was finally able to spin her body to face the gutter and climb down to the ground.

Amanda pulled her flip-flops from her back pocket and brushed pebbles and wood shavings from the front of her shorts. She stood silent in the shadow of the garage, breathing in the summer night air. There had been another dry spell for weeks, and the arid grass practically begged for an errant cigarette to be discarded from a passing car to set the neighborhood ablaze, but there was something heavy about the atmosphere that evening that suggested the drought would lift soon.

Amanda walked down the driveway and turned left to venture down a section of sidewalk she usually avoided, as it passed right by Greg's family's house; before she could get very far, she heard a noise coming from the shed. She walked further up the street to get a better view and stood under the massive oak that straddled the two properties on the tree belt. Greg and two of his friends were camped on the lawn behind the shed. They were unfolding and refolding one of those malleable, silver-colored hoses used to vent dryers. Her father had fastened an extra-long one to their gas dryer in the cellar when the vent was relocated after the addition. Amanda watched with great interest as the men attached one end of the hose to an empty glass aquarium, then lit something on fire in a small hole drilled into the side of the bowl. A cloud of pungent smoke rose from the group, who were now huddled in some sort of cabal.

They're making giant bongs out of repurposed household items, Amanda thought. *Score one for the recycling movement.* She watched as one of the three placed the end of the hose over his entire face and another lit the slide. The receiver removed the hose and exhaled, looking directly at Amanda, then began to cough violently.

"Hey, hey," he said, coughing a few more times. "Isn't that your garden hoe?" He pointed across the lawn at Amanda. The other two turned to look at her, and he slapped Greg on the back and began to laugh. "You get it? Garden HO. 'Cause she belongs in the shed!" He fell onto his side from his sitting position and continued to laugh.

Greg simply stared at Amanda and kept a cool tone. "I thought you meant because she's a real tool."

Amanda walked back down the sidewalk and up her driveway again. She climbed the trellis as quickly as she could, fearful the men would follow her. She scrambled up the gentle slope and forgetting that she still had her sandals on, slipped when she was only a few inches from her windowsill and managed to save herself from sliding on her belly down the incline only by grasping at the ridge and pulling herself back into a squatting position. As soon as she ducked back into her room and pulled the screen back into position, the insistent tapping of raindrops began to patter on the surfaces outside.

A breeze blew the wet air into her room, and Amanda stood still in the moonlight, breathing in the sweet, earthy smell. It was petrichor, the aromatic effect created when rain mixes with both the oils produced by plants during a drought and the bacteria of the soil. She had learned about the phenomenon in her botany class that year. Her teacher had described it as the fragrant cry of Mother Earth's parched skin weeping for joy.

It was the smell of relief.

At Casa di Lisa, the local Italian restaurant, Amanda sat with her mother at a table for two to celebrate her 18th birthday. It was mid-July, and the parched wind of June had been replaced with sticky humidity that would likely loiter for the next six weeks. The air conditioning blew full blast above them, but Pauline fanned herself with a menu anyway.

After the waiter delivered their drinks, a Tom Collins for Pauline and a Shirley Temple with extra maraschino cherries for Amanda, her mother raised her glass. "To being able to vote," she said, smiling.

Amanda clinked her glass against Pauline's. "And buy cigarettes. Oh—and get drunk on military bases," she said, laughing.

Pauline raised her eyebrow good-naturedly at her daughter. "To adulthood, anyway." They both took healthy swigs of their cocktail and mocktail, and Pauline stopped swinging the menu and put on her reading glasses to peruse it. "Now let's see... oh, there's that baked manicotti you like. Maybe I'll get it too."

Amanda chewed the end of her straw thoughtfully. "Only five more weeks before I'm off to the dorm." She had already made a packing list in her head. "Do you think Drea would mind if I took the big mirror with me? I guess I could buy a new one, but she already has the full-length one on the back of the bathroom door..."

Pauline removed her glasses from her face and placed her hand on Amanda's. "Listen, honey," she began. "I didn't want to bring this up until after dinner, but there's something I need to talk to you about."

Amanda didn't like the sound of her mother's tone. It was hesitant and serious, like the voice she used when Amanda came home from school to learn that Laffy, the Siberian Husky puppy the family adopted when she was nine, was sick and had to be "sent away." "What is it?" she asked. "Just tell me, Mom. I'd rather know bad news straight out."

Pauline looked at her daughter's face, but not into her eyes. She seemed to be looking somewhere past Amanda, at her earlobe or temple. "We don't have the money to send you away to school this year, Amanda. You'll have to complete your freshman year at a local school and commute."

Amanda felt her lungs turn to melted butter. "What?" she coughed. "What are you talking about?"

Pauline drummed her fingers on the menu once and took a deep breath. "Your father and I discussed this, and maybe next year you can transfer. But this year, we need you to stay at home." Amanda felt her mind drifting backwards. This couldn't be happening. Her freedom, her one chance at reprieve, at parole: it was slipping through her fingers as the beads of sweat dribbled down the sides of her glass and onto her fingers. Pauline tried to make her voice sound cheery. "We'll be sharing the car: how about that? And I think I can spare it every weekend—Jean insists on driving anywhere we go, even the casino—if you want to go out with your friends."

Amanda stared at the five red orbs in the bottom of her drink layered like beach balls in one of those big bins at the toy store. She picked up the glass and began to guzzle the sweetened ginger ale, pushing the ice cubes to the side of her mouth with her lips. When most of the liquid was gone, the five cherries toppled onto her tongue, and she let them sail into her throat without chewing them. When she breathed in through her mouth, she discovered she was choking, and on instinct, she stood up from the table and grasped at her throat.

"Amanda? AMANDA?!" Pauline stood up from her chair and felt the panic wash over her. "Amanda! Oh God... Oh God, somebody help: HELP! My daughter is choking!"

The ten seconds seemed to last a lifetime. Finally, Amanda felt two large arms wrap around her waist and a balled double fist push into her abdomen. The fruit spat from her mouth, and she could breathe again, though her windpipe burned like she had inhaled fire. She leaned forward over the table and coughed, listening to her mother thank a burly stranger for saving her daughter's life over and over. In that moment, Amanda finally acknowledged for certain something she had known deep down all of her life: no one and nothing would rescue her from her father.

Two weeks later, while Pauline was at her monthly girls' trip and Andrea slept over a friend's house, a 911 call came into Emergency Services. The caller sounded young, like a teenaged girl.

OPERATOR: 911. What is your emergency?

GIRL: The carbon monoxide detector went off in my basement and my dad won't wake up!

OPERATOR: Is he breathing? Are you still in the house?

GIRL: I turned off the alarm by unplugging it and taking out the battery. I'm on our three-season porch. I'm not sure what to do! I'm afraid to go back in the house but I'm afraid for my dad!

OPERATOR: The detector was going off?

GIRL: Yes, yes, it made, like, a piercing sound.

OPERATOR: Stay out of the house. The paramedics are on their way.

GIRL: I see them, I see them. I'm hanging up and going to meet them.

The fire department and EMTs materialized simultaneously at Amanda's home; it was encouraging to know that in such a small town, fire and rescue could be counted on to arrive on the double when called. She pointed the firefighters in the direction of her parents' bedroom. When the alarm rang out, she told them after, she sprinted down the stairs to see what was the matter. When she realized it was the carbon monoxide detector making the sound, she rushed to her parents' room to alert her father, but the door had been locked from the inside. It was one of those doorknob twist locks: it was possible her father had accidentally engaged it when he shut the door at bedtime.

In any case, Amanda had banged and banged on the door, but her father hadn't responded, so she ran around to the outside of the house and tried to push open one of the windows. The air conditioner had been running—her father always kept it going full blast at night—so although the windows were unlocked, they were shut tight. It was an older model machine, too: terribly loud. It's likely her father hadn't heard the alarm go off and had simply slept through it. To make matters worse, the air conditioner had been on recirculate: no fresh air was being funneled into the area, so any poison gas that filled the room had been trapped and continued to build.

When the last emergency vehicle pulled away from the house, her father's body in a shiny black bag inside of one of them, Amanda summoned up the strength to call her mother's cell phone. It was the middle of the night—early morning now, really—and she knew Pauline would be fast asleep and she'd have to wait ten or more rings before her mother would answer. The casino was an hour's drive away; when she finished the conversation, she plugged her cell phone into the charging station on the porch. The Fire Marshall had done readings of CO levels in the house and found that strangely, the only place they were still elevated was the master bedroom, but he warned Amanda to stay out of the house until a final inspection could be done in the daylight. However, Amanda stuck her torso into the kitchen anyway: she had to hang up her mother's car keys on the hook by the family message board.

She walked back onto the porch, grabbed her zippered sweatshirt from the coat hook and put it on, then continued through the door leading to the garage. As she walked past the front of her mother's car, she placed her palm on the hood: it had cooled slightly but was still rather warm. She grabbed one of the rags her father had piled for use when performing basic car and lawnmower maintenance and covered her hand with it, then pulled the length of dryer exhaust tube out from behind the wheelbarrow. She folded it as compactly as possible, never allowing her fingertips to touch the shiny metallic surface. As a precaution in case her neighbors were still awake after the sirens and flashing lights had retreated, she pushed open the window on the back wall of the garage and climbed out, carrying the folded hose. She looked briefly at her parents' bedroom window, only five feet from the garage's window, and walked the other way, toward Greg's house. When she was certain no one was watching from afar, she gingerly replaced the hose on the floor of the shed where she had found it.

As she walked back toward her front yard, she stuffed the rag in her jacket pocket but discovered there was already something in there. She pulled out the plastic package and examined it: an empty Chuckles wrapper.

With her father's life insurance money, she could pay for a dorm at college after all. Her mother wouldn't be home for at least another half hour, so she crouched down on the grass, then lay on her back, looking up at the sky. The starry night was turning deep blue and purple—dawn was on its way. She could see the stars themselves were beginning to disappear, swallowed by the storm clouds gathering above. She looked at the eave just above her bedroom window and noticed, for the first time, there was a small hole in the siding.

It was just the right size for a small animal to crawl in… or find its way out. Amanda closed her eyes and inhaled as much of the air as she could fill her lungs with just as the first drops of rain fell from the sky and onto her face.

Her petrichor had come at last.

SWM Seeks Release

Edward stared at the glowing laptop screen. The online dating website wanted him to create a profile. If he were being perfectly honest, it wasn't a dating site, exactly: more like one of those sly hookup apps that arranged seedy, STD-sprinkled fuck-fests in the back alleys behind dark bars or in the backseats of SUVs in the Home Depot parking lot.

Edward didn't want a date. He wanted a playmate.

Edward was 5'8" with dark, wavy hair. Dark-framed glasses surrounded his dark brown eyes. He was thin, but not overly so; the last time he had stepped on the scale, he was about 180, but he still fit into the same trousers he had purchased in his late twenties nearly thirty years ago. *Jesus! My pants are half my age*, Edward thought.

He ran his hand over his cheek, feeling the salt and pepper stubble prick his fingertips. *What do women want?* he thought. *No, what do* DTF *women want?* The shadow just below his nose began to itch. He hadn't had time to shave last night or that morning. The housework was piling up, and now his basic hygiene was taking the toll; maybe he should be placing an ad on the local odd jobs forum instead. He could use a good maid every now and again. His mind lit up. *Maybe a DTF housekeeper: 'kill two birds with one stone?* He laughed out loud, the sound taking him by surprise after enduring so many hours of dead quiet. One thing at a time, he told himself. I've paid my subscription fee to this site: let's see what gold pans out.

The first part of the questionnaire was a piece of cake: basic height/weight/physical attributes stuff. He'd have to be honest—he knew guys would sometimes stretch the truth online to attract women, but what was the point of that, really? I mean, if the end goal was to meet in person, what did those guys expect would happen once the face-to-face occurred? Did they believe they would be so charming that the chick wouldn't care that he was fifty pounds heavier, a half a foot shorter, a decade older? The last thing Edward wanted was to invest time in securing a special girl only to have her excuse herself to the ladies' room at the bar where they'd meet, never to return. The whole point was to get her to come home with him. He scratched his upper lip and began to type in the allotted boxes.

Location: Worcester metro area
Height: 5'8"
Weight: 180
Ethnicity: Caucasian

He was Italian, really. Should he specify that? I mean, in the summers, he tanned beautifully—he was a sun lover, that was for sure. His face always had that worn, outdoorsy glow usually reserved for park rangers and lumberjacks. It made him more youthful, even energetic-looking, he thought.

Age: 56

On second thought, he could shave a few years off of that number. Between his solar-tinted face and his freshly Whitestrip-bleached teeth, Edward could easily pass for someone in his late forties. Hell, if the light were dim enough, maybe even 42? He didn't want to push his luck. He changed the number to 49, and feeling secure in his white lie, he moved on to the next questions.

Gender: Male
Status: Single male seeking females
Smoking habits:

Edward paused. This was an odd piece of information to provide. I mean, he had given up the cancer sticks years ago, after the VFW where he spent the occasional Saturday afternoon had finally shown its belly and acquiesced to the state's smoking ban in private clubs. He did like to smoke a bit of pot now and again though: I mean, who didn't? Did that count?

Edward decided he was overthinking the question and answered a definitive "no." He never smoked a joint in public; if he lit up, it would be in the privacy of his own basement, and if he had made it that far to bring a woman down there, well, it was unlikely she'd be leaving because of a little reefer smoke. He laughed at the thought.

Now comes the nitty gritty. The honey in the pot, he thought. He knew that on websites like this, the ratio of women to men was defeating; the deck was stacked against the men. If he were to guess, he'd estimate there were about twenty-five men to every woman registered, and that didn't even take into account the handfuls of prostitutes, catfishes, and sugar-daddy seekers clogging the pool. He had to make his profile stand out in a way that would make a potential playmate respond to him over the fifty other locals vying for her attention. On the other hand, he had to ensure he wouldn't be wasting his time. He wanted an adventurous woman, someone who wasn't shy or only toying with the possibility of a meet up. He wanted a woman who was in decent shape... but not too athletic or fit. Someone who would be open to the idea of pursuing fantasies—specifically, his—and would be curious, or better yet, enthusiastic about trying bondage.

Limits: None—I'm very open-minded.

Encounters I am seeking: One-night stands, Short-term relationship with the right person. Not looking for online only.

What I can offer: I'll do anything, and generally everything, to ensure a pleasurable experience.

I am snipped—NO SWIMMERS—so there's no worry about unintended consequences!

I am very oral—I love to give—and I will promise you multiple climaxes if you open yourself up to my technique!

I own my own, very private, home and am available just about 24/7. I'm not looking to go outside in public with a married woman or to travel to your home: I will host and I am VERY DISCREET!

I love to kiss, and I like kissing every part of a woman's body. I like to nibble, lick, and stroke.

Soft, hard, fast, or slow: you can dictate what you want and I aim to please.

I am funny, drug and disease free, very clean, talkative, and friendly.

No pain: all pleasure!

I guarantee you will want to return!

I promise to never bother or harass you in any way after.

Edward added that last line as a final plea to show that he was safe. If there was one thing he had learned, it was that women liked dangerous men, but only in theory. No one wanted to be stalked. Women wanted attention, but they valued their privacy too. This last line about respecting boundaries was sure to earn him some points.

He hit the DONE button on the profile page and angled the laptop's camera to take a headshot. When his reflection came into view on the screen in front of him, he jumped slightly. He needed a shower. His sleep schedule had been off the past week—too many late nights and too little rejuvenating sleep had made an impact on his skin, which looked sallow. His face had the slight appearance of a slowly deflating balloon: puffy yet concave in all the wrong places. He rubbed both of his palms along his cheeks, making a sandpaper sound; there was a streak of brown dirt smeared on his temple. He stretched his arms in an exaggerated yawn, looked around the room, and stood up from the desk chair.

In the first-floor bathroom, the steam from the piping hot shower filled the tiny space like fog from a 1950s horror movie, making it nearly impossible to see clearly. Edward peeled the dingy denim and stained t-shirt from his damp body and dumped them in a pile at the edge of the tub. The clothes would serve as a makeshift foot towel in the bathmat's recent absence. He pushed his faded red gingham boxers to his ankles and stepped out of them gingerly, being careful not to trip over them. He had been wearing them so long, the long since dried bodily fluids had hardened stiffly, creating a bizarre picnic table origami shape on the floor.

Edward stepped into the volcanic spray, feeling it singe his skin like he was being branded. His body acclimated to the high temperature quickly, and he turned his face to meet the water and savored its machine gun massage on his cheeks and neck. He breathed deeply and the moist air swam around his lungs as he titled his head and watched the dirty water swirl around his feet and down the drain.

Faintly in the distance, he heard the high-pitched squeal of his cell phone's ringtone. He had plugged his phone into the charger in the kitchen that morning. It had been dead when he tried to use it when the sun just started to streak the sky and casted shadows on his lumpy furniture and dark rug, making them look wet.

When the water started to turn cold, Edward turned off the shower, reached his arm tentatively around the plastic curtain, and pawed his hands along the wall, feeling for a towel. When his fingertips felt terrycloth, he grabbed it and furiously scrubbed his body dry before any nips of cold air reached his skin. He stepped onto his dirty shirt and marched in place a few times to dry the bottoms of his feet, then wiped his hand across the clouded mirror in preparation for shaving.

When Edward was twelve, his father stood behind him in a bathroom very similar to this one. He placed his beefy hands covered in coarse, black hair onto Edward's shoulders and squeezed. "It's time you learned to shave, Eddie," he said. "And not like a woman. Real men use a straight razor. It takes a steady hand, but the effort is worth it. The shave is closer."

Edward gulped. He had watched his father shave innumerable times, seen the silver blade slide slickly along the sides of his neck, caressing his father's Adam's apple, all the while hinting at the pain and malfeasance one aggressive dip of the shaft could make at a moment's notice.

"First, prepare your skin with shaving cream," his father instructed. "Something thick, high quality. Now stretch the skin." He moved his hands up, affixing one on the bottom of Edward's jaw, pulling the skin taut. He grabbed the straight razor with his free hand and pantomimed shaving downward at a forty-five-degree angle, starting at Edward's ear and ending where his other thumb rested. "Always shave with the grain to begin, not against."

Edward had watched his father's movements carefully in the mirror, moving only his eyes as he feared any bodily shift would result in a nick in his jugular and therefore, certain death. His father repositioned his hand and turned the blade upward, laying its cold metal against Edward's hot cheek. "Go back over the area the other way, against the growth, the second time around."

It was more than four decades later, and he could still see his father's reflection in the mirror in front of him; he could make out the terror in his own pubescent face, see the beads of sweat dotting his adolescent forehead. Edward picked up the straight razor he had left to dry in the glass measuring cup on the bathroom sink. It still smelled of the rubbing alcohol he had dipped it in to disinfect it last night.

He delicately wiped shaving cream over his cheeks and chin, gingerly unfolded the razor, and positioned the shiny blade against his cheekbone. *"Always move the blade evenly, Eddie,"* he said to his reflection, mimicking his father's somber baritone. *"You must hold the razor at a slightly steeper angle along the cheekbone and above the lip if you want to maintain a sleek and smooth appearance."*

He had performed this dance so often, he could do it in his sleep. The blade glided and glinted as Edward brought it up and down his face and neck like he was spreading warm butter on toast. When he was done, he splashed his face generously, patted it dry, dressed, and did his best to take a series of devilish but trustworthy-looking selfies.

After a dinner of homemade chicken paprikash over egg noodles (Edward loved Hungarian food—he had picked up quite a few recipes in his travels and only wished he had someone to share his passion for cooking with), it was time to check the DTF website. Sure enough, one lone message had been added to his mailbox. In the subject line was only one word: *Hi.* There was no text in the message itself; just a single photograph. In it, a woman in her mid-thirties posed in a bright yellow strapless bikini, her hand planted firmly on her hip while the other arm pointed mysteriously off camera, out of frame. She was of average height with short, curly brown hair, blue eyes, and pinkish pale skin. She half-smiled, half-smirked into the camera, her small eyes frozen in a partial squint.

Smallish tits, Edward thought. Athletic thighs with the kind of bulk in them that once developed, no amount of diet or exercise could erase. *Meaty*, thought Edward. Her stomach was flat, but she was a meaty girl. Edward preferred his women thin, skinny even. He'd trade big tits for chicken legs any day. Still, one response was better than none. The best recipes are the ones made with unusual ingredients. Her screen name was BunnyGirl78. *Hippity-hop*, Edward chuckled. He composed his response.

Hello there!

You, yes YOU, made me join this site and pay the fees to send messages.

My photo should be up in my profile now. It's recent. Is yours a recent photo? I like it.

I'm a certified hypnotherapist and run my business out of my home. That's why I don't meet women at their homes—great excuse if we're ever caught here—you can say you're having a hypnosis session.

If you read my entire profile, know that I do and promise exactly what it says. I aim to rock your world and you rock mine.

I have clean hygiene, trimmed body hair, good breath, all my teeth. I am funny, passionate, romantic, and give lots of foreplay. I'm very very very very oral.

Most of all, I'm 1000% DISCREET!

See, I want YOU.

Satisfaction guaranteed. And no strings attached: I assure you.

Edward

Edward hit the SEND button and pushed his shoulders back in his chair. His spine emitted a dry crack when he lifted his chin toward the ceiling to stretch. He wondered what Bunny was looking for. He cursed himself for sounding too eager in his response—he hadn't even read the woman's profile before writing back. He clicked her screen name at the top of the message.

Location:	Worcester metro area
Height:	5'5"
Weight:	145
Ethnicity:	Caucasian
Age:	39

He had miscalculated her age—she was much older than mid-thirties. Women were so vain about their age and weight: he knew whatever numbers they listed had been tinkered and trimmed by a few years and a good ten pounds. More than likely, she was in her early forties and pushing the 160-pound mark, and he wouldn't be surprised to learn that the bikini photo was a couple of years old. Still, she was local, and she wasn't completely unattractive. There might be a few rides left in her rodeo.

Gender:	Female
Status:	Attached female seeking males
Smoking habits:	Never
Limits:	Undecided
Encounters I am seeking:	Let's play it by ear

What I can offer: Friendship, excitement, discretion, and fun. I'm an easy-going gal who'll try anything once, as long as it feels good. ;)

Edward scratched his face. More often than not, his five o'clock shadow would just begin to creep along his jawline at seven p.m. Even after daily shaving with a straight razor, he was a hairy guy. He figured he shouldn't complain: most men his age had trouble keeping their hair. He just had to keep up with his.

My little Playboy Bunny will try anything once, huh? he thought. He caressed his cheek slowly with the back of his hand. *Well, Bunny, we'll just see about that.* His mind wandered at the possibilities, and he shut his laptop, switched off the desk lamp, and made his way down to the basement.

The next morning, he checked his account activity. There were no responses in his inbox. Perhaps she hadn't seen his message yet. He flipped through the appointment book on the corner of the desk: nothing on tap for another week and a half. A decade ago, Edward had gone back to school and used his nest egg to open his own hypnotherapy business. He liked working from home and setting his own schedule, and of course, the tax write-off for the home office was a nice perk.

Most of his clients were women from town: middle-aged, married women who had drowned themselves in Kit Kats, cigarettes, or booze and had promised their husbands they'd clean up their acts. Edward preferred the self-improvement junkies, though: occasionally, a client on a quest to reinvent him or herself "just for the sake of loving myself more" (or whatever new age mantra was the most nauseating at the time) would book his services. Those clients always reminded him of Dorothy at the end of *The Wizard of Oz*: all of them clicking their sparkly heels together, squeezing their eyes closed while he spoke in his low, soothing voice, believing that if they just wanted it badly enough, they could make anything happen.

He could use a little of their optimism. When he first debated signing up the for DTF site, he had been wary. Female registrants paid nothing to join and exchange messages with others, but men had to pay: nearly sixty dollars for the profile and five dollars to send each message. He could receive messages for free, but how could he attract women without participating in a conversation?

Of course, there was that old adage: in order to make money, you had to spend money. And Edward needed it to rain soon; he was getting bored. He sent a second message to Bunny, paying the additional messaging fee to receive a read receipt.

O.K. Not trying to look desperate as I am not. I just like your photo and profile more than any other on here. Sure, there are some hot 20-30-year-olds but I am looking for a situation just like yours.

I sent you an email yesterday and nothing?
Are you worried someone will see you?

I operate a hypnosis business out of my home. You know, for quitting smoking and such. People are always coming and going, so my neighbors won't suspect a thing.

I will put my car out and let you park in the garage.
I am very discreet. Trust me-- you won't be disappointed.
:) Edward

This last part made him grimace a bit. He hated when people added emojis to emails. He knew he was no Ernest Hemingway, but with the proliferation of social media, expressing one's tone using carefully chosen diction seemed like a lost art. People today had to add illustrations to get their points across; it seemed crass and lazy. And yet, while the habit irritated him to no end, he knew he had to do it to appear like a regular, approachable guy. It seemed like adding a silly happy face to the end of a sentence could soften anything. *Hey, Bunny, you flat-chested cow: how'd ya like to come for drinks at my place so I can strangle you in the kitchen and use your limp, unconscious body as a blow-up doll? Smiley face with a tongue sticking out!* He laughed to himself, plugged in his laptop for charging, and vowed not to check it again until the next day. It was a beautiful summer day, and he had plenty of household chores to take care of that would keep him busy.

When Edward's father placed the shiny metal blade on his son's cheek, it had taken Edward every bit of courage not to flinch. He had been on the precipice of adolescence, just a few months shy of becoming a real teenager, and his father's hands had seemed like baseball gloves: large and tanned and scarred from daily use. They were hands that shook him, hard, by the shoulders whenever Edward did something stupid, which, in those days, was often. Not securing the lid on the garbage can so that a raccoon could dump their trash all over the sidewalk, exposing their business to the whole neighborhood. Adding too much ketchup to his hot dog at the Sox game so that it dribbled out the end, staining his new t-shirt and leaving him to look like an embarrassing slob. The list seemed endless.

"You have to tilt the blade just a bit," his father explained. "Or the razor will rip any stubble, encouraging ingrown hairs and negating the whole point of the straight razor." He adjusted the angle of the sheath by the tiniest margin, catching the glint of the vanity light in its reflection and temporarily blinding Edward. When his vision cleared, he placed his hands over his father's, trying to mimic his exact pose. His father slid his hands away, leaving Edward holding the razor on his own.

Edward stared at his reflection in the horizontal wipe marks in the fog of the mirror. He was holding the razor exactly the same way as on the day his father taught him to shave. He had held it this way almost every day for the past forty-four years; the topography of his face had stayed pretty constant since his early twenties, and he could shave with his eyes closed now if he really wanted. "Tilt the blade or you'll rip the stubble. Make the angle too steep and you'll cut your skin," he recited out loud, keeping his eyes locked on his own wide pupils. The blade swiped up and down, a maestro's baton conducting a symphony with ease.

When his face was clean and dry, he allowed himself to check his DTF account. It had been more than twenty-four hours since his last message: surely, she'd read at least one of them by now.

There was nothing in his mailbox, but what irritated Edward even more was that he'd received a read receipt: she had read his message but had simply chosen not to respond. That fickle bitch: who did she think she was, teasing his cock, then retreating into the silent treatment? He opened and closed his hands into fists, alternately tensing and releasing tension to calm himself. It was a trick he taught his clients who had sought his services for anger management purposes. He closed his eyes and thought of Mrs. Karney.

She had been a client who had visited his office in the hopes of overcoming claustrophobia, and Edward had hated her immediately. Mrs. Karney had been so diffident in her posture, so diminutive and weak-looking in every mannerism, that Edward found himself almost becoming physically ill when he spoke to her. For some reason, her submissiveness and lack of shame when blathering on about her stupid fears enraged him—it was as if someone had flicked a switch in his head. In the middle of the third session, just ten minutes into his guided meditation monologue, he leaped from his leatherback swivel chair, grabbed Mrs. Karney by her shoulders, and heaved her into his coat closet, which, luck would have it, was situated just behind her chair. She hadn't seen him coming as her eyes had been closed, and her relaxed state had made her body pliable and soft. When he slammed the door behind her, locking her in darkness, he felt a rush of adrenaline-surged pleasure he hadn't experienced in years. When she began to scream like an animal caught in the teeth of a metal trap, he felt himself become erect, and before opening the door again, he unbuttoned his gabardine dress pants, stroked himself quickly and furiously, and came almost immediately.

Despite seeming to convince Mrs. Karney that his outburst had been part of a planned exposure therapy technique to treat her claustrophobia, Edward knew that such behavior with his clients could not occur again. His business was built on his reputation, and if word should slip that he had the potential to make any of his clients uncomfortable, he'd be ruined. He'd have to take the same approach with Bunny and keep his cool. He dragged one finger along the newly smooth skin above his lip, then began to type.

OK. I sent you a few very long messages. No reply??

You're the reason I paid for this service.

You can always say you are getting hypnosis for one thing or another. I've done quite a few people in town. Hypnosis, that is. ;)

I promise you will not be disappointed. Just try not to fall in love. Ha ha!

You won't regret taking a chance.
Yours, Edward

He sent the message and shut his laptop. For a minute, he stared into space, his mind a jumble of mixed memories and sensations. He would never forget the sound of Mrs. Karney's scream for as long as he lived. He clenched and unfolded his hands twice more for good measure, then walked calmly down to the basement.

Three hours later, he found himself still fixated on Bunny's silence. Why had she written him if she wasn't interested? Was this some sort of ploy by the website's publisher to get him to spend more money? Had he been too late to respond and had she been scooped up by a faster suitor?

He sat in front of his laptop again and pushed open the case, absentmindedly wiping the smudge of dirt his finger left on the right corner.

Hey, you not interested anymore?

I've spent $80.00 to get you.

I CAN'T SAY THIS ENOUGH: I AM DISCREET.

Why won't you answer?
Edward.

He clicked the SEND button, then grabbed the laptop with both hands and threw it sideways toward nothing in particular. Fortunately, it landed on the old green velvet couch Edward had pushed against the wall.

The room was deafeningly quiet for a moment. Edward stood up from his chair quickly—too quickly. The straight razor, which Edward had folded and tucked into his jeans, spilled from his pocket and tumbled onto the hardwood floor, making a loud crack like a pipe hitting a metal pole. It bounced once, then came to rest, slightly ajar, five feet from Edward's toes. He closed his eyes, remembering.

"Eddie, I can't stress this enough: you must *never* use a damaged razor if you want to keep your skin safe and your shaves clean," his father said, replacing his hairy hands on his son's shoulders and meeting his eyes in the mirror. "If you drop the razor before closing it, it will likely get nicked and be damaged. If you close the blade and the hinge is loose or misaligned, it will be damaged. It will dull unevenly and can no longer be used." His double-handed squeeze burrowed through the thin material of Edward's t-shirt, pinching a nerve.

"What if I sharpen it?" Edward asked, his voice sounding tiny and hollow in contrast to his father's.

"Once a razor is damaged, it can't be fixed," his father answered.

"Fuck!" adult Edward screamed, his voice echoing throughout the empty first floor. He closed his eyes and took a deep breath to focus. *Just look what you've done now, Bunny, you rancid bitch!* he thought. *So help me, if we ever meet in person…*

He walked purposefully to the kitchen where he had plugged his cell phone into the outlet next to the stove. He pulled the cord from the phone base and scrolled through his folders until he found his video collection. There, he fingered the fifteen or so videos from the past week and clicked the latest recording. He held the phone in front of him and watched the screen as he made his way back to the study.

In the dim light, a support beam painted gunmetal grey was positioned in the center of the frame. Wrapped around the beam was a skinny woman with stringy, black hair, her arms pulled behind her, her hands tied with rope but mostly hidden by the beam's girth. She was wearing a bright red dress—*too bright, really: a cheap whore's color, but that's what you get for picking up a prostitute, isn't it?* Edward thought—that was dirty and torn in a number of places. Her exposed, bare legs were bent slightly at the knees and straddled the beam so that her ankles were tied together on one side while her butt and upper thighs gripped the slick beam like plastic wrap on the other. She wore no shoes, and the big toe of the foot closest to the camera dug into the dirt floor, half-buried. Mascara, black and oily, dripped and stuck to her cheeks, and a yellowed gingham dishrag was stuffed in her mouth.

Her wet eyes stared up at the camera and she said nothing, only blinked in exhaustion and resignation. As the camera panned closer, however, she began to whimper, then made a weak attempt at a scream, but it was muffled by the rag.

Edward's voice drifted from off-screen. "Tina… that's your name, right? Yes, Tina: you should know before I take the rag out again, I soundproofed this basement a long time ago. You can scream and scream, but no one but me will hear you. So, my advice is save your throat—it may be a while before you get more water or food, especially after the mess you made."

The camera angle bent diagonally as Edward's hand appeared in the frame and reached toward her to remove the gag. A white bathmat covered in smeared urine and feces lay discarded on the floor a foot in front of the support beam.

Edward realigned the camera's gaze and walked closer to the woman. He reached out once more and stroked the skin on her upper arm softly with his index finger. He pushed the tattered edges of her dress aside, revealing the long, bloody cuts on her chest and neck. His finger traced one as it swerved from her clavicle to the swell of her left breast.

"On second thought," Edward's voice said. "Scream as loud as you can." His volume lowered to a sinister whisper. "I want to hear just how afraid you are."

Edward's attention was snatched from the phone's screen by a high-pitched dinging coming from his still-open laptop. He walked to the couch and clicked the touchpad. He had a message in his inbox.

Edward-

So sorry I didn't get back sooner. My phone was running out of juice and I wanted to write you a proper response. However, now that I am typing, I am at a loss for words. This is my first time on a dating site, and I'm not sure what to say.

Are you free for a day drink later on today? I know you said you don't meet women in public, but just for safety reasons, I could meet you in front of the yoga studio—I teach a class there at 3. There's a hip new martini-fusion pub next door. If you're free at 4:30, the Bloody Mary's on me!

Then after, if you're game, maybe we could go to your place and I could put my limberness to some use. ;)

Hope to see you- BunnyGirl78

Edward ran his finger along the skin above his upper lip and glanced at the clock on the wall. It was 3:15. He had just enough time to change and visit the Men's Specialty Store in the upscale plaza in town to buy a new straight razor before heading over to the yoga studio.

A Bloody Mary sounded like the perfect aperitif for what he had in mind for Bunny tonight.

Déjà Vu

Charlie's hand shook when he held the gun. It was heavier, much heavier, than he had imagined it would be. He allowed his fingertip to graze the trigger softly, caressing it like he used to when he played the "Can you feel this?" game with Audrey. As she lay on her back on the living room rug, a brown braided thing his mom had procured during a hippie decor faze when the children were small, Audrey would squeeze her eyes tight, waiting for her brother's delicate tickle or wispy stroke of his hand along the peach fuzz on her cheek or arm or ankle. He could still see her scrunched-up anticipatory face, the thin rolls of skin on her forehead and beneath her eyes. They had played this game ever since Charlie could remember, and even now, as an adult, whenever he felt under stress, he found his fingers unconsciously drifting across the outside of his arm. The sensation of the soft hair on his forearms being lifted ever so slightly combined with the by-proxy heat radiating from his finger seem to penetrate his muscles, vibrate into his bones. It soothed him.

"Come on, Parker," said Carlos, chasing his borderline-threatening encouragement with a swig from a dark green bottle of beer. "Don't pussy out on us now." They were sitting in a circle on the floor of Carlos's basement. Charlie couldn't remember whose idea it had been to play the game; he knew it hadn't been his, but at the time, he'd been more than happy to participate. Lately, the numbness, the black hole he'd felt circling his body since he was a teenager, had placed itself front and center in his waking thoughts more often than not. He'd tried drinking, he'd tried getting high—hell, he'd even done a bump of coke and tossed back a valium or two—but none of it slapped his emotions awake. His soul felt as dry as desert sand. He felt nothing.

Carlos and his girlfriend Maria had come over last week for their group's traditional Sunday night television get-together. Charlie had been dumping tortilla chips into a bowl in the kitchen when Diana traipsed into the room, already slightly hammered at seven o'clock in the evening. She leaned against the counter next to Charlie and held her glass against her cheek. Beads of condensation dribbled down the side and onto her hand and face. "Jess gave me a gun," she said out of nowhere. She closed her eyes and smiled a strange, faraway smile. "Fuckin' belated birthday present, if you can believe that." When she opened her eyes, Charlie could see that the whites were bloodshot; whether from tears or alcohol, he didn't know.

"Hallmark must be revamping their violent sentiments line," Charlie said, selecting a chip from the top of the pile and rubbing it along his lower lip. He loved licking the salt from his mouth. Audrey had loved doing it to her lips, too. It must be genetic.

Diana let the comment hover in the air for a moment, then she lowered her glass onto the countertop next to the chip bowl. "Actually, the thing that pissed me off the most is, I suspect the gun was a last-minute choice. It's still registered in her name, and she says that I'll have to get my license to carry before I can register it in my name, but she works for Smith & Wesson, for Christ's sake. I mean, it's not like I've been dropping hints about how much I wish I owned a firearm or that I have a hankering for shooting up a playground or anything." Diana flashed her devilish grin again. "I mean, *not recently* or anything."

Charlie licked his lip, pulling the brackish grains onto his tongue. Diana had always had a sick and ribald sense of humor; nothing that she said fazed him anymore. "And another piece of the puzzle that is lesbian romantic bliss is placed," he said, resting his palm on her shoulder. "If only I could shatter the plaid shirt ceiling and be a part of your secret cabal."

Diana patted his hand, then reached down and patted his crotch lightly. "Baby, you don't have a ladder tall enough." She replaced her hand on her glass, took a long drink, and shifted gears. "So, when are we going target shooting?"

Charlie laughed. "I know how butch I appear, but do you really think I have experience firing any kind of weapon?" He banged the top of the jar of queso on the counter twice and then unscrewed the lid.

"Well, I have to find *some* use for it," she said. "Any secret desires for holding up a bank?"

"Who's holding up a bank?" said Carlos, sticking his head into the kitchen, then following a moment later with the rest of his body.

"I have a gun now," said Diana. "I need to find a use for it. You volunteering to be the wheelman?"

Carlos grabbed a handful of chips from the bowl. "Nah... I drive like Mr. Magoo." He tossed a chip in his mouth and chewed loudly. For a full twenty seconds, the only sound in the room was crunching. "I have an idea," he said finally. "You guys ever play Russian Roulette?"

Charlie had been leaning into the refrigerator, looking for the sliced pepper jack he'd purchased earlier that day. He grabbed the long plastic container and stood up. "Yeah, man. Old hat. Let's try something less dangerous, like throwing knives at each other's heads blindfolded or tying cement blocks to our feet and going pool hopping." He pulled a box of crackers from a cabinet.

"Seems mildly gangster," said Diana. "I'm in. Five outta six odds. Better than Vegas."

Charlie's phone rang and he checked the number. "It's Jess," he said to Diana, and held the phone out to her.

Diana recoiled from it and whispered, "I'm not here."

"Why is she calling my phone and not yours?" Charlie asked.

"I left my phone at home. Everyone I know will be here tonight. What am I gonna do, surf Instagram all evening, ignoring my friends?" She pushed the still-ringing phone toward Charlie. "Just... please. Can't deal with her tonight."

Charlie answered the phone. "Hey Jess... no, Diana's not here, at least not yet." Diana kicked him softly in the shin. "She's her own gal, but you know that...I'm sure she'll turn up soon, and I'll tell her to call you." Diana rolled her eyes; Charlie mouthed *fuck you, shady girl* back, then ended the call.

The door to the back deck jangled and opened. Corey, Charlie's roommate, was younger than Charlie by at least a decade, and he worked at the local pharmacy as an assistant while he plodded through graduate school part-time. He was still wearing his white coat with the embroidered store name on the lapel. Charlie always found the uniform slightly off-putting, like Corey was a company actor playing the doctor in a musical that ran six nights a week who neglected to take off his costume after the curtain fell. Maria walked into the kitchen just as Corey was entering from the other side; Corey nodded at her, then cast a quick glance over the rest of the crowd. "Am I missing a family meeting?" he asked.

"We were just debating the odds on accidental suicide," said Diana.

"I'm not sure *accidental* is an appropriate term when you choose to put the gun up next to your head voluntarily," Charlie retorted.

Corey snickered and pushed off his shoes, leaving them facedown by the door. "Sounds about right." He walked past the group toward the hallway. "Lemme just change: I'll be right back."

Maria leaned over and kissed Carlos on the cheek. "Be right back. Gotta pee." She turned and walked the same path down the hall that Corey had taken.

A long second passed. "Yes, I know they're fucking," Carlos said, taking a swig of his beer.

Charlie and Diana looked at each other. "Listen..." Charlie began.

Carlos held his hand up. "It's fine. She tires me out most of the time anyway," he said. "Sometimes a man needs to sleep, you know? Let the twenty-something ride that coaster for a while."

Diana raised an eyebrow, but no one said anything. Then, the back door opened again.

"Am I too late?" Sean ducked into the bright fluorescent kitchen lighting from the dark deck. He stretched in an exaggerated manner, making his enormous frame seem to grow and fill the entire room. He pulled out a vape pen. "I brought some Strawberry Cough if anyone's down."

"How high would you have to be to play Russian Roulette?" Diana asked him.

Sean put a finger to his cheek like he was lost in thought. "Hmmm. I'd say pretty goddamn high, wouldn't you? Why?"

Maria returned to the kitchen and walked directly over to the platters of food. She grabbed a slice of cheese and two crackers and made a tiny sandwich. "None of you would have the balls to play that game."

"Yeah, right, and everyone's life is so peachy keen right about now that we'd all be risking so much," said Carlos. He was staring at Maria with a blank expression.

Corey returned to the room, sans uniform. His faded t-shirt sported the insignia of the St. Louis Cardinals. "You still talking about shooting yourselves?"

"Not SHOOTING ourselves," corrected Diana.

"Playing a game of chance. A gun just happens to be involved."

Corey made himself a drink. "Is there a money bet involved as well?"

"How could there be a money bet involved?" Charlie asked. "What, whoever blows their brains out gets the pot? A lot of good it will do them then." Charlie thought back to the piles and piles of fresh flower arrangements and teddy bears his family had received after the accident; his father finally bagged all of the stuffed animals and brought them to the Children's Hospital, thinking they could do some good there, maybe make a sick kid smile, but the woman at the reception desk refused the donation, informing him that the hospital only accepted "new toys." *But they ARE new,* his father had said, genuinely confused. *My daughter never touched them… they were just sent to the house, you know, because she loved bears, but she never… I mean, she wasn't able…*

The bag returned home and stayed in Audrey's room for many months after. Charlie would glance at it when he sneaked into his sister's closed room once a week to smell her pillow. Then one day, the bag was simply gone.

Charlie, Corey, Diana, Carlos, Maria, and Sean made a pact: they'd meet at Carlos' house on Friday night. Diana would bring her gun. Whoever had the balls to play would play. No one would be forced to participate. If nothing else, it was a free country.

The carpet on Carlos' basement floor was scratchy and bright green, like a wide strip of faux grass, the kind of rug someone might put on their three-season porch or patio, even. When Charlie shifted, he felt tiny pin pricks tap the bottoms of his thighs. He looked around the room. Carlos and Maria sat side by side on a black body pillow. Next to them, Corey lay on his back with his legs pulled up, making an unfinished A shape. He held his phone a foot in front of his face; Charlie thought he could make out the screen image of a Reddit feed in the reflected glow on his glasses. To his right, Diana and her girlfriend Jess each sat on a couch cushion, and next to them, Sean sat with his butt plastered to the plastic grass-like floor covering like Charlie while he nervously puffed on a vape pen. Clouds of smoke smelling like piña colada filled the small space.

"You said you wanted to go second, dude," Diana said, resting a hand on her girlfriend's thigh and patting it twice.

Charlie HAD said that, and at the time, he had meant it. The previous day he had spent in a daze, like a zombie wandering aimlessly around his workplace. Everything, he realized, in the company's office was beige. Beige walls, beige carpets. The counter at reception was beige. In the staff break room, someone had painted the wooden cabinet fronts a pale beige color, and someone had procured one of those colored coffeemakers, the kind you could make espresso or lattes in—complete with the steamed milk pitcher—and even that was not black or stainless steel, but beige. Charlie dribbled café au lait on his tie, and as he scrubbed the stain in the men's room, he realized, he too, was mostly beige. Grey pants, but a beige dress shirt and a pale grey and beige tie. The black hole swallowing him up had already sucked most of the creativity and excitement from his soul; all that was left was an empty frame. Shooting himself seemed like a rational and positive choice: if he missed, he was sure to be invigorated with a new-found sense of life and vigor. If he succeeded... well, there wasn't much left for Charlie to miss.

Carlos, always the obnoxious alpha male, insisted on going first. He raised the gun to his head and rested the nuzzle against the tightly-cropped black hair that curved slightly around the top of his ear. He began to take deep, quick, exaggerated breaths like he was preparing for a strongman to sock him in the stomach while holding a roll of quarters. Everyone watched. No one said anything. In fact, that was the strangest part, now that Charlie thought back: no one said, "Hey, this is stupid: don't do it," or, "Carlos, are you sure?" They had all watched Jess load the revolver with one bullet, spin the chamber, and cock the trigger. They had all known that two seconds later, they could be watching Carlos's brains drift slowly down the faux oak paneling like one of those sticky plastic wall climbers. They didn't care. Charlie looked from friend to friend. No one was covering their eyes or looking down; only Carlos closed his eyes.

"Well, here we go, bitches," he said. He pulled the trigger. Everything was completely silent until the empty click rang out; then, everyone exhaled audibly at once. Carlos began to laugh. "Holy shit, that was scary." He wiped his forehead with the back of the hand that wasn't holding the gun. "Fuuuuck. Scary as shit." He unhooked his fingers and held the gun by the barrel, then leaned over and thrust the handle in my direction. "Your turn, Parker."

Charlie's last name wasn't Parker. It was Petrone, like the tequila but with an "e" at the end. In college, he had gone through a jazz faze that outlasted its welcome among his friends, and so they plopped the moniker onto him and it had stuck for over a decade. Even at weddings and funerals, when he was introduced to faraway family members by one of the group, he was Charlie Parker. The bird trapped in a cage. Charlie took the gun from Carlos. It was heavier than he had imagined it would be. He turned it over and over, stroked his fingertip gently along the trigger. This was it: the big decision.

"Come on, Parker," said Carlos, chasing his borderline-threatening encouragement with a swig from a dark green bottle of beer. "Don't pussy out on us now."

Charlie surveyed the rest of the group. All of them

were staring at him, wide-eyed and silent. Even Corey had sat up again, pushing his long legs into a pretzel-like formation and cradling his phone in his lap.

"Any last words?" asked Jess.

Charlie thought for a moment. "I guess I'd like to say that I wish I had a time machine, you know? Never did meet that one special person who really knew me; I always made safe career choices when I could have risked and won a lucrative payoff or two. I have a nice house, and a steady job, and decent lays on a regular basis… but I am miserable. I wish I could go back to my twenties and redo them." He smiled. That was the lamest speech he could have given, but hell, it was impromptu and it was the truth. He didn't have a time machine. He had made his bed and the thought of having to lie in it—for the next fifty or so odd years—was terrifying and sad.

He put the muzzle to his forehead and closed his eyes.

"No, no!" he heard Diana scream. "You'll miss and be a vegetable for the rest of your life. Through your mouth, dude. Pointing up to your brain."

Charlie opened his eyes and stared at Diana. She shrugged. "*Dateline*, dude. Blocks of repeats are on late at night. I have trouble sleeping."

"No wonder, with that bedtime entertainment," quipped Sean.

Charlie opened his mouth and turned the muzzle of the gun slightly so that he could stick it up against the roof of his mouth. It was definitely firing toward the meat of the grey matter now, he thought. Maybe this meant there would be less mess: you know, all the scrambled brains just blown up against the skull, nice and contained. Charlie would be dead, but shaken baby dead. Tidy.

He surveyed the room one last time. Carlos, Maria, Corey. Sean. Jess and Diana. They'd see to it that his body got to where it was supposed to go. They'd make sure to retrieve his personal items from his beige cubicle at work. He shut his eyes, took a deep breath, and squeezed the trigger as hard as he could.

An empty, hollow click. Charlie flinched but smiled. He'd escaped.

He didn't open his eyes, but he heard Carlos's voice loud and clear. "Oooo shit, dude. The bird flies the coop this time, dawg. High five!"

Later that night, as he lay in bed, staring at the television, watching re-runs of *The Golden Girls* on cable, he wondered, why didn't he feel any different? Where was this new lease on life that such a violent brush with death was supposed to provide? Where was the rush of euphoria, or adrenaline, even, that came with escaping the reaping? He felt nothing, and as a matter of fact, the emptiness he had been surrounded by so frequently these past months had multiplied exponentially. He didn't remember even bothering to say goodbye when he left Carlos's house. Just a quick wave, a retying of his sneakers, a snatch of his car keys, and he was out. He didn't even wait to see who had lost at Russian Roulette. He was sure Corey would tell him when he got home.

Speaking of which: where was Corey? Charlie checked the clock on his nightstand. 2:30. Charlie knew his roommate had to work the early shift that day: it was Saturday. Maybe he had crashed at Carlos's house, but that seemed unlikely with the triangular entanglement Maria had woven between the three of them. Of course, there was always the possibility…

Charlie dug out his cell phone from the nightstand drawer—he always kept it close in the event of an emergency, but in a drawer to prevent himself from making semiconscious beer-soaked calls—and hit "Favorites," then slid down to Diana's number. She would know where Corey might be.

The phone rang three times. Finally, a very groggy-sounding Diana picked up. "Hello?"

"Hey, D, it's me," Charlie said, trying to whisper. He wasn't sure why he was lowering his voice, exactly, since no one was home at his house, but who knew how high she set the volume of her phone. "Hey, what happened tonight, after I left?"

There was no noise on the other end of the phone except some heavy breathing and a snort. It sounded like Diana was still sleeping. A lot of women he knew did that—answer the phone in their sleep—he didn't know if it was a skill or an inability to shut the hell up sometimes.

"Diana, wake up. Diana, did anyone lose at Roulette? I have to know," Charlie said.

A few long inhales and exhales and a mumble or two. Then, Diana said, more clearly, "Parker? Charlie Parker?"

"Yes, yes, it's me," Charlie said. "Can you tell me? I'm dying to know what happened."

"Oh, ummmm hmmm. Poor guy. Messy too," she said, then broke out into heavy, full-bodied snores. Charlie hung up the phone.

A guy. So, it couldn't have been Maria or Jess, and obviously, it wasn't Diana. That left Corey and Sean, since Carlos had gone first. Charlie scratched his head and turned up the volume on the television. Blanche's younger brother was trying like hell to convince his sister he was gay. He'd seen this episode at least twenty times and it always frustrated him. If someone reveals a personal truth to another person, shouldn't the recipient just acknowledge and accept it, not fight like hell to disprove it? He fumbled with the remote and clicked OFF.

He hated plot holes.

When his alarm went off at nine, Charlie turned on the coffee to brew and jumped immediately into the shower; his head was killing him, although he didn't remember drinking too much at Carlos's house. He must be dehydrated. He stood under the tepid water, letting the spray's aggressive pressure swish the hair back and forth on his scalp and massage his neck. He even opened his mouth and drank some of the water and allowed himself to stay much longer than he would have had Corey been home. With only a 50-gallon tank, they easily ran out of hot water if one or the other got greedy.

When he was clean and dressed—grey t-shirt and dark grey khakis—Charlie poured himself a tall cup of coffee and dumped a generous amount of sugar into it. He popped three Advil into his mouth, chased them down his throat, and opened the refrigerator for something to eat. There was a half sleeve of pepper jack cheese left, as well as a half jar of queso. On top of the microwave, Charlie spied a bakery box full of croissants. He didn't remember buying them, but even if Corey was saving them for a special event, he wouldn't miss one. As Charlie crammed the last half of the one he'd procured into his mouth, his roommate keyed himself into the back door.

"Corey!" Charlie exclaimed. "Hey, I was worried about you. You didn't come home last night and you have work this morning, right?"

Corey took off his glasses and rummaged through the kitchen's junk drawer for a cleaning cloth. As he rubbed them, he said, "I called in sick this morning—I called the manager directly. I have a few days off, so don't worry."

"But you're okay, right?" Charlie asked.

"Yeah, yeah, I'm alright. Just one of those stupid party mistakes that haunt you the rest of your life… no biggie, right?" The sarcastic words dripped out of his mouth, making it sag and pucker, like he was trying his very best not to cry.

"Listen, I gotta go lay down. I've been up most of the night."

Charlie thought for a moment. Corey replaced the cleaning cloth in the drawer and began to walk toward the hallway. Before he reached the threshold, Charlie said, "So, Sean, huh?"

Corey turned around. "What about him?"

Charlie waved his hands to indicate there was a story to be told. When Corey didn't budge, he said, "He's the one? I mean... Diana said it was messy. I'm sorry I took off early and didn't help you guys."

Corey stared at him a long time. His face was very serious. "Yeah, that's okay. It got done, and that's all the matters, right?" He walked down the hall to his room.

"So, you'll be here for group night tomorrow, right?" Charlie yelled at his back. Corey shut his door without a response.

Charlie's phone rang. He looked at the number; it was Jess. Without thinking, he answered. "Hey Jess... no, Diana's not here, at least not yet." As he said the words, he felt a weird sense of déjà vu. "She's her own gal," he continued, "but you know that." The feeling was getting stronger. Jess was saying something, but her voice seemed far away, and Charlie couldn't hear her. "I'll tell her to call you," he said, and clicked END on his screen. Without knowing why, he mouthed *fuck you, shady girl*.

His headache was getting worse. Writing it off as a bad hangover, Charlie climbed back into bed and went to sleep. It was the weekend. He could afford to be listless and alone for a day.

He awoke confused, unaware of the time or why he was in bed with all of his clothes on. He grabbed his phone from the nightstand. 7:00. The sun was just beginning to set outside of his window and everything in his room looked muted, like he was caught in a portrait and the photographer's soft-focus filter had been draped over everything. When he turned over, he jumped to discover there was someone else in the room. She walked slowly over to his bed and climbed on top of the covers, lying on her side to meet his face.

"Audrey?" Charlie said. "What are you doing here?" He knew he must be dreaming, but the dream seemed so real... and besides, he hadn't seen his twin sister in nearly twenty years. She smiled at him, and the two just lay side by side, facing one another, searching each other's faces. "Do you remember *Can you feel this*?" she asked, still smiling. "Sometimes you'd tickle me so hard, I'd swear I was going to pee myself!" She laughed, one of her big Audrey laughs, where she tilted her head back and forth, squinted her eyes, and raised a hand instinctively to cover her mouth. She was always self-conscious about her smile, having worn much of the enamel off from grinding and heavy-handed brushing. When she had inquired about bleaching them, the dentist told her it was a loss cause: there wasn't enough enamel left to lighten. The yellow she saw was the underlayer, the dentin, glowing through.

Charlie had loved her smile, though. Although they could not have been more opposite in looks, they had one thing in common: both of them had a diastema, a noticeable space between their two front teeth, and neither of them had tried to fix it with braces. Looking at Audrey's smile was like looking at a piece of himself out in the world. It made him feel tethered. Secure.

But Audrey wasn't in the world. She had died in that car accident when they were sixteen. Three girls went joyriding on a sunny April afternoon. One of their boyfriends had decided to be the driver, squishing two of the girls in the back seat. It was a combination of high speed, driver inexperience, and the bad luck of an old oak tree planted on the tree belt right along the steepest part of the curve that did them in. Charlie wasn't even allowed to see Audrey's body in the morgue, and the services had been closed casket. For years, he swore he saw his sister everywhere: driving in a car next to him on the highway, three notches ahead of him in line at the bank, a passing face in his age range and location on Tinder. Even now, he spotted her from time to time. His very own Where's Waldo? game.

She reached over and pulled the covers down from his arm. "Close your eyes," she said, and Charlie obeyed. He felt the delicate brush of her fingertips drift from his wrist to his shoulder and then back down again, and he felt the goosebumps appear and laughed. She leaned down and kissed his cheek, then whispered ever so softly, "I hate plot holes, too. Fix them."

Charlie opened his eyes. Audrey was gone.

The next evening, Charlie pulled from the cabinet a bag of tortilla chips and a box of crackers. He poured the chips into a bowl and the crackers onto a small platter. He thought he had a log of goat cheese somewhere in the refrigerator; he could slice that up and offer it with the pepper jack and crackers. He might have an open jar of queso somewhere, but salsa would do in a pinch.

Diana traipsed into the room, already slightly hammered. Charlie glanced at the clock on the stove. It was seven o'clock in the evening. Diana leaned against the counter next to Charlie and held her glass against her cheek. Beads of condensation dribbled down the side and onto her hand and face. "Jess gave me a gun," she said out of nowhere. She closed her eyes and smiled a strange, faraway smile. "Fuckin' belated birthday present, if you can believe that."

The déjà vu feeling washed over him again, only this time, it shook him to his core. He felt a wave of nausea undulate through his abdomen, then he grabbed Diana by the shoulder and shook her.

"Why the FUCK would you need a gun?" he yelled. "You've never expressed ANY interest in hunting or going target shooting. Why the hell would you keep a gun?"

Diana let the comment hover in the air for a moment, then she lowered her glass onto the countertop next to the chip bowl. "I didn't realize you were so anti-gun: I apologize, okay? No more gun talk." She paused. "Although I've always had a secret desire to hold up a bank." She smiled.

"Who's holding up a bank?" said Carlos, sticking his head into the kitchen, then following a moment later with the rest of his body.

"I have a gun now," said Diana. "I need to find a use for it. You volunteering to be the wheelman?"

Carlos grabbed a handful of chips from the bowl. "Nah... I drive like Mr. Magoo." He tossed a chip in his mouth and chewed loudly. For a full twenty seconds, the only sound in the room was crunching. "I have an idea," he said finally. "You guys ever play Russian Roulette?"

Charlie leaned into the refrigerator, pretending to look for the goat cheese and sliced pepper jack. He was really using the distraction to stall as he breathed the frigid air in deep. The room was spinning. He counted to ten slowly. He was not going to vomit. He was not going to vomit.

"You need any help, Charlie?" Diana asked. Charlie pulled out the ingredients and closed the refrigerator door. "Are you okay?" she asked him. He ignored her and arranged the cheese on the serving plate.

fuck you, shady girl… fuck you, shady girl

The door to the back deck jangled and opened and Corey walked in. Maria walked into the kitchen just as Corey was entering from the other side; Corey nodded at her, then cast a quick glance over the rest of the crowd. "Am I missing a family meeting?" he asked.

"We were just talking about Russian Roulette," said Diana. "Ever play?"

Sean walked into the kitchen as well. "I brought some Strawberry Cough if anyone's down." He held a vape pen in his hand.

Maria grabbed a slice of cheese and two crackers and made a tiny sandwich. "None of you would have the balls to play that game."

"Yeah right, and everyone's life is so peachy keen right about now that we'd all be risking so much," said Carlos. He was staring at Maria with a blank expression.

"So, you're seriously talking about shooting yourselves?" Corey asked.

"Not SHOOTING ourselves," corrected Diana. "Playing a game of chance. A gun just happens to be involved."

Corey made himself a drink. "Is there a money bet involved?"

"How could there be a cash prize involved?!" Charlie screamed at the top of his lungs. "What you're talking about doesn't even make sense! We're going to take turns flipping a coin to see who gets to die? Have you lost your fucking minds?" He grabbed the serving plate of cheese and smashed it against the wall, shattered it and spilling cheese and porcelain everywhere. Everything was repeating. Nothing made sense to him anymore. He was going insane.

Without apologizing for his outburst or attempting to clean the mess he'd made, Charlie turned and walked down the hall to his bedroom. He walked inside and shut the door.

When Charlie woke, the television was still on. He was groggy, but he could make out a line or two from the sitcom that was playing. *Golden Girls* again. The same episode as last week. Blanche listed all of the reasons why her brother was not gay; her brother disproved each one with a reason why he was. It's hard to take the side of lunacy when someone hits you with rationale, Charlie thought. His phone rang from the drawer in the nightstand where he'd placed it.

It was Diana. "D, did you end up playing Roulette? What happened? I have to know," Charlie said.

A few long inhales and exhales and a mumble or two. Charlie felt the déjà vu creeping up his spine again.

"Diana! Did anyone shoot themselves?" he asked.

Diana mumbled. "Parker? Charlie Parker?"

"Yes—yes, it's me," Charlie said. "Can you tell me? I'm dying to know what happened."

There was a pause. Then, Diana's voice came through the phone as clear as a bell. "Yes. Parker. Charlie Parker."

She hung up the phone.

Nothing made sense. Was he going insane? Charlie thought, *Is this how people go crazy, a little bit at a time, and then, POW! full-blown loony tunes?* He switched off the television and turned on the nightstand lamp. When he did, Audrey was beside him again. At first, she said nothing, just laid the tip of her index finger on her brother's cheek and let it sail lightly downward toward his Adam's apple.

Charlie started to cry. "Audrey, what is going on? Have I lost my mind? Please tell me."

She looked at him with a serious expression for a long moment, then grabbed his hand. "C'mere. You should see something."

Charlie climbed out of bed and followed his sister down the hallway. "Where are we going?" he asked.

She put her finger to her lips. "Shhhhh. You'll see."

They continued to walk into the kitchen, and Audrey turned right and opened the door to the cellar. "What are we going to the basement for?" Charlie asked. "It's just a dirt floor with the water heater and washing machine."

Audrey said nothing but continued to lead him down the stairs. When they had reached the bottom, Charlie spun quickly in all directions. This wasn't his basement. It was Carlos's basement. "What… what are… how are we here?" Charlie asked. "I don't—I don't—I feel like I'm getting worse."

"Stand here," Audrey said, holding him back against the wall behind the couch. "And just watch. Are you ready?"

Charlie took a deep breath. He nodded his head. "Yeah. Okay."

The lights brightened in the basement room, and the seven friends sat in a circle-like formation on the floor despite there being a perfectly good couch and loveseat pair for them to use. Carlos and Maria shared a long, black body pillow. Corey sat on the artificial turf-like rug, and next to him, Sean, too, sat on the rug, but Jess and Diana had pulled cushions from the couch onto the floor for their seats. In the last part of the circle was Charlie.

Charlie stood silent next to Audrey, watching himself. Was he having an out-of-body experience? He felt self-conscious and fascinated at the same time.

Carlos handed Charlie the gun.

"Any last words?" asked Jess.

Charlie's face scrunched in a pensive expression, and then he spoke. "I guess I'd like to say that I wish I had a time machine, you know? Never did meet that one special person who really knew me, I always made safe career choices when I could have risked and won a lucrative payoff or two. I have a nice house, and a steady job, and decent lays on a regular basis… but I am miserable. I wish I could go back to my twenties and redo them." A smile crept across his face, one that those who knew him would recognize as a mask, a fraud. He put the muzzle to his forehead and closed his eyes.

"No, no!" Diana screamed. "You'll miss and be a vegetable for the rest of your life. Through your mouth, dude. Pointing up to your brain."

Charlie opened his eyes and stared at Diana. She shrugged. "*Dateline*, dude. Blocks of repeats are on late at night. I have trouble sleeping."

"No wonder, with that bedtime entertainment," quipped Sean.

Charlie opened his mouth and turned the muzzle of the gun slightly so that he could stick it up against the roof of his mouth. He opened his eyes and looked around the room one last time. Then he shut his eyes again, took a deep breath, and squeezed the trigger as hard as he could.

There was a loud bang, like a firecracker. Charlie's body flinched and a red mass shot from the backside of his head. As he watched himself, Charlie's first thought was of a shredded foam mattress topper stained with dark red jelly, but as he looked closer, he could see bits of white bone and other unknown substances. The blast had blown out his left eye, leaving a raw, ragged hole. Most of his hair on his head was gone; most of the top of his head was gone. His arm flopped to the side of his body, his finger still coiled around the trigger guide.

Carlos leaped to his feet. "Oooo shit, dude... shit, shit shit," he began pacing back and forth in front of Charlie's body. "The bird flies the coop this time, dawg." He leaned over and rested his hands on his knees and began to laugh a high-pitched, squealing laugh, the laugh of a person who'd lost touch with reality. "High five? Fucken high-five?!" He began crying hysterically, his whole body shaking. Soon, the rest of the group joined him.

Audrey turned and looked at her brother. "You didn't feel it because you weren't expecting to feel it," Audrey said. "Just like our game."

She paused and grasped her brother's hand in hers. "Now you do."

Audrey's death had been a combination of high speed, driver inexperience, and the bad luck of an old oak tree being right in the line of fire. Just like his sister's, Charlie's death had been choice and it had been chance. And neither sibling had a time machine to undo it.

A Clean Getaway

It was the same dream again. Denny had now had it three times.

She was running down the street. It was a main road from her childhood, one with a park and an ice cream place and her family's dentist's office. Her mother used to take her for ice cream after biannual cleanings, an irony apparent to Denny even as a small child. She wasn't running away from anything or anyone—she was just running, but she couldn't stop. She was naked save for a large beach towel she was clutching tightly around her like a hooded shawl. The towel was stiff and scratchy, like it had been dried outside on the clothesline.

Denny didn't know why this same image kept reappearing while she slept. This last time, Denny could see the towel clearly: it was deep pink with bright yellow stripes, the kind of towel you took to the beach with you specifically because it was easy to spot from the water and was big enough to lay on comfortably. Denny's only reserve about going to the beach was the icky feeling of exposing wet skin to the fine sand, the grains sticking to her like she was a glazed donut rolled in sugar. No matter how many times you brushed that stuck sand, you never got it off, and it irritated her to track sand everywhere until she could step out of a hot shower. She'd find remnants of it in her car, on her kitchen floor, even in her purse, for weeks afterward. She had never considered herself to be OCD, but this was a pet peeve for some reason. Thus, the larger the towel, the better. There was less chance of trace evidence.

She considered this dream as she sat in her beat-up Toyota Corolla in the parking lot of the Stop & Shop on a Wednesday evening. Denny tapped the side of the steering wheel nervously. Droplets of rain dotted the windshield, but she didn't bother turning on the wipers. Parked in an inconspicuous space in the corner of the shopping plaza, she watched a middle-aged man in a drab brown jacket run uncoordinated, one hand flailing wildly on top of his head, toward a maroon mini-van across from her. She wasn't certain if he was trying to keep his hair dry or if his hand had fallen asleep while he shopped. He carried a green reusable grocery bag, the kind she always felt emotionally blackmailed into purchasing at the checkout counter. Denny could see he had bought Pop-Tarts, a gallon jug of orange Hi-C, and two bags of generic cheese puffs. She wondered if he was a meth addict.

Truth be told, she had been much more cognizant of her surroundings over the past three weeks. The nightly news always had been saturated with histrionics, but a month previous, it had hooked its claws into a particularly juicy slab of paranoia-inducing story and refused to let go, giving daily updates even when there was nothing new to report: three local women, all around Denny's age, had disappeared from their homes without a trace. The police suspected foul play, but as far as Denny could tell, they had no leads. Denny tried to scoff it off as a slow news month—more than likely, the women had all gone on vacation and their seeming similarity was a coincidence—but the previous Saturday, when she walked to her car in the mall parking lot, she found herself gripping the can of pepper spray she kept in the bottom of her purse just the same.

Brown Jacket pressed one knee against the side of his driver's side door and fumbled with his keys. *If you're going to go around abducting women and keeping them tied up in your pantry*, she imagined saying to him, *you may want to invest in tinted windows. Or at the very least, pick up something a little more palatable for sustenance.*

She flipped the visor down, opened the lighted mirror

inside, and checked her reflection. She was wearing too much eye make-up: she looked desperate. Denny had placed her phone's music collection on shuffle, and the song had changed to one of those end-of-a-long-night-of-drinking tunes by that Boston Irish punk band that Gene, her ex, the divorce finalized just a month ago, used to call "pirate music." She ran her finger along her lower lash line, a futile attempt to wipe some of the waterproof liner away. Brown Jacket had started up his mini-van and was backing cautiously out of his space.

What the fuck am I doing? she asked her reflection.

The bar where they had agreed to meet was just a few blocks away. The dashboard clock read 7:00. She was supposed to be there at 7:00.

Denny smoothed the neckline of her sweater and checked the backings on her earrings for security. She had chosen to wear jeans and a form-fitting but not tight top, one Gene had given her for her birthday last year—just two weeks before he moved out, as a matter of fact. He had known her favorite color was blue, and it was a beautiful sea glass blue that made her eyes appear as luminescent marbles glowing from her pale skin. Simple pearl stud earrings. The worry ring she had purchased for herself at Christmas to take the place of her wedding ring. And the perfume she always had worn since she and Gene had gotten married. People had always complimented her on her perfume: heck, even strangers approached her to tell her that she "smelled amazing."

What the FUCK am I doing?

She had begun talking to Jason just two weeks ago; she found him on the dating site with the subscription her friends had gifted her last month as a "congratulations on your freedom" present. He was handsome—built like a lumberjack with a broad chest and hulking arm muscles—but it was his quick wit that had convinced her to take the plunge and meet him in person.

He probably wasn't even showing up. She will probably be sitting at that bar for an hour, waiting like a schmuck, wondering how she became so pitiful.

Or maybe he WOULD show up, and despite having seen the handful of photos Denny sent him, he would find her unappealing. Ugly. Old.

Unsexy.

She stared at her reflection again. *You're thirty-seven years old. You're not one hundred and five. Sometimes you have to say, 'Why the fuck not?'* She knew she wouldn't be able to do this in ten years. She wouldn't have been able to do it ten years ago, despite having a firmer body, shinier hair, and moral sovereignty. It was now or never.

Denny took a deep breath, smiled widely in the mirror to check for stray embarrassments, and shut the visor. She put the car into drive and headed toward the bar.

She refused to pause between locking her car and opening the door to Frankie's Pub. She consciously made one fluid movement: click, beep-beep, walk walk walk, swing the arm and pull the handle. If she paused, she would chicken out and go back, or, at the very least, she would start to over-think the situation. She had done all the thinking necessary in the week leading up to this meeting. If she made a fool of herself, well, no one she knew was here to witness it, so who cared, right? She hadn't even told her friends about the meeting. She hadn't wanted to jinx herself.

The bar itself was shaped like a giant letter C and appeared just inside the door to the right; to the left were rows and rows of booths and tables, mostly empty. The lighting was dim, almost orange-tinted, like every lamp had a red scarf draped over it. From Denny's vantage point just inside the foyer, two coffee-colored women leaned toward one another at four o'clock, two bartenders—a slim Asian man and a young, blonde woman—stood still inside of the C, and a lone white man wearing a worn Yankees baseball cap sat at the far end, near eleven o'clock, with his back to the wall. He made eye contact with Denny immediately and flashed a sideways grin.

"Here she is," Jason said loudly. "That's her." He didn't appear to be speaking to anyone in particular, but the male bartender smiled broadly and laughed lightheartedly. Denny paused. He looked different than his photo. Not bad, but different. Better, actually. He hadn't been smiling in any of the pictures they had exchanged. More often than not, he had been dressed in his state trooper uniform in each shot: Jason sitting in the barracks at the close of his shift, Jason standing next to his new patrol car, Jason leaning over to pet his division's newest police dog. Now he was grinning like a cat who had not only eaten the canary but was sitting on a cage full of follow-up birds. His white teeth glowed. "Come on over. Have a drink."

Denny walked to the end of the bar, shimmied out of her coat, and draped it over the back of the barstool. She held out her hand. "Denise."

His smile didn't move. He grabbed her hand and shook it. "Nice to finally meet you, Denise. Now sit down. Stay a while."

She pulled out the stool and climbed onto it, suddenly self-conscious. She felt his eyes as they drifted over her face, chest, waist, and thighs. "Have you been waiting long? I'm sorry I'm a little late."

The male bartender approached them. "Oh no—he's fine. He's been keeping us company." He winked at Denny. "I'm Frank and this is Sue. We love our trooper here. So funny!" He had a heavy accent: Vietnamese, a bit effeminate. He shook a silver shaker for a few seconds and poured its contents evenly within two rocks glasses and put one of the glasses in front of Denny. For a moment, she thought of all of the date rape PSAs she had seen while in college. Wow, you spend your undergrad career thinking every frat boy has a rufee hidden in his championship ring, when all along it's being slipped into drinks by gay bartenders at townie pubs. "You try? It's fruity: you'll like."

Denny stared at the glass. As if reading her mind, Jason grabbed it and put it to his lips, emptying the contents into his throat, then slamming the glass back onto the bar. "She thinks we're trying to poison her, Frank." His face grimaced suddenly, then returned to its happy countenance. "Uggh—quite a kick to that one. What did you put in it?"

Frank smiled coyly and turned his back to us, busying himself at the sink. Denny picked up the remaining glass and drank its contents quickly before she could lose her nerve. It tasted like pineapple and raspberries, but after she swallowed, the unmistakable sting of cheap vodka burned her throat. She looked at Jason. He was still smiling. "So what'll it be, Denise?" he asked.

"Lemondrop martini," she replied.

"Me too," he said, and waved at Sue, who was fixated on the big screen TV on the wall above them.

As Jason ordered their drinks, Denny focused on his hands. They were tanned and slightly worn, like he worked with wood or tools on a semi-regular basis instead of patrolling the interstate for speeders, drug dealers, and murderers. He folded his fingers together and arranged them on his abdomen, then leaned forward like he was her high school guidance counselor about to deliver a life lesson. His smile remained fixed in place. Denny shifted in her seat. She could not stop feeling self-conscious, but she forced herself to keep eye contact with him. Jason's eyes were a deep blue, almost violet, and they were glazed over like he had been drinking for a while before she arrived. She let her eyes graze over his body. He was broad-chested and firm: his arm muscles pushed out insistently from his shirt sleeves and his neck was wide and tan, like his fingers. He wore tight, faded jeans and clean sneakers.

Sue placed the two martinis in front of them. Jason immediately grabbed one and held it in front of her. "So, what are we drinking to?" he asked.

She grabbed the remaining glass and touched it to his. "How about to leaving politics alone for the night and talking about something we agree on?" The topic had been a bottomless source of banter between them in text messages and on the phone: Jason was a staunch conservative and she, a left-leaning moderate.

Jason pulled his glass back dramatically and feigned shock. "What?! And miss the chance to debate the merits of Republicanism with you in person? No way." He lifted the glass to his mouth and drained the glass in three swallows, then replaced the glass in its ring of sweat on the bar.

Denny timidly took a healthy gulp and placed her glass down as well. She spun her chair slightly to the left to face him, brushing her knees against his, and flashed her widest grin. "Bring it on," she purred.

Denny glanced at the television above the bar. *American Horror Story* was starting. That meant it was 10:00. She had to get going—she had work in the morning, and although she'd traded martinis for ice water an hour ago, she was certain she'd have to keep her hands firmly at ten and two on the wheel to avoid swerving on the drive home. Jason, on the other hand, had maintained a steady diet of alcohol and bar Chex Mix the whole time they had talked. Still, his voice remained steady, absent of even a hint of slurring. Denny doubted he'd have any trouble if he were pulled over, anyway, being a cop and all. They had gotten along better than she had anticipated: arguing good-naturedly about politics and culture, his conservative views always colored with a sprinkle of impish teasing so that Denny wondered if it were all an act. At one point in the conversation, Jason had grabbed her thigh insistently to emphasize a point, and it had startled Denny, not because she didn't want him to touch her, but rather because it had sent a jolt of desire through her body. She couldn't stop looking at him. And yet, time had run out.

"Well, it's getting late. I really have to take off," she said apologetically.

Jason looked away, glancing first at the television, then at the arrangement of liquor bottles stacked colorfully behind the bar. For the first time that evening, he looked shy. Neither of them said anything for a full minute. Then, Jason looked at her, flashed a sideways grin, and said, "Wanna get outta here?"

Denny paused. "What did you have in mind?"

"My hotel room," Jason replied, his eyes suddenly darting about the bar as if he had misplaced his keys and was trying to remember where he had last seen them.

"You have a hotel room?" Denny was surprised. If this had been the plan all along, why had it taken him so long to ask her?

He smiled sheepishly and looked at his hands. "Yeah. It's just around the corner. Maybe five minutes from here."

His sudden reticence filled Denny with a sense of power. Here was this incredibly funny, smart, handsome man—a man's man, to boot—who wanted her. Her. *Now or never, right?* she thought. She glanced at the television one last time. Sarah Paulsen was taking a long drag on a cigarette while a mysterious dark shape skulked behind her ominously. Denny met Jason's eyes, which were searching hers expectantly. "Let's go."

He drove so quickly to the hotel, Denny began to wonder if he had changed his mind on the way to his car and was trying to lose her. In order to keep him in her sight, she was driving twenty miles over the speed limit: not a great choice in a semi-impaired state. Between the rain and the darkness, she had difficulty making out his vehicle in the first place—it was some sort of dark sedan or elongated coupe, but Denny couldn't be sure which brand. When they reached the hotel—a swanky one, the kind that had all-night room service and a workout room with shiny ellipticals and Nautilus machines—Denny found the only spot left in the lot and parked. As she climbed out of her car and shut the door, Jason was walking toward her.

He began talking nervously about the hotel's amenities, something about going for a swim before he had driven to the bar, and Denny realized for the first time in hours that she no longer felt apprehensive about being with him. Why wasn't she nervous? Why wasn't she feeling pangs of self-consciousness? She imagined Gene, likely sound asleep in his new apartment on the West Side, an array of take-out menus splayed on his kitchen countertop—he was never one to cook—and a glass of water on the nightstand. When they were first married, they had climbed into bed together naked at the same time every evening. After a few years, they came to bed when they were tired, wearing pajamas, and each only cared about the other being there if sex was a possibility. And now, here she was, following a state trooper who practically oozed primal lust into a strange hotel room, unsure what lay beyond the door. She turned off the ringer of her iPhone and shoved it to the bottom of her purse.

Denny walked quickly alongside Jason as he sauntered past the front desk, took a hard right, and bounded to the end of the first-floor hallway. She had to double her pace to keep up with him, but finally, he stopped at the last door on the right, inserted his key card into the slot, and walked inside.

The room was wide with high ceilings, the far wall almost entirely glass but draped in opaque, ivory curtains. A king-sized bed jutted out from the left wall and faced a broad dresser, desk, and small refrigerator. Jason fished a wallet out of his pocket and dumped it and the room key on the dresser; he began to fumble with his phone awkwardly. Denny tentatively placed her purse on the desk and looked around. The only illumination came from the foyer and bathroom lights, and it gave the room an ethereal, somewhat surreal feeling. It was only then that Denny realized that Jason was swaying slightly, and not purposefully. *Is he drunk? Am I seducing a drunk man? Should I consider this rape? Jesus! Am I a rapist?* Denny thought again of those college PSAs. *Should she ask him if he consents?* She smiled to herself and decided she would wait and see what would happen next. For the first time in a long time, Denny felt grounded while the world spun around her.

Jason shifted from one foot to the other, sliding his finger frantically along his phone's screen. "How about some music?" he asked. "What d'ya wanna hear?" His voice slurred just slightly, and he took his eyes off of the screen and met Denny's. Unwavering, he tapped the screen without looking down, and a grungy, late '90s band began to play. The song was fast, dark, and slightly violent. His jaw relaxed into the smile Denny had watched all evening. She smiled back at him but said nothing.

Suddenly, he reached into his back pocket and pulled out a pack of gum, removing two, then three pieces and shoving them into his mouth. *Is he hiding them from a Nazi invasion?* she thought. "I have a problem with chewing tobacco," he explained. "But this is better, right?" He flashed the toothy grin again at Denny like they were sharing a delicious secret, a gob of minty white peeking out from his left cheek.

Denny took a deep breath and walked toward him. She slowly placed her hands on the sides of his face, feeling the five o'clock shadow that had developed. She took off his baseball cap and placed it delicately on the dresser beside them, then replaced her hand on his cheek. He kept his eyes intent on hers, and she searched them for a minute. Then, trying her very best not to appear like a parent, she grabbed a tissue from the box on the desk and handed it to him. "Spit it out," she commanded. He did as he was told but made no further move.

She stroked his stubble gently again, then leaned in and kissed him softly on the mouth, gently sucking first his lower then his upper lip. He kissed her back, hard, then pushed her away and glided his glance along her face with a serious expression, as if he were trying to commit her every feature to memory. "That hair… it's like the sun is reflecting off of it," he said dreamily. She smiled and, without a word, grabbed the bottom of her shirt, the one Gene had given her for her birthday, and pulled it over her head, spilling her hair messily around her shoulders. Jason didn't move, but his eyes began to caress her body lecherously. He raised his arm above his head and rested his hand on the back of his neck like a cat stretching before dinner. Keeping as much eye contact with him as possible, Denny unbuttoned her jeans, pushed them to the floor, and stepped out of them, pushing her boots off as inawkwardly as she could manage. She felt slightly unsteady on her feet, like a colt, but knew it was the pure rush of excitement that was doing this to her. She liked it. She liked it a lot. The song changed to a slower, more bass-heavy number, and Jason finally moved forward.

He grabbed her face hard, holding her firmly along the jaw, and kissed her, aggressively sticking his tongue in her mouth. She responded by pulling on his shirt, pushing it higher until he broke away and pulled it off over his head. His chest was hard, tanned, and muscular—he was even better looking naked than Denny had imagined all evening. She touched his shoulders and moved her hands to his upper arms, feeling him flex with vanity. He kissed her again, then picked her up by the waist and turned her body so that it was in front of the bed. She broke free of his grasp and let herself fall carefully onto the bed, scooting backward and stretching her body long so he could look at her. "Take off your pants," she instructed, surprised at her own boldness. He smiled broadly, unbuttoned his jeans, and took them and his sneakers off as gracefully as a dancer. He was no longer swaying, but his eyes had glazed over again, and once he stood only in a pair of navy and yellow striped boxer briefs, he was still and simply stared at her on the bed.

She smiled coyly at him and flipped over to show him the lace back of her dark pink panties, then flipped again and positioned her body so that her head was closer to the pillows but her body was in the middle of the bed. Jason grabbed one of her legs and pulled her closer to the edge, then brought her foot up to his face and kissed her ankle. He bent down between her knees and started to kiss the inside of her thigh, keeping his hands firmly on her hipbones. Denny looked up at the ceiling. It had been years—*years*—since someone had wanted her like this. She still didn't feel self-conscious. Not one bit.

Jason latched his fingers inside the sides of her underwear and pulled them down slowly, continuing to kiss her inner thigh. When he had taken them off, he pushed his body up so that he was kneeling between her legs. He pushed his own briefs down and off. In the dim light, Denny could see his eyes darting over her body. He was at once a frightened bird and a hungry animal, and she shivered without meaning to. She reached behind her back, unclasped her bra, and pulled it from her body, and like a starter pistol shot had been fired, he was on her.

He began sucking her neck, her shoulders, then her chest violently, and Denny pushed him off of her and met his eyes. "Do you have a condom?" she asked.

"'Course," he replied, but made no move to find one. Instead, he moved his face further down her body and began sucking at the skin on her stomach and hips. His hands were strong and held her body fixed as her legs shook nervously. She sat up and met his face with her own, kissing him as hard as he had kissed her. He moved his mouth again to her shoulders and sucked hard, and she winced in pain and pushed him away.

"Ow! Fuck, that hurt!" she yelled, louder than she intended. He smiled and began kissing her torso, turned her on her side and kissed her hip and down the outside of her thigh. It tickled and Denny began to laugh. Jason turned her onto her stomach and spread her legs. He began to kiss the back of her thighs, then moved his face and began to suck on the inside of her thighs. Again, Denny winced in pain, kicked him away, and turned over onto her back and sat up.

"Cut it out—I'm serious. That hurts," she stated with as much authority as she could muster. She didn't want him to stop touching her, but she needed him to be gentler. "And how about that condom?"

Jason rolled over and stretched to open the nightstand drawer. His hand emerged with a small, dark grey box and he pulled a single packet out, but instead of putting it on, he began to kiss her again. He kissed her shoulders gently, and Denny began to moan quietly. He moved his head to her breast and sucked her nipple gently, then more forcefully until he began to bite, and on instinct, Denny lashed out and struck his shoulder to make him stop. He moved his head down to between her thighs and began to suck the skin hard there instead, and Denny pulled back and slapped him across the face as hard as she could. Jason straightened his torso in surprise and grinned broadly, and she couldn't help but laugh when she saw his expression. She was a wildcat. She wanted to wrestle. And wrestle they did.

This dance of kissing and pain, of desire and punishment, continued until finally, he reluctantly put on a condom. And another. And another. Denny began to wonder how it was possible that a man who was so intoxicated could fuck her so many ways and so many times. When he finally relented with exhaustion, she glanced over to the digital clock on the nightstand. It was 2:10. She had to leave. She had to be up for work in four hours.

Denny rolled away from Jason and got up from the bed, tossing her jeans and shirt from the floor onto the dresser while searching for her underwear. Jason began to moan like a wounded child. "Where are you going? Don't go. Don't leave," he pleaded.

Jason poured his body over the bed, lying on his stomach, looking up at her like a petulant boy. "That beautiful hair… like sunlight," he muttered wearily. His eyes started to close. Denny caught something pink peeking out from under the bed skirt. Shit, that was just her bra. Where were her panties? She hastily got dressed from the waist up and ran her fingers through her hair. "I have to go—I have work in the morning."

"Stay… just stay and go to work in the morning," he whined. He pushed himself up and climbed out of bed. Drowsily stepping into his boxer briefs and yanking them up to his waist, he grabbed his shirt and pulled it over his head. "Wait: hold on just a sec," he said, and grabbing his jeans from the floor, ran into the bathroom and shut the door. She heard the sound of urine pattering into the toilet bowl.

Denny looked everywhere around the bed but still couldn't find her underwear, so she surrendered and put her jeans back on without them. "I had an amazing time," she said to the closed door, zipping up her boot. She felt like a B-actor in a 1970s porn film. What was she supposed to say? "I had a great time, Jason," she repeated weakly. Her clothing successfully reapplied, sans panties, she grabbed her purse and walked out of the room, shutting the door softly behind her.

She had done it: a one night stand and a clean getaway! This must be how the hip twenty-somethings on all of those crass reality shows must feel after a sexual conquest. Her friends were going to love this story. She made her way across the parking lot, breathing in the starry air and listening to her boot heels click-click-click on the asphalt, the night's stillness racquetballing an echo of every step.

It was when she was a few feet from her car that she heard it: a faint yelling, like a woman calling out from deep inside a closet, her voice muffled by wool jackets. She looked around but could not decipher its origin, until she saw it. Five spaces from her Toyota, a shiny black 1980s vintage vehicle was parked. On the bottom of its trunk lid read the words "Monte Carlo" in red. To the right of the lettering was a woman's hand sticking out from a broken tail light; the hand was twisting frantically and waving up and down.

Denny ran to the car: click-click, click-click, click-click, but realized when she was in front of its trunk that she had no idea what to do. Could she pry the trunk lid open? Maybe she should just call the police. She fished through her bag, wishing she had placed her cell phone in the zippered pocket next to her wallet.

"Oh my god—what the hell is this?" the voice said behind her. She turned to see Jason walking toward her from the direction of the hotel entrance. His eyes were fixed on the hand waving from the hole in the Monte Carlo's trunk.

"I don't know! She just started yelling and I looked over, and—Jesus!" Denny babbled nervously, forgetting that she had just spent the last three hours naked with the man in front of her. Thank goodness he was a police officer. He would know what to do.

Jason walked closer to the car and crouched down slightly. "Ma'am, are you hurt?" He didn't wait for her to respond before he stood back up and walked to the front of the car. He tried the driver's side door, and finding it locked, he continued to walk around to the front of the car. He spotted something on the ground and bent down to pick it up.

Denny looked back at the trunk. "It's okay… we're going to help you," she said to the hand, which had stopped waving and was just slightly bobbing. "He's a police officer. We're going to get you out of there." Denny leaned down and tried to peer through the hole in the tail light to see the woman's face. She could hear her crying softly inside.

Jason reappeared at the back of the vehicle holding a long, silver-colored spike that looked like it had fallen from a jersey barrier or concrete barricade. "Stand back: I'm going to try to pry the trunk open with it," he said. Denny complied silently, crossing her arms in front of her chest.

After a minute or two of jimmying, the lock made a creaking snap and unlatched, and the trunk door bobbed open halfway. Jason grabbed the center of the door with his left hand and pulled it open. Then everything happened so fast, Denny hardly had a chance to take a breath.

The woman was curled into a ball on her side the floor of the trunk, although it seemed obvious she was in the position not for lack of room—the space was surprisingly cavernous—but because it was the most comfortable position for her to reach her hand out of the broken fixture. When the door was raised, she paused a moment before pushing her torso up and facing the man who had saved her. Then, her face dropped and she began to scream, a sound that was immediately cut short by Jason's quick and violent strike across her face with the makeshift crowbar. Her cry was silenced like a radio's cord had been yanked from its electrical socket.

He hit her twice more, and Denny felt droplets of blood splatter her face and chest. "What the—" Denny began, and then she saw them: a pair of white cotton panties were balled up on the left side of the trunk. They were wet with saliva and mucous and... blood. The woman collapsed sideways back into the trunk. Denny could see pieces of her skull poking out from the side of her eye socket. The woman's pupils grew large and black, swallowing her irises whole.

Denny was watching their hazel color fade away when she felt the blow to the back of her head. Confused, she tried to speak, but the air felt heavy and thick, and she felt her legs turn rubbery and dissolve.

Jason picked Denny up and laid her in the trunk on top of the now dead woman. He snatched her purse and slung it over his shoulder, then pulled Denny's pink lace panties out of his back pocket and shoved them in her mouth, and she felt her tongue dry up like a sponge and fold backwards like an accordion.

"Thanks for making me fuck up the trunk latch on my brand-new Monte Carlo," said Jason. "We had such a good time, Denise, and you had to spoil it." He slammed the trunk door and the world went dark. The last thing Denny thought of as she felt her body slide downward and onto the gritty carpet was how the embedded dirt pressed into the skin of her cheeks, making them burn. She would never get the sand out.

All Bets Are Off

The Blue Moon Rising Bar wasn't the cleanest place to meet for drinks, but it was that or the college pub, and in October, with rush week in full swing, Rachel and Trish agreed that the Blue was a better choice. It wasn't a dangerous place, just a townie dive joint with a big, U-shaped bar, single-stall bathrooms with doors that barely closed, and more mounted televisions than sturdy stools. Two game machines, one, a KISS pinball, and the other, a Big Buck Hunter with one of the two plastic rifles suspiciously absent, lined one of the walls alongside an electronic jukebox. Patrons wandered out the back and onto the small patio to have a cigarette or a joint, and since the door was perpetually ajar, smoke weaved through the dimly lit room like fog on a lake after a storm.

Rachel was doing her best to stifle a cough with her sweater sleeve while she fondled her phone with her other hand as Trish walked in. Even in lighting that consisted mainly of neon beer signs and the glow from KENO games, Rachel was striking: too pretty and refined to be sitting at the Blue, that was for certain. As if she could hear Trish's approach over the music's volume, she looked up and smiled at her friend.

Trish shucked the black pea coat from her shoulders and slung it over the back of the stool. "Hey," she said, and Rachel nodded and closed the screen on her phone with a finger swipe and placed the cell face down on the bar. "I'm sorry I'm late," Trish added. "I got stuck behind a school bus. What the hell is a school bus doing letting off kids at six o'clock at night?"

"No worries. I just got here a minute ago," said

Rachel.

The bartender, a tall, plain-looking man wearing a red plaid flannel shirt and jeans, appeared in front of them. He wiped a limp rag halfheartedly across the space on the bar in front of them. "What can I get ya, ladies?" he asked, his eyes glancing at the TV on the wall behind them. The Patriots game had just started.

"Tito's and soda, with lemon," said Trish. She looked at Rachel.

"Cabernet Sauvignon if you have it. Or a Merlot."

The bartender withdrew his rag and stuffed it under the bar, out of sight. "You got it."

Rachel tucked a strand of her straight, dark brown hair behind her ear. "So, how's Phil?"

Trish smirked. "Just fantastic… I think." She watched the bartender place the glass of red wine in front of her friend. "Haven't seen him conscious since Saturday afternoon. I guess that's the one advantage of working opposite shifts: you never really get bored of talking to each other." Phil was a foreman for a gas pipeline construction company stationed two counties away, and he and Trish had been married for nearly a decade. They didn't have kids, which was just as well; although someone would be home to care for children just about twenty-four hours a day, neither Phil nor Trish were the nurturing type. They hadn't even discussed the possibility, and fortunately, no one ever brought it up in awkward inquiry at family gatherings or barbecues.

The bartender placed a short glass of clear liquid in front of Trish, and she immediately began to squeeze into the drink the lemon wedge that balanced on the rim. A bit of the juice dribbled down her index finger and stung where she had chewed the cuticles from her nail bed. "How's Nate?" she asked, shoving the finger into her mouth to stop the pain. "And Olivia?"

Rachel smiled into her wine glass and laughed softly. "Liv is good. She loves second grade. She's starting soccer this weekend. I don't know how long it will last, but it gets her out of the house." She paused and ran her pinky up and down the stem of her glass. "And Nate... well, you know how that goes." Rachel and Nate had been together since college, and although the days of frat parties and binge drinking were two decades in the past for most of their friends, Nate was still the party guest whose keys had to be hidden in a drawer long before his departure, and in recent years, there had been the occasional week that he hadn't come home, not for hours but for days. Rachel initially called hospitals and police stations looking for him, but finally resorted to raising the payout on his life insurance policy as a preventative compromise. At least he is a happy drunk, she told herself, even if he's a piss-poor father.

When Rachel was young, she had had big dreams. She had always been one of those people who was blessed with intelligence, an even disposition, and naturally good looks. Since she was six years old, she had worn her hair long and shiny, and its deep chestnut hue had been almost black when she was a teenager—a striking contrast to her poreless, alabaster skin and round blue eyes. In junior high, she had gone to modeling school and came home every Saturday afternoon with a new beauty tip to share with Trish. At thirteen, the two stood in Rachel's lavender-painted bathroom, staring at their reflections in the mirror. "You have to start from the ends, like this," Rachel said, holding her paddle brush against the handful of hair she had pulled in front of her shoulder, mimicking what the instructor had demonstrated. *"Hold tight to the base of the hair to prevent breakage, and make your way up the shaft."* She ran the brush through the section of hair three times, the strands singing through the bristles with a shushing sound. Now, at 42, Rachel had the tiniest hint of silver peeking out from her locks, but it was so inconsequential, she didn't bother to color it. In the dim light of the Blue, no one could even see it. Sure, she had had big plans for her life once upon a time, and at no point had they included being a single parent or the wife of an absentee partner, but things never went as planned. Along the way, she had added realistic expectations to her list of attributes.

Trish's family had moved down the street from Rachel when the two were eleven. As the moving company workers shuttled box after box into the tiny ranch home like a three-man assembly line, Rachel teetered on her purple bike, watching the activity from the sidewalk. A man with a fuzzy head of orange marmalade hair and fearfully long mutton chops pushed an awkward girl with equally fuzzy hair to the end of the walkway in front of Rachel. He rested his hand on the girl's head and said, "Hey, do you live in this neighborhood?"

Rachel looked around, both to see if he was speaking to her and to reassure herself that responding would not constitute talking to a stranger. She was the only one around, but he was now a neighbor in full view of every house on the block, so she ventured an answer. "Yeah," she pointed to the left. "Down there."

The fluffy-haired girl's eyes did not leave their focal point on the sidewalk. Her cheeks burned pink, but Rachel couldn't tell if it was from the sun or embarrassment. "Will you play with my little girl?" the man asked. He gave his ward a little shove and suddenly distracted, turned and walked toward the moving van to inspect the progress without a word. The girl looked up at Rachel. They had the same eyes—a detail that would cause people to remark, for the rest of their lives, that they could be sisters—and Rachel found herself smiling.

"My name's Patricia," the girl said. She was shorter

than Rachel, but not short by any means. As she grew into adolescence and adulthood, Trish's ruddy complexion never evened out, and her wavy, warm blonde hair frizzed and dulled after years of flat-irons and dime store dye jobs, but she had somehow grown into her awkward beauty, had become more attractive as she aged. People called it the Princess Diana phenomenon. Although she would always be the less polished of the two childhood friends, Trish finally settled into herself.

Her mother had been only nineteen when she had Trish, and the family often consisted of Trish, Trish's mom, and Trish's mom's flavor of the month. Mutton chops had split only two weeks after introducing Trish and Rachel. She never had a stable father figure, and her mother had worked a multitude of second- and third-shift jobs to keep the pair afloat during most of Trish's teen years, so accepting a marriage where she interacted with her husband on a limited basis had been as easy as sliding into a warm bath. It didn't make a pretty Christmas card, but it was comfortable.

The music changed on the jukebox, and a Tom Petty tune from the 1970's began to play. Rachel swirled the wine in her glass and threw her shoulders back. "Enough about Phil and Nate. What have you been up to lately?"

"Same ol', same ol'," said Trish. "Work is good. That Michael Fassbender movie is finally on HBO—did you see it?"

"Jesus, did I! That man is too good-looking." Rachel laughed. "To be honest, I have no idea what the hell happened at the end—I had to pick up Liv from her friend's house—but damn, I could've just muted the damn TV and watched him walk across the screen all night."

Trish swallowed a mouthful of her drink. "Yeah, he's on the list. Phil and I have this list of celebrities that if we ever had the chance to sleep with, we could do so with impunity.

You know, like a hall pass of sorts." She raised her eyebrow and smiled. "Because you never know: it could happen!" She laughed.

"Who else is on there?" Rachel asked.

Trish thought for a moment. "Let's see... well, Benicio Del Toro... Tom Hardy... hmm, who else? What about you—who would be on your list?"

"Johnny Depp," she responded without hesitation. "Like, on the top. No lie. Even though he probably smells like an ashtray."

"And he's friends with Roman Polanski, the child rapist." Trish held her hand up sarcastically to an imaginary jury. "Oh, wait, I'm sorry. I think he pled down to unlawful sex with a minor. Totally different."

"Isn't all sex by an adult man with a minor unlawful?" Rachel asked, then emptied the rest of the wine into her mouth. She replaced the glass on the bar and pushed it forward slightly.

As if on cue, the flannelled bartender removed the glass and placed a freshly filled one in front of her. "From the gentleman at the end of the bar," he explained. Trish and Rachel simultaneously crooked their necks to take a look at Rachel's benefactor. A tall—very tall—man wearing a stained t-shirt looked back at them and raised his hand to his forehead like he was tipping an invisible hat. He swayed a bit in his stool.

Rachel smiled her tight-lipped grin, the expression she reserved for lecherous admirers and stupid people. "Thank you," she said, purposely not making full eye contact with the patron.

Trish tipped her head backwards to down the rest of her drink. She placed the glass down as far in front of her as possible and said to no one in particular, "Yes, I'll be buying myself another, thank you."

Rachel put her hand on Trish's forearm, suddenly remembered where they had been in their conversation. "You know who is danger-sexy? Jon Bernthal. That guy, that actor from *The Walking Dead*."

The bartender removed Trish's glass and walked away to make her another. "Danger-sexy? What is that?" Trish asked.

Rachel removed her hand. "A guy who isn't traditionally sexy because he doesn't have that movie star perfection handsomeness... maybe he has a strange jawline or pock-marked skin... or maybe his nose is way too big, but there's something, I don't know, sensual and provocative about him."

Trish considered this for a moment. "Danger-sexy. Yeah, I can see it." The bartender set a fresh drink in front of them and wandered back to check on other customers. "So, what do you think?" Trish asked with a sideways grin. "Is Tall Drink of Too Many Budweisers your next boyfriend?" She jutted her chin toward the man at the end of the bar.

Rachel laughed. "I don't know: that group on the other side of the bar has been eyeing us off and on since you got here," she said. "And the only woman who's with them keeps shooting me death glares, like I'm sending subliminal messages to whichever one is her boyfriend or husband or whatever and need to cease and desist immediately."

Trish casually glanced in the direction Rachel was describing and took a quick overview of the group in question. There appeared to be five or six men together, most standing and facing one another behind the one male and one female who were sitting in stools and facing Trish and Rachel. Trish only looked for a moment, but she caught the eye of the woman in question; she was, indeed, glaring at Rachel for no apparent reason. Seeing Trish's interest, she switched her glower to her, and Trish looked away quickly.

"Now *there's* a woman with more issues than *Sports Illustrated*," Trish said.

Rachel looked over at the group again, unfettered by the woman's expression. "I think some of those guys are from the neighborhood... they look familiar." She squinted her eyes a bit. All of a sudden, she turned her head and looked down at her drink. "You want to go somewhere else? Somewhere less... I don't know, dive-y?" She swirled her wine, then drank the remainder in one gulp, something Trish had never seen her friend do.

Trish looked at her full drink. "Uh, sure, let me just drink a little of this," she said, bringing the full glass to her mouth. The soda was cold and hurt her teeth, and as she was pulling it away from her lips, she saw him.

Rachel was halfway off of her stool and pulling her handbag strap onto her shoulder with one hand and a wad of cash out of her pocket with the other. Trish put her hand on Rachel's forearm and squeezed. The two women exchanged a silent glance and Rachel climbed back onto her chair without a word. On the other side of the bar, a man with coarse black hair and sagging round eyes roared with laughter. He touched his scarred face, then placed his hand, palm open, on his friend's chest and pushed slightly to punctuate his amusement.

Then

It had seemed like a good idea to Trish at the time. After all, the window was only a few feet off the ground, and Rachel's boyfriend Floyd had been there to wrap his arms around her thick waist as she shimmied feet-first from Rachel's bedroom sill onto the cold grass of her backyard. She hadn't anticipated the sharp metal frame of the screen sticking up and scraping her freckled thighs as they slid awkwardly outside, her jean skirt pushed upwards and bunching around her waist. When her feet finally hit solid ground, she brushed her knees and shook her legs one by one like a professional gymnast limbering up for a routine. Rachel's feet and legs and black skirt followed effortlessly behind her, and when the three were standing together in Rachel's backyard at last, Floyd reached up and carefully closed the drop screen. As they tip-toed across the lawn and over the fence into the neighbor's backyard, Trish looked back at their exit door wistfully. She hadn't thought about how she was going to climb back in, but she supposed that would be a problem for after the party.

Ten blocks away, older kids from the neighborhood were drinking and smoking and playing Rock 102's Fourth of July party music on the radio. Neither Trish nor Rachel knew most of the people there: they were only fifteen, after all, and these kids were seventeen and older. Even the host was a stranger, a man in his early twenties home from college for the summer, aimlessly drifting through dead-end jobs to make beer and cigarette money. His parents were at the Cape with his little sister and her friends for the week, he told the girls as they were introduced upon entering. "I'm Justin," he said, shaking Trish's hand like he was running for Congress. "I'm glad you decided to come."

Trish blushed and discreetly wiped the sweat from her palm on her hip. "Trish."

Justin smiled. His hair was dark with thick waves running across it. Its pattern reminded Trish of those photographs of desert sand, the ripples prodded and kneaded into the landscape by the wind. His eyes were round and drooped slightly, and his jaw was slightly too big for his head. His face was pitted with acne scars and shaving casualties, but there was something sweet about him. He was wearing a white t-shirt ringed with brown trim and faded Led Zeppelin album cover art in the center. "Hey, do you like dragons?" he asked her, a non-sequitur for a keg party, but somehow, it was endearing, and Trish smiled back.

"Um… who doesn't, I guess?" she stammered, trying her best to sound nonchalant.

Justin grabbed her by the wrist. "Then you're gonna love this!" He pulled her away from Rachel and Floyd and through the crowd of people gathered in small groups around the next room—Trish thought it might be the dining room—and around the corner to a doorway with a set of stairs going down. He was walking so quickly, Trish practically had to run to keep up with him, and she became slightly anxious that she might topple down the stairs if she misstepped. The basement was finished and had been transformed into a rec room, complete with a pair of worn, mismatched sofas, a wet bar, and a full-sized pool table. There was a radio blaring in this room, too, while three college boys played pool and drank beer from brown bottles.

"C'mon," Justin said. "It's over here." He brought her to a large glass curio cabinet wedged in the corner between the two couches. Inside was a sizable collection of grey stone figurines, all of them dragons, each enhanced with a jewel or tiny pieces of tinted glass. One dragon had shiny red eyes; another, a set of shimmering green scales along its tail. One figurine, displayed on the middle shelf at the edge of the glass, stood out among the rest: instead of grey, the dragon was a deep, blood red, and on it, there was a woman wearing a red cloak and drinking from a gold-colored chalice. She rode side-saddle, and her empty hand rested on the base of the dragon's enormous tail which was pointed up, its end sharp like a spear.

"Cool, right?" Justin said. His hands had released Trish's and were placed firmly on his hips.

There had to be twenty dragons in the case. "Yeah, cool," she agreed, although she was only mildly interested. Dragons weren't really her thing.

Justin plopped down on the couch closest to the pool table and reached behind it. When his arms reappeared, they were holding a bong as tall as the sofa back. One of the pool players yelled over the music. "Yeaaaah!" he whooped and dropped his cue on the table. The three boys joined Justin on the couches.

Justin motioned to the couches with his arm wide, like a model on The Price is Right. "Sit down," he told Trish. To the boys, he said, "Guys, this is Trish. She came with her friend and her friend's boyfriend."

Trish looked for an empty place on one of the sofas, then settled for squeezing between Justin and the whooping boy. She placed her purse gingerly on the floor in front of the curio cabinet. Justin lit the slide on the bong while the whooper sucked hard on the top of the long pipe and created a wet bubbling sound. Trish could see the smoke gather behind the glass of the tall base. Whooper pulled his head away and Justin leaned down and drew all of the smoke into his lungs. He sat back onto the couch and exhaled, and the room seemed instantly foggy. Justin and the whooper switched positions and Justin pulled the smoke into the chamber for his friend. As Whooper sank deep into the couch cushions, Justin pulled another cloud of smoke into the chamber, then held his palm tight over the top. He motioned to Trish with his chin. "C'mere, come take this," he commanded. Never having smoked pot before, Trish figured she'd give it a try. She inhaled all of the smoke just as the boys had done, then sat back on the couch and exhaled deeply, surprising herself by transforming into a smog machine when she breathed out.

By the time the two remaining boys had taken their turns on the bong, Trish was floating; at least, her head was floating. Her eyes felt like they were hovering somewhere just above her head; she had to tie strings to them like helium balloons and weigh the ends down to keep her vision from drifting up and through the ceiling. The boys were talking all at once, but she couldn't follow what they were saying. On the radio, Paul Rodgers was singing about being radioactive. Then, everyone but Justin and Trish stood up.

"We'll catch you upstairs, dude," one of the boys said. Trish could have sworn she saw him wink at Justin.

The whooper leaned down and whispered something into Justin's ear. As he turned to walk away, he said, "Just remember what's in the cigar box." He backtracked two steps and grabbed Justin's hand in an odd, secret-society shake.

Trish looked at Justin. The air was still foggy, tendrils of smoke hovering in long trails in the air around her. She wondered why the fire alarm wasn't going off. "What's in the cigar box?" she asked, only then recognizing that the voice she was hearing was her own.

The boys laughed and walked up the stairs, shutting the door behind them and muffling the cacophony of crowd chatter above. "What's in the cigar box?" Trish repeated. She rearranged her question. "Where is the cigar box? What cigar box?" She realized that this was the most she had spoken to Justin all night.

Justin reached under the couch where he was sitting and pulled out a small cardboard box with a faded painting of a red parrot flying above a cluster of palm-treed islands on its cover. A thought popped into Trish's head. "Are there condoms in that box?" she asked, and then she began to laugh at the absurdity. "Not really, right? There aren't really condoms in there, are there?"

Justin ignored her and lit the bong again. He pulled more smoke and motioned for Trish to take it. She did, then sat back on the soft couch and stared through the glass next to her at the red dragon figurine. It had many heads, each of them turned in a different direction, their needle teeth glinting in the dim recessed lighting. Trish leaned her head back on the pillow-back and felt her mind turn soft and airy, sugary and pliable like cotton candy. Her body was heavy and warm. Justin leaned over and put his hand on her bare knee.

Now

The raucous group across the bar was dissolving; the scowler and her tightly leashed boyfriend left first, then a few more of the men, until all that remained were Justin and a man with thinning hair and a wiry build. As Justin clapped his friend on the back and put his jacket on, Rachel nudged Trish and the two of them followed Justin out of the bar and into the parking lot.

Trish pulled on the arm of Rachel's sweater and motioned toward her car. Without a word, the two climbed into Trish's Honda Civic. They watched Justin slide into an older model white SUV and turn on his lights, temporarily blinding them. "You ready for this?" Rachel asked, holding her arm in front of her face to block the headlight beam.

Trish tossed her coat into the back seat and started up her car. "Yep. Let's find out where he lives."

The two drove in silence for a few minutes, following far enough behind the white truck so that they were inconspicuous but close enough so that they didn't lose sight of it. After a long while, Trish spoke. "I should've told my mom. I should've had him arrested," she said, not taking her eyes off of the white beacon in the distance.

Rachel paused. "No," she said. "We should've gone back into his house the next day and killed him," she said flatly. Neither woman spoke for the rest of the ride.

When the SUV pulled into a side street and then into a driveway three houses down, Trish pulled her car over and shut off her headlights. They watched as Justin exited his car, turned on his alarm, and began to stroll toward a dark-colored cottage-style house with chipping paint. He tossed his keys in the air and caught them as he walked. When Trish turned off her engine, she could have sworn she heard him whistling. He jogged the three steps onto the tiny porch, fumbled with the key in the lock for a moment, and disappeared inside.

Rachel placed her hand on the handle, but Trish stopped her before she opened the door. "Wait," she said, reaching up toward the ceiling and shutting off the interior light switch. "Okay." Both car doors opened in the darkness. Both doors closed quickly but quietly. In the midnight stillness, Trish's heels clicked and echoed, so she balanced on her toes and skulked silently across the street and along Justin's side yard. A light illuminated a window in the back of the house and both women ducked instinctively. Rachel paused for a moment, her high-heeled boots sinking into the wet earth, then continued along the side of the house until she was standing just before the glowing window.

"It looks like a bedroom," Trish whispered from her stance five feet back. Rachel put her finger to her lips. Despite the closed window, the two heard a television come to life and snippets of dialogue trickled down on them like raindrops.

Trish slid soundlessly under the window and stood opposite Rachel on the other side of the frame. "I need to know, Rach," she whispered. "I need to know what his life is like." Rachel motioned with her hand for Trish to stay back, then she climbed onto an overturned flower pot near the window and slowly stretched her neck to peer inside. She stood watching for ten seconds, then ducked, climbed down, and pulled on Trish's arm. The two walked back to the sidewalk.

"I couldn't see anything, really," Rachel said once they were out of earshot. "I think he's getting ready for bed or in another room."

Trish thought for a moment. "I have an idea," she

said. Then she walked over to the porch, climbed the three stairs, and pressed the doorbell.

Then

If Rachel had to listen to one more AC/DC song, she was going to scream. They had been at the party for a few hours, and the crowd was slowly beginning to dissipate. She hadn't seen Trish since they'd arrived. She had to pee and prayed there would be toilet paper: she had only seen a handful of female guests the entire night.

The door to the first-floor bathroom was closed, and two people were in line next to it. "Is there another bathroom?" Rachel asked a boy she didn't recognize. He nodded his head and pointed up the open staircase. When she reached the second floor, she saw that the bathroom was on her immediate right. The door was ajar and the light was on. She wasn't prepared for what she found inside.

Trish was sitting on the floor, her legs bent in front of her and her arms wrapped around her knees. Her skirt was pushed up to her waist. The bathroom's sink was filled with water, and Trish's panties floated on top. They were stained with blood. Trish looked at Rachel quickly, then looked down at her knees and began to cry.

"Oh my God, what the fuck?" Rachel said. She knelt down next to her friend. "What happened? What happened? Oh my God," she repeated. Now that she had gotten closer, she could see the smear of blood on the tile beneath Trish's thighs, the torn neck of her t-shirt. There were swollen bite marks peeking out from her lower neck and shoulder blade, some so deep they were crusted with blood. "Oh my God, Trish," was all Rachel could say. She wrapped her arms around Trish and hugged her. "Oh my God. What the fuck?!"

After a moment, Rachel stood up and opened the medicine cabinet. She grabbed a bottle of hydrogen peroxide and ripped a handful of toilet paper from the roll. She soaked the paper in peroxide and dabbed at Trish's bite wounds. "Someone fucking bit you?" she said. "Was it that Justin guy? What the fuck?!"

Trish grabbed her friend's arm. "You can't tell anyone," she said. "You can't. My mom thinks I am sleeping over your house. She will kill me if she finds out." She started to cry, big tears now, making her nose red and swollen.

Rachel put her hands on Trish's shoulders. "Listen to me. I want you to clean yourself up." She reached over and snatched a box of baby wipes from atop the wicker hamper and handed it to Trish. "Then go directly downstairs and out of the door we came in. Wait for me outside. I am grabbing Floyd and we are getting out of here. Now." She pulled Trish's panties from the water and squeezed as much of the liquid out as she could, then dumped them into her purse and began to walk toward the door.

"Wait," said Trish. "My purse. My purse is still in the basement. It's in front of the display case with all the dragons. Will you grab it for me?"

Rachel nodded. "I'll see you outside." She walked downstairs, through the dining room where people were standing around a chip bowl, talking and crunching, and around the corner to the cellar stairs.

Now

"What the hell are you doing?" whispered Rachel loudly. Trish only turned her head and looked at her friend in response. A moment passed, and the small ceiling light in the enclosed foyer lit. The inside door opened, and Justin stepped onto the porch. Only a thin screen door separated Trish from him.

He opened the door a few inches and looked down at the women. "Can I help you?" he asked, sounding more curious than irritated.

Trish wrapped her arms around to her back and pasted a smile on her face. "Hi… we are SO sorry to bother you, but we saw your light and thought you might be our best chance at help. Our car died," she paused and motioned nebulously down the street a ways. "And we were wondering if we could use your phone to call AAA."

Justin stared at her for a moment. In the awkward silence, Rachel cleared her throat. "We… we are really sorry. We wouldn't have bothered you, but we have no way of getting home, to be honest."

Justin let the door close in front of him. He peered at them, his face shadowed by the screen. "Neither of you has a cell phone?" he asked suspiciously.

"No—no, mine's at home," said Trish quickly. "It was dead anyway," she added.

"And mine is dead in the car," added Rachel.

The women stood holding their breath and waiting for his response. Finally, Justin pushed the door open again, holding it wide with an extended arm. "Yeah, come on in. My phone's in the living room." He cocked his head and looked back into the house.

Trish climbed the final step and placed her hand on the door to keep it open. Justin walked back into the house. The women quietly followed him through dining room then an out-of-date kitchen dimly lit by a nightlight next to the stove and into a spacious front living room full of dark wood and leather furniture. A big-screen television was mounted on one wall. The tall display case in one corner caught Trish's eye immediately.

"The phone's on the side table." Justin pointed. "I think I'm the only person left on earth who still has a landline."

Both women stayed grounded in place for a moment,

then Rachel walked slowly over to the phone. She picked up the receiver and glanced at Trish. Realizing she needed to provide a distraction, Trish walked to the other end of the room to the display case. The same tiny grey figurines were arranged behind the glass; in the center of the middle shelf was the red dragon with many heads.

"Dragons, huh?" Trish said, leaning over to get a better look at the woman riding. In all of the years that had passed, Trish had relived the evening in her head over and over, and nowhere in the reenactment had the woman riding the dragon been smiling. She saw now that, indeed, she was, and it made her stomach turn.

Rachel dialed the only number she could think of: 1-800-JUMPING, a bounce house rental company with whom she had been trying to book Liv's birthday party activity. The irritating television jingle was engrained in her head. As the company's answering machine picked up, she casually hit the switch and hung up but continued to speak as if she were calling Nate for assistance.

"Yeah… sweetheart, I know: we should've checked that before we left," she said into the receiver, pressing the earpiece as hard as she could into her ear to muffle the dial tone. She glanced at Justin. He was staring at Trish. More specifically, he was staring at Trish's lower back. Rachel followed his gaze and saw what has captured his interest: sticking out of her back pocket was Trish's iPhone.

Without turning around, Trish said, "Hey, do you mind if I take one of them out for a closer look?"

"Excuse me," Rachel called out, holding her hand over the mouthpiece of the phone as if to mute it. "Where are we, exactly? My husband is calling a tow truck and is on his way over to get us."

Justin's stare broke from Trish and he turned to look at Rachel. "76 Pheasant Street."

Rachel took her hand off the receiver. "76 Pheasant Street," she repeated. She paused. "Okay, see you then." She replaced the receiver quickly and shoved her hands into her pockets nervously. "He put it into his GPS. He should be here shortly." Justin's focus had returned to Trish. He seemed to be lost in thought. "Uh," Rachel continued. "We really appreciate your help. Should we wait outside?"

Trish turned around, her interest in the figurines finally broken. "Yeah, thanks a lot," she agreed, smiling a customer-service grin and placing her hands on her hips.

All three of them were quiet. Justin continued to stare at Trish awkwardly. Without looking away, he said, "You're welcome to stay inside until your husband comes. The window there looks right out into the street," he motioned to the curtain abutting the curio cabinet. "And yeah, take one out if you'd like. I've had them forever: collected them when I was a kid. Would you like a glass of water or anything?"

"You know," Trish said, the smile still affixed rigidly on her jaw, "I'd love one. If you don't mind, that is."

Justin exited the room, and Rachel walked over to Trish just as her friend was opening the door to the cabinet. "We have to get out of here," Rachel whispered, grabbing Trish's elbow for emphasis. "I think he recognizes you."

Trish jerked her arm away. "Yeah? Good," she said angrily. "I hope he does. Then maybe I'll take one of those fucking dragons and smash it into his face so he'll never forget again." She turned to look at Rachel head-on. "Just what did you think we were going to do when I rang that bell? Invite ourselves to tea?"

Rachel searched her friend's face with her eyes. "We aren't doing anything, Trish. This isn't a Lifetime movie: this is real life. You want to go to prison? Let's just get out of here, okay?"

Trish stared back. They could both hear the faucet

running in the next room. Justin would return any second. "You don't know, Rach. You don't know how it feels to carry this every day of your life. To have other women tell stories about their first time and know that yours was this horrible, brutal trick. To dread being kissed on the neck or the shoulder because you immediately think every guy's going to take a chunk of your flesh with it." She looked down at the floor. "To not be able to tell your own husband how you lost your virginity because you're so fucking ashamed." She sniffed. "You just don't fucking know."

Justin reappeared in the room, holding the glass of water.

Then

Rachel could hear the boys talking and laughing at the pool table, so she walked as softly as possible down the stairs, hoping to grab the handbag, turn around, and walk right back up the stairs without anyone acknowledging her. It wasn't until she had reached the bottom two steps that she saw what the boys were so amused by: Justin had his t-shirt off, but he was holding it in front of himself, his left hand parallel to the floor like a makeshift table. There were streaks of wet red and drying brownish blood on the front beneath the Zeppelin logo. The other boys took turns slapping him high-fives, then slapping twenty-dollar bills into his open right palm.

"Told you I could do it," Justin was saying. "And here's the proof, boys."

When the group saw Rachel, they froze for only a moment, then began laughing again. Rachel walked as fast as she could to the corner, grabbed Trish's purse, and ran back up the stairs. When she had reached the top, their laugher dissolved into cackling.

Now

Justin walked casually over to the women, holding the glass of water far in front of him like a soiled piece of laundry. When he was within arm's reach, Trish took the glass from his hand. "Thanks," she said immediately, then sipped from the glass.

Justin pointed to the window. "You can watch right here for your car," he said. He pulled the curtain aside and leaned over to take a look for himself.

It was at that moment that Rachel did it.

Without saying anything, without looking at Trish for acknowledgment or permission, she grabbed the largest dragon, the red one with the heads and the woman riding, from the case. She raised it above her head, then brought it down hard on the back of Justin's skull. There was a sickening crunch, and for a moment, the women believed that the impact had broken the stone figurine in half. Instead, they discovered, as Justin leaned backwards and fell awkwardly to his knees, the red dragon's long, spear-like tail had lodged itself in his skull, piercing his brainstem. The woman's hand, once resting on the base of the beast's tail, now seemed to be reaching inside Justin's head: a magician's assistant pulling out the rabbit for the audience. Justin teetered on his knees for a moment, then slid sideways and onto the floor in front of them.

Trish looked at Rachel, speechless. Both women had tiny freckles of red dotting their faces. They were silent for a long minute, then Rachel spoke. Her voice was soft and gravelly.

"I do know, Trish," she said. "I do."

Boundaries

Broadway actors were shrinking. Lin-Manuel Miranda was 5' 9". Before him, the big name was Neil Patrick Harris. He was 6" even. And before that? Hugh Jackman at 6' 3". Richard Felling worked as an actor for twenty years. At 6' 2", he sometimes towered over his female partners, and because of his height, was at times banished to the back of the chorus line. Occasionally, his scene partners were forced to wear higher heels to balance him, which of course made them cranky and in turn, made the entire run a pain in the ass, especially when they went on tour.

He didn't go on tour anymore.

He had been married for more than eighteen years: a child's lifespan. When he met Jacquelynn, he hadn't even been old enough to drink, let alone make rational, lifelong decisions, but at twenty, he asked her to marry him. He spent the next two decades auditioning for shows, sleeping in buses, drinking in applause like water, and fucking waitresses and co-stars. Finally, Lynn—Lynn, not Jackie: Jackie was a white trash nickname, he told her—rounded thirty and began prodding him for a family, which meant stability: a perfect little house with a tidy picket fence and a round little Corgi for whom he was perpetually picking up poop each time he returned home on break. His children began to walk and talk, and suddenly, no longer was he phoning home from cheap motels halfway across the country, some fan's mouth suction-cupped tightly around his cock as he wished his wife goodnight, the phone receiver pressed tightly to his face so no background noise petered in. No, at the ominous age of forty, he had a real job, a secure job, a job that kept him home 365 days a year.

He was a middle school drama teacher.

It was in Richard's second year of teaching that he started to notice the grey along his temples. One night, while he was flossing his teeth, he saw the crow's feet crinkle beneath his green eyes. He had barely dipped a toe into middle age: he shouldn't look like a grandfather. It was as if when he stopped chasing his dreams, the world caught up with him, tapped him on the shoulder, and yelled "You're It," leaving him to hold a leaky bag of hourglass sand.

At ten o'clock at night, he sat in bed, thumbing his phone surreptitiously around porn sites while his wife snored loudly beside him. He turned from his screen to look at her in the television's glow. She had never been a slight woman, and although she had a decidedly pretty face that lacked the garishness of makeup or the ostentatiousness of expensive creams, she had always been what people described as Rubenesque (on a good day, voluptuous), and carrying two children hadn't done her body any favors. Moreover, since he had left the road, she had really let herself go. She rarely if ever shaved her legs anymore, never mind any other feminine parts, and with the additional weight had come the unpleasant side effect of monstrous snoring, the kind that woke him from a deep sleep each night.

Lynn's primary care physician had sent her to an overnight sleep study. Richard used the opportunity to sneak one of his local girlfriends into their marital bed, and the next morning, as he was stripping the sheets and poking around the trash to make certain the condom wrappers were sufficiently hidden, she returned with her diagnosis: sleep apnea. She could wear a CPAP machine or she could lose weight. Her high blood pressure and use of birth control pills already made her a walking stroke candidate; the apnea was just icing on the risk factor cake. She had promised to lose weight, to get healthy, if only for the children's sake, but six months had passed and the nocturnal cacophony had only worsened.

Richard opened up his Facebook app. Although he had abandoned the stage, he kept in contact with some of his regular "roadies," as he liked to call them, through innocuous social media sites. They sent him covert emails and private messages every now and again, then justified their online friendship by attaching enthusiastic *Love!* emojis to his family photos and compilation videos. There was a message from Marielle, the plain-looking but petite brunette he'd met in Chicago a few years back. Each time a tour brought him to the Windy City, Richard would drop Marielle a note, and within an hour's time, she'd be straddling him on her basement office desk chair, covering his mouth as he came so that her husband, sound asleep in the bedroom two floors up, wouldn't hear them. Marielle had two children under the age of six but she managed to keep her figure in check for him. The tiny green dot next to her name indicated she was online.

Hey, sexy, the screen read.

Richard shifted his weight so that he could finger the screen with one hand. *Hey there yourself,* he wrote back.

Three grey dots danced to indicate she was typing. *What are you up to this evening?* she asked.

Richard glanced at his wife's noisily heaving body. *Just listening to my wife shake the house with her snoring,* he wrote. It would be so easy, he thought, to simply roll Lynn onto her stomach and press her face into the pillow until she suffocated. The doctors would rule it an accident, considering the havoc she had been wreaking on her circulatory system. He didn't understand why she took the birth control pills in the first place. She was thirty-nine. Their last child had been born three years ago, and he could count on one hand the number of times they'd had sex since then. He could count on his closed fist how many of those times she'd been on top, his favorite position.

I bet I could make it shake, too, Marielle's reply read.

Richard clicked off the television with the remote and turned slightly onto his side, his left leg bent to tent the sheet and blanket. *Send me a pic to help me imagine*, he wrote back. He muted the sound on his phone and watched the screen swell into a darkly lit live stream of Marielle, lying on her back in her underwear, Lynn's snores humming a raucous soundtrack in the background.

The next morning at work, Richard received an email from the school's Guidance office. One of the students in his class, Susan Davis, had submitted a note from her mother to the school. She has an eating disorder, the email explained, and as part of her treatment, she should be allowed to eat food anytime, anywhere. Richard snorted. *Another helicopter parent coming in for a landing*, he thought. He didn't know when mothers and fathers had lost their balls, but his generation had definitely been castrated. Kids demanded instant gratification these days, and their parents were too lazy to say no.

Susan, or Suzy, as her friends called her, was a bossy eighth grader with long, greasy hair and a perpetual look of indignation on her face: she always seemed to be smelling someone else's crop-dusted fart. Last week, he had caught her eating a bag of Fritos. Richard's number one rule was no food or drink on the stage—not only was it unhygienic, but unintentional spills or crumbles could cause a fall. He had assigned Suzy detention and she had refused to attend, making a grand show of her public pronouncement. Now she was shoving his nose in it: she could violate his authority with impunity.

That afternoon, Suzy's class filed into the auditorium for class, and he instructed the students to line up on stage and face the long mirror he had pushed to the back wall. "Are we going to dance?" asked one of the children.

"No, no," explained Richard. "We are going to do some work on our postures. Now stand an arm's length away from the person next to you so that you have some movement space." He paused and watched the line wiggle and expand. "Okay, now deep breaths."

Richard walked slowly behind each of the students, watching their inhales and exhales in the mirror. When he got to Suzy, he stood immediately behind her. He amused himself by watching his body disappear behind her broad hips and meaty thighs. She was barely five feet tall and thirteen; he was a grown man of two hundred and sixty pounds, and yet, she exceeded him in width. *Fat Suzy, that's your name from now on*, he thought to himself, *if only in my head*. Fat Suzy sneered at her teacher in the mirror and Richard smiled prettily back. "Good work, Ms. Davis. Keep it up," he said cheerfully.

"Excuse me, Mr. Felling?" a voice called from the theater door. It was the front office secretary, someone whose name he had never bothered to learn. "You have a new student." Alongside the anonymous office worker appeared a tall girl with straight brown hair. She walked carefully down the aisle to the stairway and onto the stage and handed Richard her schedule card. The secretary disappeared without a word.

Richard skimmed the card. "Edith?" he said tentatively. He could barely read without his cheaters anymore. The letters were fuzzy and melted together. "Is that right? The lighting is terrible in here."

"Yes, that's right. Edie, please," a small but husky voice said. Richard took a long look at the girl. She wore a plain burgundy dress and a long-sleeved cardigan sweater, and her face was plastered with so much makeup, Richard had the urge to scrape it with a putty knife.

"Edie, like Édie Piaf, the famous French chanteuse and international film star," Richard said, smiling. "Or is it more like Edie Sedgwick, the avant-garde muse to Andy

Warhol?" Richard was always doing that, making references to things and people he knew his students were too young to recognize. It made him feel important and knowledgeable, even though he knew he'd probably come off as a pompous narcissist to any adult who overheard him.

To his surprise, Edie replied softly and evenly, "I'd say the latter, but I'd like to live past twenty-eight." She took the schedule card back from Richard, shoved it in her purse, and walked to the end of the line and faced the mirror. For the remainder of the class, Richard said nothing to Edie directly, but he watched her with great interest. There was something about this young girl that drew his attention. It wasn't sexual; it was something else. He found himself thinking about her for the rest of the afternoon.

There was another email from the Guidance office in his inbox the next morning.

Dear teachers-
This is an email to let you know some information on your new student, Edith Wells. Please be aware that Edith is transitioning and should be allowed to use the bathroom in the nurse's office should she wish. Also, should any paperwork with Edith's birth name, Elliott, be forwarded to you, we wanted you to understand that it would be referring to Edith. Edith's parents are very supportive of her journey and we encourage you to contact them should any problems, academic or otherwise, develop.

Richard leaned back in his chair. Edith had been born a boy? He could hardly believe it. Usually, he could sniff out the gays and trans from a mile away; he worked in the theater for half of his life, for Christ's sake, and he'd had his share of one-night stands with men and even a couple with women who turned out to be biologically male. An orgasm was an orgasm, as far as he was concerned. But Edie... she looked more like a full-fledged girl than Fat Suzy did.

That afternoon, Edie lingered after the dismissal bell. Gathering her books and jacket, she seemed to be waiting for Richard to notice her. When he looked up from his plan book, she was staring at him. "Have a good evening," he said dismissively. He didn't like having to stay after school if he didn't have a preplanned commitment. That was one thing that teaching had over acting: the show was over early enough in the day that he could still do something productive.

"You were on Broadway, right?" asked Edie. "I mean, I heard some of the kids talking about it."

Richard smiled. He loved telling the students stories of his stage adventures: the PG-rated ones, that is. He could afford to stick around for a few minutes. "That is true, young lady. I was a stage actor once." He turned to walk toward his office beside the emergency exit off stage right.

Edie took this as an invitation to follow. "Anything Tony-winning?" she asked, walking briskly behind him.

Richard pushed the heavy velvet curtain aside and held it so that Edie could walk past. He motioned forward, toward backstage. The area was only dimly lit, and he walked carefully over a few cables and around a casually strewn folding chair. "Sure. I was in quite a few of the touring companies. Most of the actors weren't from the original production, but the show was the same. You should have seen some of the intricate costuming." He didn't know why he had added that last part: maybe he figured a girl would be more interested in the clothing than in the performance itself. Maybe he was nervous, but why? He was talking to a child. He talked to more than one hundred children every day. He opened the door to his office, switched on the desk lamp, and sat down heavily in his rolling chair.

Edie stood in the doorway and shrugged nonchalantly. "I don't know much about fashion or costumes. To be honest, I don't know much about plays or musicals in general. I've never acted before. I just saw your class on the list of electives and decided to try it out."

"Well, that's okay," said Richard. "There's a first time for everything, right?" The two were silent for a moment. Edie was making Richard a little uncomfortable, hovering in the doorway like she was. He was about to make up an excuse to leave for the afternoon when she suddenly spoke.

"Do you mind if I sit down?" she asked, pointing to the one other chair in the room, a vinyl-covered vintage knockoff. Richard had brought it from home because he liked looking at its color, a seventies-funk burnt orange.

"Oh, sure, of course not," stammered Richard, embarrassed that he hadn't offered her a seat earlier.

Edie sat down delicately and crossed her ankles. She was wearing a blood red dress with black tights and shoes. "She folded one arm beneath her chest and rested the elbow of the other awkwardly on her forearm, then propped her chin with her fist. "So, Mr. Felling," she began. "Tell me about your strangest experiences as an actor on Broadway. I want to hear everything."

Richard felt his face blush, the first time he'd reddened from embarrassment in recent memory. "Edie, that's a tall order. We could be here for days."

She laughed and rearranged her arms so that she could entwine her fingers while resting her hands in her lap. "My ride doesn't come until four."

By the time Richard got home, his children were getting restless and the babysitter, annoyed. She expected to leave by three-thirty each weekday, about a half hour after his oldest son disembarked the yellow bus from school. Richard gave her an additional twenty dollars and opened the refrigerator door to assess the possibilities for dinner. "What do you think, guys? Taco salad?" he said, more to the air than anyone in particular. He pulled out a package of hamburger, a head of lettuce, and a bag of shredded cheddar. He began dicing the ripe tomato that had been sitting on the windowsill.

Lynn didn't cook. If he didn't plan out the meals and make an effort, they would be ordering take-out every night. He wondered if the children had developed mild cases of scurvy while he was on the road; they *did* seem to lose their baby teeth much earlier than he thought children should. A year ago, he decided to stop planning and making dinner as an experiment; he wanted to know what his wife would do. Sure enough, she pulled out a pile of menus and the family ate nothing but submarine sandwiches, pizza, and Chinese food for a week. When he stepped on the scale and discovered he'd gained five pounds after only seven days of his strike, Richard drove to the grocery store and resumed his daily dinner preparation.

He rinsed the knife in the sink and glanced out the window. Along the back edge of his property was a moderately tall wood fence. He had installed it a month after they bought the house, even though the neighbor's property had a chain-link fence surrounding it. He left a five-inch gap between the neighbor's fence and his, and over the years, from the dead space an army of weeds had banded together and woven opaque nets of vines that peeked over the tops of his fence posts and lolled in the breeze. He refused to trim them: after all, he couldn't see them unless they drooped onto his side of the barricade, and quite frankly, the rogue vegetation was probably growing from his neighbor's property anyhow—why should he be responsible?

Suddenly, from over the top of the fence poked the blades of an electric hedge trimmer. He watched the instrument zip and shear the top six inches of weeds along the perimeter of the fence, the clippings falling carelessly onto his lawn. "What the fuck?!" Richard yelled and ran outside into the backyard. "Hey!" he yelled over the fence. "Hey! You're leaving weed clippings all over my grass!"

The lopper continued to whir and chop without commentary. When it had finished trimming all of the weeds, Richard bent down and scooped as much of the debris as he could carry, then lobbed the pile back over the fence. "Here!" he called snidely. "You dropped something!" He brushed his hands on his khakis and stomped back inside, muttering to himself. He hated passive-aggressive people.

The next morning, as he stirred sugar-free creamer into his coffee, he saw it.

A pile of weed clippings was stacked neatly on his chaise lounge in the middle of his backyard.

For the next month, Edie came to visit Richard every day after school. They never referred to her visits during class time, and occasionally, Richard would fool himself into thinking there were *two* Edies, one who was his student and one who was his captive audience of one. After a few weeks of her stopping in after the last bell, Richard began to expect her; he even started stocking cans of diet soda in his mini-fridge in case she was thirsty.

They didn't have conversations; rather, Richard talked and Edie listened. They were a therapy patient and physician, a one-man show and the sole ticket holder. At first, Richard censored his stories; he provided a public television version of the truth. However, after a few weeks, Richard spoke as if thirteen-year-old Edie were a colleague, an equal.

The release he received from unburdening his memories onto her became addictive; when the weekend arrived, he found himself restless, unable to concentrate. He wondered what Edie was doing. Did her family plan day trips to the movies? Museum walks? Picnics in the park? Had she made friends? Did she have a boyfriend? He had never asked her about her life or even how she was adjusting to a new school. He'd make a mental note to inquire first thing when she showed up on Monday afternoon, but then he'd forget and as soon as she arrived, his own life spilled from his mouth uncontrollably like a dam had broken. Soon, he was telling her about his wife, his children, his family. He was complaining about the neighbor who had taunted him with the weed trimmings. He was reminiscing about his love affairs on the road. He admitted to her that he wished he had never gotten married so young. Perhaps, if he had remained single, he'd be a great actor today. A star.

All the while, Edie would smile at him, a broad, gentle smile framed by pouty, burgundy-painted lips and accented by a spontaneous giggle now and again. She reassured him that he was a good father, a devoted husband, and a dedicated teacher. She pushed him to investigate the local community theaters, to get up on stage again.

She absolved him.

And then, one Monday afternoon, she stopped coming.

Richard told himself something must have come up: a family emergency, an adolescent hormonal crisis, an alien abduction. Certainly, she would have told him if she had known she could not visit. The next day in class, as the students were practicing their monologues in preparation for their graded performances later that week, he stealthily bent down and whispered into her ear. "What happened to you yesterday?"

She visibly shrank from his presence and did not turn her head to meet his eyes. "I joined the volleyball team. I have practice now every day after school," she said quietly, matter-of-factly.

She joined the volleyball team? Richard didn't know Edie had an athletic bone in her body. He'd never seen her wear anything but dresses and delicate, feminine shoes: not the clothing a jock would wear. "Oh," he replied. "I didn't realize. Well, good luck with that," he stammered. He walked swiftly to the next student and pretended he was checking in with every child's progress, but out of the corner of his eye, he watched Edie. She was lost in concentration in her pantomime, gesturing broadly with her arms as she recited her soliloquy. She seemed unfazed by the abrupt cessation in their daily meetings.

Her abandonment meant Richard would be alone with his thoughts once again. On the bright side, he could head home right after the last bell again. He'd have some coveted alone time if he arrived before the sitter appeared. It was a positive readjustment, he told himself. And yet, that evening, as he lay in bed, attempting to block out Lynn's snorting and squealing as it grew progressively more obnoxious, he typed every variation of Edie's name into Facebook's search bar to try and locate her page. She was nowhere to be found. He tried Instagram, Snapchat, Twitter. Nothing. He put his phone down onto the bed and sighed. Realizing how naked he felt without it in his hand, though, he picked it back up and returned to Facebook.

To distract himself, he waded through his newsfeed. He could see by his friends list that Marielle was signed on; he wondered what she was doing. A couple he and Lynn saw socially every once in a while announced that their five-year-old was graduating from preschool in May; they were having a barbecue to celebrate and wanted all of their Facebook friends to attend. *Really?* thought Richard. *A daycare graduation? How the hell could a kid* fail *out of daycare? Eat too many crayons and projectile puke on the reading circle carpet? Jesus, some parents were idiots.* Richard clicked "maybe" on the response.

He closed the app and surfed through his standby porn

site but found nothing that struck his interest. Irritated, he turned onto his side and fluffed his pillows violently, not caring if he woke Lynn. She continued to snore uninterrupted and he rested his ear on the pillow and watched her face for a moment. This was it. This was what he had signed on for when he slipped the ring onto her finger so many years ago. There was no undoing it now. He closed his eyes and drifted off to sleep.

Wednesday afternoon, Richard walked across campus to the gymnasium entrance. The co-ed volleyball team was playing in its first game of the season, and faculty and staff had been encouraged to attend, so the bleachers were already packed with spectators by the time he arrived. He climbed the stairs until he found a small opening on the fifth level and shimmied over to the vacant spot. The man next to him, a squat, balding man in his thirties, sat with his legs spread wide like a predatory animal staking his claim on the hunting ground. Richard shifted his weight away from him to keep the man's knees from bumping his, but with his every movement away, the man encroached even further into Richard's space. Finally, Richard opened his legs and bumped the man's leg with some force, and his neighbor, after shooting him a look of annoyance, slid away from Richard a few inches.

A whistle blew on the court. Richard searched the players' faces for Edie's familiar countenance but did not see her. The teams batted the ball back and forth over the net. Richard did not know the formal rules of volleyball, but he managed to surmise the basics as the game progressed. Finally, the visiting team served and the ball sailed over the net and to the back of the home team's court. It hit the boundary line and bounced away. Richard didn't understand the referee's ruling, but neither team seemed happy, and soon both coaches were on the court, yelling and gesturing loudly, while the children fidgeted and looked uncomfortable in their polyester uniforms.

Richard figured this was his opportunity to escape the game and go home. He wiggled past the people sitting to the left of him and hobbled carefully down the wide stairs, taking extra care not to trip and fall: there was nothing worse than looking stupid in front of middle school students. Their mouths were loud, their memories were long, and their empathy levels were on par with burgeoning serial killers. Should he fall, he would have to hear about his accident for weeks to come. Luckily, he made it to the bottom unscathed, and he could finally look up and in front of him, just in time to run straight into Edie.

He pushed into her and immediately began to apologize before he realized who she was. "I... oh, Edie. Edie, I'm so sorry: I didn't see you," he said, both surprised and embarrassed. Then he recognized that she was dressed in her everyday school clothes, not in a team uniform. "I... what are you doing here? Why aren't you playing?" he asked.

She stared at him, unashamed at being caught in her lie. "Oh, I decided not to play volleyball after all," she said. "See you tomorrow, Mr. F," she added dismissively, then stepped to the side and began to walk around him without waiting for his response.

Seeing her brought a wave of relief he hadn't felt since she had last sat in his office and listened to him talk. When she began to leave, he felt that relief fall to the pit of his stomach. Without thinking, he grabbed her by the shoulders to keep her from leaving. "Wait, where are you going?" he asked loudly. He tightened his grip and shook her slightly to punctuate his desperate longing. He needed her to come back.

Her face changed. Her ambivalence transformed into incredulity. "What are you doing?!" she screamed at him suddenly. "Don't touch me!" She pushed his chest with both of her hands, his firm stance sending her reeling backward slightly. The gym fell silent. The coaches stopped arguing and waving their arms. The players topped teetering. The crowd stopped chatting amongst themselves. "Stay the fuck away from me!" Edie yelled. "You're old enough to be my dad! Why don't you get friends your own age?!"

Richard froze in place. He felt a deluge of shame wash over him as every adult stared at him ferociously, their glares piercing and stinging his flesh. Edie walked quickly and determinedly to the gymnasium door, her kitten heels clicking like a metronome. Richard turned and skulked to other door on the other wall of the gym. He kept his head pointed down as he concentrated on placing his feet firmly on the floor with every step. He did not look up again until he had reached his car and climbed inside.

When he arrived home, the house was quiet. His wife should have come home from work by now, or the kids and the babysitter should have been running around the backyard or shooting hoops through the basket in the driveway. Instead, he found Lynn's handwritten note taped to the refrigerator. *Kids were starving. Couldn't wait any longer. Went to Chuck E. Cheese.* It was just as well; he wasn't very hungry anyway.

He glanced out of the big window over the sink. With the prodigious amount of rain that had fallen in the past weeks, the weeds behind the fence had accelerated their growth and once again lolled over the top of his posts. He needed something to distract his mind, so he wandered outside and into the garage and grabbed his manual hedge trimmers. This garden tool always made Richard a little uneasy, as it reminded Richard of a scene in the movie *The Exorcist III*. In it, a nurse quietly goes about her rounds on a hospital ward until suddenly, without warning, a figure in a white nun's uniform appears behind her, holding an enormous pair of shears even with the nurse's neck.

Richard thought of the scene again as he held the tool and walked toward the fence. It played on a loop in his mind as he held the trimmers high in the air and he opened and shut the hinge over and over on the vines. He could see the nurse's red cardigan sweater, her white nurse hat, her white nurse shoes. He snapped the shears open and shut, open and shut, faster and faster, and watched the green heads and necks fall helplessly in front of him and behind the barrier.

Snip snip snip

He thought of Edie's smile as it had appeared as she sat, listening intently, on the burnt orange chair in his office.

Snip Snip Snip

He thought of her angry sneer as she berated him in the gymnasium.

SNip SNip SNip

He thought of Marielle's smile as she faced him on her basement's desk chair, her head tilted backwards and her bare breasts bouncing softly up and down as she rode him.

SNIP SNIP SNIP

He thought of Lynn's face as she lay dead asleep, her mouth slightly ajar, her lip quivering with each snort and grunt.

SNIP SNI—

"Richard, we br—"

He felt a hand grip his shoulder, and startled, he spun, reeling the sharp blades around to confront the person behind him. It wasn't until he saw the look of surprise and horror that he realized what he had done. Lynn's mouth formed a deflated oval, and her eyes widened; saliva dripped from her lips, and she spasmed a cough, spraying a fine mist of bright red blood over his shirt.

As she collapsed, Richard let go of the tool's handle

and watched it sail backwards with her, the better part of the blade still planted firmly in her neck like a garden stake in fresh earth. She lay on the ground, groaning and writhing in agony.

Richard looked at her for a long minute. Then he leaned over, pulled the trimmer from her flesh, and stabbed it over and over into her chest until there was nothing left of her breasts and neck but a sticky mound of bloody pulp and bone.

Richard had crossed the boundary.

He wasn't coming back.

A Shot of Knowledge

Sherry Clancy stood outside of room 351, her arms folded like Japanese origami around the fat three-ring binder containing the class attendance lists, worksheets, and miscellaneous paper weaponry necessary to act as substitute teacher for the day. *Who takes a summer school teaching job knowing that she's due to give birth in the middle of July?* she wondered. Sherry hated irresponsible people. If everyone just followed the rules and did as they were told, the world would be a happier, and certainly more peaceful, place. The tiny slit of a window in the middle of the classroom door was greasy, streaked with fingerprints and hot breath. Sherry tried to peer inside without touching her skin to the glass; she didn't want to catch anything. The room was dark. Even the windows to the outside world offered no light: all of the shades had been drawn.

Next to the door, framed by a pale grey plastic block, were the words "CLASSROOM 351." The words were spelled out in individual white, plastic, raised letters about an inch high. From where she stood, Sherry scanned the rest of the doorways along the hall; each had a similar looking room identification posted.

The door to the stairwell thrust open with a crackling bang, and from it emerged a petite woman who looked to be in her early thirties. She had long, dark hair and carried a briefcase duct-taped on one corner. Her boots made echoing clicks in the empty hallway as she walked toward Sherry with purpose, like a frustrated parent ready to scold her child. Sherry half expected her to grab her by the upper arm and yank her back when she was close enough.

"Can I help you?" she asked Sherry curtly. She pulled a set of jangling keys from her blazer pocket and fished through them; when she discovered the one she was looking for, she jammed it into the lock for room 351 and turned it quickly. *Everything about this woman screams aggression*, Sherry thought. *She should really learn to relax.*

"Hi—I'm Sherry Clancy. I'm subbing for Mrs. Nestle—I mean, Nettles," Sherry stammered. "At least for the rest of the month." She stuck out her hand in a way she hoped evoked friendliness tempered with submission. Sometimes it was better to just cow to the Alpha females of the world. It reduced the drama potential. "Thanks for opening the door for me: they said they can't give me keys until this afternoon."

Alpha turned the door handle but stopped before entering. "This isn't Nettles' room. This is *my* room," she said. "I'm 351. Nettles is 315."

Sherry looked down at her paperwork and felt her cheeks flush. She scanned the itinerary madly: now she felt like a complete idiot. Had she really flipped the numbers? No, no: here it was—room 351, written right on the assignment. She started to twist the paper toward Alpha to show her that the mistake hadn't been hers.

"315 is right around the corner there," Alpha said, pointing with the hand that still held the keys so that her palm appeared to have grown ten extra metallic digits. "By the way, my name is Elizabeth Rogers. Please call me Betty. If you need anything, don't hesitate to ask." She ducked into her room and began to kick a wooden stop under the door to hold it open. "Nilda—Nettles— and I used to eat lunch together, so I know we have the same lunch block. Maybe I'll see you then." She smiled quickly and turned her back.

Sherry walked slowly down the hall and around the corner, checking the room sign numbers as she passed. When she reached 315, she couldn't help but notice the classroom signage. Some of the raised digits that should have collaborated to read "CLASSROOM 315" had been pried off.

Specifically, the C, L, and M were missing, and the front leg of the R had been chipped away. "*ASS POO 315*. Very clever, kids," Sherry said out loud, her voice echoing like Alpha Betty's shoes had in the cavernous space.

315 was a science lab room, so it was large and airy, and it boasted large storage closets with thin air circulation slits along its back wall. The window shades had been left rolled up, and the counters and desks had recently been wiped down. Next to the teacher's desk was a large wire cage. When Sherry approached it, she could see a fat white mouse scurrying madly along the perimeter. There was water but no food in the cage, and Sherry panicked for a moment. There were no instructions on feeding a pet in the sub plans; there was no mention of the tiny animal at all. Then she spied the bag of food on the floor under the desk. Mrs. Nettles must have assumed she would know the amount or frequency to feed. Or she had pregnancy brain and had simply forgotten there was a living thing still under her care. Sherry scooped a bit of the food into the mouse's dish and made a mental note to bring back a bottle of water to refill the dropper.

When the bell rang for the morning block, Sherry took a deep breath and steeled herself for some resistance. She knew students never adapted well to a change in teacher, whether it was a substitute for the day or a permanent replacement. The reason for the change never mattered: Mrs. Nettles could have been hit by a bus and the students still would have treated her like dirt.

As she introduced herself to the class of twenty-five eleventh graders, two girls in the front row began to snicker and murmur to each other. She gave them the stink eye, but when that did nothing, she stopped trying to talk over them. "Do you mind waiting until I am finished to talk? I'm trying to explain the game plan for the rest of the summer semester," she said to the taller of the two, a skinny girl with tightly curled black hair and a bony nose.

"I'm not talking loud," Skinny said. She moved her head slightly in a side-to-side tilt to emphasize her irritation.

"I'm asking you to not talk at all," Sherry said quickly, keeping her voice even.

Skinny's sidekick, a plumper girl with large blue eyes, straight blonde hair, and teeth that jutted out slightly like a woodchuck, rolled her eyes in an exaggerated manner and leaned in closer to Skinny. She said something under her breath and the two girls began giggling uncontrollably.

"I'm not going to ask you again," Sherry warned. Skinny kept her eyes on Sherry and said something low, almost under her breath. "I'm sorry, what was that?" Sherry asked.

"I wasn't talking to you, bitch," Skinny said, in a louder voice this time. The rest of the class began to twitter and chuckle, and Chuck Teeth turned her face to meet Sherry's and broke into a wide grin—so wide, it forced her eyes closed and Sherry could practically count every one of her teeth individually.

It was going to be that kind of substitute assignment.

When she had finally calmed the class down to a dull roar, and the students were working semi-diligently on coloring a dissected model of a frog and identifying each organ, Sherry walked inconspicuously to the back of the classroom, where the door to the adjoining room had been left slightly ajar. She wondered if the room was unoccupied—she hadn't heard a sound all morning, hadn't even realized the door was open until she happened to glance at the back wall while waiting for two boys to stop chuckling over the wet farting sound one of them had emitted during her lecture. When she silently pushed the door further open, she was surprised to see that a full class—at least twenty-five students—was in progress. The teacher, a tall, barrel-chested man with closely shaved red hair and wet blue eyes, walked back and forth across the front of the room in front of the SMART Board, occasionally touching items on it and making notations as he delivered his lecture.

None of the students were talking. In fact, it looked from her vantage point that all of them were sitting rigidly straight in their seats, their eyes plastered to the teacher, who stopped only briefly to acknowledge Sherry with a quick glance before resuming his explanation. Embarrassed to have been caught spying, Sherry closed the door softly and returned to the front of her classroom.

At lunch, Sherry selected a chair next to Alpha Betty in the teachers' lounge and proceeded to nibble on the sad turkey sandwich she had slapped together the night before. Two other teachers joined them: a tall, greying man in his early sixties and a pretty, cherub-like woman who hardly looked old enough to vote, never mind lead a class of children. Each time she spoke, she ran her hand through her wavy, chestnut brown hair and adjusted her black framed eyeglasses nervously, like a twitchy gangster under the glare of a police interrogation spotlight.

"So, how did the first morning go?" Betty asked, her mouth half full with something wet and green.

Sherry put down her sandwich. "Alright, I suppose," she said. "I didn't realize Mrs. Nettles had a pet mouse. Who takes care of it during vacations?"

Grey Sixties let out a guffaw. "Ah! You must mean Lazarus. He's not exactly a pet... more like a scientific anomaly."

Betty swallowed and wiped her mouth with a napkin. "So, get this. The head of the history department—this white-haired spinster with like, fifty cats in her house—she discovers a mouse in her kitchen sink: how's that for irony? She didn't catch it on purpose: I guess it fell in there and couldn't climb back out. Anyhow, she scooped it up in a box but couldn't bring herself to kill it with a trap or poison or whatever, so she decided to smother it."

Sherry had been reaching for her sandwich but paused, her hand hovering awkwardly upon hearing this last detail. "What do you mean, she decided to smother it?"

Betty laughed. It was a strange laugh, though; one that sounded hollow, like it was coming from a long-distance phone call in the 1970s. "Yeah, she—I guess—thought it would be a better death for ol' Mousie there. Or maybe she's just a sadistic bitch: who knows?"

This prompted another guffaw from Grey, and the round hair swirler let out a nervous cough.

"So, she scooped it up in a small box," Betty continued, "and dumped it into a Ziploc sandwich bag. You know the kind: you can seal it up and turn it upside down and nothing leaks out?"

"Yellow and blue make green, baby," laughed Grey.

"And then she threw the bag in a kitchen drawer, figuring she could take it out the next day and toss the bag out, mouse corpse and all. But here's the creepy part." Betty leaned in. Sherry could smell her lunch on her breath: pesto, maybe? "She forgot she had thrown the mouse in there. She forgot for three days! I guess she discovered the bag when she opened the drawer to find something. And lo and behold, the mouse was still alive!"

Round Hair Swirl tucked a strand behind her ear. "Yeah, she was so freaked out that the mouse had lasted so long that she brought it in to Nilda to show her. And Nilda decided to keep him as a pet."

"So... Lazarus: escaping death. I get the name now," Sherry said.

"Yeah. No one is supposed to know the story; it makes the history teacher seem like kind of a psycho. But nothing is kept a secret here for long," said Betty. "At least not the juicy ones."

The four were quiet for a moment. Sherry's throat felt drier than usual. She had to concentrate to swallow each mushed mouthful of her sandwich. Finally, Round Hair Swirl spoke.

"Why are there so many autistic kids in my class? I mean, in my *summer* school class?" she asked. "I must have fifteen kids: like, diagnosed, IEPs, the works. For a *Spanish* class, for Christ's sake."

Betty waved her hands in the air like she was casting a spell. "Wooooo! The scary vaccines strike again!" She wiggled her fingers for emphasis.

"Oh, Jesus, not this discussion again," Grey rolled his eyes.

A teacher across the table from them removed his fork from his Lean Cuisine and pointed it at them. "Hey, maybe it's not bullshit: you guys see the influx of spectrum kids. More and more every year. Something's gotta be causing it."

"The only vaccinations required now are MMR, hep, and varicella," Betty said. "They eliminated the bad one years ago."

"MMR?" Sherry asked.

"Measles, Mumps, and Rubella," Round explained. "Plus Hepatitis B and Chicken Pox."

Sherry thought for a minute. "Didn't there used to be one for whooping cough or scarlet fever or something too?"

"Ah yes, the DTaP." The Lean Cuisine teacher took a sip of something from a travel mug with the tagline *Make America Grope Again!* written in purple script. "D-T-A-P. Diphtheria, Tetanus, and Pertussis. Don't you remember? That batch five years ago that caused all the brain hemorrhages?

Something funky in the development made the shots deadly... whole lot of eleven-year-olds dropping dead with blood oozing out of their noses on the playground and *pow*! They were yanked off the market before you could say Class Action. I mean, there are new shots now that are perfectly safe—it was just an isolated, wonky shipment—but shit, did that scare the bejesus out of parents. No more DTaP boosters for their kids, no sir. That's when the state made the vaccine voluntary."

"Who the hell gets whooping cough these days anyway?" said Grey. "Or polio? I mean, we aren't vaccinated against anthrax or smallpox, something a terrorist might shovel into the water system with abandon, but some ancient disease from fifty years ago, that's on the menu? Give me a break."

Sherry balled up her napkin and twisted the cap back on her water bottle. She nodded at her lunch partners and walked quickly back to 315.

The next day, Sherry brought with her the container of mouse treats she had purchased from the big-name pet store on her way home. She dropped a few in Lazarus's cage. The mouse wandered cautiously over to them and sniffed. Sherry could have sworn he turned his little pink eyes to meet hers in suspicion.

"I'm not trying to trick you, Lazarus," she said out loud, her voice echoing slightly off the cement walls and glass cabinets. "You and I both know you've been through enough: am I right?" As if in agreement, the little furry creature began to chew thoughtfully on one of the treats.

That day's assignment was to create an online presentation comparing the reproductive system of a frog to that of a human. Sherry ducked "green dick" and "smells fishy" exchanges between the students and did her best to maintain order. Chuck Teeth was in a particularly energetic mood, throwing pencils across the room and even lodging one in the particle board ceiling at one point.

Skinny, on the other hand, kept her mouth formed in an angry sneer and her eyes on Sherry for most of the class, something that began to unnerve Sherry rather quickly. She moved toward her, eyeing the girl's laptop screen to check on her progress. Skinny had done nothing. "Do you need my help?" Sherry asked earnestly.

Skinny said nothing but stared ferociously into Sherry's eyes like a predatory animal waiting for a flinch. After a long minute, Sherry focused on keeping her face steady and said, "Okay, well if you need anything, please let me know—I'll be walking around the classroom." She flashed what she hoped was a carefree and pleasant smile and turned her back to walk to the next lab table, all the while expecting a sharp object to be lobbed into the flesh of her back.

After the bell rang for lunch and dismissal of the morning session, Sherry cautiously pushed the door connecting the next classroom open. She wanted to introduce herself to her neighbor. They would be sharing a wall for the rest of the summer, and truth be told, Sherry was curious to learn his classroom management secret. Surely she had simply caught him on a lucky day. However, the room was as silent as the previous day had been. Moreover, despite the fact that the students had been free to leave for a half hour, all of the children had remained in their seats, their heads held rigidly erect, facing the front of the room.

Sherry backed away from the doorway and closed it in front of her. Deciding to negotiate a better view, she grabbed her lunch tote, hurried outside to the hallway, and walked purposefully by the room next door. She peered through the slit of window. Sure enough, the kids were sitting rigid in their seats, their heads not moving and their eyes following the movement of the male teacher as he moved about the front of the room. She could see drool glistening along the bottoms of some of their mouths, which were fixed in unsettling, Jokeresque grins. Sherry jumped back instinctively. It was as if she had opened a coffin only to find a corpse inside staring with eyes wide open.

In the teachers' lounge, eating another sad turkey sandwich—this one with extra brown mustard—Sherry described what she had seen to Betty. Betty shrugged her shoulders.

"You must mean Mr. Allen. He has a double block class of standardized test prep," she explained. "That's why they weren't leaving for lunch. He probably gives them breaks throughout the day because they have to stay there from nine to three."

"Six hours of standardized test preparation? Ugh: I can't imagine what it's like to take that class," Sherry said.

"I can't imagine what it's like to *teach* it: it must be some sort of coming attraction of hell," Betty said. "His whole roster is comprised of students who have failed or are labeled likely to fail the state exam. If the school's scores trail downward, we might be taken over by the state, so any teacher who shows success in raising scores is given *carte blanche* to teach as he or she wishes. Allen has the highest turnaround success rate in the school, so administration just lets him do as he pleases." She shoveled a pile of red-sauced tortellini into her mouth. "More power to him," she added, her cheeks puffed with pasta.

"All I know is, he's some kind of Svengali when it comes to classroom management," Sherry said. "I wonder what his secret is. Maybe I'll try to catch him at three and ask."

Betty let out a low chuckle. "Good luck with that. Allen talks to no one. Comes in early, leaves late, and skulks around the building on weekends. Rumor is, he does his own science experiments using the school's equipment." She paused to stab a few more tortellini onto her fork. "Nilda told me once that he has this very rigid pacing: three weeks of instruction followed by a three-day lab and three days of lab analysis. Then the three weeks of instruction again. Wash, rinse, repeat."

Sherry left the lounge a few minutes earlier than she needed to; she wanted another long look at Mr. Allen's class before she welcomed her afternoon group and repeated that morning's routine with them. Once again, she looked through the slice of window; this time, she focused her attention on the children sitting in the front row. One boy, tall, with a mop of dark hair and a curiously long torso, was sitting so straight, his back appeared to be bowing backward slightly, like his neck was being pulled toward the back of his chair with an invisible string. His eyes were wide and he bore his teeth slightly, like a rabid dog in a frozen growl. Suddenly, his eyes darted to meet Sherry's, and she watched a puddle of gelatinous drool escape from the corner of his mouth, wind lazily down his chin and onto his neck. Sherry shivered and moved along to 315.

After three weeks, Sherry's sub assignment came to an abrupt end. The school had decided to hire a full-time replacement for Mrs. Nettles, who had filed notice to take a child-rearing leave of absence for the upcoming school year. The principal wanted the long-term substitute to acclimate to the environment before classes began in the fall. Sherry was disappointed for the loss of income, but she was mostly relieved to be free of Skinny and Chuck Teeth and their gang of merry terrors. Over the course of eighteen school days, her lunch had disappeared twice, her car had been keyed one afternoon, and she had soaked her blouse with anxiety sweat more mornings than not. That day, she could lock up 315 and never see the inside of the room again. The night before, she pondered whether to take Lazarus home with her. Who knew what kind of person was replacing her? If a mild-mannered schoolteacher could torture him without batting an eye, who knew what others were capable of?

She still didn't know Mr. Allen's secret, and she knew as soon as she pulled her rusting two-door hatchback into the parking lot that morning, she was going to find out. She would put her plan into motion that morning.

The junior class had an assembly in the theater scheduled before the morning session. The students would be an hour late to her class, if they even bothered to show up at all. She had monitored Mr. Allen over the past two weeks, noting his comings and goings, his habits and compulsions. He walked to the teachers' lounge to fill his travel mug with coffee a half hour before his class began. Ten minutes later, he visited the men's room for exactly two minutes. He did not leave for lunch, and he did not leave the building until long after every colleague packed their things and sauntered to the parking lot on their way to Stafford Cidery, the local townie bar where the teachers often met for drinks.

Sherry waited until she heard Mr. Allen leave for the lounge. When she was sure he was gone, she crept into his classroom, opened one of the storage closets in the back of the room, and climbed inside, squeezing her shoulders around the stacks of glass beakers and test tubes. The tight slats along the front of the doors were there only to encourage air circulation, but having practiced in her own classroom next door, Sherry knew that with some contorting, she would be able to see and hear the classroom as well from that vantage point.

Mr. Allen's students shuffled in and fell into their seats. The order, *the blind obedience*, in his room was like nothing she had seen anywhere else in the school, or in any other school in the area, for that matter. The education system was turning into Thunderdome with every teacher and child for himself. Thank goodness a new Commissioner of Education had been appointed, Sherry thought. People groused about the new czar not having any experience in education—she had been a nurse by trade: I mean, what was the President thinking? However, he was quoted as calling her the "cure for the sickness that public education had developed." Sherry hadn't voted for him, but she secretly hoped his intention was true.

The peacefulness of the room was interrupted jarringly by a strange noise. Sherry had to readjust her body slightly to peer out of the slit and see what had happened. In the far front corner of the room, a tall boy with sandy, almost grey, hair was convulsing. His head and shoulders vibrated wildly, like he had placed a wet finger into an electric socket. "Herrrrhummmmmmmmmm!" the student yelled out in agony, a garbled mess that sounded like a halfhearted cry of protest: against what, Sherry did not know.

His body twisted like a burnt pancake on a hot griddle: quickly and as one solid, overdone piece. His head did not turn from his shoulders but remained fixed in place like a steel bar had been attached to his spine. When he fell, shaking violently, out of his chair and onto the floor, Sherry glimpsed his face, which was now turned awkwardly toward her. His eyes stared straight ahead, wide and unblinking. Most disturbing, though, was his mouth—it was pulled back naturally in a wide, toothy grin, like a Halloween mask had melted onto the boy's skin. The incongruous combination of the frantic primal screams of pain combined with the broad, fixed smile, was unnerving.

More disconcerting was the lack of reaction by any of the other students in the room. No one's body moved. No heads turned. Even the feet remained rigid under the desks.

Mr. Allen walked calmly over to the student, removed a small syringe from his lab coat, and injected the boy with it. The convulsions stopped. Mr. Allen gently pulled the boy to his feet and placed him delicately back in his chair, ignoring the puddle of urine that had formed on the floor below.

Sherry felt her armpits begin to dampen. Not only was it airless in her tight, dark hiding space, but she was starting to regret having climbed into it in the first place. She began to worry that if Mr. Allen were to discover her, she would suffer a punishment much more severe than a simple scolding or unkind word from her neighbor.

There was a quick knock at the door. Sherry readjusted herself again, feeling the round glass beakers push against her shoulder from the abutting shelf. From the tunnel of vision she was able to glean from her place in the closet, she could see Mr. Allen cross to the classroom door, but the door itself was out of view. When he reappeared, a small, Asian-American girl followed behind him. Sherry saw her eyes dart around the room nervously, but Mr. Allen turned back to look at her as he spoke, and she returned her eyes to him.

"Alright, Caitlin, well, you have a bit of work to make up, but I'm sure we can get you up to speed," he said. "First, we started our third lab two weeks ago. Come right over here and put your bag down."

Caitlin did as she was told. Mr. Allen bent down to remove a tray from the refrigerator under his desk. "I... I really need to pass the science exam, Mr. Allen," Caitlin stammered. "I just have trouble staying focused. My mom... she doesn't believe in drugs, you know? I wanted to go on Adderall, but..."

"Nonsense. I'll help you focus." Mr. Allen removed the frosted plastic top from the tray, revealing a selection of Petri dishes. He pulled a slim white cylinder from the other pocket in his lab coat. "Give me your hand, please," he instructed.

Tentatively, Caitlin held out her hand. Mr. Allen grabbed it gingerly and turned her hand over, exposing the pink, delicate flesh of her palm. "This will be just like a shot at the doctor's office," he said with a small smile. His eyes danced for a moment.

"Oh, we don't get shots in my family. We're Christian Scientists," Caitlin said. Her face flushed like she was embarrassed.

"Even better," said Mr. Allen, pushing the white cylinder onto her index finger and clicking a button to make a quick snapping sound. Caitlin winced, but he held her hand steady, then guided it to one of the Petri dishes. "This is the first lab. Rub your fingertip all over the top."

Caitlin obeyed, but looked at Mr. Allen inquisitively. "What's in the dish? It feels kind of slimy."

"That's just the gel medium that the bacteria feeds on."

Caitlin stopped moving her hand but did not remove her finger from the dish. "Bacteria?"

"Oh, Caitlin: there is bacteria on your bag, on the desk, even on your skin itself: it's everywhere. We're just testing the effects of this particular bacteria. It's nothing to be concerned about," Mr. Allen smiled again, revealing a chip on the bottom of his left front tooth. "Now. Go to the library and catch up on these three chapters. On Monday, when you return, you should be on track to join us in our lesson."

Caitlin pulled her hand away and looked around, searching for something to wipe her finger on; finding nothing, she put her hand in the pocket of her jeans awkwardly. She grabbed her bag and slung it over her shoulder, then turned and walked toward the door without a word. Sherry shifted herself again to follow her with her eyes but could not manage to see the door. Perhaps with a little twist of her shoulder, she could...

The glass bottles tumbled from the shelf by Sherry's back and smashed on the metal shelves and flooring of the closet in a painful crash. Sherry looked frantically out of the slit and saw Mr. Allen's body walking quickly toward the sound. There was nowhere to run. She was trapped. When the closet door opened wide, she looked downward in shame.

"What are you doing?!" Mr. Allen asked brusquely. "Are you spying on me?"

"I... I... I'm sorry: I was just so impressed with your classroom management, I just, I... I wanted to know what your secret was. No one seems to know," Sherry blathered, feeling her face grow warm and red.

"My secret? Hmmm..." Mr. Allen paused for a moment, then he grabbed Sherry's arm and guided her out of the closet. "Well, I don't know what to tell you. It's always been my belief that if you can get a child's undivided attention, you can teach them anything," he said. He put one hand in the pocket of his lab coat. "Of course, with technology and ADHD, ADD, ODD, whatever the acronym of the month is, it's harder than ever to achieve that."

Sherry glanced around the room, her view finally uninhibited. The students continued to face forward, unmoving. She heard a low growl that made her shiver. She could not place from which student it was coming. Her attention was broken by a sharp pain in the side of her neck. She turned to feel Mr. Allen's hand on her shoulder, the warmth of his other hand pressing against the underside of her face as he pushed the plunger on the syringe.

"Clostridium tetani." Mr. Allen's voice shot into her ear, his breath hot on her skin. "Found everywhere in nature. It's why you should wear gloves when handling soil in the garden. The tiniest of cuts on your hand can be a way in for the bacteria."

Sherry felt her head fill with fog. The room began to spin.

"Did you get your tetanus booster recently? Let's see if you're one of the morons who let those bogus vaccine scares convince you to avoid it," Mr. Allen whispered. "I hope, for your sake, you were smarter than that."

Mr. Allen left Sherry where she had fallen on the floor, her muscles becoming rigid and her body bent like a bow, like her heels were straining to touch the back of her neck. She watched his worn brown canvas loafers pad away from her body to the classroom door and outside of it. She heard the key catch metallically in the lock. Her heart raced, sending rhythmic pounding sensations echoing from her ribcage to her stomach. She tried to catch her breath, but her lungs were growing smaller, smaller, smaller: a paper bag of air being folded over once, twice, three times until it was only a fraction of its original size. Her jaw ached, and despite her hardest efforts to open her mouth wide to force air inside, she felt her teeth clench together in a lockjaw grin.

As she felt the drool escape in a river down the side of her cheek, she looked straight ahead, unable to move. From her vantage point on the cold, dank floor, among the dust bunnies, paper scraps, and forgotten gum wrappers, she could see that something had been swept under the radiator by the window. Sherry concentrated hard and tried to blink but found it was a useless endeavor. Through her failing, hazy vision, she spotted three things: three white, spider-like things only an inch high. Sherry could make them out if she focused hard enough: a plastic C, L, and M, and a tiny chip of white plastic like an elongated comma.

The One That Got Away

I'm the one that got away.

Not the one you wanted to marry who said *no*, not the one who smiled coyly at you during third period English but you never rousted up the nerve to ask out. No, I'm that other one: the one you took to the movies freshman year of college, who kissed you wet and long in your dorm room after but never returned your calls in the weeks following. I'm the coworker who flirted with you all fall but didn't attend the Christmas party, then quit the second January appeared. I'm your best friend's fiancé, your boss's daughter, your son's older, wiser American Beauty. And I'm back to give you another chance.

When I say *you*, I mean men. Preferably married or otherwise attached men. Men with families, steady jobs, reliable cars, Christmas photos on annual greeting cards and Disney timeshare vacations. You are so easy to spot, even when your wedding ring is muffled by woolen gloves or surreptitiously hidden in a pocket. Your look of resignation as you wait patiently in line at the bank in front of me (*Excuse me, but may I borrow your pen? Mine just ran out of ink*), your nervous energy hovering along the edge of pained restraint as you walk purposefully through the parking lot (*Gosh, I'm so embarrassed, but my door lock appears to be frozen: would you lend me a hand?*), your barely hidden exasperation at having to buy a whole case of baby formula, a bright green box of super-strength Tampax, or an industrial-sized can of Metamucil for your prenatal vitamin-chugging wife at the pharmacy at ten o'clock at night (*you are too kind—I am such a klutz, tripping over nothing!*).

As they say in poker, everyone has a tell. Yours are just easier to recognize.

You are so quick to accept appreciation (*you've been so nice: please, let me make this up to you*) and just as quick to acknowledge that my thanks will be in a currency best kept secret from your significant other (*do you know that place on Worthington Street? They make great martinis, I hear!*). Once you've walked through the door, you've sealed your fate.

We both know where this is leading. Don't play coy with me.

You like to talk. You're lonely. Unappreciated. I understand, and I'm here for you with a sympathetic ear and a razor-sharp memory.

Of course, that makes it easy as pie to find out everything I need to know about you. In this age of social-media-cum-perpetual-narcissism, I know that if you don't have an active Facebook, Instagram, or Twitter account that provides regular updates on your job, Saturday barbecues, and likes/dislikes, it's a sure bet you have a spouse who does. It's the rule of overcompensation: the more of a straying dog you've been, the happier Stepford-family posts your wife will display for the world to view: a desperate ploy to convince everyone, including herself, that everything is just fine, that your increased irritation with her, lack of interest in the bedroom, and well, sudden regular gym attendance is *definitely not* because you have a pussycat girl on the down low. No, you're just distracted from work, and working all of those late hours, isn't it selfless of you to make certain you're taking the best care of your health so that you can be there for her and the kids?

So, I sift through your Thanksgiving snapshots, trying not to judge your goofy selfies at the shore, ignoring the halfhearted *Like* emojis you slap under each of the Mrs.'s pics of her latest casserole, your daughter's dance recital, and the whole brood wearing matching pajamas, crowded around the television to watch Green Bay finally secure that Super Bowl trophy. Within a fortnight, you're thankful for my coming into your life. You can't remember being this happy before I did. Finally: a woman who anticipates your every desire, who seems to know what you need before you ever vocalize it to her. A girl Friday, aide-de-camp, abettor and attendant, not for your paperwork but for your personal pleasure.

I've been a partner in crime to so many of you.

First, there was the city planner. Three kids, a dog, and a mousy wife with stringy hair and a pained expression in every family photo op. His fiscal year budget granted a surplus of new iPhones for the whole staff: surely they wouldn't miss one? And wouldn't you know it—I left my beaten-up Android on the subway last night. I'd never want to be out of touch. I am always appreciative of your generosity, and of a phone that allows me to switch numbers as easily as flipping a SIM card.

Then there was the redheaded HVAC mechanic with the stretched lobes, arm sleeve tattoos, and pregnant wife bedridden with twins on the way. My condo fees were becoming exorbitant, and wouldn't you know it? They don't cover heating repair. How toasty and warm I was that winter with the installation of a new furnace. And to think it was a manufacturer return that was lost in the mail? My luck could not have been better.

The childless beat cop who raised Weimaraners and complained about his wife's dismissal of his Cross-Fit discovery didn't last long, but it was his name I dropped when I was caught making out in a parked car in the back of the movie parking lot. Yeah, that's right: I'm a friend of Jerry's. We were gym partners—you know, he threw the big tire as I air-jogged to nowhere on the elliptical. *Of course* I'll give his poor widow your condolences at the memorial this weekend. The body shop mechanic with the four-year-old son and ten-year-old marriage was more than happy to come to my aid when a hit-and-run damaged my front fender—one late night at the shop is worth it for your special girl—and the short-statured locksmith with the guitar-playing girlfriend helped me out in a caper or two until he got a little too clingy.

It always happens. You think you're getting the best of both worlds: cake and eating, fork and spoon, a family and a fantasy, and I am around just often enough to leave you satisfied but elusive enough to make you crave me for days following. When you call on a Tuesday and it goes straight to voicemail, you assume I am with my mother, I am shopping with friends, I am working late. I must be driving and don't want to endanger other commuters. I must be on the train, outside of service range. But it's an hour later, and I still do not pick up. Am I with someone else? Have you been replaced? You mind races, panic sets in. Maybe you should set me up with an apartment. That way, you'd know I was safe and sound. The hotel charges are adding up to a monthly rental anyhow.

Oh, there will be no evidence tying me to you, your family, or your circle of friends. We're strangers, and we'll stay strangers, long after you've booked and paid for king bed suites while I wait patiently in my own car until it's safe to make my way up the elevator to meet you inside. We'll never go to my house (*I have a cranky roommate, a sick dog, an active neighborhood watch: it's just too risky!*), never discuss my day job (*I'd put you to sleep, it's so boring! Besides, I'm much more interested in hearing how YOUR day was, darling*), and never quite commit to which high school I attended or what year I graduated: those pesky Classmates pages and Facebook alumni groups can be so informational.

Your wife will cry fat tears for the media. If only you hadn't been so stressed at work: maybe you wouldn't have mixed those Xanax and martinis. She didn't even know you had a prescription: no one did! You must have procured the pills from a friend out of desperation.

Your wife will wear her best navy pantsuit to your wake. Poor thing: you ran yourself ragged, between your job, your family, and your workouts—it's no wonder your reflexes were too weak to prevent that terrible fall from the fourth-floor balcony at your company's flat. You were such a trooper, dropping off a last-minute welcome basket for the visiting client who was due to check in the following morning.

Your wife will file her claim on your life insurance within two weeks after she's mailed her last thank you for the condolence cards. You were a provider right up until the end, and even afterward: it's so tragic that the jack spontaneously collapsed on your Nissan while you were stranded on the side of the road with an inopportune flat. They should really make those zippy sports coupes higher off the ground.

And me? Oh, I'll be simply devastated to learn of your passing. You were so kind to help a stranger in need, and so personable once we met... and of course, the fringe benefits were lovely as well. But I'm off to the bank: I want to make a quick transaction before the sun sets and it gets really chilly. I never know how my car locks will perform once the wind starts blowing.

Look for me, and you'll glance right past me. I hide in plain sight.

I'm the one that got away... over and over again.

Appreciation & Acknowledgments

To Kevin Bell, who reads my stories and worries that there's something very wrong with me but sleeps next to me with both eyes closed anyway.

To Anthony Santiago, for allowing me to pick his brain about the damage slipping tetanus and other deadly biologics into unsuspecting individuals might do but not calling the authorities.

To Liz Lane, who knows that a friend will listen while you plot a fantasy murder but a good friend will lend you the fantasy shovel.

To Jen Danio, for listening to me brainstorm the most disturbing of characters and book ideas (and *life* ideas) yet continuing to be seen and heard in public with me.

To Ann Michaels, for introducing me to Flannery O'Connor and having the best (and sometimes darkest) sense of humor north of the tofu curtain.

To Susan Amaral, for scaring the bejesus out of me with a seemingly innocuous doll and in turn, inspiring me to explore what lurks in dark corners, preparing to bite.

To Dylan Burakiewicz, for his endless generosity in books and in spirit and always being the first person to stand up to any bully who targets one of his "girls."

To Greg Rubeck, for brainstorming creative cover ideas, to Alicia Mattern, for flushing out the fabulous final design, and to David McCutchen, for copyediting with a keen but kind eye.

And to Michael Aloisi, for trading Easter eggs with me for many, many piles of cheese.
Without you, this collection would be only a jumble of unpleasant ideas in my head.

I Forgive You Foundation

The **I Forgive You Foundation** is an important and selfless cause built and nurtured by Zori Alfonso; please visit www.gofundme.com/i-forgive-you for more information on helping her achieve her goal of breaking the silence about one of the most terrible horrors of them all.